MW00475773

Praise for Brooke Lea Foster's
On Gin Lane

"Set on the tony East End of Long Island where the beautiful people play, *On Gin Lane* encapsulates the very best of historical fiction, delving into timeless questions about the traditional expectations of women versus the challenges and rewards of pursuing a creative career. An exciting, fast-paced, enchanting read."

—Fiona Davis, *New York Times* bestselling author of *The Magnolia Palace*

"What a lovely summer novel! [. . .] The exquisite care given to vintage detail in this novel was utterly captivating—I felt like I was eating tomato sandwiches, bumping into romantic rivals at the Maidstone Club, and dancing in the street in my espadrilles."

—Elin Hilderbrand, #1 *New York Times* bestselling author of *The Hotel Nantucket*

"Brooke Lea Foster brilliantly captures a bygone era in this sparkling tale of self-discovery that has it all: mystery, romance, and life-changing friendship. *On Gin Lane* is the perfect summer escape."

—Jamie Brenner, bestselling author of *Blush*

"*On Gin Lane* begins as a languid, sensual glimpse into the lives of women in the late 1950s until a shocking event—and the ensuing investigation—ratchets up the tension. The book is at once a page-turner that kept me reading into the night, and a reminder of the importance of carving out a place for ourselves, whether it is by creating art or finding where we belong."

—Janet Skeslien Charles, *New York Times* bestselling author of *The Paris Library*

"If you're looking to dive into historical fiction this summer, look no further than Brooke Lea Foster's *On Gin Lane*."

—*Town & Country*

"*On Gin Lane* first seduces with everything readers want in a sun-drenched tale: glamorous and colorful characters, evocative settings, and enough secrets to topple a town. But as our heroine battles a suspicious fire, fiancé, and social circle, author Foster slyly starts adding all the heady thrills of a modern-day *Rebecca* to the intoxicating mix. An un-put-downable, irresistible summer read."

—Natalie Jenner, author of the international bestseller *The Jane Austen Society* and *Bloomsbury Girls*

"In this atmospheric new novel, Brooke Lea Foster explores the glittering and bohemian world of the Hamptons in the 1950s—and the dark underbelly that her protagonist never could have imagined. A page-turning mix of historical fiction and coming-of-age, readers will devour *On Gin Lane*, and its lessons of self-discovery and following one's heart will remain long after the final page. An utterly enchanting tale."

—Kristy Woodson Harvey, *New York Times* bestselling author of *Under the Southern Sky*

"The glitzy late '50s Hamptons sparkles like a coupe of champagne in this tantalizing novel from the talented Brooke Lea Foster. . . . A delightfully complex tale of deceit, social maneuvering, and self-determination that will have you cheering for the gutsy main character as she fights for the right to control her own fate."

—Kristin Harmel, *New York Times* bestselling author of *The Forest of Vanishing Stars*

"Brooke Lea Foster pivots from Martha's Vineyard to the Hamptons for another perceptive beach drama. *On Gin Lane* expertly builds out the various characters, revealing the ugly truths hidden by their wealth and social status. This story of a young woman's self-discovery captivates."

—*Publishers Weekly*

"An engaging story that pairs a strong, female protagonist's self-discovery with vivid descriptions of both setting and characters throughout."

—*Booklist*

"Prepare to pack your beach bag this summer with the ultimate historical summer read from Brooke Lea Foster."

—Women.com

"*On Gin Lane* takes readers to a beautiful location. We can smell the ocean, we are poolside for Bellinis and luncheons, and on the courts for daily tennis matches. But behind the aesthetically pleasing atmosphere, there are cracks and lies in the façade. [. . .] What other lies, misleading untruths, and fraud are behind all the glamour? It's a perfect summer read for the pool or beach."

—*Chick Lit Central*

Praise for Brooke Lea Foster's
Summer Darlings

"I was immediately seduced by *Summer Darlings*. Foster cleverly conceals her characters' deceits and betrayal beneath a stunning, sun-spangled surface, and Martha's Vineyard is portrayed with glamorous period detail. This is one terrific summer read."

—Elin Hilderbrand, #1 *New York Times* bestselling author of *The Hotel Nantucket*

"A perfect summer book, packed with posh people, glamour, mystery, and one clever, brave, young nanny. This book just might be the most fun you'll have all summer."

—Nancy Thayer, *New York Times* bestselling author of *Surfside Sisters*

"Engrossing . . . Foster's musings on money and class, along with her believable depictions of over-the-top behavior, elevate this tale above typical summer fare."

—*Publishers Weekly*

"Innocent intrigue segues into a love triangle—and goes out with a blackmail-backstabbing bang."

—*People*

"Beautifully written and richly detailed—it pulled me in from the very first page. Heddy is an unforgettable heroine, and I'll be recommending this book to everyone I know."
—Sarah Pekkanen, #1 *New York Times* bestselling author of *You Are Not Alone*

"Foster has written a coming-of-age story that exposes the sparkling glamour and dark underbelly of the haves and have-nots in the 1960s. *Summer Darlings* is utterly atmospheric and compelling."
—Julia Kelly, author of *The Last Garden in England* and *The Light Over London*

"I was swept away by *Summer Darlings* and its fiercely unforgettable heroine, Heddy Winsome. This perfect summer read blends it all: intrigue, romance, a gilded atmosphere, and gorgeous writing."
—*Entertainment Weekly*

"A fresh new voice in historical fiction! Filled with 1960s nostalgia and a host of deftly drawn characters, this is a novel that gives us an intimate look at the world of privilege, proving once again that money does not buy happiness."
—Renée Rosen, bestselling author of *Park Avenue Summer*

"The enchanting beaches, dazzling parties, and elusive social circles of Brooke Lea Foster's 1962 Martha's Vineyard carry secrets and twists that keep us breathless. A delicious read filled with an acute sense of place and unexpected discoveries about class, status, and ambition."
—Marjan Kamali, bestselling author of *The Stationery Shop*

"*Summer Darlings* has all the ingredients of a delightfully fizzy beach cocktail: A spunky, working-class Wellesley student determined to make her mark, the deceptively 'perfect' wealthy couple that employs her, two alluring suitors, and a bombshell movie star with a heart of gold. If you like your summer escapism with a nostalgic splash of *Mad Men*-era glamour, you'll love this surprisingly twisty debut."
—Karen Dukess, author of *The Last Book Party*

"A delicious romp through mid-century Martha's Vineyard replete with movie stars, sun-drenched beaches, and fancy outings to the club. *Summer Darlings* is about the human desire to strive toward something more, and the strength a woman will find within herself when she listens to her inner voice."

—Susie Orman Schnall, author of *We Came Here to Shine* and
The Subway Girls

"The romantic entanglements and the scandalous exploits of the rich and entitled makes this suitable for a quick beach read."

—*Booklist*

"This luminous novel feels like the summer you first fell in love. This unputdownable novel sparkles with wit and insight, captures the Vineyard's beauty, and, most of all, reveals Heddy with truth and tenderness."

—Luanne Rice, *New York Times* bestselling author of *Last Day*

"A taut portrait of money and social status, and of a young woman navigating her place in the world. Foster offers a glittering glimpse into the private lives of New England's elite families, while exposing the dark underbelly of privilege. I couldn't stop turning the pages until I had reached the breathless, satisfying conclusion."

—Meredith Jaeger, author of *Boardwalk Summer*
and *The Dressmaker's Dowry*

"A solid beach read."

—*Library Journal*

ALSO BY BROOKE LEA FOSTER

Summer Darlings

On Gin Lane

All the Summers in Between

BROOKE LEA FOSTER

G

GALLERY BOOKS

New York   London   Toronto   Sydney   New Delhi

Gallery Books
An Imprint of Simon & Schuster, LLC
1230 Avenue of the Americas
New York, NY 10020

This book is a work of fiction. Any references to historical events, real people, or real places are used fictitiously. Other names, characters, places, and events are products of the author's imagination, and any resemblance to actual events or places or persons, living or dead, is entirely coincidental.

Copyright © 2024 by BLF LLC

All rights reserved, including the right to reproduce this book or portions thereof in any form whatsoever. For information, address Gallery Books Subsidiary Rights Department, 1230 Avenue of the Americas, New York, NY 10020.

First Gallery Books hardcover edition June 2024

GALLERY BOOKS and colophon are registered trademarks of Simon & Schuster, LLC

Simon & Schuster: Celebrating 100 Years of Publishing in 2024

For information about special discounts for bulk purchases, please contact Simon & Schuster Special Sales at 1-866-506-1949 or business@simonandschuster.com.

The Simon & Schuster Speakers Bureau can bring authors to your live event. For more information or to book an event, contact the Simon & Schuster Speakers Bureau at 1-866-248-3049 or visit our website at www.simonspeakers.com.

Interior design by Jaime Putorti

Manufactured in the United States of America

10 9 8 7 6 5 4 3 2 1

Library of Congress Cataloging-in-Publication Data is available.

ISBN 978-1-6680-3437-8
ISBN 978-1-6680-3439-2 (ebook)

To John, my best friend

All the Summers in Between

"Think about me every now and then, old friend."

— John Lennon's last words to Paul McCartney,
just before Lennon's death.

Chapter One

June 1977

Thea set the vegetable platter she'd prepared on the covered picnic table, the din of cocktail party conversation humming around her. Her friend Midge had just arrived, forty-five-minutes late and without an apology. Thea pretended not to notice. Instead, she asked her: "Midge, do you ever feel like your life is a watercolor painting blurring at the edges?"

It was mid-June in East Hampton, and Thea and her husband, Felix, had a lucky break in the weather for her thirtieth birthday party. All the guests mingled on the brick patio of their pretty yellow Victorian with its wide-open views of shimmering Gardiners Bay, dusk settling in. It was just after seven o'clock. A "Happy Birthday" banner hung over the back door.

"Midge?"

Her friend had spun around to greet someone else while holding a tray of appetizers she'd brought. Thea pretended to be interested in the two women's conversation about a rude housekeeper. It was probably better that Midge hadn't heard Thea. She and Midge didn't talk about the "malcontents," as Thea had come to think of the thoughts that sometimes popped into her head lately; theirs was a friendship based on a shared love of racquetball, their kids, and the soaps. And how could Thea say something negative when all these nice people had come to celebrate her? She needed to smile. Even if she was having one of those moments when she felt like she was playing a part in someone else's movie rather than the lead in her own.

Midge finished her conversation and turned to Thea.

"You told me deviled eggs were your favorite, but I sprinkled them with cumin rather than paprika," Midge said, handing off the platter. She had straight auburn hair and freckled skin and was always dressed in some variation of a frilly top, big necklace, and Bermuda shorts, a cute look, thanks to her elfin nose and round pixie face. "Your mother used to make them for you, right?"

Had Thea talked to Midge about her mother? Perhaps one night after a few drinks.

"Yes, she did. Thank you!" Thea, standing there in her denim bell-bottoms and floral blouse, tucked her long, wavy blond hair behind her ear and reached for one of the eggs. The taste of the cumin transported Thea to an image of the Beatles emerging out of an Indian ashram back in 1968. Thea had so badly wanted to travel back then. She'd spent one year at junior college upstate, but she'd never gone anywhere other than New York.

"Oh, Midge. You're such a good friend." Thea smiled, hugging Midge just as someone turned up the record player: "Hooked on a Feeling" by B. J. Thomas. She and Midge had gone to high school together but hadn't become friends until they were both chasing after their toddlers at the playground in Sag Harbor.

Midge's husband, the financier George Bells, hadn't been spending weekends at the beach as much lately, and when Thea asked her about it last week, Midge had snapped at her. Thea didn't dare ask her where George was tonight. Midge nodded at the spread of food Thea had put out. "You should experiment with new recipes like I do. Obviously, these dishes look wonderful, but during the week . . ."

"I should," Thea said. Midge was always lecturing her to try new things, like the pu pu platter at the new Chinese place in Southampton. But they both knew that she wouldn't. Thea loved the long-held traditions of summer. Like everyone else who called these shores home, she held on fiercely to memories of July corn slathered in butter, lobster bakes in August, walks down the tidy streets of charming old towns, and annual events like July Fourth parades. Everyone here, except maybe Midge, wanted every single summer to feel as special (and as similar) as the last one. These would be a glowy three months filled with crisp white wine at sunset, sandy sandwiches, oceanfront barbecues, and juicy berries picked ripe from the vine. The promise of an East Hampton summer was why Thea endured the icy winds of January, the muddy tracks of April.

Thea's husband, Felix, walked over to them. He was already tanned, thanks to his love of gardening, even though there had been only a handful of warm days in May. Felix had the tortoiseshell glasses and austere confidence of an intellectual, but a down-to-earth nature that made everyone want to befriend him. Thea thought he was the perfect mix of hard and soft: he had inherited the expansive mind of his artist mother, and the hearty masculinity of his Norwegian immigrant father. Leaning down, he popped a kiss on Thea's smooth cheek. "Can you believe she's thirty?"

"And I've got the puckering thighs to prove it," Thea laughed, self-conscious that she'd put on a few pounds recently. She'd started jogging and promised herself she'd cut back on the ice cream, even if it was summer.

Felix playfully squeezed a fleshy part of her hip; he was still hand-some, with that slender frame, those long, boyish eyelashes. "You look like you did when I first met you."

Thea wasn't sure how she felt about turning thirty. Some days she felt like her youth was slipping away from her. If her twenties had been defined by becoming a mother, what would her thirties be? She'd always wanted to go back to school and earn her degree, but it was too late for anything like that now. Imagine the embarrassment wandering around campus with kids the age of her babysitter?

"Your birthday is next," Midge said to Felix. His milestone was at the end of the summer.

"Shall we have another party for you, honey?" Thea sipped her char-donnay, squeezing his hand. "Maybe a vacation somewhere?" *Maybe that is what she had actually wanted*, she thought. A hotel room and a bubble bath. A nice dinner out.

Felix scratched the part of his temple where his hair still curled even though it was cut short. "My perfect thirty would be Thea and Penny gifting me time to start that novel I have bouncing around. Thea would have a steak waiting for me and one of those ice cream cakes from Carvel, and Penny would beg to eat ice cream for dinner, and I'd say 'Yes!'"

It was sweet, but they both knew what he really wanted for his birthday was a second baby.

"A weekend I can give you," Thea laughed, popping another deviled egg, dabbing her lips with a napkin. Since she'd met Felix ten years ago, she'd supported him emotionally and financially through graduate school, then through his rise as an editor at a local publishing house. Some days he'd get home, loosen his tie, and put on a record by the Rolling Stones, while complaining that he could write a better book than some of the novelists trying to sell their work. *Someday I'm going to do it*, he'd say, and Thea would encourage him, while wondering if it would ever be her turn to go after something she wanted.

Besides another baby, of course.

The phone was ringing, and Felix excused himself to answer it, letting the screen door slam behind him. In that moment, Thea noticed a sailboat gliding into the harbor. It wasn't uncommon for exploring sailors to push into the small, shimmering inlet of Gardiners Bay that faced Thea and Felix's house, but few ever stopped to moor for more than a few hours for swimming. She wondered what the boat was doing in the harbor at this hour, the white sails flapping in the breeze.

It was getting late, and she needed to serve dinner. Teetering in her wedge heels, Thea went into the kitchen to get the lasagna. From upstairs, she could hear Felix in a discussion with an author. All day she'd busied herself with her to-do list for the party, trying not to think about those that *wouldn't* be there to celebrate. Her mother, whose grave she'd visited yesterday. Her sister, Cara, who couldn't afford the ticket from California. Her old summer friend, Margot, who she still missed, even after all that had transpired between them. All three had known Thea when she was nineteen or twenty; it saddened her that only her sister would know her at thirty.

Thea removed the foil off the salad, pretty rows of cucumbers and tomatoes arranged in concentric circles, and while admiring her handiwork, she smelled smoke. "No! No! No!" Thea yelled, rushing about to get a hand towel to fan the gray plumes coming from the oven. Using an oven mitt, she pulled out the lasagna, the noodles charred.

"Dammit!" she said. She opened the window higher and called through to Midge. "Can you help me a second?"

Midge's cheeks were flushed with punch when she came inside. Quickly assessing the scene, Midge said: "No one really cares about sitting down to dinner anyway."

Thea pressed her hand against her face, trying to pretend she didn't have a burnt lasagna with twenty-five hungry people outside. Had her tears smudged her mascara? She probably had black circles around her eyes like the guy in *The Rocky Horror Picture Show.* "Midge, I told everyone there would be food."

"It's fine. Come outside and have fun," Midge said, pushing open the squeaky screen door and stepping out. Dismissed. That's how it was with Midge.

When Felix had asked her a month before what she'd wanted for her birthday, Thea had said a big party. She hadn't had one since she was eighteen, when her mother brought her and a few friends roller skating up island, and thirty seemed like a year worth marking. But what Thea hadn't considered was that having a party meant she would do all the work. Thea wished that Felix had reached out to Midge early on, that Midge had taken over the details. It was something Thea would have done for her friend. She would have insisted that Midge relax on the night of her birthday. She would have hosted the party at her house. Felix hadn't done anything other than buy beer and toss it in ice in a cooler.

Thea fiddled with the pendant hanging from her neck. Should she order pizzas? She peeked outside the kitchen window to look at the

patio table where the crudité platter she'd made was still half-full. There
were pigs in a blanket, cheese and crackers, and shrimp cocktail. Then, of
course, there was the platter of Midge's deviled eggs. No one was really
eating anyway. *We still have cake,* Thea thought. Her birthday party could
still be lovely. She wished Felix would hang up on whoever he was talking to. For a second, she considered cutting the phone line with a pair
of kitchen shears.

"Mama, I'm sleepy," Penny suddenly said, tugging on Thea's jeans,
the smell of the charred lasagna overwhelming the kitchen. Thea had let
her daughter stay up watching *The Love Boat* and whatever else came on
in the living room, which probably wasn't the best idea. But with Felix
on the phone, she'd have to put Penny to bed herself. Cake would have
to wait.

As she tucked Penny in, Thea heard the sound of laughter outside.
Someone else's good time. Penny announced she needed to go potty.
She begged Thea to sing her a song. Then she wanted Thea to rub her
forehead. It was so hard for Thea to say no, so she sat there feeling a bit
like a prisoner. She didn't want to make her daughter cry. Not tonight.

Downstairs, after Penny had finally settled, Thea tossed the lasagna
in the trash, then carried the chocolate cake she'd baked herself outside.
The frosting was beginning to melt.

The partygoers clapped as she set it down. Midge was right: no one
seemed to care about dinner. A light on the horizon caught her eye. It
was the sailboat, lazily rocking from side to side in the calm harbor. A
single glow from the cabin, another from the back deck. Who would
park overnight in someone's private inlet?

Thea began to slice the cake, serving each wedge on a paper plate
with confetti printed on it. She cut herself the last piece, joining a group
of friends at the picnic table. She was thirty now, a grown-up. So why
was she so upset that no one thought to sing?

Chapter Two

"**Y**ou're as pretty as a parakeet." Thea kissed the top of her daughter's smooth hair after braiding it. The six-year-old was a dead ringer for her father, the dimple in her left cheek deep and rounded like Felix's. When they first met, Thea loved to make her husband smile, just so she could insert the tip of her finger into his dimple. She loved that dimple on her little girl now, even if sometimes she wished that Penny had a little more of Thea in her. When perfect strangers told Thea that her daughter looked like her, she saw nothing but Felix's charisma, his curious eyes, his desire to take things apart and put them back together.

What Thea and her little girl shared was the ability to focus and observe in quiet: The two of them could hunt minnows for hours. They kept logs of the phases of the moon and lay in the grass searching for four-leaf clovers. They pet their rescue dog Bee's belly, or "Old Girl," as they called her now, and laughed when she shook her leg. Sometimes Thea set up a still life scene—a vase with flowers, a book, a clock—and they'd draw it. Other times they caught fireflies and tried to draw those as they flickered. It was like magic when they spent days like this, and it was so different from the ones where Penny threw a tantrum and Thea grew so overwhelmed with her daughter that she'd pretend to use the bathroom and cry into a musty bath towel while ignoring her daughter's shrieks outside the door.

"Can you put carrots, crackers, and pepperoni in my lunch?" Penny said, trying to hold a bundle of dolls without dropping them while brushing her teeth. Her daughter was also a bit of a list maker. Perhaps that was something else she got from Thea. A desire to feel like you were getting things done. Felix sometimes looked at Penny's morning list—the items led with: make bed, eat breakfast, feed Bee—and her husband would wink at Penny. "This is why women should rule the world," he'd tell her.

Thea had to stop herself from saying aloud the malcontent that popped into her head. *Stop patronizing our daughter like you actually believe she might be president someday. No matter what Gloria Steinem says or does, women are still at home. Doing everything but what they really want.*

Today was Penny's first day of summer camp. And as Thea flipped the French toast on the griddle, she looked out over the calm blue inlet. There was the same sailboat, gently bobbing in the harbor, the gleam of its shiny steel captain's wheel catching the sun. Not only was the boat built of polished teak wood with crisp white cushions positioned in a right-angled U at the back, it had a cabin below with a mysterious name painted on the shiny wooden back: *Dalliance, New York, New York.* She half expected a leggy Italian model to emerge from it.

She'd considered rowing out to the boat, telling the mysterious sailor that this wasn't Three Mile Harbor where yachts moored off the marina. This was a residential inlet, across from the privately owned Gardiners Island and inland from the choppy mouth of the Atlantic Ocean. With the exception of one other house on the crescent of land that curved moonlike around to their small, grassy backyard, the harbor was quiet and still and their own.

"It's always sunny on the hill," the realtor had playfully sung out to her and Felix when they stood in this spot in the kitchen seven years before, asking particulars about the appliances, opening and closing kitchen cabinets, inquiring about the age of the windows. Felix was beginning his job as an editor at a small publishing house in Sag Harbor. Thea's stomach rounded to a ball that winter, their hopes pinned only on their future together. Even after purchasing the house, they still sang the silly song sometimes. The tune—and the house—had become a symbol of all that was right about them.

Thea wondered how her modest yellow Victorian looked from the bow of the sailboat. Even if it was much smaller than the grand old-money estates near the ocean, she and Felix counted their house the loveliest. It had a small private dock where Felix kept two canoes, as well as a floating wooden platform for swimming. Penny had only recently made it to the dock on her own while swimming the doggie paddle, and Thea had sat on the platform cheering when a funny thought crossed her mind. She wanted to be little again, all those unlived years ahead of her daughter, all those dreams with plenty of time to chase.

Yesterday afternoon, when her sister Cara called to wish her a happy birthday, Thea had pulled the telephone into the blackness of the coat closet so the only thing she could hear was Cara's voice coming through the line. It was how she preferred to talk to her, like they were still little girls in their old bedroom, lying on their backs and whispering in the dark. "Everyone is telling me how great your thirties are," Thea said, trying to sound chipper, despite the fact that the shearling of her winter coat kept itching at her nose. "Even the dentist said that women don't get wrinkles until forty, and he stares at people's faces all day long."

"Well, I expect to work long into my fifties, even if that means I have to play a grandmother," Cara laughed. She was waitressing in Los Angeles and reading for bit parts in movies. Her most famous role was a mother giving a child a bath in a Mr. Bubble advertisement. "You know who is thirty and looks amazing? Farrah Fawcett."

"Wow. She's thirty?" Thea ran her hand down her thigh in the dark, imagining for a moment her legs were as fabulous. "I mean, thirty is good, right? No, it will be great. I definitely feel better than I did at twenty."

"At twenty, that summer with Margot . . . you were a mess, and I was a ten-year-old following you around. Don't you remember?"

"Was I? Were you? But I didn't have mortgage payments to manage or a child to raise." *I didn't have memories of practicing an alibi while drifting on a boat in the dark.*

"But you love your house and you love Penny. Why don't you come visit me? A little sunshine, palm trees."

"You think Los Angeles fixes everything." There was a hint of sarcasm in her tone. And still, Thea did imagine folding her clothes into neat stacks into Felix's blue leather suitcase, buying a new bikini, and wearing it on a beach in Malibu.

Her sister snorted. "California does fix everything."

They'd hung up, and even as her birthday came and went, one thought stayed with her: oh, how she wished she was twenty again. She'd been thinking of her younger self in the oddest moments, like when she tucked her daughter into bed last night and was overcome with the memory of when her mother did the same to her, even if the image of her mother's face sometimes felt out of focus. She missed her mother, an ache that formed just before she and Felix had met, but which persisted to this day. To be motherless was to be unmoored, like that sailboat drifting in the harbor.

Thea returned to her house on the hill after taking Penny to camp. Penny, who was excited to make macaroni necklaces with a camp counselor, even if it meant she'd be separated from her mom all day. For the moment, Thea ignored the breakfast dishes and left the laundry to pile up. Because she'd decided, without mentioning anything to Felix or Midge or anyone else, that the first thing she planned to accomplish in her thirtieth year was to get a job. It wasn't about the money; they lived fine on his salary. In fact, she hadn't worked since she had Penny. She'd focused on getting Felix settled into his career and on raising their little girl: nursing and bottle-feeding and trying to get her to nap, and, in later years, teaching her how to read or bake chocolate chip cookies, taking her to the playground or leading her Daisy troop in a community service project.

Yesterday, though, the morning after her birthday party, she'd woken with a deep sadness pulling up from her solar plexus. With Penny in front of the TV and Felix reading outside, she had dialed her sister, but Cara hadn't picked up. After trudging down into the basement and tossing a load of clothes into the washer, she'd collapsed into the laundry pile on the cool concrete floors, the stale clothes smelling sour, and wondered: *Is this all there is?* Because what was she in this life other than the mortar that kept the house glued together?

Thea wondered if she just got out of the house more, if her days weren't built only around making lunches or tending the vegetable garden, beating the summer crowds at Bohack's market or building the menu for a Friday night barbecue, she'd feel less restless.

After fixing herself a piece of toast with the radio tuned to the news, she climbed the stairs to a desk positioned under the slanted ceilings of the third-floor bedroom where Felix often took calls with authors. She'd started coming up here lately, appreciating how blank the room was, how there was never anything that needed to be tidied. She thumbed through the Classified ads. *Cabana boy at the Maidstone. Fryer at John's Drive-In.*

Through the small square window above the wobbly wooden desk, her eyes were once again distracted by the sailboat. Looking for a flicker of movement in her sightline, a hint that someone was inside. But since the cabin light on the night of her party, there was no change in the height of the American flag flapping off the back, no towel drying on the rails.

Thea returned to the Classifieds.

Person of Interest needs someone local to assist in high-profile operations; creative thinkers encouraged.

Could she be counted as a creative or a thinker? She was mostly a woman who kept cantaloupe cut in Tupperware in the refrigerator, who kept clothes folded neatly in her daughter's drawers, who went to the library every Monday to return and check out books. *Waitress at a clam bar. Lifeguard at Gin Beach.* She crossed both out with a Flair pen.

"What's wrong with you?" Felix had asked her this morning after she huffed that he hadn't cleared his dish from the breakfast table.

"Nothing, I'm *fine*," she said, forcing a smile as he'd kissed her neck softly, a tenderness she couldn't resent him for. How could she tell him she still thought of the baby that had been forming inside her only months before? How she wondered whether the child's face had hints of Penny's button nose, the reddish-brown hair of her mother. She didn't want another baby, she wanted *that* baby, and once she'd lost it, it was hard to imagine trying to create another one in its place. It was like trying to pretend your aunt was actually your mother, using a warm body to fill the emptiness of the one that left you behind.

Outside in the harbor, a head popped out of the boat, a small-framed figure wearing a navy baseball cap. It was a woman with a delicate shape, a red tank top tucked into dungarees. The stranger pulled on a thick rope attached to the mooring, and for a moment Thea smiled to herself: the stranger was finally leaving.

Thea went back to the Classified ad about a local in "high-profile operations." It had piqued her interest. There wasn't a phone number, only a P.O. Box. Opening the drawer, she pulled out a note card and wrote: *Dear Sir, I've lived in East Hampton since I was born. I know most local businesses and I can draw, if that's helpful. Thank you.* She sealed the envelope, addressed it, and would post it on her way to pick up Penny. Thea had vowed to start drawing more often this summer. She'd even picked up a fresh set of shading pencils and a sketchbook with firm pages. But every time she sat down to draw, she heard a critical voice say: *What is the point?* She'd spent years attempting elaborate scenes of the sea, painting watercolors of beach roses growing along the dunes, but she'd never felt confident enough to sell them at the annual summer art fair. Instead, a few summers back, she'd gathered the abandoned pile of old paintings in the garage and driven them to the town dump.

A noise rattled a floorboard downstairs.

Thea rested her pen on the paper. Listening with the intensity of her dog, Bee, who also lifted her head, Thea heard another creak. Then a faucet turned on, the echo of the pipe traveling up to the third floor where she sat. Was the sound coming from the kitchen or a bathroom? She couldn't tell. Bee—who had the ears of a Beagle, the tail of a German Shepherd—flew down the steps, ready to greet any intruder with welcoming licks.

"Hello?" Thea rose cautiously from her wooden swivel chair and leaned over the third-floor landing, her eyes looking for answers in the beige carpeted hallway. Felix was at the office. Perhaps their handyman was finally stopping by to fix that leaky basement pipe.

Her movement down the honey-colored wood stairs was slow and deliberate, her ears waiting for another sound, a voice. She wasn't scared, not really, not in this resort town where nothing ever happened. Yet she was certain that someone who hadn't knocked or announced themselves was in her house.

As she rounded the bend of the second-floor hallway, Thea reached for the first thing she could find: a toilet plunger they kept in the hall bath.

"Hello?" she called again.

A woman cleared her throat downstairs in the kitchen. Most definitely a woman.

Thea raised the plunger over her shoulder like a baseball bat, ready to swing, as she came down the last few steps. Perhaps it was the woman on the boat. Had she opened the drawer to fetch a butcher knife? What if the woman was poised to rob her? What if Thea wasn't at the four p.m. pickup for Penny, and her daughter began to cry, fear in her round eyes, because her mother never returned?

"Thea," someone whispered from the next room. "I don't want to frighten you."

"Who's there?" She raised the plunger higher, her pearl necklace stuck to her glistening neck.

"It's me." The woman's voice was quiet.

Thea rounded the green living room couches, passing through the formal dining room, ready to whack whoever was there.

When she stepped into her sunny kitchen, Thea dropped the plunger, the rubber bouncing off the wood floors in the silence. The thorny parts of her past barreled right into the present, slamming into the center of her chest like she'd stepped in front of a car.

A waif of a woman sat at Thea's table, a half-empty glass of water on the placemat in front of her. Thea placed a hand against the doorjamb to steady herself, the heavy feeling lingering in her chest. The air felt too warm suddenly, stifling even with the windows open.

It had been ten years since she'd seen her. And now Margot Lazure was here. In person. Sitting in her kitchen as though a day hadn't passed between them, sipping a glass of water that she'd helped herself to.

Thea remained completely still. "What are you doing here?"

Margot's long blond hair had been cut into a choppy bob, the blunt cut creating an uneven line under her Yankees baseball hat. It was severe compared to the long, flowing skirts and handmade sack dresses she once wore, the multiple strands of simple beaded necklaces that had hung from her neck. They'd been replaced with faded Lee jeans, a red-striped tank cut low into her modest cleavage.

Her friend opened her pert little mouth and said, "I'm—," before pressing her lips back together. While Thea couldn't be sure what Margot was about to say, it had looked like the beginning of "I'm sorry." Which would be more than appropriate.

The tiny muscles in Thea's right eyelid began to twitch, and she rubbed at them as though she might rub the discomfort away. Her brain wasn't working right, and she struggled with what to say. "I thought you'd call me on my birthday, not just show up here like this," Thea said.

Margot's face brightened. "That's right. Happy birthday. Thirty!"

Bee wagged her tail at the stranger, and Margot pet her fluffy ears. Was it possible for a dog to remember someone it hadn't sniffed or seen for ten years?

"Well, are you going to explain yourself?" Thea didn't care that she sounded short. "Why are you sitting in my kitchen right now?"

Margot cleared her throat. "I just, well, I needed to see you, and I wasn't sure you'd let me in." She swallowed once more.

Thea had written her off when she didn't return her letters several years ago, and even if she daydreamed about a reunion, she'd long ago given up the fantasy of one. They'd separated because they'd needed to leave behind the memory of that awful summer night; because staying close friends meant having to relive the very thing they were trying to forget.

A dull ache escalated from the front of Thea's head—what the psychologist who she'd met with once had deemed her "worry spots." Her senses were overloaded with the reality of Margot's arrival. That it was just the two of them, the clock sliding to ten in the morning.

"I had a really fun party for my birthday, but Cara couldn't make it." Thea needed to say *something*, the silence pressing in on them. "What did you do for your thirtieth?"

"Monte Carlo." Margot shrugged. "But I'm sure your party was much better."

"Doubtful." Thea stopped herself from rolling her eyes.

Just below her shoulder, Margot had an ugly bruise the size of a plum, deep purple with blue streaks. She licked her lips once, pressing them inward, noting Thea's eyes on her skin, placing a hand protectively on the part of her arm that was hurt. *But if she'd really wanted to hide it,* Thea thought, *she would have worn a long-sleeve shirt.*

Thea looked out at the technicolor sky, wishing she could swoop away like the chickadees outside her window. Margot was in some kind of trouble, it wasn't hard to see, and it had left Thea with a wormy feeling in her stomach. "I don't understand you or this or anything right now. I can't figure out why you're here."

Margot took off her baseball cap, tucked her hair behind her ears, each lobe studded with a diamond. "I'm sorry. I'm being rude. First, tell me how you've been? You and Felix?"

A pang of heartache flashed through Thea, that gnawing sensation she used to get whenever she felt Margot wasn't being entirely truthful. "Fine, great. We have a daughter."

A knowingness crossed Margot's blue eyes. It was where her and Margot's looks differed: while they both had light hair and fair skin, Thea's eyes were hazel, her skin freckled, while Margot was alabaster, like one of those porcelain dolls her mother used to collect.

"Penny," Margot said.

"Yes."

Thea's fingers curled over the backrest of the kitchen chair. She wondered how long Margot had been in the house then, since she'd always been very comfortable moving through other people's houses, handling other people's things. Did she know Penny's name because she'd already climbed the stairs to Penny's room and seen her name on her glittery jewelry box? It was within reason that she'd padded down the hall and stood in front of Margot and Felix's modest bed, that she climbed the stairs on tiptoe to the third floor, watching as Thea penned an answer to the Classified ad.

Thea ran her hands down the seams of her denim cutoff shorts while trying to decide what she should do or say next. The coffeepot was still on, and it would seem less awkward if she could take a drink as they talked, the movement a distraction from the intense volley of emotions ping-ponging around her.

"Would you like a cup of coffee?" Thea nodded at the Black & Decker. How many cups of coffee had she had with other women in this kitchen since the last time she saw Margot? At least a hundred, she surmised, and she counted few of them as close as she'd once counted Margot. Her mind flashed back to them driving Margot's Mercedes to Montauk, the radio blasting and the windows down. How they'd pricked their fingertips with a discarded fishhook they'd found on the beach by the lighthouse, pressing the pads of their fingers together and promising to remain best friends. "Let's agree to always be there for each other, no matter what," Thea had said, and Margot had smiled and repeated: "No matter what."

Thea brought Margot the coffee, a pitcher of cream, and her treasured crystal bowl, a wedding gift from her old boss at the record store, the shop where Margot and Thea once worked. "I'm not sure how you take it," she said, realizing that she didn't really know anything about her anymore.

Margot stirred in a sugar cube. "It's nice being together again, isn't it?"

The way she said it irked Thea. It was so Margot to act as though nothing had ever happened and that Thea should forgive her long absence in an instant. She wouldn't.

"Stop avoiding the question, Margot."

Margot gulped the coffee in a way that belied her years of finishing school, like she was completely unaware of the strange reality of the situation. "Can I just hand you a big crystal ball, so you can watch my life as a movie? With a disco music soundtrack."

"I don't care for disco," Thea said, folding her arms across her chest.

The charm in Margot's face vanished into the steam over her coffee. "Okay, fine. Have it your way and we'll stay angry. I'm here because of my husband. Willy."

After that summer when Margot disappeared from her life and East Hampton in general, Thea had heard things about her comings and goings in the gossip columns. She certainly read the snippets published around the time she'd married William Crane, a restauranteur in Manhattan who the FBI had once investigated for having ties to the mob. Thea also knew that Margot's mother had gotten her daughter a job in the Fashions & Styles section at the *New York Herald* newspaper, only to be embarrassed when Margot stopped showing up for work. Thea had seethed with jealousy from afar at how easily Margot had thrown it away. Thea had even seen a photograph of her in *Vogue*. She was in the background of a party in Cannes, wearing a sunhat, a long floral sundress, and aviator sunglasses, the photo capturing her wide smile with her perfect row of teeth. She'd flitted through a carefree, glamorous life in New York, while Thea had settled into the shadows of a quiet town and spent mornings with other housewives, drinking Earl Grey.

Still, no one knew the kinds of things that Thea knew about Margot, the lies that Thea had caught her in.

"What about Willy?" Thea turned on the radio, needing a break in the quiet.

Margot folded her hands on the table. "Well, Willy is in deep. I need your help, but . . ."

"But you feel bad asking for it considering you haven't tried to contact me in all these years." Thea plated a few shortbread cookies, walking the biscuits over to the table. "Well, I agree. It's pretty lousy showing up like this."

Margot stared into her coffee. "You were my best friend, Thea. Do you know that I drove out here once? I parked in front of your house, watching you cradle Penny in your arms on the porch. But I couldn't get out of the car. Why would I mess all this up for you? Remember what my mother used to say about me?"

If there was fire, Margot would find it. Of course Thea remembered. But she never saw her as calamitous as that. Other than that one fateful night, she'd had nothing but fun with Margot, and she imagined Margot approaching her porch steps years ago. How much she could have benefited from the reemergence of an old friend during those lonesome early days of motherhood when her only company was Joni Mitchell's album *Blue*.

Oh, I wish I had a river . . .

"You left, Margot. You left me alone after everything that happened."

They sat in the quiet drone of the radio. Thea rose to wash the breakfast dishes, keeping the water on a weak flow so she could hear Margot's eventual response.

"I treated you badly. You're right. But you're not innocent. You share the same story."

Thea switched off the water, turning and resting her back against the sink, wiping her hands dry on a clean white dishcloth. The back of her throat began to burn. "I thought none of it ever happened," Thea said, watching Margot as she sat up straighter against the rough cane of the chair. "Isn't that what your mother told us?" Margot held her gaze. "Sometimes it feels like that summer didn't happen at all."

The song on the radio ended, and an announcer's voice roared on. Thea moved to turn the volume down but caught Margot's name in the headline. The tin speaker crackled. "Dubbed the 'Ink Heiress' due to her mother's storied career, Mrs. Lazure vanished from her Manhattan apartment just as authorities went to question her about her husband's mysterious disappearance. While the millionaire socialite isn't considered dangerous, she is wanted by police for questioning. Please contact authorities if you see her at Studio 54."

The announcer broke into laughter.

Thea locked her gaze on her friend, just as Margot's deep-blue irises narrowed and darkened. If Thea stretched out her arm, she could lift the earpiece of the wall phone. She could call the police in seconds.

Margot pulled a small, shiny locket from her pocket, dangling it from the delicate chain, the familiar hummingbird silhouette engraved in black on the face. Margot's family heirloom. The identical one she'd once given to Thea as a gift.

A part of Thea wanted to reach out and take it, hold it in her hands and clasp it to her heart. Was the picture of the two of them still inside? The photo had been no bigger than a thumbprint: two girls basking in the orangey glow of sunset, posing in a lifeguard chair with sweaters over their sundresses since there had been a chill in the air.

Margot unclasped the necklace and put it around her neck. "Do you still have yours?"

It was terrible to think of what Thea had done with it, that it was gone. "It's upstairs," she lied.

Margot nodded. "Please, Thea. I wouldn't come to you if there was anyone else."

Thea stopped thinking about picking up the phone. She folded her trembling fingers behind her back. "What did you do that authorities are *looking for you*?"

"It's not what it seems." Margot shifted in her seat. "Let me stay in your barn. Just for a night or two. Please, Thea. I'm afraid someone is going to find me in the darkness."

Thea kicked at one of the square table legs, and Margot looked away, like she couldn't take the sight of Thea's frustration. She needed Margot to leave. It was that simple. Felix wouldn't want the law to follow them home. Thea turned her coffee cup in circles on the table and a memory wrestled its way into her thoughts. She and Margot working at the record shop one afternoon when they were twenty, Margot urging her to say hello to Felix. Would she have met Felix at all without Margot nearly pushing her headfirst into the path of her future husband? Margot had done things for her. Big things.

"You're so crummy, Margot, you know that? Showing up here like this. You know I'm not going to turn you away."

Margot was a hugger. She might have hugged the grocery store clerk if she was so inclined, so Thea took a step back from her to avoid the embrace. It was one thing to help Margot, quite another to get all syrupy and pledge allegiance to their friendship once more.

"We're like sisters, you and me." Margot dropped her arms to her sides. "You could have shown up at any point, and I would do the same for you."

Thea liked to think that was true, even if she'd never show up unannounced on anyone's doorstep.

"One night," she said. "But keep yourself invisible."

"You know how good I am at blending in." Margot brightened, and her sarcasm amused both of them. "But I agree. Felix can't know I'm here."

That thought wasn't nearly as amusing, and Thea didn't know yet how she'd keep her hidden away; the gossip in the town came in every morning with the tide. Plus, Thea wasn't sure she could keep a secret from her husband. Although she'd kept things from him before, hadn't she?

Chapter Three

That night, just before bed, Thea stepped inside the lemon-themed nursery to return a few baby books Penny had taken off the shelf. *I love this house*, Thea thought, with its sagging wooden floors, polished mahogany stair banister, and crisp, white-painted ceiling moldings adorned with rosettes. When it came to decorating, Thea didn't follow the latest trends—she despised most of the bright orange bathrooms and geometric patterns in magazines. Instead, Thea preferred to fill her home with secondhand furniture she picked up at East Hampton estate sales, solid traditional-style dressers, desks, or sideboards that she'd sand and paint (or stain) the surfaces of. Just like her turn-of-the-century house, those pieces had a story, and that had always been a comfort to her, knowing that the past could remain with you, if you wanted it to.

The nursery, which Penny had outgrown and moved down the hall from, had always been Thea's favorite bedroom in the Victorian, even if it was the smallest and set aside for a baby that still wasn't here. The room got sun all day long, and it had pretty views of the sea and the yard. She had mostly avoided this room lately, keeping the door closed as she moved through the house vacuuming and dusting, chasing Penny into the bath and then into bed. She hated seeing the empty crib inside.

Her husband, with dark features like his mother, a man whose tortoise-rimmed glasses were often buried in a novel, was already in bed when Thea lay down beside him on top of the freshly ironed sheets.

He immediately placed his bookmark into the pages while slipping his other hand under the silky polyester of her peach nightgown. *Not now,* she thought, her mind elsewhere. Nagging at her, of course, was the reality that an hour earlier Thea had dropped a stack of sheets, two pillows, and a blanket on the old couch in the barn so that Margot could row onto shore when darkness fell. There were a million reasons why Thea didn't want Felix to slip off her nightgown in that moment, and still, as his kisses traveled up her neck, she thought of one reason why she should. Felix couldn't think anything was amiss. She raised herself up to switch off her bedside lamp, even though Felix preferred to make love in the light, and arched her body up to him, doing all the things that drove him bananas, just so they could get to the end. When he was satisfied, Felix switched on the light and put a Beach Boys record on low; they often fell asleep listening to music.

He lay on his side, resting a rosy cheek against his palm and glowing at her. "You know *Pet Sounds* is better than *Revolver*. Admit it, once and for all." How many years could this debate carry on? She yawned.

"Brian Wilson was a genius, yes. But overall best album? *Revolver.* There's 'Eleanor Rigby' and 'Good Day Sunshine.'"

"That song is the fluff." He smiled at her. They listened for a moment more, then he said, "I noticed the pink plastic shell in the medicine cabinet. Are you back on the pill?"

The downturn of her eyes to the chenille bedspread, her fingertips finding the raised pattern, revealed the truth. She'd been caught, but doing what? Trying to keep her body from entering into a certain kind of hell ever again.

"I know this hasn't been easy," he said, reaching his calloused fingers for her hand. "But I want to be a young father, Thea. You always said you wanted to be a young mother."

Thea sat up, feeling around for her nightgown and pulling it back over her head. "It took us so long to get pregnant the second time." She worked to sound calm and adjusted her chest into the ruched bosom of her nightdress. "The doctor thought we could test you. Your mother thought it would help too." She loved his mother, an artist active in the

Nuyorican movement in New York City, who had decamped to Miami only recently.

"Even the doctor said it's unlikely my fault. We have to be patient and keep trying the basal thermometer." He snuggled up to her upright position. "Besides, going on the pill pretty much negates this entire conversation."

It was inconsiderate not to have told him she was back on the pill; she'd just seen them in the medicine cabinet and was so tired of trying, the waiting every month to see if her period arrived. It took two years last time. "Isn't this my decision anyway? Whether I want my body to be taken over by aliens again?"

He laughed. "Last I checked, Penny is rather humanlike." With a sleepiness in his boyish brown eyes, he waited for Thea to lay back down and tenderly brushed a piece of hair off her slender neck, where two moles aligned like stars—her and her daughter, she liked to say. "Have you changed your mind?"

Thea stared at the ceiling. "Of course not," she lied, afraid to tell him that sometimes she felt certain, other times not so much. "I want another baby as much as you do."

They had been on a winter walk at the Montauk Lighthouse earlier that year when she'd told Felix she was pregnant, Penny climbing on the rocks ahead of them, the Block Island Sound pooling around the cliffs and rocky shoreline. He couldn't stop smiling that day, the woolen strap of his hat blowing with the icy wind into the black stubble of his chin. He'd intertwined his warm hand in her cold one, pulling her next to him on a boulder and kissing her like they were newlyweds, sweet and tender and uncertain and certain all at once.

Of course Felix had handled everything perfectly after the miscarriage started. Thea had found a light brown smidge in her underwear, and the nurse reassured them: *It's probably nothing.* But then the bleeding started in earnest. After the doctor had given her a pill to help with the discomfort and she had finally lifted herself out of bed to walk Penny to the bus stop, Felix had sat with her and handed her tissues and made her cups of tea with those little honey sticks she adored. He had reassured her that she had done nothing to cause this misfortune, bought her clean underwear after the bleeding ruined many others, washed sheets, and ran her baths, and still—still!—she couldn't stop the frustration she felt with him. These days, while remaining patient on the outside, she could tell that he was beginning to tire of her never-ending emotions about the miscarriage, the fact that she wasn't moving on.

"I'll stop taking the pill. I'm sorry. I'm just so afraid that if I get pregnant, I might lose that one, too." *There*, she thought, *I've said it*. She bit into the fleshy insides of her cheeks, girding for his response.

"Well, we can wait longer for you to be ready. But the doctor did say your body is ready, and I promise it won't happen like last time." Felix kissed her shoulder, turning his head toward her until she returned his gaze. "Don't be scared, Thea. You and me, everything always works out for us. It's the golden rule." She kissed him back on the lips because she knew he'd always believed this to be true, that she and him shared some kind of cosmic destiny, even as guilt niggled at her for a lifetime of dishonesty—for the fact that, even now, she was hiding Margot in the barn. After switching off the light once more, she waited for his breath to grow quiet. He deserved to be happy, and he was right: it was time. She'd stop taking the pill, for their marriage's sake, and just knowing that on impulse she'd made the decision, rather than avoided it, made her feel better.

Closing her eyes at the album's end, Thea tuned into the sounds of night, remembering then about Margot in the barn. She listened for sirens or the putter of a motor pulling into their driveway, evidence that someone was coming for her. But Thea heard only crickets trilling, the rhythmic lapping of water against the pebbly shoreline, and later, the quiet glide of water over oars as Margot rowed to shore. They agreed she'd drag the dinghy up into the sand. She'd hide it behind a large boulder Thea knew couldn't be seen from their windows. She'd enter the barn in silence. And then she'd wait.

Thea woke earlier than normal, rising and immediately peeking out the paned window, relieved that she couldn't see Margot's boat from there.

In the kitchen, she found Felix and Penny huddled over the movie listings in the newspaper, making plans to go to the Bridgehampton drive-in that night. *Star Wars* was playing, and both of them wanted to see it. Shouldn't Penny be scared of that awful Darth Vader she kept seeing in television commercials? Lately, though, her lanky, big-hearted six-year-old was showing signs of change, her outsized opinions and moody personality coming into focus, and it occurred to Thea then that she had only a handful of years left before the child grew into a know-it-all twelve-year-old, then an insecure teenager who said awful things to her mother. Mothers liked to think their child would never get there, but from what Thea had seen, they all did. She cringed thinking about the time that she had told her own mother, who wouldn't budge on her curfew, that none of the other mothers in the neighborhood even liked her. Rather than reprimand Thea, her mother had actually looked pained: *Is that true?* she'd asked with a tremble in her voice, and worst of all, Thea had screamed back at her: *YES!*

"Will you come with us, Mommy?" Penny said, sucking on a mouthful of Trix as Thea bent over to kiss her daughter on her milk-stained cheek.

Thea placed a quick kiss on her husband's lips, then twisted her daughter's hair into loops. Nothing felt certain today now that Margot was *here*. All night Thea had tossed and turned, waiting for a uniformed officer to bang on her door and demand that she hand Margot over, and the anxiety had awakened her: She'd let Margot stay without knowing what she had done wrong. "Okay, fine, we can go to the movies. But only if you let me do your hair like that Princess Leia I saw on the commercial."

"Yes, yes!" Penny jumped up and clasped her hands around her mother's neck, swinging like a monkey, pulling every muscle in Thea's lower back. Thea lowered Penny to the kitchen table while Felix announced he was leaving and pretended to fight Thea with an invisible sword.

"Watch the light saber." He smiled, whispering into her ear: "I love you. Remember I'm in the city tomorrow until Friday"

The city. She had forgotten. By the time he returned home, Margot would be gone. Guilt washed over her. "Yes, right. I love you too."

After dropping Penny off at camp and stopping by the post office to pop her response to the Classified ad in the mail, Thea rushed home. She'd chosen to wear her red peasant dress with a gingham belt to prove to herself (and maybe even to Margot) that she hadn't fallen so far out of fashion as a mother. She'd applied mascara and a generous stroke of blush.

Thea slid open the large, heavy barn doors, finding nothing but a stack of neatly folded blankets on a green velour couch with frayed cushions that she had saved from a falling-down mansion in South-ampton. Outside, from the lawn, Thea couldn't tell if Margot was back on her boat, because she couldn't see the dinghy. It left her with a pathetic feeling, the way she'd felt as a child when she was the only girl in the class not to get invited to a sleepover. The way she had felt, years ago, when Margot had left without saying goodbye. Thea wanted to talk to Margot—really talk to her—and she wanted a chance to tell her something about their friendship that she'd wished she had much earlier. That Margot had been her best friend. That she'd been the clos-est friend Thea had ever had.

Thea went inside, glancing at her reflection in the round mirror over the dining room credenza. Her blond wavy hair was clipped to one side, her wide-set amber eyes set into her ruddy Irish complexion, her skin perpetually dry and freckled from the sun. Most days she didn't recognize the person staring back at her: tired eyes, pale lips. Sometimes she pre-tended to be Felix rushing out the front door to work, donning a shoul-der bag and gliding past the mirror like she was on her way somewhere important, when she was only headed to the grocer. Today, though, there was a lightness in her expression that hadn't been there the day before, a hope in her gaze. It was silly to fight against what was inevitable; she would have a second baby, whether it was now or two years from now, and maybe Felix was right: carrying a second child would change everything for the better. She would finally be able to move on from this strange purgatory. She was tired of the judgment imposed on her by other women for having one child, the invitations that sometimes passed them over for birthday parties of younger siblings.

As she prepared cucumber-and–cream cheese sandwiches on pumpernickel, Thea spotted Margot steering her boat back toward Thea's dock with a nylon knapsack and suitcase in the bow. Watching Margot putter across the harbor, with her sleek haircut and precious Louis Vuitton suitcase, Thea remembered all of her friend's contradictions, how she was exactly the kind of woman people loved to hate. How much fun the summer people had picking apart her seemingly glamorous life.

Margot tied up the boat, the rubber squeaking under her weight as she hoisted herself up onto the dock, and Thea called out to her through the kitchen window. "I have lunch for us."

"Can we eat outside?" Margot said.

She gave her a thumbs-up, smiling on the inside. Is this what Thea had truly wanted all along? To have Margot here again? To ask Margot to attend a dinner party with her and Felix so she could watch them interact as a married couple? She wanted her to see how Felix knitted his brows at Penny's sweet turns of phrase. How inquisitive Penny was and how she loved to ask for stories about when Thea was a little girl. Her favorites were the ones Thea shared about her friend Margot, who had worked alongside her at Sunshine Records, who did all sorts of crazy things and got Thea to do some of them with her. Rebellion fascinated Penny, which shouldn't have surprised Thea at all—it was a trait she'd also inherited from her mother. Thea, too, loved girls that stepped out of line.

Cool air ruffled the roses as Thea walked outside to the smell of honeysuckle. She carried two glasses of iced tea along with two paper plates as she headed down to the dock, where Margot stared pensively into the shallow waters from her perch on the warm wooden slats. After handing Margot the drink, Thea lowered herself down beside her, kicking off her sandals and dipping her feet into the cool water.

Margot was looking at her with an openness, smiling. It was a chance for them to start from the beginning. *After you left, I ran home and bawled in my bed, my sister Cara running washcloths under the sink and dabbing them against my forehead.* But there was time for that. Her eyes grew wet in the corners. Her connection with Margot was always so natural, so steady, that it sent the truth out of Thea in a burst.

"God, life isn't what I expected it would be," Thea heard herself saying. Of all the things she could express, she wished she hadn't started there. And still, it was the truth.

The warm sunshine beamed down on them, and Margot rested her head on Thea's shoulder, the way she used to whenever Thea was upset. "For me too," Margot said. "No one ever warned us that entire years could be shitty."

"Or that friends could be." Thea didn't meet Margot's eye, instead dangling her legs off the dock like she'd said nothing of consequence. "I'm curious: Did you ever finish at Barnard?"

Margot offered a small smile. "Barnard doesn't give degrees to shitty people."

"And thank goodness for it." Thea tried not to laugh. Instead, questions swam through her head. She was about to ask another when Margot interrupted her.

"Did you ever go to art school?"

The memory of what it felt like to be twenty, to be beside Margot for some of the most important decisions of her life, flooded back to her. "For a bit, but then they realized I can't draw."

Margot's eyes glowed. "Not possible."

A swish of her feet in the water. "I also became a mother, and that kind of took over. I must seem so boring to you."

"Nah. You are exactly where I left you, but you're changed. In a good way."

Thea flushed as she pictured her daily routine of laundry, dishes, tidying, grocery shopping, and roasting chicken after chicken. With a heavy heart, she said, "I suppose I am."

They each took a few bites of their sandwiches, the water shimmering before them. But Thea couldn't go on talking, she couldn't attempt to know Margot again until she knew what had brought her here in the first place. "Tell me what really happened," Thea said.

"Okay." Margot sighed like it hurt, tilting her face to the sky; the bruise on her arm looking yellowy. She noticed Thea staring at it, and her nostrils flared. "Willy did this."

She spoke quickly then. Her husband had fallen into gambling with some guys in New York. Although she didn't know *all the details*, Margot knew he had a back-door blackjack problem; he loved it a little too much. One day last month, muscled men appeared outside their apartment, following him to and from his restaurants, and they'd mostly left Margot alone, except for one time when they'd followed her to the dry cleaner, trailing her home, too. Soon after that incident, Willy disappeared. He and Margot had a vicious fight that grew violent on account of the fact that Willy had started getting home later and later. When he didn't come home two nights in a row, Margot assumed the worst: That maybe the goons waiting outside their apartment had gotten to him.

Margot had stopped eating her sandwich. "I don't know if Willy is dead or alive, or if I should call the police. I don't know what to do, Thea."

Thea was still trying to understand. "But why come here?"

Margot continued on. When she had seen another dark-windowed sedan parked outside the apartment a few days earlier, she had decided she wouldn't wait for them to come for her, too. At dawn the following morning, Margot had grabbed a single backpack and suitcase and loaded them up with her belongings, taking a taxi across town to her father's sailboat that sat unused at the Boat Basin marina. At first, she had planned to sail to Greenwich. Then she'd thought of Thea. How Willy didn't know about their friendship. Thea's contact information wasn't even in the address book Margot kept near the telephone table in her Park Avenue foyer.

A sad little detail, Thea thought. But a telling detail, too, since it lifted the feeling of a five-hundred-pound barbell constricting her chest as she'd been listening with a certain amount of fear. Margot was right. It would be difficult for anyone, let alone those men, to trace her here. It seemed unlikely to Thea that they'd come for her anyway. Those were Willy's debts, not Margot's.

"Why do the police think you had something to do with Willy going missing?"

Margot rolled her eyes, disgust turning down her mouth. "Because this nosy neighbor of ours, Betta Gregory, who could write a newsletter on everyone in the building, said she'd heard us fighting and gabbed to the police." Margot exhaled and calmed herself. "Anyway, I suppose Betta was only doing her due diligence. We used to be friends, and maybe she was frightened for me."

"Well, we both know how easy it is to fall away from someone." It had scared Thea back then how she, too, could write a friend out of her life, how she could busy herself with a marriage, a baby, a series of mystery novels, and distract herself from missing someone. "Weeks turn to months, and months turn to years, and suddenly, you can't remember what you're really angry about."

"But not you." Margot clipped her with her eyes. "You know why you were angry at me."

Thea wasn't sure if Margot was making a statement or posing a question. Over the years, she had wanted to talk to Margot only to nail down exactly who had done what, to clarify the guilt and regret that she carried. "I suppose."

Margot pulled her skinny legs into her chest. "And still, it feels good to know that we can forgive each other."

"I suppose we can try, yes." It had a harder edge than Thea had intended, but she didn't work to right it. A part of her needed to keep her guard up. Thea knew, deep down, that Margot would probably leave as abruptly as she had arrived.

And yet.

If they didn't have endless time together, what they did have was this moment. They had their shared youth, the summer they met, their enduring connection. Because they weren't just friends. They were the guardians of each other's secrets, the keepers of each other's deeply held dreams, the survivors of a terrible night that bound them together like pages in a book.

Chapter Four

June 1967

Ten Years Earlier

Thea struggled to knock on the front door of the imposing Arts and Crafts mansion while cradling the wriggling puppy under her arm. The small Cape where Thea lived was nearby, no more than two winding bends and a left turn down a dusty dirt road, but standing on the mansion's expansive slate landing—with its grand white columns and sprawling green lawn—provided a more charmed view of the neighborhood.

A young woman in a long floral sundress suddenly opened the door, barefoot and with her blond wavy hair parted down the center. She glowed as if she'd spent the morning at the beach. After running her hand over the neat shape of her own darker blond hair, pleased that nothing was out of place in her thick elastic headband, Thea's words tumbled out in a single breath. "Hi. I found this puppy, and I've been going door to door looking for the dog's owner and . . ."

"Oh, thank goodness, you're back, little friend," the young woman's face took on a dreamy quality, and her smooth cheeks rounded with joy as she smothered the dog's tiny pink nose in kisses.

Relief flooded through Thea as she handed over the dog. "So she's yours, then? I'm so happy. I found her running through the garden in our backyard, and she bolted into the front, nearly getting hit by a car, too." Thea didn't actually have a garden, but there were the remnants of the one her mother had kept, a sorry tangle of tomato plants she kept telling herself to rip out to avoid thinking of her mother every time she saw them.

"Don't tell me this pup was nearly hit! I'll hurt anyone that harms you, puppy." *She's loyal,* Thea thought. She had to be Thea's age. Thea had just turned twenty, with a year of junior college completed, though judging by the size of the young woman's house, Thea guessed that her parents could afford to send her for a four-year degree. Thea imagined that she was the sort of girl who grew up attending horse riding camps and swimming at coveted beach clubs. The girl whose parents applauded her every jump off the diving board, gave into every one of her whims. "I'm Margot. Want to come in for something to drink? Then I can properly thank you."

"Sure. I can stay a moment, I suppose. I'm Thea." Thea was curious to see the inside the mansion. The biggest house she'd ever been in was when she filled in for a friend on a cleaning crew, and that one was only half the size.

Her swallow went down hard as she stepped into the lavish entryway, glancing around at the elaborate crystal chandelier and artwork in gilded frames. The foyer was quiet and cavernous, and when Thea spoke, her voice echoed. "What's the puppy's name?"

Nuzzling the golden fur of the dog's face, Margot said, "Her name is Bee, after Joan Baez. Joan is pure of voice like Bee is pure of heart."

Closing her eyes and snuggling the dog, Margot hummed a folk song made famous by Dylan and Baez at the Newport Jazz Festival, as Thea awkwardly watched her sway. *What is she going to do next?* Thea thought. *Get out a guitar and ask a complete stranger to sing along with her?* It was becoming apparent that she was exactly the kind of person that bugged Thea: the type at a party that worked at getting everyone to hold hands and sing a protest song in the name of freedom, when some just wanted to dance and forget their reality. Thea was against the war, too, as was everyone else her age, but she didn't hang her disagreement out for everyone to see. She didn't act as though walking around half-naked and *feeling* music rather than *listening* to it at some crowded music festival made her more important than anyone else. Thea knew she'd still be stuck living with her stepfather in a cottage that smelled of mildew, writing him a check for rent, and helping him care for her little sister. Being against the war didn't make her immune from the responsibilities of daily life.

Thea raised her voice to snap Margot out of her reverie. "Bee is a sweet name, but if I had a dog, I'd prefer John, Paul, Ringo, or George. I saw them last summer at Shea. Second level, tenth row." Margot didn't respond, and Thea laughed to fill the silence, then rattled off something about their encore. The dog was on the floor now, Margot kneeling beside it—was that a mood ring on her finger, or a giant emerald? The latter, Thea decided, while Margot draped a long, beaded necklace around the animal's soft neck.

Thea cleared her throat. "That won't really work as a collar. You must have a real one around?"

"We must, but where?" Margot opened what appeared to be a wall of built-in drawers and slammed them shut, rifling her fingers through each while still humming the Baez song. The puppy wagged its tail, circling and sniffing. It suddenly squatted, making a small piddle on the thick oriental rug.

"Oh! Where is her leash?" Thea glanced around, expecting a parent to spring out of the walls and yell at them. "We need to take her outside."

"Take her outside. Right." Margot folded her long dress behind her knees, returning to the rug and breaking into laughter, calling the puppy onto her lap. "Oh, Bee. We have some work to do, don't we?"

In her white knee socks, loafers, and fitted marigold romper—perhaps a bit too fitted, thanks to a love of butter pecan ice cream when she was stressed, Thea stared at the pee on the ornate Oriental carpet. The woman wasn't going to clean it up? She wasn't upset? Margot hadn't even been looking for the dog, and now that the dog had made it in the house, Margot acted amused, as though it was the first time it had ever happened. Which probably meant that it was.

Thea scooped the puppy back into her arms. "You're lying to me. The dog isn't yours, is she?"

Margot blinked her catlike eyes. "Of course she is."

Thea examined the puppy, fixating on a white spot on its belly. "Then tell me what color its stomach is," she tested.

Margot padded deeper into the house, the puppy wriggling out of Thea's arms and trotting after her. "If you're going to quiz me, I might as well get us a drink."

Thea reluctantly followed, hoping to God that she was wrong about Margot lying. Glancing at the family photographs lining the hallway, her breath caught as she recognized some of the individuals in the pictures. There was everybody's favorite news anchor Brett Lazure, now a morning show host on NBC, posing with Margot at every age. *My god. Brett Lazure is her father?* A rock lodged in her throat as Thea saw the next photo: Margot's well-dressed parents posing with President Kennedy and his wife, Jackie, the caption identifying Margot's mother as Julianna Lazure, the legendary heiress and editor-in-chief of the *New York Herald*.

How could someone so utterly glamorous live so close without Thea having had any wind of it? Then again, the summer people were so different from Thea, their lives so otherworldly, that to Thea, they were nothing more than a blur of money and faces and houses. Her own world carried on with little fanfare: She warmed her little sister's hot cereal and brewed Dale's coffee. She went to work at the record shop and spent her weekends lying on a beach while the summer people arrived on trains or backed up traffic in fancy cars, living out a rarified existence that had nothing to do with her.

"Sorry about all of this," Margot called over her shoulder as they entered the mint-green kitchen. A housekeeper in uniform slipped out as soon as they stepped inside. "Bee must have gotten out the back door." The puppy sniffed the perimeter of the terra-cotta floors while Margot unlatched a carafe of lemonade, splitting it between two glasses and dropping a slice of strawberry in each. She opened an unlabeled bottle, pouring some of its liquid in each glass. She handed Thea one, beaming with pride.

"The puppy's tummy is white. Any other questions? My mother bought me the puppy just last week. An early birthday present."

"Happy birthday." *Cough.* Thea spat out her lemonade in the sink, resisting the urge to pour the rest down the drain.

Margot fell into giggles, shrugging: "What? It's just a little splash of Beefeater."

Voices drifted in through the back door, a man and a woman's, and Margot quickly dumped her drink down the drain, running the faucet while chewing at the inside of her lip. Just before the couple entered the kitchen, Margot snatched up Bee and thrust her into Thea's arms. "Just follow my lead. Okay?"

And then there she was: pint-sized Julianna Lazure surveying the kitchen and her daughter, who Thea quickly realized got her height from her tall, anchorman father. The sight of this woman—someone else's *mother*—with her vulnerable bare legs so exposed in a tennis skirt, sent Thea's heart into a plummet as she remembered how skinny her own mother's legs were in the end, how sharp the angles of her elbows, as if she were using a pencil to erase her limbs altogether. Thea had just started illustrating for the campus newspaper when Dale had called her home to help. Just before she had gone home, she'd turned in a witty illustration to accompany an article about cheating, and oh—*oh!*—how she had daydreamed about designing the campus paper the following year.

Instead, she had spent the next few months at her mother's bedside, the last few weeks next to her in the hospital, machines whirring and beeping, nurses shuffling in and out, the ubiquitous odor of cleaning spray and floor wax. Thea had tried to remain vigilant but cheery, even as her heart spliced into a million little pieces. "You will be okay without me, Thea. You will," her mother said once, after they'd finished a cross-word puzzle, growing serious. "I've taught you how to be a strong girl, and I need you to remember that. For Cara."

Two weeks later, the night before she'd died from a cancer that was unexpectedly swift, she had gripped Thea's hand as though she were about to fall off a cliff. "My little lark, you need to look for happiness in all the nooks and crannies of life, okay? There are pockets of it, all around you, but you have to keep your eyes open and look. Really look." Thea nodded back like she'd understood completely, and when she'd asked Thea to watch over her stepfather and her sister after that, Thea had nodded again. She would have said yes to anything. In return, she'd whispered the only words she could think of: "Please don't leave me, Mommy."

Little lark. Thea had taken to calling her sister that.

"Margot? Why are you still here?" Julianna's voice broke through Thea's thoughts. Her tennis whites were pressed pin-straight, her tone insinuating a crime. She stroked her neck with disgust, and if she noticed Thea or the dog, she didn't acknowledge either.

Margot put an arm around her father's waist, a white belt anchoring his tennis shorts. "Oh, Daddy. Will you explain to Mommy that I don't want some boring summer job? I don't want to be a member of this abhorrent capitalist culture you both center your world on."

Her mother pinched her eyebrows together. "We will not have this conversation again. We've been too soft on her, Brett."

"Oh, sweetheart, that's hardly the point." He unhooked Margot's arm from his waist, pivoting so he could see his daughter, and spoke as though he was delivering a headline. "It will be nice for you to get out and meet new people, Margot." He glanced at Thea, his eyes saucering at the sight of the dog. "Who is this?" he said, while Julianna turned to fill a glass with water.

"See! I already have friends here, Daddy. This is Thea, a brand-new friend, and besides, half of New York is in East Hampton, remember? I don't need to be wasting away at a local real estate office or running around some dinky newspaper kissing up to somebody I'll never see again."

The record store. Sunshine Records. They needed another salesperson. One of the owners, Shelly Burns, had just recently complained to Thea that she and her husband, Jay, couldn't find any women to hire—only men were responding to their Classified ad. "And everyone knows women sell more records," Shelly had laughed, her thick black hair braided in

two parts, one hanging over each shoulder, her bangs falling straight to
her shapely brows. But Thea couldn't recommend Margot for the job.
She might as well have been from Mars. What if Margot did something
to offend Shelly, and it was Thea's fault for bringing her in in the first
place? Thea loved her job at the record store. It wasn't much to be a clerk
whose job was to restock albums, shelve sheet music, or book bands who
wanted to use the recording studio Jay had set up in the back. But the
rotating cast of music lovers filling the store, the smell of plastic envel-
oping the albums, the satisfaction that came with matching a patron
with the perfect vinyl record—it filled Thea with something close to joy.
Of course, it also allowed Thea to make her own money so that she and
Cara could get out of there someday.

Julianna slammed her glass down. "You're not laying around all summer smoking grass and telling me you're not going back to Barnard."

"You're a total witch, Mother."

"Same to you." Julianna rubbed her temples as though a headache
was forming.

"Now, girls," Brett spoke as though he were brokering a peace agree-
ment. "Stop getting so emotional."

"Shut up," both women said in unison, chuckling in a momentary
truce.

Thea couldn't figure out how to put the puppy down and slip out
the French doors without being noticed. She had *never* spoken to her
mother that way, and a part of her wanted to yell at Margot: *Your mother
could leave you in a matter of months. She could leave you with a hole in
your heart so big that some days it feels like you've been hollowed out like that
swimming pool outside.*

Working not to call attention to herself, Thea crouched down to
release the animal onto the kitchen's wood floors. She felt Julianna's
piercing blue eyes pin her and the woman emitted a high-pitched howl.
It became very clear to Thea that Bee was not, in fact, the family dog.

"MARGOT!" Julianna grabbed Margot by the ear, tugging her to
the back door of the kitchen. "That's it. If you don't get a job by the end
of the day, you're out on your ass."

Thea cradled the puppy as she tripped on her own two feet trying to rush outside behind Margot, jamming one of the French doors into her toes. She yelped in pain, not even registering what Margot was saying back to her mother, both women yelling through the screen. The last thing Thea heard was Julianna's voice: "I will change the locks, that's how. Don't tempt me."

Margot slammed the door shut. She and Thea hurried along the stone terrace until they were standing beside the tiled pool glimmering at the center of the lush formal gardens.

The puppy was a birthday present from her mother! It was an utter lie.

There were four loungers in a neat row on one side of the pool. Margot fell back into one, draping the back of her wrist across her forehead as though she were catching a fever, her stack of silver bangles sliding with a jingle down her arm. Thea trembled, holding the dog.

"I'm in trouble," Margot whined.

"You're in trouble? *You?!*" Thea said, not really feeling sorry for the woman, who appeared to be a spoiled brat. "What am I going to do with this puppy?"

Neither said a word for a moment. There was birdsong, a car revving in the distance.

"Wait, I have an idea." Margot sat up, blinking to adjust to the blazing sunlight. "Give the dog to me. I'll make a bed for her in the pool house. My parents will never be the wiser. They're not even here during the week."

"But it's Monday, and they're still here." Thea glanced at her watch. Ten thirty. She had to be at work in thirty minutes. She wasn't sure if her boss tolerated lateness because she had never been tardy. "I don't think—"

"Listen, this could work. They're leaving at two."

Thea didn't want to bring the dog to the pound, but trust Margot? How could she? "Why should I believe you?"

Margot collapsed against the lounger's plastic slats, turning onto her side in defeat. There was something familiar about the way she curled into a fetal position, how she stared at the blue sky, her cheeks slack with disappointment. It reminded Thea of herself on the days when she couldn't get out of bed. That elephantine feeling that pressed on her chest. When she'd switch on her turntable and play her scratched "Yesterday" single from her senior year of high school. Then she'd realize all over again that for her problems to truly go away, the memory of her mother needed to grow dim. She needed to forget.

Instead, she held tighter.

Thea wanted to remember everything about her mother: how she smelled of Johnson's baby powder, how she closed her eyes in concentration when Thea read aloud to her from Hemingway novels, how she loved to sing along to Broadway show tunes, how tight her slender arms could wrap a person, could wrap Thea.

"I'm sorry," Margot said. "I've wanted a dog my entire life, but she's always refused. I don't have a sister or a brother or anyone really, and then you showed up, and I thought: *I'll do it*. I'll give this puppy a home."

"You don't have anyone? I hardly think someone like you—"

"What do you know about me?" Margot snapped, and her pain softened something that had been forming in Thea. Not to assume that anyone is without problem—it was the first thing that her mother had taught her. *Just think of that nice First Lady and the pain she's had to carry.*

But how could this girl possibly have felt she had nobody? She had two successful parents concerned for her well-being. She was going to *Barnard College*. She could study whatever she wanted. Then again, Thea's mother had never spoken to her with so much hate, like everything about her daughter disgusted her. Thea suddenly wanted to be Margot's friend. Perhaps every single person on earth got a little lonely sometimes, and all one could do to survive was to be there for someone else, even in the most fleeting sense.

"I lied once about having a dog, too. In third grade," Thea said, and laughed.

Margot sat up with a smile, hugging her arms around bent knees. "Well, maybe I'm eight years old in spirit, then."

They agreed to take in Bee as their dog and share care for her in the pool house. And suddenly, Thea felt like she was fourteen years old and at a sleepover, her mother in the next room shushing her as she and Margot giggled and daydreamed about things they wanted to do together. She forgot that Margot had lied to her. She understood how desperate Margot was to love something, and to be loved. It was how Thea felt most days: a desire to connect to something she wasn't sure was out there.

Even as she opened her mouth, Thea hoped it wasn't a mistake. "After you get her settled, I'll ride back over on my bike and we can head to Sunshine Records. I clerk there, and they're desperate for help. Working together will make things easier on us, and it will certainly get your mom off your back."

Margot smiled. "You would do that for me?"

There was a split second where Thea could see into the future—she and Margot swimming at the beach, sharing a dinner salad, going on a double date. She could use a friend. The corners of her mouth turned up. "I have a good feeling about you."

Chapter Five

When they entered Sunshine Records at a quiet end of East Hampton village, the shop housed in a brick building separate from the boutiques that catered to the summer people, Shelly Burns was behind the circular counter. A pair of metallic headphones covered her small ears. Her blue-shadowed eyes closed, she listened to an album playing on a turntable she kept at the front counter. Whenever a new record came in, particularly one people had been reading about in *Tiger Beat* or *Record World*, the record store owner and her husband, Jay, treated it like a prize and listened to it before they allowed customers to purchase it. They wrote reviews of the albums on index cards and taped them to each record in the music store, which sold everything from folk to rock, jazz to blues.

Aware that the brass bells inside the shop door sounded, Shelly waved to the two young women, quickly removing her headphones and placing them on the glass counter. "You have to hear this new Jefferson Airplane song. Grace Slick is pretty much singing about LSD, and they're going to have to play it on the radio." Shelly loved to pinpoint controversial lyrics.

"Why? Is it too good not to?" Thea tossed her sack purse under the counter.

"'White Rabbit' is going to be our biggest seller of the summer. I guarantee it." Shelly held up the album *Surrealistic Pillow*. A black-and-white photograph of the band graced the cover, each member posing with kind eyes. Grace Slick looked as though she could teach first grade, and her neat line of bangs meeting her eyebrows mimicked Shelly's.

Thea reached for the headphones, holding one earpiece up to listen. The beginning, she was reluctant to admit, was *trippy*, the word she hated using since so many of those who used it were stoned out of their minds. Maybe musicians could make a great song while on a mind-expanding drug, but plenty of songs continued to be made without the use of one. Thea bucked against the idea that you needed to be *on something* to really enjoy a song, what some people at parties believed.

She was about to write off the song when Grace Slick cut to the chorus, hitting a guttural darkness with her voice that made Thea feel something she didn't expect: understood. "Ooh. I dig this." She returned the headset to Shelly, the rhythms sticking in her mind.

"I told you." Shelly was pleased as she lifted the needle.

"Grace Slick is my hero," Margot said, and pretended to hold a microphone as though she was the rock-and-roll singer yelling into a crowd of concertgoers. "'We are the people our parents warned us about.'"

Thea laughed. "Well, she certainly doesn't mind standing in the ocean during a hurricane." Thea herself didn't have the courage to speak her mind quite like Grace Slick, declaring herself something so different from everyone else around her. To be something that went against the grain. She supposed quitting on Dale and taking the job at the record store six weeks ago had been a small act of rebellion, but telling everyone around her to fudge off? It wasn't in her.

She was about to introduce Margot to her boss when Shelly asked, "Who's your friend?" Before Thea could get a word in, Margot jutted out her slender hand, pretty gold cocktail rings with pastel stones gleaming on two of her fingers.

"I'm Margot. I live in town."

Shelly's eyes traveled down to Margot's long skirt and bare feet, her pink painted toes peeking out, a toe ring on one. "Nice to meet you. I'm Shelly."

Shelly didn't seem to care that Margot looked as though she were walking on a beach. "Margot lives in town, part of the time."

"Right. We city people invade in summer." Margot pretended to be a creepy-crawly traveling up Thea's spine, and they laughed. Then she turned to look around the shop's music posters in awe, pointing out all the ones covering the walls like wallpaper: the Doors, Marvin Gaye, the Supremes.

Shelly spoke in Margot's direction. "We've been collecting those posters since we opened two years ago. We used to be a small room off the old pharmacy, but when the pharmacist retired, we took over the whole space."

Thea used to come into the store with her mother most weekends to buy records. Shelly knew them, but one rainy day in April, after Thea had already been coming in by herself for months, Shelly had asked where her mother was. "She's not with us anymore," Thea had said, and Shelly had dropped her eyes to the cash register. The next time Thea browsed the shop, she and Shelly struck up a conversation about the latest Beatles single "Penny Lane," with "Strawberry Fields" on the flip. "I notice you love music," Shelly had said after, her gentle manner already apparent as she pointed to the "Help Wanted" sign taped to the cashier's desk. "You interested in applying? We pay a dollar-sixty cents an hour."

Of course Thea had been interested. She couldn't take answering phones for her stepfather Dale's plumbing business any longer. They didn't get along even when her mother was alive, and things had gone from bad to worse with her mother gone. Still, she had worried about how to tell her stepfather that she'd found another job that Tuesday night in April. Fortunately, when she'd delivered the news along with his dinner—Shake 'N Bake pork chops and green beans out of a can— he hadn't flinched. But she still lived with him. His home was the only one she had known since she was ten, and she had promised her mother that she would help raise Cara, who her mother had had with Dale.

Margot picked up a Simon & Garfunkel record to examine the list of songs, then put it back on the shelf. "I can't believe I've never been in here. Your shop is yet another thing in this town that my parents keep me from enjoying."

Thea cringed. Margot's comment was worse than her insistence on being barefoot. Why would she admit she had never gone into the very shop where she was trying to get a job?

Margot moved on to the jazz section and admired a red-and-gold-bubble-letter concert poster from a performance of the Muddy Waters Blues Band last summer at the Fillmore.

Shelly stood beside her. "My husband Jay's brother lives in San Francisco and sent us that—isn't the artwork unique? I imagine some-day these rock posters will sell at Sotheby's."

"Doubtful," Margot laughed. "My parents are the kind of people that attend auctions at Sotheby's and they'd rather spend a night in the sewer than admit that anything our generation creates is of value. Mother won't even wear a skirt higher than an inch over her knee."

Thea, a bit disheartened, signed into the hardback employee log while feeling uncertain about whether or not she should still suggest Margot as a new hire. But Shelly seemed unfazed by Margot, more curious than irritated, so Thea closed the employee log, readying herself behind the cash register.

"We just met this morning," Thea explained to Shelly, "but you're going to love these circumstances." She explained about the lost dog, and how she'd overheard Margot's mother insisting her daughter get a job. "Are we still hiring?"

Thea had never been the most obvious person to work there. She didn't play an instrument, and while she loved music, she did not have the catalog of musical knowledge that Shelly had, although she was get-ting better. Thea had been to one concert in her life, and she was fully aware that she dressed fairly square, more preppy than cool, exactly how parents these days *wanted* their grown children to look: denim cuffed shorts with button blouses, Keds on her feet. Still, as girlish as her style was, she'd been told she was an old soul by more than one teacher over the years, and this quality came in handy when recommending albums to customers.

But Margot. Margot with her rose quartz crystal dangling from her neck, her arms stacked with silver bracelets—she looked the part of record store employee.

"Do you want to work here?" Shelly asked Margot, who grinned back.

"It's dreamy. Of course I do."

The two women talked a while longer about Sunshine Records, and Thea knew Margot was hired once Shelly gave her the particulars: hours were eleven to five, three days a week, sometimes Saturdays. She and Thea overlapped on their busiest days: Mondays, Thursdays, and Fridays, when weekenders were coming and going to and from the city from the Long Island Railroad train stop.

"Could you start tomorrow?" Shelly asked.

Margot hugged her. "Of course I can start tomorrow."

"You think you can wear some shoes?"

Margot dropped her shoes on the checkered floor, slipping each foot inside. "Of course—I just love going barefoot in summer."

"Well, you will need to wear shoes while you're working." Shelly returned behind the front counter. "Can you train her these next few days?" she asked Thea.

The idea buoyed Thea. "Sure. I'll get her up to speed in no time."

The record shop was bright with buttery light and smelled of the sandalwood incense that burned in a holder on the front counter. The near-perfect beach day made the crowd in the store even more surprising; the shop was usually busiest when it rained, but it was Monday, over a week after Margot started the position, and they had plenty to do. Shelly reached for the Turtles' hit single "Happy Together" and set it on the turntable at the front counter, dropping the needle on the catchy song and turning up the volume so shoppers could hear it.

Imagine me and you, and you and me . . .

Whenever Thea heard the song, she envisioned she was singing it to someone she was falling in love with—someone twirling her through the pretty streets of Southampton or rowing her in a boat in the pond at Cedar Point State Park. She blushed when Shelly caught her in a daydream, her eyes refocusing from their far-off stare. "This song makes me want to be in love."

"What is this about being in love?" Margot said, popping between them behind the counter with a Jimi Hendrix album; a young man about their age opened his wallet and waited for Shelly to ring him up. Margot had settled in rather nicely at the shop these last few days. Even with Jay working in the stockroom and sometimes emerging to help out in front, the three women made the shop feel like a clubhouse as they spent the day chatting and laughing in between waiting on customers.

"You mean, what is this about *the lack of* being in love?" Thea said. She had had exactly three boyfriends since she turned sixteen: Lawrence, her first, was a guitarist in a local high school band; Matthew, who she'd lifeguarded with at a local summer camp, returned to Horace Mann and never called her again; and Brad, the college freshman boyfriend who kissed like a horse but also gave her flowers every time they went out. Thea had never been in love, and she didn't want a boyfriend as a savior, either. Her mother had tried that, and it backfired.

Shelly counted the man's change back, then popped a square of Chiclets chewing gum in her mouth, which she said eased her digestion. "Oh, girls. You'll find someone when you're not looking. Do you know my good friend sat down next to a handsome guy on a Pan Am flight? When they landed in Honolulu, he asked for her number, and they got engaged a year later."

"Wowwwww," Thea said dreamily. The idea of being on a plane was enough to turn Thea's gears—the thought that one might step inside a shiny jet and step out with an entirely new life.

"And they lived happily ever after?" said Margot, giggling, leaning down to pet Bee, who was asleep at Shelly's feet behind the counter. When Shelly got wind that they were leaving the dog in Margot's pool house, she had insisted they bring Bee to the shop. "Customers will love it," she had told them, "even if Jay is allergic." So far, though, he hadn't shown any reaction to the dog, and the person who buried her face in the dog's fur most often was Shelly.

"They're divorced now, but still." Shelly worked to keep a straight face as Thea playfully smacked her with the telephone cord.

A pudgy man with a clean shave and sunburned arms waddled toward them for help, and Thea nudged Margot. "Is he *my* happily ever after?"

Margot turned around so the man didn't see her burst into laughter.

The man wanted to surprise his seventeen-year-old daughter with a record. "It can't be anything that sounds like Frankie Valli, or she'll never touch it," he said. His close crop of hair set him squarely in middle age, which meant he most likely favored the war, and he was probably from the summer colony since his smooth leather loafers looked expensive and not at all like Dale's cracked, faded pair.

Thea showed him a brand-new Beach Boys single that was pretty popular. ("It will be on their new album in September," she said, an air of professorial knowledge in her tone.) Then she showed him the recent "Ruby Tuesday" single by the Rolling Stones, which was edgier and just right for a teenager. The father curled his lip with disgust.

"I wouldn't even want my daughter to go near a guy like that, let alone have him singing to her," he blurted, pointing to Mick Jagger's long hair and smug expression.

Thea pivoted, holding in a sigh. What this father wanted was something *safe* that counteracted any possible rebellion in his daughter. *That's what the older people have wrong these days,* she thought. *Music isn't the enemy dividing one generation from the next—it's capturing a sentiment that's already there.* Thea led him over to the pop section and pulled out two albums by Dusty Springfield.

"The first record is a few years old," Thea said, "but honestly, the song 'I Only Want to Be with You' is the best one. Maybe write your daughter a little note saying as much to her in black marker on the back." Thea pushed up onto her tiptoes for a moment, pleased with herself, and the man grinned, heading straight for the cashier.

"Don't forget to tell your daughter that you love her," she called out to him, even though she felt a dull ache rising in her chest as soon as the words left her mouth. She sighed, trying to push away thoughts of her own father, the one that left when she was a child. Sometimes she couldn't help but remember his clean shave, his giraffe-like legs, the stuffed mouse he gave her the day he left. He lived about an hour west in a suburb called Deer Park, but he might as well have been shipped off to Vietnam—that was how little she'd heard from him.

There were several listening stations in the back of the store where Jay had attached headphones to record players so customers could try before they buy. The shop, which was packed with crowds of shoppers for most of the morning, was quiet then, and after guzzling a Tab, Thea noticed Margot was stacking discarded albums left behind at the listening station.

"Do you need help?" Thea asked. Margot's bare back was visible in her sundress, the skin smooth where a bra strap normally drew a line.

"If there aren't any other customers left, sure." Margot handed her a stack of 45s. It was easier if they divided up the 33s and the 45s since they were on opposite sides of the store. Thea slid a few more into her arms and accidentally kicked over the trash can. She put the records down to right it.

Bending to collect a newspaper that had fallen out, Thea glanced at the front page: a photograph of three of the most stunning necklaces she'd ever seen and a headline—BRIDGEHAMPTON BURGLAR STRIKES AGAIN.

"Look at this jewelry that went missing. One is a replica of Elizabeth Taylor's." Thea held up the front page for Margot to see.

"They look like fakes." Margot wrinkled her nose, returning to filing away the albums.

The dismissive statement riled Thea; did Margot's monied background make her some kind of expert in jewelry quality? "Margot! They're priceless necklaces. Don't tell me that you wouldn't wear one."

Margot snatched the newspaper, walking to the listening stations and tossing it back in the trash can. "It infuriates me that the news is focused on the property thefts—what about the fact that residents of this town are so wasteful that they spend exorbitant amounts of money on something that sits in a jewelry box?"

There were times when Thea felt resentful of the summer residents too; how they had so much when she and her little sister had so little. But why would Margot feel that way? She was one of them.

"I suppose that's true," Thea said, pulling the newspaper out of the trash and pointing at the ruby-and-diamond necklace. "But just once I would love to arrive somewhere special wearing one of those."

Margot pushed forward two albums in the *M* section, slipping in a record by the Monkees. "It's like people want everyone to know how much money they have by looking at what hangs around their necks. Do you know in India, women wear gold, but the pieces mean something to them? They're symbolic. You tell me what those necklaces symbolize?"

Thea thought for a moment. "Excess."

"Exactly. Isn't that just awful?"

So your parents' money is awful, too. Thea felt nothing but reproach— how easy it was to hate wealth when you had so much of it. Instead, she fell quiet, turning to find the *B* section and sliding in an album by Harry Belafonte.

Later in the day Shelly needed to run an errand, and with Jay in the back stockroom cataloging inventory and phoning in orders with the record companies, it was just Margot and Thea in the front of the shop. Margot sat at a listening station wearing headphones. After stifling a yawn, Thea removed a sketchbook and pencil out of her canvas bag and arranged it on the glass counter. It didn't get that slow often, but when it did, she liked to pluck a record out of one of the shelves and draw her own version. This time, she picked an obscure band called the Left Banke. Rather than the bland photo of the band depicted on the front, she envisioned redrawing the type in a swirling burst of neon bubble letters. One pencil line turned into many, the blank page filling with her bold colorful illustration. She was so immersed in her design that she didn't notice when thirty minutes later Margot turned off the record player and leaned over her shoulder on tiptoe.

Thea snapped her sketchbook shut. She returned it to her tote. "Sorry, I was just jotting something down."

Margot tugged at the bag between Thea's feet. "You drew something?"

The clock over the shop door read five o'clock, and Thea gathered up her belongings. "You ready?"

Margot put a hand to Thea's elbow. "Can I see it? Please."

Thea hesitated. Sharing her work was as natural to her as riding a unicycle, in part because she was always afraid of being judged. These drawings were all she had that were hers and only hers, and drawing without an audience meant she didn't have to worry whether or not she was any good. She'd harbored many embarrassing fantasies over these last several months, hoping that someone—an older man, probably an editor at a famous magazine—might see her drawing in a public park and *discover* her, hiring her on the spot and giving her staff work.

But few people even glanced her way; mothers pushing strollers breezed by, and if a man strode past, he was more interested in her face than what was on the paper in front of her. At home, it was worse, since Dale referred to her drawings as "doodles." No, Thea worked hard on her illustrations; she'd spend hours erasing pencil lines, more time inking or painting them with watercolors. They were not doodles. They were her heart. And she hoped one day she might make a living off them.

Reluctantly, Thea removed her sketchbook and placed it on the counter.

As Margot flipped through the pages, Thea had the overwhelming desire to run out the shop door and not stop until she hit the ocean.

"This one, no, don't look at that . . . well, it could be better. I'm still working on that one, too, you know." Thea watched Margot's face for a reaction but she held her expression still while studying the drawings. There were only a few, since it was a fairly new notebook. She blinked, turned the page. Finally, Margot closed the sketchbook. "Thea! You're so incredibly talented."

The tension in Thea's jaw loosened, and it sounded like she'd sighed, but really she'd exhaled with relief. "You like them?"

"Oh, Thea, they're so impressive. Why didn't you tell me you could draw?"

"We didn't get to that part yet."

This made Margot laugh. They had only known each other a little over a week. "You have a goddamn special talent."

Bee jumped up from sleep, wagged her tail, and Thea bent down to pick her up. "Tell my stepfather that."

Mischief slipped into Margot's smile as she pet Bee, too. "You know what? I will."

A glow appeared in Thea's mind as though a match had been lit inside her. She didn't even know if Margot meant what she'd said about her drawings. Nearly every day she gave her little sister a compliment about how beautiful her handwriting was, when it was actually worse than a doctor's scrawl. It was just what people did to build each other up. And still, Thea felt as light as a seagull feather floating through the air at the beach. When they reached the sidewalk, Thea kicked off her sandals, just like Margot had, tossing them into her bike basket. *Margot.* This strange girl was turning out to be a kind soul. A good friend.

They pedaled their bikes under the sweeping elm trees lining the back streets of East Hampton, Margot riding with no hands on the handlebars, her back straight against the breeze, her porcelain nose looking a bit like a cherry. "Everyone needs a special talent, mother says. You're lucky you found yours. She wishes I'd find mine."

Thea rode with her hands gripping the handlebars, careful to avoid the pebbles on the roadside so her bike wouldn't slip. The dog trotted beside them on the grass, stopping every so often to sniff about. "You strike me as a girl that's good at just about everything."

"Mother thinks I'm *incapable* of just about everything. She wants my special talent to be writing, but I'm not a writer."

Kindness welled up inside Thea, a generosity that came only when she was at her best, something she hadn't felt for a very long time. "Well, you're not incapable at your new job. The customers really respond to your advice."

Margot pulled out several strands of hair blowing into her mouth, grinning. "Thank you! That means a lot coming from the shopkeeper's pet."

Thea liked that Margot noticed how well she and Shelly got on. The world no longer felt like it was on a tilt, and she was filled with another emotion that had become foreign to her this last year. A sense of hope. Of possibility. She threw her head back with the lightest of laughter.

"You know," Thea said. "I'm a teacher's pet too. And a parent's pet. And a friend's pet."

They were belly laughing then, the late-day sun shining on their hair and unleashing a golden feeling inside them. Even after they passed Margot's house and Bee plopped down in the grass momentarily to catch her breath, they pedaled around the block a second time just so they could keep talking. The dog hopped up, running to catch up to them, barking to get their attention.

Chapter Six

A few days later, Thea prepared breakfast in the kitchen. The room still smelled of last night's meatloaf, even though Thea had scrubbed the pots and wiped the faux-brick linoleum countertops more than once before bed. Popping a sugar cube in her mouth, a bad habit started only recently, she tied up the trash and walked it to the front door, empty beer bottles clanging inside, so Dale could carry it out on his way to work. Then she returned to the rusted toaster to remove two slices of bread and slathered them with butter, not bothering to switch on the handheld radio on the counter. She didn't want to hear anything upbeat today.

Her stepfather ate the same thing for breakfast every day—two sunny-side up eggs, a banana, black coffee, and the toast. She knew to arrange it on the solid blue stoneware dessert plate he favored, and not to pour his coffee, letting it sit in the coffee pot, since he'd want to reach for the same mug he pulled out every day—one of two jade-colored coffee cups that he and her mother had once used together.

Dale finished in the bathroom, she could hear him coming, and while feeling a bit like the robot housekeeper in the futuristic cartoon Cara loved, Thea dried her hands on her mother's old lime-green apron. Her little sister was crunching on Apple O's at the table, and out of boredom, Thea snuck another sugar cube into her mouth. She really needed to stop, but the problem was that no one even noticed Thea sucking on them, and the little burst of sweetness on her tongue tasted like a gift. Something only for her.

Dale offered his good morning by way of a guttural clearing of the throat and a subtle dip of his chin. Even after all these years, he was alien to her.

Within minutes, Dale had the jade mug in hand, steam rising off the surface, taking his seat in front of his breakfast. *His perfect breakfast,* Thea hoped, tensing inside and glancing to make sure his left palm remained open and flat against the table. When something was amiss in the routine, which it often was in those first few weeks after Dale made clear that he expected her to help out after Mother passed, Thea had learned that a closed fist meant that he was getting "that wiggly feeling" inside his body. He wasn't a violent man; he hadn't ever hit her mother. But a clenched fist was where he balled up his nervous energy, where he stored all the words he didn't know how to express, and an escalation of "that wiggly feeling," as her mother once explained with a straight face, was the precursor to an unpredictable temper. "Dale just needs everything the way he likes it to feel calm," her mother Irene, "Reenie," as friends called her, said after one of his outbursts. "Routine settles him."

Thea poured herself a glass of Tropicana and sat at the third seat at the rectangular table, trying to ignore the empty one. No one was saying the thing that she couldn't get out of her mind. She wasn't sure if she should acknowledge it, and if she did, what kind of effect it would have on her sister and stepfather.

"Yesterday something funny happened, Thea," Cara said, breaking the rhythm of Dale's chewing, a grin spreading over her sister's tulip lips. "Out on the busy road, little Jimmy Hoover was trying to ride his bike with no hands." Here Cara spat out a mouthful of Apple O's, since she'd started laughing.

It dulled the heartbreak weighing on Thea—her thinking that maybe Dale had forgotten about the anniversary the same way he'd once forgotten her mother's birthday. But her sister, who had no idea Thea had been tracking the date so closely, laughed hard at her own story, snorting even, and Thea couldn't help but smile with her. "What? Tell me."

Her sister pushed back a chunk of hair that dipped into the cereal bowl. Hers was the same reddish color hair as their mother's. "So he was on the road, saying 'Cara, Cara! Watch!' And he crashed straight into the telephone pole."

Thea raised her hand to her mouth. "Was he okay?"

He was, and Cara proceeded to throw her hands in the air and pretend to crash into the kitchen table, laughing even harder, but on the second attempt, she misjudged her weight and banged so hard into the edge of the wood that Dale lost his grip on his coffee. The contents didn't dump entirely, but the liquid slopped onto his plate, where he'd only eaten one of his two eggs.

"Jesus Christ," Dale snapped, his fist closing as he rose out of his chair, his arms curled with tension. "If you wanted to be clowns, then you should have joined the circus."

Thea worked to steady her expression, partly because of the hilarity of his statement, but also out of nerves. Cara stared into her cereal.

Dale shook the spilled coffee off his hands, his palms opening and clenching back into fists. Thea's heart skipped fast now, like a rock on the surface of the sea. Last year, she'd been sitting in the living room reading a book when the mirror over the fireplace had unexpectedly fallen to the floor and shattered. That confused state of fear, of not really knowing what happened, reminded her of this feeling. How nothing was ever wrong with Dale, until suddenly it was.

"Cara, get him a washcloth," Thea said, hoping that the appearance of the item would help tamper his frustration. But Dale had already left the table to get himself a hand towel from the hall closet where he began mumbling. Cara ducked under the kitchen table to hide, her body crouched low and round like she was trying to disappear. "It's okay," Thea leaned down to rub the delicate vertebrae curving along her sister's back, but then it came—the inevitable yell of Thea's name. Cara hated the yelling most.

Dale called Thea into the hallway by the bathroom, the spot where a single lightbulb was fixed to the ceiling, a silver pull cord comprised of small silver beads dangling. Standing next to him now, Dale hurled the linens, every single one folded and ironed by her, a growing mountain of sheets and towels at her bare feet.

"Some—Someone needs to take—care of this," Dale stammered, breathless. He had a particular obsession with the order of things in this closet, and she'd become accustomed to following it. The sheets were only ever on the top shelf. Towels were stacked side by side in the middle. Hand towels and washcloths went on the bottom. Everything *had* been in place, she'd just checked recently.

Thea gulped like she was swallowing glass. She'd watched her mother enough to know that when he got like this, she needed to tread lightly to appease him. "Of course. I'll get it right this time. I'll reorganize it."

Inside, she thought: *If I ever have my own linen closet, I will purposely toss everything together like a salad, putting pillowcases with hand towels just because I can.* The subversive daydream lifted her spirit, even though she was licking her lips like she couldn't get them clean enough.

Thea considered leaving. Forever. She could pull out that old suitcase she stored under her bed. It was beat-up, with a torn undergarments pocket, but it would do. She could stuff all her clothes inside. She could march off to the train station and board the next train to Manhattan, and then . . . then . . . She could go visit her mother's sister in Poughkeepsie. Her mother's *drunk* sister in Poughkeepsie.

Thea restacked a set of sheets onto the shelf, her heart falling ever so slightly. The only place she was going to was to work at eleven.

Dale returned to the kitchen, pulling open drawers and slamming them closed, and he stammered, "The hell this is living." Seconds later, a clatter of silverware fell to the floor. Thea rushed into the kitchen, where she found Cara gathering teaspoons in one small hand, big spoons in the other, her narrow cheeks flushed and wet.

The counter was all that was holding Dale up where he leaned against it, sweat circles seeping into the armpits of his navy-blue plumbing uniform, an oval patch with "Dale" scripted in red thread. He'd fixed his eyes to the calendar on the refrigerator, where Thea had drawn a circle over today's date. That was when he finally spoke, his voice hoarse.

"I didn't think we would make it a year."

"Me neither," she said, feeling sorry then. *So he* had *remembered*, Thea thought. With a heaviness weighing in her limbs, Thea lowered to her knees to gather butter knives and place them back into the proper slot.

Sometime in the morning . . .

It was a Monkees song in her head, one that was popular just after her mother became sick. Thea played it for her as she lay in bed, her body limp, her spirit slipping away from them. Normally, her mother was energized and in the kitchen early, her thick hair held back with a wide headband. Dale once joked that her mother had so much stamina, she could run to Montauk and back before most people took a shower. She'd lean in to kiss Thea on the cheek as she entered the kitchen, the smell of melted butter, cinnamon, and sugar wafting from a stack of French toast or the salty-sweet of bacon frying on the stove. The table was always set with this very silverware, a vase of flowers at the center.

The memories became too much to hold inside.

"Remember how she used to put notes in our lunch bags?" Thea blurted out, even if her voice was unsteady and trembly. "'I love you like the astronauts love the moon,' she'd say."

Cara grinned, her eyes puddling into glossy pools. "'Why did Humpty Dumpty have a great fall?'" She crawled over to Thea, who was sitting cross-legged, holding a bunch of forks.

"To make up for a bad summer." Thea delivered the punch line with a chuckle, glancing at Dale, who hadn't peeled his eyes off the calendar. It heartened her to know he was struggling with the day like she was, even if she had borne the brunt of his temper. "But we never had bad summers, did we? Mom made sure of it."

Dale cleared his throat and leaned his sausagey back against the white metal cabinets, exhaling with the most exhausted sigh she'd ever heard. She'd never seen him cry, not even at the funeral, but right now he looked as though he might never find the energy to stand up again.

"I still have one of those notes," Dale said, pausing so long, seconds passed like hours. The sprinkler was on in the backyard, and Thea listened to its pitter-patter against the cellar door.

With an even gentler voice, Dale said, "Cara, fetch me my shaving kit, will you?" It was a brown leather satchel he stored under the bathroom sink, and her sister was back in minutes with it clutched to her chest. She handed it to him, and the sisters leaned forward to watch him unzip it. Dale wasn't the type to share anything personal, and seeing him open up the leather bag felt colossal, like for the first time in their lives, he might reveal a part of himself they'd never seen before.

Out of a tiny pocket sewn into the lining, he slid out a small rectangle of folded paper. It was a watercolor painting of the night sky, the moon and stars nestled into the darkness, and her mother's unmistakable loopy script: *I see you in the stars, Daley. I love you.*

A bee, or at least the sensation of one, began stinging an outline in Thea's heart. She remained still, while Cara sprung up, flinging her small frame against the polyester uniform that hung loose on her father's chest. He let her stay there, resting his hand atop Cara's small skinny shoulder. It was one thing Thea could say about Dale—he showed her sister an affection that no father had ever shown Thea. Nothing overt, just small things—reading Cara a bedtime story, or scooping her an extra dollop of ice cream.

"You kept this? For how many years now?" Thea hadn't saved any of her mother's notes. She didn't have reason to think she'd never get another one.

"I did," he said, rather definitively, like there was nothing else to say. Thea wanted to know when her mother wrote this, and where Dale was when he'd read it. Thea tried to imagine her mother slipping the note into his lunch pail, how Dale's stocky shoulders might have softened as he'd read it, how her mother likely grinned when he got home, Dale coming up behind her at the sink, planting a kiss softly on her neck. Suddenly, she couldn't match the Dale who hollered this morning with the sentimental man sitting beside her now. Her mother used to say that Thea focused only on his negative traits. But she told Dale similar things about Thea, too. "Just give her a hug, Daley," Thea had once heard her mother pleading with him in bed, soon after they had married. "It would change things between you. Really."

Dale hadn't ever tried to hug Thea. She didn't want him anywhere near her. But in that moment, seeing the way Cara sank so easily into her father's lap, and sensing the comfort that passed through them without any words exchanged, Thea wished Dale had hugged her when she was young. Because it would mean he could hug her now.

The doorbell chimed, and the shock of the sound made them all aware of how unconventional the scene had become. Dale seemed most uncomfortable with it, and Thea tried to see it through his eyes. A grown man and two girls sitting on an un-swept kitchen floor, each of them longing for a woman, a wife, a mother, who had left them just as love-sick twelve months ago. Dale lifted Cara off his lap and stood, brushing off his pants and clearing his throat. Thea wished the spell hadn't been broken, that he'd had a chance to say more.

"May I help you?" Dale said rather formally to someone outside.

It was the singsong voice of a woman. All at once it registered who was at the door. Margot. "Is Thea here?" her friend said.

Thea was grateful they'd already cleaned up the silverware in the kitchen, but she rushed into the hallway to pick up the sheets. Her house was a mess. It was worse than it normally was, and the realization that Margot stood on her front steps, the cement cracking into pebbles in multiple places under her feet, might be worse than Dale's earlier tirade. The last thing Thea wanted was for Margot to see where she lived, the reality of her house with its chipping white clapboard, the only pool a giant mud pit in the driveway from a recent heavy rain. Her bedroom was so small it didn't even have a closet. She and Cara hung their clothes on hangers from a steel wire her mother fashioned across the back of their room.

Dale called Thea's name in a bland voice, and she rushed to the aluminum screen door, stepping outside with her body angled so Margot couldn't peek inside the house.

"Bye," Dale said, his shoulders slumped as he trudged to his van holding a toolbox. He glanced back once, a sad smile on his face.

Thea folded the pillowcase she was holding, in half, then in thirds, until it was a neat package resting in her palm. She turned to Margot. "Hi."

Margot waited until Dale started the van. "Hi. Sorry for dropping in so early."

There was something funny happening in Margot's concerned expression, like she was searching Thea for signs that she'd been in some kind of accident. Thea glanced toward the driveway where Margot's dark green Mercedes convertible was parked next to Dale's van, her stepfather taking inventory of the young woman's leather interior as he backed out.

"How long have you been outside?" Thea asked. She ran her hand through her unbrushed hair, her fingers catching in a knot. If Thea could hide in her middle-parted hair right now, she would.

"Long enough. I was about to knock on the door when, I heard . . . well, then I waited in my car until things quieted down." Margot had brought the dog, and Bee pulled on her leash to say hello, jumping up on Thea's bare legs and leaving wet paw prints on her thighs. "And I'm sorry, Thea. Truly." For a second Thea thought she was apologizing for the dog. But then Margot kicked at one of the loose bricks, releasing more of the crumbling concrete. "He's terrible."

A trio of sparrows chirped in a nearby bush, jumping to another flowering tree, then flew off. *Can I come with you, little birds?* she thought. There was no way that Thea wanted to talk about Dale's fits or the dreaded anniversary of her mother's passing—not after glimpsing Margot's life. She liked it better when Margot didn't know anything about where Thea lived, when she might have imagined that Thea's house had pretty painted shutters with stars cut out of them. Now Margot would certainly categorize her as just another down-on-her-luck local girl, someone who lived with an awful stepfather in a crumbling house in a wealthy resort town.

The front door clicked open behind them. Thea turned and saw Cara in her stained T-shirt from breakfast. She stared at Margot with mistrust.

"Yes, he's got a temper," said Thea. "But he's gone most of the day."

"Are you sure?"

Cara spotted the puppy, falling to her knees beside Bee. She was quickly smothered with licks and kisses and erupted into happy giggles.

"He's not that bad," Thea said. She wouldn't invite Margot inside. She could form whatever opinion she was going to form of Thea based on the view from these junky old steps. "What is that you're holding?"

Margot grinned. It was a dress made of a pretty blue fabric with a cinched waist and tank sleeves. "I sewed this for you. I thought the color suited you. And you said you have long legs and it's hard to find dresses that fit at the right length, so I made the hem so it would fall just right."

As she held up the dress, Thea could see that Margot had somehow gotten her measurements perfect. The dress hung to her ankles like Margot's dresses did, with only her toes showing. It was a dress that should be worn by someone carefree, a dreamer. Someone who twirled about at a beach bonfire just to feel the dress billowing around her. The other day at the record shop, Thea had complimented one of Margot's dresses, admiring the long strand of beads she paired with each of her outfits. She never imagined Margot driving home and sewing her one. But she had, and it was so incredibly nice, so overwhelming that she'd spent her free time making this, that Thea could feel herself turn to stone, afraid that if she said anything, even a thank-you, she might burst into a sob.

Margot shooed her inside to try it on. "Come on, I want to see it."

Inside the bathroom, Thea was met with her reflection—red-rimmed eyes and sunken cheeks—and she knew that this was the boost she needed today. She pulled the lightweight dress overhead, relaxing under the satin slip that Margot sewed into the sheer fabric, the pattern a swirl of blue and lilac blooms. It was loose and soft and it made her feel like she should pin flowers in her hair. It was a wonder that she'd lived twenty years and never felt this beautiful. In this dress, she channeled Margot's carefree spirit. Her wonderful life. Because like Margot, this dress had everything.

Stepping outside, Margot and Cara applauded. "It's perfect, Thea. You can wear it to work."

"Do I look silly?" Thea asked, even though she thought she might never take it off. She felt ready to meet up with old high school friends and reveal this version of herself. Could a dress do that for you? Make you feel like an entirely new person?

"Please, Thea." Cara begged. "You never look this pretty."

"Hey!" Thea put her hands on her hips, laughing. But it was true. Her clothes were rather serious—even she could admit that. "I'll wear it. Thank you so much, Margot." They embraced, and she felt it when Margot squeezed her tighter, holding her for an extra minute. Thea squeezed her back. "Maybe this is your special talent," Thea whispered in her ear.

Margot shook her head like it was the craziest thing she'd ever heard. "My mother calls my creations *rags*."

"Your mother is awful." For a second, Thea relaxed about Margot overhearing Dale, because Margot had a complicated home life too, albeit a different one.

"Oh, she's way worse than your stepfather." Margot adjusted the waist of Thea's dress, pulling it straight. "Speaking of Mother. I have a favor. My parents come back tomorrow night. Lucky me!" Margot pretended she was strangling herself, gasping for air. Then she laughed. "They're having a few people over on Saturday. Will you come? You can wear the dress!"

Thea laughed, because she couldn't wear the dress every day of her life. But despite the day's rough start, she had the inspired feeling she got on the ocean at sunset, when the sky streaked with color and possibility. A party? With Julianna and Brett Lazure, and their glamorous friends? And yet—what kind of impression had she made on them?

"My parents have short memories," Margot continued, recognizing Thea's hesitation. "They'll be too busy trying to sound smart to notice anything else."

"Margot, your parents *are* smart."

"Suuuurre." Her cornflower hair was braided into two plaits down her back. Margot tugged on the dog's leash, spinning around to head to her car. Climbing in, she idled in reverse as she leaned out her window to yell to Thea: "Just remember. When it comes to my parents or anyone else . . . Don't trust anyone over thirty. They know nothing of the young."

Chapter Seven

The party was in full swing when Thea arrived at Margot's house a couple of nights later. She walked along the soggy, curved brick entryway to the front door and knocked the brass lion's head. This time, a butler ushered her inside. With an unexpected change in the weather, the cheese platters and crudité had been moved inside to the shining mahogany dining room table, most of the guests roving about in the living room with its pinch-pleated curtains and floral sofas. Gentlemen in white jackets delivered meatballs in grape jelly and pineapple shrimp on bamboo platters, while guests socialized to low-playing classical music. Thea straightened nervously in the flowy dress Margot sewed for her and the white strappy sandals she had found on clearance at the end of the season last year. Most of the other women wore tailored summer prints with cinched waists, and for a moment, Thea worried she looked too artsy. Then she saw Margot perched on the arm of the sofa in a sack dress with visible stitching at the hem—another one of her creations, perhaps. The boredom immediately left Margot's face and she sprung up to grab Thea's hand.

"Thank god you're here," Margot said. "Let's go to my bedroom."

"Why? Are you not having fun?" The last thing Thea wanted to do was leave the party. The guests seemed like the kind of people she waited on sometimes at the store—surely the wives of lawyers and judges, clumps of businessmen with collared shirts and self-important tones of voice. One especially handsome gentleman in a chambray suit looked ready to take a call from the president himself.

Thea reluctantly followed Margot up the emerald-green carpeting on the curving staircase, slipping off her sandals in her girlish bedroom. Margot flounced onto her perfectly made bed, a dotted quilt pulled taut to the six overstuffed pillows. "Am I having fun? No, not especially."

"I'm sorry. Is it that bad?" Thea supposed it was an older crowd: stiff and serious, conversations about the long-term implications of the war. She'd overheard at least one woman complaining of how dirty San Francisco looked these days with a bunch of rotten kids littering the streets with marijuana smoke—the lingering effect of the Monterey Pop Festival, which was just about the coolest concert ever held in America. Shelly had gone with Jay back in June and said she regretted getting so high that she didn't remember anything except a performer named Janis Joplin, who sang differently than any white girl she'd ever heard.

Margot arranged her dress under her knees on her bed, narrating whatever Thea's eyes landed on in the bedroom. There was a sewing machine on her desk, a pair of pants with the seams half-stitched arranged under the needle. "I'm going to finish those later," she said.

Thea complimented the stitching; the seams in the dress that Margot made her were taut and even. She could also afford any fabric she wanted, like that roll of purple velvet leaning against her desk. Thea could see it becoming a pair of bell-bottoms. "So what's so bad about the party?"

"My father is at a 'work event' in the city," Margot sighed, lighting an incense stick, the smell of vanilla pooling around the room. "But I don't know why my mother tells these lies to herself when her job is to seek out the truth. We both know that he's with Alexandra McKinnon in some fancy hotel room on the Upper East Side. Mother hates to host parties on her own, so she makes me attend, and tonight I've been standing next to her like I'm her husband. I could scream."

Thea knew she should show sympathy, but *Alexandra McKinnon?* The famous television news reporter? "What do you mean he's in some hotel room with Alexandra McKinnon?"

Margot sniffed. "Don't you read the *Tattler*?"

Thea didn't read anything if it wasn't a novel, a music weekly, or the *East Hampton Star*. She sometimes caught a television report by Walter Cronkite, but he didn't report gossip. "You seem upset."

"I'm beyond upset. I'm falling apart." Margot rolled an icicle-sized purple crystal in her palm, dropping back into the rows of plumped white pillows. "I've been reaching for my amethyst all afternoon."

"It's incredibly lousy of your father, I'm sorry." Thea sat down on the beautiful quilt, trying not to notice that her own thighs were unattractively splayed out under her dress; she was envious of the way Margot's slender legs narrowed to her ankles. She bet Margot's inner thighs didn't touch when she stood up, that they didn't chafe against her shorts when she rode a bike. Still, they were both blond, equal there at least, even if Margot's hair was much lighter and prettier than Thea's.

She could tell Margot was crying by the shudder in her body, and Thea leaned back onto the pillows next to her, like she did when Cara threw a fit and she needed to calm her. "I hate him," Margot said.

"You don't."

"How do you know what I feel?"

"Okay, maybe you hate him." Thea sucked in a breath. "But I do know this. My father ran out on us with some woman he met at the VFW hall. Her name was Sharon, and she had this awful stringy dyed hair. Chicken legs. She tried to make it up to me by bringing me silver dollars. I was nine."

"Oh," Margot said. "So you get it, then."

Thea chewed the inside of her cheek. She'd never admitted that story to anyone, and she regretted sharing it now. Her mind reeled back to that icy winter's day when her father left. He was wearing his freshly polished black dress shoes and a tan plaid scarf tossed sloppily around his neck, and he'd walked out the front door with his arms balancing a cumbersome stack of boxes. Before starting his Chevy, he got down on one knee, promising Thea he'd pick her up the following Saturday. But he never did. In the gloomy winter weeks after, Thea ran her mother hot baths and worked on her handwriting extra hard at school to try to make her mother happy again, but nothing worked until her mother met Dale at bingo that spring at the local church. Dale ran his own plumbing business, fell hard for her mother, and they'd married a year later. Recently, Thea's real father, who worked as a vacuum salesman, had sent a note to Thea apologizing for not coming to her mother's funeral. She'd tossed it in the trash.

"You know men," Thea tried to make light, rising from the bed. "They have urges, and they're not very good at controlling them. But my mother and me survived just fine. You will too, if you have to. I'm not saying it won't hurt, just that there is the other side of a mess like this, and you'll get to it." Thea glanced around the pretty pink bedroom that had marks of Margot's adult self now imprinted into it: a Timothy Leary book on her nightstand, a record player on her dresser alongside a shimmering cloth lined with crystals of various sizes, colors, and shapes.

"Are you reading *Robin Hood*?" Thea was restless in Margot's bedroom, and she looked about, picking up the children's adaptation of the novel that was open on her desk. She had been forced to read it in high school.

"Let the rich give to the poor and not just in Nottingham Forest," Margot proclaimed in a terrible British accent, making Thea laugh. She slithered off the bed and bent down under her box spring, pulling out a wooden wine box and sliding the top off to reveal shredded paper grass and a bottle of red wine. She held it up like a trophy. "May we help the poor—and may we find better men than our fathers."

"And our stepfathers." Thea lifted up a finger as if she was giving an important speech, but she was laughing and caught sight of herself in the mirror. Her mod eye makeup was still in place; she had tried to mimic Twiggy's cat-eye liner and layers of mascara. "Gosh, what a mess our parents have made of their lives."

And our lives, Thea thought. Not only was Dale relying on Thea to help raise her little sister, but Cara was counting on her too. Every afternoon she'd wait on the front steps for Thea to get home from work so she could follow her around the kitchen while she cooked, and it was hard for Thea to pinpoint why she felt so much pressure to be attentive to her. Her sister went to Thea for help with homework, for advice on what to wear to a birthday party. A few weeks ago, when Cara got her first period, she had so many questions for Thea. Why was this happening to her body? How could she make it stop? Thea took her sister shopping for maxi pads, delivered the most awkward explanation of how a baby is made, and found herself saying uncomfortable things like, "You can't wear a tampon until you're eighteen because Mommy said it's like losing your virginity." But then Cara would ask twenty-five more questions, and Thea buried her face in a book and begged her sister to please, please leave her alone.

"Do you ever think about who you'd be if you had different parents? What's the one word that comes to mind?" Margot snapped her fingers at Thea, egging her on. "Just say the word that pops into your head. What is it?"

Assuming her mother was still alive . . . *daring*. No, not that, Thea thought. *Contented*. She didn't want to admit that either; her mother would roll over in her grave if she thought she'd made Thea unhappy, and that wasn't the point she was trying to make. "I don't know. Foolhardy."

Margot squinted at her. "Foolhardy? That makes zero sense."

Thea crouched down to look into Margot's dollhouse. The miniature bed was made with a real tiny pink comforter, a teeny dog sleeping at the foot of it.

"No, it does make sense," Thea said. "Because my mother taught me to be practical and to do the right thing. Another set of parents might have pressured me to be perfect, making me do all these reckless things to get their attention. What's yours?" Thea repositioned some of the furniture in the dollhouse's formal living room. A miniature end table had fallen over, and she positioned it upright. Was it weird that she wished she could live in this dollhouse with its tiny little fireplace, a pair of small sconces on either side of the mantel? She could choose swatches of chintz wallpaper for the dining room, furnish the space with a long mahogany table. It wasn't the décor that excited her, really—it was that the house looked so happy, so free of problems. She would invite Cara to move in, of course. She'd give her a room with wall-to-wall lavender carpet, a white canopy bed at the center.

"Hmm." Margot picked the bottle of wine back up, pouring them each a generous glass. She crossed back to the bed near the dollhouse, where Thea was still marveling at the tiny mirrors inside, the coatrack with little coats hanging on hooks, the telephone that was no bigger than her pinkie nail. If she could shrink herself, Thea would live in that house. She would.

Margot handed her the goblet of wine. "Free. I would be unencumbered by all these things they want me to be and how they want me to act and talk and dress."

Free? Thea couldn't hold back her scoff, and Margot made a face. If only Thea could have Margot's closet of clothes, her beautiful house, her own fancy car to drive wherever she wanted. "I'm sorry," Thea said. "I see things differently."

The way Margot turned away from her to look out the window made plain she was hurt. "Will you stop making assumptions about me?"

Thea moved the tiny fake houseplant from the kitchen window to the mini fireplace mantel. "You're right. It's just that your new parents might expect things out of you too, just different things. You might feel just as pressured."

"I suppose." Margot considered this, then brightened with a new thought. "Here's a game. Let's pretend that I can pick new parents. Ooh. This is fun. I would pick someone that doesn't care about that dumb newspaper she's inherited, and instead waits for me after school, bakes me fresh cookies, and comes to my piano recitals. I'd pick a father that took me to breakfast once a week, taught me how to surf, and encouraged me to travel." Margot raised an eyebrow, challenging Thea to top that.

"So you basically want a 1940s housewife for a mother? And a hunk for a father? What would the women's libbers think?"

Now they both giggled. "I take it back. I want the strong, uncaring, selfish witch downstairs."

"Cheers," Thea said, and after they gulped some wine down, she held up her glass. "I would have loved it if my mom was like Shelly at the record store. She's swell, isn't she?" Thea didn't like feeling guilty for looking at her boss in a motherly way, so she tried to explain herself, believing that she was betraying her mother somehow. "I bet she'd be the kind of mom that would be more like a friend, diving into your bed at night to talk about boys and music and the latest cool color lipstick." Her mother had always been too busy pleasing Dale and raising a baby to have that kind of time for Thea.

Margot sat down next to Thea, clutching a green notebook to her chest—a journal with a tiny lock fastening the pages together where she recorded her secrets. "Mothers are never as cool as Shelly, but I adore her and Jay as a couple. Do you know that they were set up on a blind date? She arrived at the restaurant and he was reading from Shirley Jackson's *We Have Always Lived in the Castle*."

Thea swooned, clasping her hands together at her heart. "I know, her favorite book. The novel is actually quite creepy, but Shelly loves mysteries. She has me reading Patricia Highsmith's *The Two Faces of January*."

Margot snatched up a copy of *The Maltese Falcon*. "She gave me this one, but I can't get through it." Both women basked in the attention of Shelly's affections, and neither one admitted it, but there was something intoxicating about an older woman sharing her favorite things with them. Thea wasn't just drawn to Shelly's fun-loving personality. She was in awe that she owned a record shop, that she'd chosen to be something so utterly cool rather than something predictable and boring like a secretary.

"Sorry if the wine isn't great. Mother throws away most bottles that people bring as hostess gifts, so I fish them out of the trash and save them. For celebrations."

Another sip and already Thea's cheeks were warm and fuzzy. That was the other thing about being young, Thea thought. It was so thoroughly entertaining to pretend to be an adult. "We're celebrating?"

"Yes, we're celebrating. We're celebrating me and you becoming friends."

Margot lowered the needle on the record, the latest summer hit "Angel of the Morning." Merrilee Rush's voice was loud, even with the party carrying on downstairs, and after setting her drink down on her nightstand, Margot begged Thea to dance with her. They moved about in an exaggerated version of a ballroom dance while singing to each other.

On one wall in Margot's room there were album covers arranged into neat rows and attached to the wall haphazardly with long skinny nails. Two from Joan Baez and one of Bob Dylan's latest, which wasn't surprising, and then there was the Rolling Stones and the trippy-sounding Beach Boys album. Thea was relieved to see the latest Beatles record, *Sgt. Pepper's Lonely Hearts Club Band*—she couldn't be friends with anyone who didn't share her love of them, even if some had started to prefer bands that felt like the anti-Beatles, like Jimi Hendrix.

"You know I have the utmost respect for the Beatles," Thea started, as she moved to put a song on the turntable herself, "because their influence reigns eternal. Everyone jeers Dylan for going electric, but do you know who has supported his switch from acoustic guitar? George Harrison. He called Dylan's angry fans a bunch of 'idiots.'"

Margot twirled about the bedroom. "The latest Beatles album is the best, hands down. I was at Shea, too, you know." She picked up on the conversation they'd had the day that Thea had knocked on her door, the wriggling puppy balanced in her forearms.

"You were?!"

"I even got backstage, thanks to the music reporter at the *Herald* who smuggled me back there, but the boys left before we could get to them."

"The boys." Thea smiled. "I like that."

"I did get this." Margot opened her top drawer and pulled out a ruby cuff link, cradling it in her palm. "Found it on the floor of Paul's dressing room, and the *Herald* reporter said I could keep it."

"Margot! Is it real?"

Margot giggled. "I told the reporter that I planned to sell it and give the money to orphans in Vietnam."

"So why do you still have it?" Thea would have killed to get her mitts on anything that had once belonged to the Beatles.

She said she couldn't prove it belonged to McCartney, so it wasn't worth much. "But the thought of the money did lead me to call an organization in Washington that sends supplies to Vietnamese children, and they told me what they needed help with. I believe it's my destiny to help people who need it. All people."

"Wow," Thea said. Her dreams sounded big, important.

Thea slid one of her favorite Simon & Garfunkel records out of its cover and centered it on the record player, setting down the needle. The wavy sound of the record catching filled the room, then the famous guitar strums and lyrics about going home in one of her favorite songs, "Homeward Bound."

Balancing their refilled wineglasses in hand, they swam their hands through the air and lip-synced to one another, their faces contorting with extra emotion at the chorus. The record skipped, then skipped again. Just three words on repeat: *long to be, long to be.* They fell into laughter on the bed. "I forgot I scratched that album. I think I stepped on it," Margot said.

This made Thea laugh even harder, until she noticed that her friend was looking outside and grimacing.

"This is bad," Margot said. "Very, very bad."

Pushing the frilly curtains out of the way, Thea saw the dog. Outside. Free. Tracing a path across the wet lawn in full view of the French doors overlooking the pool, which could be seen from the room where the party was unfolding. Margot tossed Thea a rain jacket, and they hurried their shoes on, rushed down the stairs wearing sophisticated matching trench coats, slowed as they walked by the party and passed a waiter in the wall-papered hallway. Margot picked off the platter in a rush and popped a pig in a blanket in her mouth, while Thea breezed right by, her eye catching the waiter's for an instant. The caramel hue of the young man's slender jawline, the way he was studying her with recognition as she passed. It was his side profile that gave him away. He was a young man she'd noticed recently at the record shop, the one she couldn't stop looking at.

The back door had been left open by the caterers, and Margot and Thea stepped into the pelting rain into the sopping field, calling Bee's name. The puppy trotted straight to them, jumping with its muddy paws up on Thea, then Margot, and bolted off again before either of them could grab her.

"One of the caterers must have let her out." They chased after the animal, soaking their feet through their sandals and stockings, their dresses wet to the undergarments. A shaggy-haired young man walked straight up to them, his mustache curving around his lips like an upside-down horseshoe. Margot called out to him, sounding desperate: "I can't get her, Shawn."

The man's untucked blue-collared short-sleeve shirt was stained, like he'd just finished fixing a car engine, and without a word he crouched down behind the pool house where no one from the party could see them. He dangled what looked like a piece of liverwurst, calling the puppy over. Bee pranced to him, wagging her tail, and as Shawn offered her the meat, he grabbed the dog by her collar, which itself was nothing more than a sailor's rope that Margot had braided and fitted rather cleverly around her neck.

"Here I am, taking care of you again, little lady," the man said, roughing up the fur of the puppy's head. Margot bent down to hook on the leash, something left unsaid in his light eyes as he smiled with amusement. Thea disliked him immediately, especially since his mustache made him look like a walrus.

Margot giggled. "How can I thank you, Mr. Strider?"

Was it Shawn or Mr. Strider? Thea would call him Walrus, at least in her head. She leaned in to pet the dog, the fur wet and matted in the rain, but her true focus was the way the man was cataloging Margot's figure.

"Who is this?" the Walrus said, training his eyes on Thea now, and she squirmed under his gaze. He was older than them by at least ten years. Shelly's age. But he had the look of a guitarist in a rock band, and almost immediately, Thea could see that he carried himself with a cool edge. The guy who tended the bonfire at a beach party, the guy who pulled out his personal stash of Acapulco Gold, rolling a joint and passing it around to friends and strangers.

Margot draped an arm around Thea's shoulder. "Thea, this is our caretaker, Shawn Strider. Shawn, this is my friend Thea. Shawn keeps me company when Mommy and Daddy are away. Just in case I have a bad dream." There was mischief in Margot's expression.

The Walrus waited for Thea to look up at him before he said, "A pleasure," and he locked his eyes on her one beat longer than Thea found comfortable. He pushed his hair, long like Jim Morrison's, off his wet, chiseled face. She immediately tried not to imagine what he would look like with his shirt off, but there it was in her mind. It was off, and he was unzipping her dress, pulling her face to his.

Thea blushed. "Nice to meet you too."

The rain showered their faces, and Margot began to twirl like she had in her bedroom, saying something nonsensical about how they were already drenched, they might as well enjoy themselves. "If there wasn't a party, we'd jump straight into the pool, wouldn't we? Even you, Thea."

The idea sobered Thea, even as the Walrus smirked at the possibility of all three of them doing just that. No doubt he'd suggest they take off their clothes. "I don't think so." Her feet were speckled with mud, and she bent over because it was awkward with this man and Margot. Just as she wiped off her foot, something jabbed into her side. It was sharp and hard, and it hurt. It was coming from the pocket—two pin-like needles. A pair of earrings? she wondered. Thea dug inside the trench coat to pull whatever was inside, out, but the seam of the pocket had been sewn shut from the inside.

How strange, to sew a pocket shut.

"I want to see you girls again, okay?" The Walrus turned to cross the lawn. In the distance, Thea could see where he was headed: a small cedar-shingled cottage about half the size of her own house, located at the edge of the property. Perhaps the house fit a bed and a small couch, a hot plate and a compact refrigerator. Thea knew there were bachelors that lived on farms and the grounds of local estates, but they never befriended the people who lived in the houses, and they certainly didn't speak to the owner's daughter in the same tone that he had.

"Isn't he a sweetheart?" Margot said to Thea as they dried Bee in the pool house.

Thea folded the damp towel out of habit and handed it to Margot to put in the washer. "Uh, sure . . . But he's your groundskeeper."

"He's just so real. You know what he told me the other day. 'I'm not ashamed of who I am.' It struck me as so honest. I'm *always* ashamed of who I am, Thea. People are interested in me only because of my father, because of who my mother is."

"That can't be true."

Thea and Margot slipped back inside and changed, smoothing their hair with Margot's fancy hand-held hair dryer in her bedroom; before this, Thea had only seen such dryers in hair salons. "We need to make an appearance or Mother will kill me," Margot said.

Thea shook out the tan trench, handing it back to her. "What in the world do you have in here?" She pointed to the pocket that had been sewn shut. "Do you do this to all your coats?"

Margot grabbed the jacket and hung it on a hook in her closet, shushing Thea. "A little grass, that's all. Want me to sew some into your denim jacket? Then no one can find anything, if you ever need to hide something."

"That's okay. I don't smoke much." She didn't smoke at all. Thea hated how out of control she felt after smoking weed, the way the world spun, and she had no way to stop it.

Down the stairs they entered into the living room and nibbled on shrimp cocktail while circulating through the diminishing crowd. Thea made polite conversation with two elderly sisters whose husbands co-owned a string of undergarment stores up island. When Margot sat down at the baby grand piano to play Beethoven, the sisters asked Thea if she'd heard about the jewelry thefts in town.

"One of the women is Marge Runion, a friend of mine, who lives in Southampton. Her diamond ring was stolen right from her jewelry box."

"I heard that another woman had her grandmother's ruby necklace taken," Thea said. During three different high-profile parties, the paper reported, valuable jewelry had gone missing upstairs as guests mingled downstairs.

The older woman, her hair cut into a short bob, frowned. "That was Izzy Lewis; her husband is a federal judge back in the city. It's just terrible. Who would take these? They're family heirlooms."

Someone who needed money, Thea guessed. If she had that kind of money in an instant, she would buy a car, pack it to the gills, and drive straight through to Los Angeles, kidnapping her sister and stowing her in the passenger seat. Her mother had dreamed of being a performer, a singer or an actress, and she'd always promised to take them to the southern California city where, she said, you could walk off the sidewalk and straight onto a movie set.

"It's the City of Angels," she'd told Thea one rainy winter afternoon while they snuggled on the couch. "Which means as soon as you get there, the angels find you and watch over you. We'll make it there, little lark. Someday."

After Thea finished her plate of shrimp cocktail, she excused herself to the bar to order a soda. There he was again. The gentleman from the record store who she'd seen in Margot's hallway earlier. Now he mixed drinks in his bow tie, showing off his striking features as he charmed the older women lining up for cocktails. She wanted to say hello, but when it was her turn, he barely looked up at her as he filled her glass. As she was about to turn away, he glanced up and smiled at her, just for a second. His eyelashes were long and dark, the sweetest dimple below the chisel of his cheek, and she smiled back. Then he turned to shake a martini.

After rejoining Margot at the piano, Thea gazed at the other women in their gauzy sundresses, the gilded mirror over the unlit fireplace, the ambient glow of the large candles in the room that cast a rosiness across Margot's cheeks.

What a magical world I've entered into, Thea thought, sipping her fruity punch, the bubbles popping inside her. They seemed to travel all the way down to her toes. Just for a moment, she felt like one of the lucky ones.

Chapter Eight

June 1977

"Mama, there's a stranger in the barn."

Penny's dark hair was tangled, the thick brows she'd inherited from her father pulled together like she was struggling to provide an answer on *The $20,000 Pyramid*. Thea pushed the sheets off in her white wicker bed, noting, with a sense of panic, how high the sun was in the sky. How late had she slept? She leaned over the side of the mattress to see into the driveway.

"Daddy already left," Penny said, climbing onto the bed and burying her face into Thea's neck. "I was watching cartoons." Thea rested her head back on her pillow and pulled her daughter close, needing to feel the child's warmth against her chest, the simple act of pressing together enough to calm Thea's heartbeat.

"Now, what happened?"

"I'm scared, Mama. I saw the doors open and a woman came out." At dawn, Penny had climbed between her and Felix, pulling the blanket over her head and shrieking nonsensical sentences about Darth Vader being in her closet.

Thea yawned, trying to think of a good explanation. "Are you sure your eyes aren't playing tricks on you?" She immediately felt guilty for trying to convince Penny that she was seeing things and changed tack.

She threaded her daughter's knotty hair into a ponytail, then released it to fall down her pink nightgown. "It must be the gardener I hired to help trim the roses."

"But Daddy told you he would trim the roses." Daddy, in fact, *always* trimmed the roses.

Thea lifted her daughter gently, placed her down on the bed, tickling the soft of her belly. "Well, don't tell Daddy, then."

Penny fanned her fingers out like she was counting them. "It's our number one secret."

Thea pulled on her denim skirt, then hooked her bra around her back. Childbirth had left the skin around her middle resembling a walnut, with a wrinkled outer layer and all. She wished sometimes the clothing styles would revert back to the loose, flowing silhouettes of her teenage years. These days everything was so high-waisted and form-fitting. Sometimes, when Thea fantasized about the past, mentioning to Felix how much better things used to be in the sixties, he'd remind her it wasn't true. "Look at all those hippies who hollered about free love," Felix said.

There was a controversial piece in a rock magazine recently that had reported how many women at Woodstock and other music festivals had been violated in the spirit of "free love." How ideas about sexual freedom meant something different to each gender, and for some, it had confused consent. She had thought about Margot when she'd heard that, how easy it would have been for Margot to believe that all men saw women as powerless as the Walrus did—that all women accepted the demands of someone as charismatic as he was. If Margot hadn't been so focused on appearing carefree back then, things might have turned out differently for her. For them.

"Yes, a secret for us girls." Thea leaned down to her little girl's cherubic face, kissing her eyelashes. Her daughter could drive her to madness sometimes, but when she was sweet, Thea wanted to inhale her.

Secrets.

The night before came back to Thea. After they returned from the drive-in movie, Penny falling asleep in the car on the way home, she and

Felix had a glass of wine in the living room, falling into each other on the navy-blue corduroy couch, Otis Redding playing on the turntable. Felix couldn't stop talking about *Star Wars*, what "the force" symbolized, how insightful it was when Darth Vader said, "I find your lack of faith alarming." It had been a good movie—she enjoyed it as much as he did—but she found herself irritated by Princess Leia. That she wore virginal white robes and needed the help of men and monsters to save her planet, that she couldn't simply save it herself.

The movie had also made her think of the choices Luke and Leia had made, how far they had traveled to find their destiny. "Do you think we're meant to be in East Hampton for the rest of our lives?" she asked Felix.

He pulled her up from the couch to slow dance. "These Arms of Mine" was their favorite Redding song, something he played for her on their first date when they'd listened to albums in his parents' basement. Felix always said that Redding put his whole heart into singing that song, that when the singer declared he wanted to be in the embrace of his dream girl for all of time, Felix wanted to be in Thea's arms, too. "I think we're meant to be here now. Maybe forever."

"But what if you were fired from your job at the publishing house? What would we do? I mean, you'd obviously get another job. But maybe I would have to work, too."

He kissed the side of her temple, the music drawing their bodies closer like two puzzle pieces fitting just right. "Being able to take care of us, to own this house together—it's my biggest source of pride. If I got fired, I would wash dishes or paint houses if I had to, whatever it took to give you the life I promised."

She thought his words kind, yet something niggled at her. "You say it like a soldier reporting for duty."

"My father told me once that a good man takes care of the people he loves."

"Well, you're a good man, then." He kissed her again, and when the song ended, they sat in the quiet, watching the sea breeze billow the curtains about the open windows.

Around midnight, Felix announced he was going to bed—he had an early train to the city. "I'll be up in a moment," she'd said, relieved that he didn't pressure her to come upstairs. Nights alone in the house calmed Thea, rooted her in her own head, and she could hear herself think. Sometimes she'd get restless and rearrange their bookshelves. Other nights, she'd sink into the quiet and build a fire in the living room, falling asleep with a book in her lap, her night throw wrapped around her shoulders.

Last night, though, she'd had an urge to listen to her old albums, songs she hadn't heard in ages, each one bringing forth a memory of that summer ten years before with Margot. From a wooden chest in the living room, she pulled out photo albums, their pages sticky with age, and flipped through, laughing at pictures: She and Margot stacking records on their heads and competing to see who could balance them longest. She and Margot having a popcorn fight at the drive-in. She and Margot on bikes. She and Margot at the beach. The memory-seeking sending her even deeper into the past, and she looked at photos from childhood: she and her mother blowing out candles on her fifth birthday cake. Her father was in that picture, a gleam in his eye as he clapped behind her. Who had taken it? Then there was the image of her and her mother in front of the Majestic Theater in New York City for her sixteenth birthday, her mother in a pillbox hat.

Every photograph painted a picture of who Thea once was, what used to be important to her, and she felt something inside her reignite. A recognition that she used to be someone who could lose herself in the words of a rock song. Someone with strong opinions and someone with a grief so deep it split her in two. It was good that she'd left some of those pieces of herself behind, but she'd forgotten things about herself, too: how hard she'd studied to get into college, earning straight As and Bs; how determined she and her mother were to get her there, her mother taking a second job in her teenage years to pay for her applications and tuition. How her life seemed destined to go in a different direction than it had.

Penny began jumping on the unmade bed, and Thea scolded her to stop. The child fell to her knees bouncing on the mattress in a *Scooby-Doo* T-shirt, then clasped her hands together like Princess Leia, kneeling regal and proud on a pillow. "Help me, Obi-Wan Kachobi." Penny giggled.

What they needed help with, Thea thought, was getting out the door. Camp started in thirty minutes; Thea had to get moving. "It's Obi-Wan Kenobi, silly. Did Daddy feed you breakfast?"

"Wheaties." Penny nodded and jumped off the bed, landing her chubby feet on the wood floors.

She and Penny somehow pulled into the Laurel Oaks Country Day Camp on time, even though they had gotten stuck behind a gas truck that kept stopping and starting. It struck Thea then that when you needed the world to move fast, it always moved slow. But it would be the opposite with Penny, she thought, glancing at her daughter in the back seat in her pigtails. Her days as a little girl who lined up her stuffed animals in rows and taught them school, who insisted on burying a dead mouse they found in the road, who could be hoisted up onto Thea's hip and carried—those days might move slow, but for Thea, they were moving too fast. Hadn't her daughter changed so much just this year? In ten years, she'd be sixteen and plotting to get away from her mother.

Thea reached an arm back to squeeze her bare leg, her daughter's grin enough to satisfy her. "Let's play dolls when you get home today."

"Okay, Mommy."

After walking Penny up to the camp counselor, a college girl with bright blue eyeliner, Thea noticed that Midge was on the opposite side of the parking lot talking to other moms. For a second, she considered pretending she didn't see her and getting in her car, but Midge waved her down. "You didn't come to racquetball yesterday—what happened?"

Did they have a match? Thea had completely blanked.

"I'm sorry, I didn't feel well," she lied. "A headache. I should have called." Midge asked if she was going to Peg's for coffee that afternoon—Peg had called to invite her last night—and when Thea made an excuse for that, too, Midge eyed her. "Are you okay?"

Thea turned to get into her car but stopped for a moment. She faced Midge, her elfin face soft and pillowy and covered in foundation. Midge loved her "Jag," as she called it, the green sports car parked perfectly centered in the lot, her key chain a small gold jaguar with real rubies for spots (both gifts from a husband who stayed in the city all week). Was Midge asking after Thea because she truly cared—or was she simply looking for gossip? She had *very* loose lips. And now that Margot was here, Thea couldn't help but compare her best friend from childhood with her best friend today. It wasn't that one seemed more or less true, but even after all these years, Thea felt so much closer to Margot than she did Midge. Had Midge been nothing but a placeholder until Margot returned? Sometimes Thea wasn't even sure she liked Midge and all her judgments about Thea's way of doing things. All those times Midge had encouraged Thea to be a better cook or to pack up her summer clothes in the attic (rather than letting them mingle with winter's long sleeves and pants), to let her pots soak with Bar Keepers Friend—wasn't it all a way of criticizing Thea for not being more like her? But Margot didn't want Thea to be just like her. In fact, she seemed to enjoy that they were different, and part of what drew them together was rediscovering just how much.

"I'm fine. No, I'm good. Just catching up on some stuff." *To say the least.*

"With the person in your barn?" Midge smiled with a knowingness. "I stopped by the other day."

Thea dropped into the driver's seat. She needed to act as though it was perfectly normal that someone was at her house. Midge wouldn't know who it was. Midge didn't even *know* Margot. "It was one of Felix's authors coming for lunch." What a whopper she'd come up with! "Next time, be sure to knock."

Midge flicked her eyes. "I didn't want to be a bother."

"You never are." Thea turned over the engine, her nerves shifting with the gears. This was a small town. People talked. How much longer would she be able to keep this secret?

*   *   *

There was a grumble in Thea's stomach as she pulled up to the house on the hill and walked up the front steps, immediately going around back to pick hydrangeas to put in a vase on her kitchen table. Margot was outside at the picnic table overlooking the deep blue bay, writing in a leather notebook. Her hand was moving quickly, the words flying across the page. When she spotted Thea snapping off large blooms, Margot waved, dropping her pen and closing the book.

"Any news on Willy?" Thea asked, curious about what she had been writing in the blank notebook. Something about how hunched Margot had looked a minute before had given Thea the impression that there was a development, that maybe she'd received discouraging news. Then again, Margot was wearing a strapless terrycloth romper with string ties at the chest and looking rather fabulous for someone with a missing husband. It both impressed and irritated Thea.

Margot helped Thea arrange the bouquet. "I rung his mother in Chicago—I hope you don't mind the long-distance call. She barely remembers her own name these days, but I begged her to call me if he gets in touch with her."

It was already warm and humid, and with Penny in camp until four, they had the entire day ahead of them. It was the kind of summer morning that would have kept them outside all day when they were younger. Everything always seemed interesting back then, even laying on a blanket and staring up at the clouds, trying to catch the world spinning. Mick Jagger's voice popped into her head: *What a drag it is getting old.*

"Remember when we used to ride our bikes to work and try to reach up and tear the leaves off the trees overhead?" Margot handed Thea the bright pink bunch and she smiled at the memory.

"I forgot how fun that was." They went inside, and Thea hunted in her cabinets for a vase, then spun around, remembering, "I've got to show you this picture of us that I found." The photo was of the two of them with their hair blown out big and voluminous and Twiggy-short skirts. The Walrus had snapped the picture with Margot's camera, right before they left for a concert on the beach for some local band. "Is that the Wheezy Brothers, those three guys trying to sound like the Beach Boys?"

"Yes! That was them. Didn't one of them like you?" Thea filled the vase with water, arranging the bouquet to fill out the glass.

Margot laughed. "I kissed him. Remember?"

She and Margot hadn't been able to stop remembering since they started talking yesterday, and looking back made everything seem more charming. In one moment they couldn't stop laughing about the time that Margot dressed as a chauffeur and drove Thea around the Hamptons in the back seat of her Mercedes, pretending that Thea was Scottish royalty, if there even was such a thing. And then there was the time that Margot convinced Thea to go on her horse with her, and she'd ridden out of the paddock, taking her across the meadow at galloping speed; how Thea had thrown up when she got off, her head not having enough time to catch up to the horse's pace.

"Remember when I took you to Ditch Plains, and you met that surfer and he took us to his van, where it turned out he had a bed in the back?" Thea snorted.

Margot hiccupped with laughter. "That was disgusting! But I actually thought it was kind of cool at the time."

"Didn't you spend the night with him?" Thea rumpled up her face with disgust. "Ew."

"He WAS gorgeous."

Thea popped two slices of bread into the toaster. They never did mention the Walrus.

It had become a familiar pattern, with Felix in the city these last couple of days. Thea prepared breakfast and drove Penny to camp. She'd make small talk with Midge and the other moms, often making plans she didn't intend to keep. Then she'd return home and find Margot, either in the barn folding the blankets off the couch where she'd slept, or rowing out to her sailboat, or in Thea's kitchen, ready to launch into a funny story. Thea had things to do—she needed to go to the bank and order new checkbooks, pick up dish soap, and get Penny a stack of elastics because her hair was getting long and unruly this summer. But Thea put all of it off—the vacuuming and dusting, even the laundry—because suddenly, everything other than spending time with Margot felt like a waste.

She'd felt a similar tug when Cara had come home for Christmas this year. Her sister hadn't been back to Long Island in three years, and there was so much Thea had wanted to show her—what restaurant had replaced the old soda fountain they loved, the colossal houses that were being built along the dunes. Long hours passed when the sisters read in the living room while Penny napped, when they'd bake and decorate cookies in the shape of angels and stars while a winter wind howled off the sea. They shared nightly cups of chamomile tea and flipped through the latest issues of *Cosmo* and *Vogue* and remarked on their favorite outfits or quotes or sex tips, all while Felix worked late or remained in the attic with a stack of manuscripts, knowing the sisters wanted to be alone.

On that same trip home, Cara had spent a day with her father, who still lived in the same Cape Cod with the crumbling steps and rusted appliances that Thea had grown up in. Since moving out, Thea had only seen Dale a dozen times: he'd come to her wedding, and he'd visited after Penny was born. Sometimes she'd run into him at the grocery store or Easter mass. That night, after her visit with her father, Cara had tried to go along with Thea's plans for a fancy dinner at The Palm and a viewing of *Rosemary's Baby*, but Cara was quieter than usual on the drive to the restaurant, a sure sign that something was wrong. After some prodding, and as the chorus of "Bohemian Rhapsody" played on the car radio, it came out that Dale, now fifty-nine, had hurt his back on the job and could barely walk, and was hobbling around with a cane.

"He's in pain, and the house smelled, Thea." Cara had pulled Thea's coat tighter around her chest; her sister didn't have one warm enough to bring home from California. "And in his fridge there was all this rotted fruit, a few bottles of beer, a gray-looking tray of chop meat. I don't even think he can get to the grocery store."

"I had no idea, I'm sorry." Thea had worried about Dale in a distant sense now that he was alone, but never enough to check in on him more than every couple of months. His longtime girlfriend Becky had left him a few years before, just after Cara moved out.

Her sister had paused, the headlights of another car blinding them both as it passed. "I might come back for a while to help out," Cara had said, pulling a cigarette from her embroidered suede purse, pressing in the car's silver lighter. "Then you and I don't have to squeeze everything in, you know? I can go into the city for auditions, maybe try for Broadway. It's not like I'm doing much more than waitressing out there anyway." Cara sounded hopeful, and Thea had thought: *It's amazing the drudgery that we can convince ourselves of when we love someone.*

Before the cigarette lighter even popped, Thea had told her sister that she'd check on her stepfather every week. She'd bring him prepared meals, drive him to his doctor's appointments. All in the name of keeping Cara on the West Coast. Thea insisted she keep her apartment, go to auditions in Hollywood or Burbank or wherever. "I don't want you to push off everything just because Dale is having a tough few months."

After dropping Penny at camp on a drizzly morning, Thea drove straight to Dale's with a platter of food on her passenger seat. With Margot's arrival, she'd neglected to stop by her stepfather's since last week, and she was beginning to worry that too much time was passing. Going back to her old house had gotten easier these last few months. At first, she had struggled to feel comfortable around her stepfather, wading only into safe territory, like how his aspirin had run out or his coffee was running low. She rarely spoke of anything going on in her own life, and they didn't really have conversations. Instead, they spoke in checklists of doctor's visits and news headlines. By now the effect of Dale's rants had long dulled, and in those early weeks of January, Dale felt nothing but old to Thea. She felt sorry for him that his body had given out on him, the same body he'd relied on his entire life to make a living.

With the car parked next to his old plumbing van, she knocked on the door.

"Pop, are you awake?" Thea hollered, but when he didn't answer, she used her key to unlock it.

"In the kitchen," he yelled, his voice muffled. She found him on his hands and knees under the sink.

"Pop! You're going to hurt yourself all over again."

The change in name had happened so easily after Penny started coming over regularly with the steady stream of tuna casseroles and beef stroganoffs that Thea had made. "Grandpop!" Penny called him, and from there, it had been easy for Thea to shorten it, to create a role for this man who had never had a clear purpose in her life. Calling him her stepfather had always felt hollow, since he wasn't a truly paternal figure to her in his actions or affections, and she'd never felt attached enough to call him "Dad." But Dale was Penny's grandfather—and that one small adjustment had given Thea and Dale something to connect on. She tried to bring Penny every time she came over, even if just to break the ice between them, but on the days she didn't, Dale actually asked about her. Sometimes the way he inquired about Penny's teachers or her progress in tap dancing had made Thea understand what her own mother had seen in him.

Dale grumbled. "There's a leak under here, and I'll be damned if I'm paying someone to do what I've done a million and one times."

Thea set down the plate of chicken wings she'd grilled, a big enough portion of potatoes she'd roasted to last him a few days. When he ran out of her home-cooked meals, she kept a steady stream of Swanson TV dinners in his freezer. He loved the cherry pies.

Dale got up slowly, like he wasn't sure what might hurt if he moved an inch in the wrong direction. "Where's my granddaughter?"

"Camp," Thea said with a shrug, sitting for a moment at the kitchen table. She always felt a little tired here. Emotional nerves, she thought. "Penny loves that camp so much, I couldn't beg her to stay home."

He shook his head with a disapproving smile, and he didn't have to say a word for her to know what he was thinking. In Dale's mind, camp was for the wealthy summer people who didn't know what to do with their kids all year long, not the locals who knew the best beaches and fishing spots and ran barefoot through town. But Thea had always dreamed of attending camp as a kid, and she'd vowed that if she and Felix could afford the weekly fee—and boy, did she scrimp on extras all year to cobble it together—she would send her.

Thea immediately changed the subject. "Did you make your appointment with Doc Robbins? He said six weeks."

"August 12 at eleven. But I don't think I need those shots anymore."

Thea rolled her eyes as he rambled about why he wouldn't go. "Discuss that one with Cara."

It was a waste of time to banter like this, Thea thought. They both knew that he'd go to his appointment and they both knew he'd get his shot. It was funny, too, because they also both knew he was feeling better. That he could buy his own groceries and fix his own meals, maybe even drive himself to the doctor. But Thea kept stopping by to see him, and Dale kept phoning her with items from the grocery store that he needed. Maybe it was just their shared love of Penny, or maybe it was because they'd both started to look forward to this time together. No matter how flawed he was, Thea decided, it was a comfort to be around him since he was the *only* person that remembered her mother the way Thea did. Even Cara's memory was shaky.

Two months ago, Thea had overheard Dale in his woodshop in the garage telling her daughter a story about Thea's mother, how she would have loved to have met Penny.

"Oh, how that woman loved her girls," Dale said.

The sentiment hit Thea like a train crashing straight into her heart. She'd been drying dishes by the open window, but suddenly, Thea was steadying herself on the countertop around the kitchen sink, gripping the faux brick linoleum like it was all she could do to keep from falling to the floor.

Chapter Nine

Thea spread mayo on turkey sandwiches in her kitchen while envisioning what kind of trouble she'd get in if the police pulled up to her house right that minute. She could pretend she didn't know Margot was staying in the barn, or Thea could say that her friend had asked to spend a week's vacation, clueless there was any kind of trouble. More snapshots passed like a flipbook: Margot being led away in handcuffs, Felix's disapproving face, police ripping Penny out of her arms.

"You're certain you told me the truth?" Thea said as she arranged carrot and celery sticks on two plates to accompany the sandwiches.

From the kitchen table, Margot tugged on the hummingbird pendant she'd been wearing around her neck since she'd arrived; seeing it made Thea feel guilty that she'd tossed her matching one in the dark swirl of the ocean years earlier. "Everything with Willy? Yes."

The insides of Thea's body quivered with a strange kind of chill. She needed to expel some of this nervous energy.

"After we eat lunch, do you want to go for a bike ride?" She was back home, the drizzle had stopped, the fog had burned off, and it was still early on Friday. Her husband returned that night, but not until dinnertime.

"But someone might see me."

"I have an idea." Inside the hall closet by the front door, Thea hunted for a large sunhat and the big black Jackie Kennedy sunglasses she used to wear. She dropped both items on the wooden picnic table outside along with brown bags holding their sandwiches. "You can go in disguise."

They pedaled out of the driveway twenty minutes later, determined to ride the thirty minutes it took to get to the ocean. Thea had a disguise of her own—a men's baseball hat, aviator sunglasses.

Margot took her hands off the handlebars, singing aloud to Elton John's "Goodbye Yellow Brick Road" coming through the transistor radio attached to Thea's bike. The lyrics had been Thea's favorite of the last several years, the ballad unfolding like a bittersweet farewell to childhood. Elton's voice always tugged at Thea to revisit her own past, and his words filled her with a longing to be young, to be home with her mother, to be a teenager falling in love for the first time. She considered Dorothy and Toto following the yellow brick road to Oz in the movies, only for Dorothy to discover that she had what made her happy all along.

Thea wanted to think that everything she needed to be happy was right here in front of her, too, but she wasn't sure sometimes.

"Look, I can still ride with no hands," Margot yelled, sailing along the tree-lined streets. Thea could never do it and still couldn't, but she loved the gentle glide of the wind across her face. These days she often stood outside while talking to the other moms as Penny rode her bike in the neighborhood; why had Thea stopped riding herself? When Felix asked her recently to bike to town for breakfast at the diner, she'd thought it would be easier to drive, especially with Penny trailing behind. But the smooth tires on pavement, the invigorating speed, the balancing act—all of it brought her back in time. How had she thought she was overburdened at twenty?

"Are you glad you stayed here?" Margot asked, speckles of sun funneling through the stately trees and dappling the roadway. "I forgot how special summer feels out here. I would stay just for that farmer's strawberry rhubarb pie we picked up."

Thea felt a tightness unfurl inside her. She'd been consumed by this thought lately—*had she made the right choice in staying in East*

Hampton?—and when the honest answer came to her, it was a comfort. "I am glad, but I wouldn't mind seeing a little more of the world like you have."

"You know where I think you would love? The south of France. We hated glitzy St. Tropez and ended up in an old town on the water named Antibes. They have artists and a jazz festival. I thought of you when I was sitting on the old wall looking out on the water."

"Did you?" Thea liked the idea, since she had thought of Margot numerous times while walking an ocean beach in East Hampton. "The oddest things would remind me of you too. I was at a yard sale and saw a political button against nuclear war. 'Hell No, We Won't Glow.'"

Margot laughed. "Do you think if my mother hadn't left, I would have stayed out here for good?"

"Probably not," Thea said. "You had so many open doors."

Margot might have visited more often had her mother stayed, but a quiet country life didn't suit Margot any more than it had suited her mother. The newspaper woman and her daughter had the mindset of summer people: The "country" was worth visiting only because everyone else from the city and its suburbs were visiting too. They hired locals to keep their floors free of sand and stock their bar carts. They paraded around in designer bathing suits at members-only beach clubs as if that was the entire point of going to the beach. And most of them abandoned it all come Labor Day, as house staff dragged inside overpriced outdoor furniture, installed storm windows, cleaned out the food cabinets, and drained the pool.

They biked in the quiet, the rattle of the spokes spinning underneath them. "Felix made it all worth staying, I bet," Margot said.

"Sure. Staying out here with Felix's job has definitely connected us with people I never thought I'd be friends with," Thea said. "It has surprised me how alike we all are."

Summer people found Thea's knowledge of where to go clamming and where to find ponds where kids could catch frogs utterly charming, and rather than hide that she grew up in the area, she often let it "slip," basking in the attention it brought on her. "What is winter like out here?" some women asked, confiding in her as they admitted how exhausting life was in their busy suburb. Sometimes she'd see those women at the grocery come January, but only the heartiest stayed a second winter. Still, it didn't matter how long people stayed; all of them were knitted together by their love of summer. Just like the rest of them, she and Felix paid their yearly dues at the Maidstone Club, even if they were heavily discounted because Felix's boss was on the board, and Thea spent long mornings at the pool talking with other moms about the best swim instructor, the tennis pro worth registering with, and how to barbecue the juiciest steak. Class, it turned out, wasn't as much of a divider as she'd once thought.

And still. *Still.* Thea kept up walls with these friends. She never did confide in any of them about the stormier years of her childhood or how she wished she could have finished college or how she hadn't expected to be a mother so young herself or how she worried she wouldn't be a good mother and Penny would find a reason to hate her someday or how life could be so incredibly boring one day and colossally fascinating the next. Did anyone else feel as though they lived on the same roller coaster of emotions in a single afternoon, the desire to be everything and to admit that you'd become nothing in the very same breath?

"Do you remember when Penny was born?" Margot steered her bike directly beside Thea, pedaling at the same speed, their legs in sync. "Did you get a gift in the mail? A pretty crocheted dress and winter bonnet. Yellow, with a small lamb sewn onto the pocket?"

Thea did recall. It had come in a small box with a Florida postmark, without a return address. "That was from you? Felix said it must have been from his great-aunt down in Port Charlotte."

Margot laughed, then reached up to an overhanging oak branch, grabbing a leaf, then letting it flutter out of her hands. "This is what I was trying to tell you. I was here with you, before this mess I'm in now, just not in the normal way."

Thea scrambled to understand. Why would she keep it a secret? It would have meant something to her to know that Margot was following her life from afar; she'd always assumed she'd simply moved on.

"Why didn't you just sign your name in a card? 'Congratulations! From, Margot.' Easy."

"Because I didn't have the energy to apologize and bring up all this tension. I just wanted to give you a present and congratulate you, not stir the pot."

In those early weeks, Thea had been too overwhelmed with new motherhood to question something as trivial as who sent it; she could barely keep up with her engorged breasts. "How did you even know I was pregnant?"

"I went to camp with a lot of women out here. Word gets around."

Thea gulped the honeysuckle air. Her legs pushed harder to keep the bike moving. It had been easier to think that Margot hadn't thought of her again after their friendship drifted apart. The knowledge that Margot had wanted to make amends all these years made Thea feel guilty that she hadn't tried harder herself. But it was different with a friend like Margot; you wanted them in your life, but you didn't *need* them. It wasn't as though they were former lovers rekindling a fire. She and Margot had simply been there for each other at a critical juncture in their early lives, and what they needed then was so different from what they'd probably needed in the coming years. Or even now? What could they even offer to each other now other than memories?

"I wish you would have come to visit—even just to say hello."

Margot shrugged. "You could have found me too."

Thea slammed her foot against the pedal with frustration. "I wrote you letters. I called."

Her friend seemed surprised. "Mother never gave me any letters. That was her way, though: she'd told me the day we packed up our beach house and returned to the city that I should stop talking to you." Margot parroted her mother's condescending voice. "'She's an innocent in this, Margot.'"

"You never listened to her before." Thea couldn't help her sarcasm; she'd always looked up to Margot's mother. To think that she'd likely opened Thea's letters before throwing them in the trash, that she'd read her apologies and pleas for Margot to call her. How weak Thea must have sounded.

Margot did a zigzag in the roadway, hollering behind her. "I know, but I thought it would be better for you, honestly."

Thea tried to decide if it was true, if she would have struggled with Margot in her life. They might have fixated on their guilt, one or both of them feeling an overwhelming desire to tell—and then what? There was no turning back. But Margot was right. Thea had stopped trying to connect after those first few months too, and it was for one reason, a reason that had popped into her head now: because she'd never truly believed she was good enough for Margot. That entire summer, she'd been waiting for Margot to discard her.

Thea pedaled harder to catch up with Margot, who was gliding down a small hill. When they were side by side again, Thea asked after her family, trying to connect the dots of Margot's past. "So why did you ice your parents out of your life?"

"Are you really asking me that question?" Margot snapped, their bikes passing by a large red barn, an American flag flapping off the front. A whaling cottage came into view, a tidy picket fence wrapping the property. Slowing down, Margot said: "For a long time, Willy defined me, and I adored him for that. For taking away any of my confusion about how the world should look. Because I liked his view of a well-lived life. It was full of distractions and late nights out and plenty of books and travel, and I needed that. For him to simplify things for me. My parents did nothing but confuse me with their perplexing show of love and hate."

Willy's disappearance had been on Thea's mind this entire conversation. "Have you tried calling your apartment?" Thea pressed. "To see if Willy's come back?"

"He's not coming back." Margot tucked a chunk of her hair into the sunhat. "And anyway, what if I do call, and someone else answers? Someone waiting for me to reveal where I am."

They'd scoured the newspaper together every morning after it arrived this week, and there had been only one article about Willy, buried toward the back, three-quarters of a column with one new detail. Reporters knew: He'd disappeared from his Park Avenue apartment, his wife vanishing soon after. His body had not been found, and investigators believed he was on the run and wanted for questioning in a possible Ponzi scheme involving a string of restaurants in Miami. "Nonsense," Margot had slammed the paper shut yesterday morning. "We own those restaurants free and clear. I helped buy them for god's sake. Can't they just look up a title?"

It had surprised Thea how easy it had been for Margot to take Willy's side. *Accused of a Ponzi scheme?* That was a serious crime. She'd arrived saying that Willy had hurt her, hinting that he might have endangered her, but she seemed to be reversing that stance now, playing the role of supportive wife. And yet, Margot wasn't doing much to try and connect with him, either. If Felix disappeared, Thea would be frantic, doing everything in her power to try to locate him. But Margot seemed to know something more, and Thea suspected that she wasn't telling the whole truth. Margot was always good at leaving things out when it was convenient.

"Maybe you should call the police, so they don't think you did something bad." Thea didn't feel thirty saying that. She felt twenty, still the uncertain young adult looking to Margot to prop up her confidence.

But old friends were bound like siblings; there were roles to play, and if she'd been passive in the past, it was hard not to be now.

Margot's foot slipped off the pedal, and she pushed on. "But if the police know where I am, then someone else can find me. I have this bad feeling."

"But you could prove to them that you bought the restaurants. You could clear Willy's name."

"You're missing the point, Thea. The feds are looking for one thing, and those goons outside the apartment are after him for another. It's not the cops I'm scared of."

A more disturbing thought came to Thea then. Perhaps Margot didn't actually care what happened to her husband. Maybe after he gave her that giant bruise and she discovered his crimes, she'd decided that the only way to protect herself was to disappear. She would tell an invented tale of scary mobsters chasing after them, when really it was just the feds looking for Willy because he'd broken actual laws. Maybe Margot had too.

Thea sighed. She really hoped she was wrong.

They took a break under the shade of a large pine tree, drinking from a Mickey Mouse–themed thermos that Thea packed in her woven bike basket. Thea wanted to state the obvious: if Margot wasn't ever going home, where was she planning on going? It was only a matter of time before the harbormaster discovered her sailboat on one of his routine tours of the shoreline. Thea's daughter had already seen her in the barn. Felix would return tonight, and at some point, he'd find out too. Then she'd be in a marital sparring match of her own.

As they saddled back on their bikes, Margot reached out to steady Thea's handlebars as she fiddled with her kickstand, seemingly reading her mind. "Don't worry. I have a plan to get out of your hair. I will hide out in the Caymans until I figure out what is really going on."

Thea winced at the thought of this far-fetched plan. Margot would sail alone? For weeks? It sounded suspicious holing up on an island in the Caribbean, too. She wished she could trust her friend to be innocent. Then again, Margot had lied to her before. Thea had seen how easy it was to lose yourself in a flash of anger, how Margot's face had contorted that night when she saw Thea holding the umbrella overhead next to her illuminated pool, the adrenaline they'd both felt that fueled them when they'd needed their strength. Fear was always the first domino in the collapse of rational thinking.

"Do you know how nuts you sound?" Thea exaggerated her cadence to make clear how dubious the circumstances were. "You're going to sail to the Cayman Islands? Alone? On your father's boat? Margot, have you lost your mind?"

"Of course not." Margot lifted her feet off the pedals, suspending them in midair. "I've hired a local sailor. I only need you to drive me to the dock in Montauk next Friday at five o'clock. The eighth of July."

"For the record, this is a terrible idea."

Margot laughed. But Thea began planning out how it could work. Felix would return tonight, and Margot planned to take her boat to hide in the next cove. They'd go to the beach on Sunday as a family and watch the fireworks; Thea would attend Midge's July Fourth barbecue with Felix on Monday, and when Felix left for the train bound for New York on Tuesday, Thea had four more days to help Margot. That Friday, they would say a tearful goodbye, and she would drop Margot at the Montauk dock and hope that Willy's demons never found their way back to her.

She and Margot walked along the dunes to a point far from the crowds of the public beach and concession stands, the pound of the surf roaring. Margot set up her towel and Thea unrolled hers right beside it. They lay down in the sand, found safer lines of conversation.

Margot said she never did return to Barnard, and that San Francisco wasn't what she thought it would be back then. She fell in with a group of people living in a mansion in the Haight, a commune of sorts, where everyone had a job like scrubbing carrots or toilets or tubs, and at night, they all cooked elaborate dinners because the owner of the house, a friend of a friend she knew from her Manhattan private school, had just graduated from culinary school. After a year of Margot standing on sidewalks singing peace songs with a hat overturned in front of her, a year of selling her dresses at flea markets, a year of learning how to read the energy of her housemates (her roommate taught her to see auras), Willy came to visit a friend at the house. Their attraction was instant, a physical one that didn't make sense since his nose was as big as an elephant's, she laughed, "a true schnoz."

But Margot was drawn to him, in part because he wasn't at all like the stoned, flaky men she was used to spending time with. She was so sick of tie-dyed T-shirts she could scream, sick of people trying to pretend that communal living made them socialists. Instead, every one of her housemates, including her, was empty; their auras were blank. Then Willy had shown up in a suit, looking like an ad from *Gentlemen's Quarterly*, and he had this blue glow around him. Everyone in the house had heckled him for being square, but it had only made him stand taller and announce: "While all you sorry kids are wasting your life, I'm going to make something of mine."

Now that was an energy Margot wanted in her life. Willy knew exactly what he wanted; his trajectory was so clear. It made her feel pulled together, like she suddenly had a plane to catch. Two weeks after he arrived, Margot climbed into the passenger seat of his black Mercury Cougar and they'd driven straight across the country to Manhattan. They moved into a studio on Thompson Street, lingering most mornings in bed together, leaving sometimes for picnics or concerts in Washington Square Park. It took seven days for Willy to have his first big idea: He was opening a restaurant. He'd name it Divisadero for the street where they had met in the Haight. Margot gave him a small loan to secure a space and hire a chef, and her mother, feeling a bit enthralled by the change in her daughter, appointed her a Styles editor at the paper. She and Willy got engaged, and rather quickly, they had a New York life.

"It was a relief really," Margot said now. "All my crystals had lost their energy, and then I could see them glowing again. I was glowing again."

"Why didn't you and Willy ever have children?" Thea asked, turning on her side and facing Margot, who was laying on her back with her eyes closed. She and Margot used to promise that they'd be "cool" parents, but now that Thea was a mom, she could see that being cool had little to do with parenting.

A sigh from Margot. "Well, my hoo-hoo is sick."

"What the hell is a hoo-hoo? Do you mean your 'lady garden'?" Thea tried to keep a straight face but failed miserably, belly laughing.

"Yuck. What man looked at a woman's parts and thought these names were any good? My god." Margot reached for Thea's Coppertone, slathering it on her chest and shoulders. "In all seriousness, though, I think that's partly why Willy and I drifted apart. We both wanted kids."

"I'm sorry, Margot. I know how hard that is." Thea weighed how much she wanted to get into her own pregnancy struggles, even though she already had Penny, which was more than Margot might ever have. "I bet you the problem was Willy. You'll meet someone else, you'll see, and the first time he digs into your 'lady garden,' you'll get a nice juicy tomato plant."

"This conversation is getting weird." Still, Thea saw the corners of Margot's mouth turn up. "Well, with polycystic ovarian syndrome, some women get lucky and some don't. I was the latter."

Thea sat up. She watched a woman in a black bathing suit running after a large loose sheepdog down the beach. "You could adopt."

"I could." Margot pulled the large-brimmed hat lower over her eyes. "I've got a question for you now. Why did you stop drawing?"

The question niggled at her. Thea fidgeted with her hair, deciding to braid it; separating the strands sometimes helped her separate her thoughts. *She did draw.* She drew with Penny all the time. Every year on her daughter's birthday, she'd work from a photograph to document her child's changing face. She'd doodle when she was on the phone with Cara. Sometimes she'd grab a sketchbook and trace out the inside of houses, just like she did as a kid.

But that wasn't the kind of drawing Margot was asking about. Thea didn't want to sound defensive and admit that it bothered her, too. "It just never added up to anything."

"Thea, you were designing concert posters for local bands. You nearly had illustrations in the *Star*. Mother thought you were wonderful. Why did you stop?"

Thea gave Margot's shoulder a playful nudge. "You never told me your mother thought anything I did was worthwhile. I would have remembered that." She and her mother had left without giving her any feedback on the illustrations she'd done for the paper, and she'd been too upset with Margot leaving to focus on her designs.

Why *had* Thea stopped? She got busy, that was all, and she'd stopped feeling inspired. Doodling didn't seem as important as shaping the life of a newborn baby. "I don't know. Penny was born, and I just wanted to do everything right, be a good mother to her, so she knew how much I loved her. And I felt like—"

Margot cut her off, holding a finger up to her face, waving it. "No, no, no. You don't get to do that."

Thea flipped over onto her stomach to escape the fire in Margot's glare. She stared down at the small loops in the striped beach towel. "I can't do what?"

"Put everyone else first. That's what you used to do. Don't you ever learn? It's like we all have these demons we try to fend off, but they just keep finding us."

"You're the only one that thought my stuff was that good, okay?"

"That's not true, and you know it. I just told you my mother liked your stuff!"

"Well, that piece of information is ten years too late." Thea realized she was yelling. "She never called me or asked to print anything I sent."

Margot tipped up her hat, even though she shouldn't. How many people she must know on this beach, and here they were raising their voices. "Sometimes I daydream about that day. What if I hadn't called Shawn? What if you hadn't come to check on me?"

Thea felt the urge to run to the water's edge and dive straight into the ocean, the water erasing the words that Margot had just said. The darkness came back to her, the moment Margot cried out, the cool of the aluminum umbrella pole under her fingers, the rocking of the boat in midnight waters.

"Let's not talk about it," Thea said, suggesting they walk down to the water.

Margot shook her head with frustration. "We have to talk about it. Because I need you to know that everything I did, I did for you. You deserved a second chance after what happened with your mother."

That wasn't the way Thea saw it. The scuffle with the Walrus had little to do with Thea at all. In that shadowy hour, after the humiliation of discovering Margot's secret, Thea had been poised to go home, her footsteps crunching along the gravel driveway. That's when she'd heard Margot scream.

Thea had run, her legs pushed by a current of anxiety. The terror of what she'd seen, of what she'd had to do. To this day, she believed it had been worth it. Something worse could have happened.

"*Margot!* You didn't give me a second chance. I saved you. If I hadn't come back . . ."

Margot stood, swiping the towel off the sand and draping it over her arm. "Well, then you and I see things very, very differently."

Margot didn't wait for her until she got to the parked bikes, and Thea was left to wonder what she'd done wrong. Had Margot tried to justify what happened by telling herself that she'd saved Thea in the process? She had, but there was a hiccup in her thinking—Thea hadn't put herself in that bad situation; it was Margot's mess that Thea had walked in on.

They didn't speak much on the bike ride back to the house, and when they arrived, they each drank a glass of water at the kitchen sink. Margot sunk down into a cane dining chair, resting her forehead in her palms.

"What is it?" Thea assumed that Margot was going to apologize for snapping at her earlier.

"I've been looking for the right moment to ask you something." Margot leaned back in the chair, resting her palms atop the tablecloth Thea had put on.

"You're making me nervous," Thea said.

Suddenly, Margot rose and scurried to the bathroom, slamming the door. Thea heard her gagging. She'd always had a nervous stomach.

"It's going to be okay." Thea handed her a cool washcloth as Margot returned to the kitchen table, and she nodded, pressing it to her forehead.

"So I've been thinking," Margot said, slowly, carefully. "No one can know I'm here or that I ever was. It will be too easy to track me when I leave. So before you take me to the dock next Friday, I'm going to need to get rid of my boat."

Did Margot plan to sell it? Would she use the cash to fund her journey south to the islands? But how would she find someone to buy it in one night? Did she expect Thea to take this on? She couldn't—what if someone realized what she was trying to do? "But there's not enough time," Thea said. "You won't find a buyer."

"You misunderstand." Margot glanced out the window where the boat bobbed near the buoy bell. "We need to go out on the water on

Tuesday night. We'll bring the dinghy, and before we head back, we'll sink the *Dalliance*."

Thea's brain went muddy. Nighttime. Water. Bobbing in a harbor whispering with ghosts. "No, Margot. I can't—what if someone finds out? What if someone sees us, or your father presses charges?"

"He won't."

"Margot, you realize it's still Fourth of July weekend, the busiest time in the entire summer. You know how many people will be on the water, who might see you sinking a boat?"

Margot twisted the small crystal beads dangling from her ear. "It will be after dark. No one will see a thing."

Thea's heartbeat thrashed in her ear. "What you're asking . . . it's a really big deal. I have a daughter, a husband. I can't just . . ." Her voice trailed off.

Margot nodded with understanding. "I know this is crazy, and I swear I won't put you in harm's way. But I promise you, Thea, I promise with all of my being, that even if we get caught, I'll tell them I held you hostage. I will tell them that I forced you. I didn't let anyone touch you after what happened ten years ago, and if you help me this one final time, I promise I will never ask you to do anything for me again." She blinked once, then a second time.

"You don't have to cry." Thea opened the refrigerator and pulled out the strawberry pie Margot loved, slicing her a piece and sliding the plate in front of her. Thea took a bite from the pie pan. "Why do I need to come at all?"

"Because I'm scared, and something could go wrong. There would be no one to go get help." Margot wiped at the corners of her eyes. "We have to go deep so no one can find the boat."

Thea agreed with that point. As soon as someone placed Margot in East Hampton, it would be easier to trace her whereabouts. Thea rubbed her temples, her mind racing to what was likely to happen. Even if they did get caught, if she promised to say Thea hadn't agreed to any of it, Thea would be fine—and she could trust Margot to tell a lie for her.

Thea forked off another chunk of pie in the pan. "Fine. That's our story, then. You held me hostage and made me help you. I wasn't a willing partner. Promise?"

Margot pressed her hands to her heart, doing a quick Hail Mary prayer. "I'll say I had a gun and walked you to the boat with it at your back."

Thea stopped chewing. "You don't have a gun, do you?"

"No, I don't have a gun." Margot pointed a finger at her head. "Thea, it's still me in here. You need to trust that everything will be fine."

A part of Thea would never fully trust anything about Margot, and yet she felt a familiar tug. She wanted to help. She couldn't just stop caring for someone because it made logical sense. "Okay, I'll do it."

Chapter Ten

The following Tuesday, as the wind blew her bangs off her forehead, Thea closed her eyes at the open horizon, gripping the white leather seat in the back of the boat like she might disappear if she didn't.

She hadn't been on a boat since the summer she and Margot met, and no matter how Felix had tried to coax her onto one over the years—they had always said they were going to sail to Block Island—she never budged. Boats were such a romantic notion, weren't they? The idea that you could board a boat and go somewhere far away, docking it in a new place with new people and new pursuits.

But in truth, Thea had always been a little leery of boats. Even if daylight made swimming and canoeing benign, Thea couldn't stand on a beach at night and not think of the sea as she did that night: as a monster.

It was why she closed her eyes now as Margot pulled back the throttle, steering the silver captain's wheel toward the open water. Every time Thea looked out into the fading light, the swirl of darkening water brought the question coursing through her: Why had she let Margot coax her onto this sailboat? She was disappointed with herself for being so willing to please, for being afraid to say no. But then Margot had made that tender comment so breezily, and that had convinced Thea to do it. They were painting their toenails on the sunny patio last Friday, and while applying the second coat of red, Margot had said, "Next time I come here, it will be on our terms, and we'll do whatever we want."

It was a fleeting thought, a forgettable sentence if Thea hadn't homed in on its subtle suggestion, warming her like she'd just tucked herself into her porch blanket. *There would be a next time.* When Margot left East Hampton on Friday night, she wouldn't be leaving for good. Their time together had been the start of something new between them, and accompanying Margot on this boat was just another test of loyalty. Of friendship. Of a story that they'd laugh about *the next time* they got together.

When she and Margot parted ways ten years ago, Thea hadn't had a clue how hard it would be to make a friend where everything felt as easy and natural as it had with Margot. Most of her friends had come into her life after Penny was born, women looking to connect over the shock of new motherhood, or ones she'd bonded with poolside at the club in summer. Sometimes Thea looked out on all the children in the pool, all the mothers lining the cement perimeter with their feet swishing in the crystalline water, and wondered: *Where have all the men gone?* Husbands were like weekenders, showing up Friday for social hours and on Saturday for Little League practices and Sunday night for barbecues, but otherwise, Thea lived in a community of women. Lunches with women. Racquetball with women. Walking dogs with women. It wasn't bad, just different from what she'd thought domestic life would be.

"You get to be like Mom now," Cara told her over the telephone back in the early days when Thea walked the halls with a fussing newborn at night while Felix slept since he had to get up for work. In those conversations, she'd picture her sister's curly red hair twisted into a bun, how when she smiled her upper lip disappeared, just like their mother's. "Remember how many groups that Mom tried to be involved in. It was to make friends! Go join one of those mommy play groups at the church."

And Thea had listened to her little sister. On one of those outings, she'd met Midge. But getting to know someone took so much energy, often with little payoff, since so many came and went after a few months. Over a string of coffee dates or playground meet-ups, she and her new friend showed their shiniest sides, courting each other while gauging the level of commitment to the friendship, comparing values through seemingly benign stories about parenting. Then the friend let down their guard and offered a glimpse into what was behind all that pretty wallpaper, and that's when things got awkward. Because then you had to back your way out of a relationship with someone who you'd continue to see at every stage of your child's life.

But these friends were different from the ones she'd made in her formative years. The friends made when young were perhaps the most important because those friends knew all the cumulative versions of you—the you then, the you now—and they could somehow sense the years in between. And while time could change the face, adding laugh lines or age spots, it rarely changed the soul. Margot knew her before Thea had taken on any of the ubiquitous labels, before she was someone's wife or mother, before she was another woman at the club swishing her feet in the pool. Margot knew her when Thea was only the culmination of a million little moments she'd spent alongside her.

Felix was in the city until Friday, so she'd phoned Dale earlier in the day, her anxiety spiking over asking him for a favor. She'd never asked him for anything. "You wouldn't mind if I dropped Penny for a few hours, would you? I'll send her with her crayons." Dale sounded pleased, possibly even thrilled, saying he'd heat them both a TV dinner. It was like aging had scraped off his hardest edges, his heart hiding under one of those instant lottery tickets you'd scratch away to find a prize.

After dropping Penny off, Thea had parked under the cover of a pine grove in the "meeting spot." She couldn't stop itching her neck, then her arms, her eczema flaring all at once—she itched as she peeled off her clothes, folded them, and placed them on the back seat of the car. She couldn't escape the sense that she was being set up to fail, that Margot knew the decision to help would backfire and yet she didn't care. If Felix ever discovered that she was taking a boat out into the middle of the sea to sink it, that she'd changed into her bathing suit in the car so Penny didn't ask her why she couldn't come swimming, Thea could probably deny all of it and he'd believe her. That's how outlandish the accusations sounded.

And still, Thea had waded into the pebbly water along the shore at the park, diving into the chilly sea, swimming against a current pushing her away from the large sailboat with its unfurled sails, the water stinging at the red streaks on her arms. "The water is more dangerous than it looks," Thea had said as she pressed up onto the boat. Margot was dressed as though they were on holiday: a string bikini, her hair tucked behind her ears, large sunglasses on her face.

She tossed Thea a towel. "Come warm up in the sun." The days were still long, and sunset wasn't for two hours. Positioned at the helm of the boat, Margot switched on the engine. "There isn't enough wind for the sail."

Now the wind sent goose bumps up her arms and legs as the boat crested over the waves. Thea watched the jagged cliffs whip by, the blur of a sprawling Georgian estate with white columns.

The dinghy, tied to the back of the boat by thick roping, dragged behind the sailboat as Margot steered. She'd insisted they go farther east around Gardiners Island and beyond, where the sandy bottom dipped twenty feet down, maybe deeper. Thea dreaded getting home in the dinghy, with its weak outboard motor and bench seats and sides that barely provided cover from water and wind. By then it would be pitch-black, the waves picking up if the breeze did. Thea double-checked for life jackets.

The bow of the sailboat cut through the sea, and Thea felt faint with every rise and fall. Scrambling into the cabin, feeling a bit seasick, she steadied herself by holding on to the glossy teak countertop. There were no glasses or plates or blankets or clothes. Two days before, Thea and Margot had loaded up the dinghy three times, carrying everything from the boat to the back of Thea's station wagon, driving everything to the local dump. But there was a nautical map still hanging on the wall, and Thea stared at the swirls of concentric shapes with small numbers written at each line. Felix had once pointed a finger to the same map, showing her where the bay meets the Block Island Sound, then the ocean, explaining how boats could run into rough water near here since the currents slammed into each other like opposing linebackers. She hoped to God they weren't going that far.

Rejoining Margot at the helm, Thea yelled over the motor. "I think this is good enough. We haven't passed one other person."

The engine roared on. "I see too much land."

After what seemed like the duration of Thea's entire childhood, Margot slowed the boat and threw over the anchor. Pink and purple skies painted the sea a dark navy, all the colors alight and shimmering with the sunset. To the south, in the far-off horizon, Thea spotted five distant dots of light. Shoreline. The relief caused her to release the fleshy meat of her thigh she'd been gripping.

With the water lapping against the boat, Margot hopped over a pile of braided mooring line to shut off the engine. Without birds or boats or voices traveling across the water, the night fell silent. A reminder that, out here, they were completely alone. Thea scratched at a flare of itchy skin on her arm.

"Calm down. You're going to get welts," Margot said, glancing at the red bumps on Thea's forearms. "This isn't like last time."

"It feels like last time." Self-conscious and suddenly freezing, Thea pulled on her East Hampton sweatshirt.

There are sounds out here, Thea thought, as Margot ducked down into the cabin. The splash of a fish, the listing of the boat, the gentle knocking of the dinghy thumping against the stern as it floated.

Up the steps came Margot holding two Colt 45 beers. "For a little courage." She'd popped off the tops, and she handed Thea one. They would wait for utter darkness. "To the worst good times," she said.

Thea said a little prayer in her head before she sipped. "To the worst good times."

Margot curled into the white leather boat cushions and sighed audibly. "Don't you think those days with Jay and Shelly were the best? Maybe it was having the puppy or maybe it was because you and I did everything together. And that was two summers before Woodstock."

Thea wouldn't drink much. She needed to stay alert on the water. "Before the Beatles last performance on the rooftop at Apple Records in London."

"Before we put a man on the moon."

"Before I walked down the aisle."

Margot smashed her palm against her forehead, wincing. "Before my father remarried. Oh, it was just happening then, wasn't it?"

"It was. Do you ever talk to him? He's out here, right?"

Margot shook her head. "In the end, he was so cruel to my mother. I took his side at first, but he was the one who mucked everything up."

There was a fantasy they'd shared as young women, that leaving behind the people who hurt them would keep them from feeling the tender ache of any more sorrow. By now they both had learned the same lesson: Your past followed you wherever you went, worming inside your brain, popping up at the oddest of moments. Even if you were on a boat in the loneliest middle of Gardiners Bay.

"When Penny was in the Christmas pageant last winter, I found myself bawling when she came out dressed like a lamb. I looked at Felix and how adoringly he stared at her, and I squeezed his hand, and I thought: *I don't deserve this happy life. Something terrible is going to happen.* Sometimes I wait for it."

"Oh, Thea. You simply picked well. You made this life for yourself. I was strategic in a different way: I did the opposite of whatever my parents wanted, and I rather deserve everything coming to me."

It wasn't entirely true: Margot had "worked" at the paper, she'd gotten married, she went to the parties her mother requested her presence at. But she did it on her own terms.

In the distance, a strobe from a lighthouse flashed. It couldn't be Montauk, could it?

"I'm not always sure I'm happy though," Thea said. "Sometimes I'm just so bored. I can't focus on reading a novel. My thoughts wander during TV shows. Is it normal to feel so restless sometimes?"

Margot patted Thea's leg with tenderness. "Yes, it's normal. If the housewives out here are pretending otherwise, they're filled with fluff.

Do you know what my mother told me once? 'Times change every decade and yet they don't change at all.' Being a woman is a full-time job. Finding satisfaction is a full-time job."

Thea let out a huge breath. "God, that makes me feel better. Sometimes I feel like I'm the only one searching for some kind of purpose."

Margot looked out into the nothingness. "If it makes you feel better, I'm disappointed with myself nearly every day of the week. I know how much more I should have amounted to, how I didn't live up to anyone's hopes, including my own."

Thea paused, watching the light strobe once more. Her mind slipped to the past again. "I waited for you that day. Why did you leave without me?"

Margot pulled her knees tight to her chest. "I think I just wanted to go alone by then. If I could erase you from my life, I could erase that night. But I couldn't erase the memories any better than you could, I'm guessing. I had nightmares all the time until I met Willy." She used the sleeve of a battered men's sweatshirt to wipe at her eyes. "Remember that picture you drew me of my summer house?"

It came back to Thea. How she'd sat cross-legged on Margot's large front lawn with a sketch pad, drawing the detailed lines of the lovely Craftsman-style estate. "So you'd always remember that place."

"I made you sign the drawing," Margot said. Thea nodded, smiling at the thought of it.

"Well, I framed it and hung it in my bedroom near my vanity."

"I loved your summer house," Thea said. "Did you see they tore it down? Someone is building a house twice the size in that spot, if you can believe it."

"I wish you hadn't told me that." Margot sank lower. Then she guzzled the last of her beer, soldiering into action. She glanced around the boat. "You ready?"

It was actually quite easy to sink a boat. Every boat, whether it was an old-fashioned sailboat, or a sprawling powerboat, relied on a single instrument to keep it afloat: a sea cock. These small valves opened and closed to let water come in and out of the cabin. It was a sea cock that diverted water away from a boat's tiny sinks and toilets; even the bilge pump relied on a sea cock to control the outward flow. If you cut a hose connecting, say, the cabin's kitchen sink to the hull, where it typically pushed water out, and disconnected the sea cock, the water would flood in. The sea cock effectively sank the boat for you.

So far, everything was going according to plan. Margot descended into the cabin to disconnect the sea cocks, four of them to effectively make four holes for water to pour into the boat. That was Thea's cue to step into the dinghy, detach it from the sailboat, and lower a small anchor. Thea looked at the horizon, searching for any sign that another boat was approaching, but there was none. She saw only the brackish and blackness of the sea at night. It unsettled her to think about the stripers and sea bass, the eels and sharks swimming around beneath the dinghy.

The waves plunked against the bottom, a thwacking that made her think something was banging against the boat, but it was only water playing tricks with her ears. Margot's silhouette rose up from the darkness. "It's working," she called out, and for the next twenty minutes, Thea could just make out Margot going below and coming back up. At the forty-five-minute mark, the boat was listing.

"You should hop on now," Thea called, using the oars to keep the dinghy near as it continued to drift from the anchor.

"I'm coming." Margot stood up on the angled sailboat, its small portholes beginning to submerge.

She heard a thud, then saw Margot teetering in the dark. The silence broken suddenly with screaming. Margot was on her knees on the listing side of the boat. She must have tripped. Standing up, nearly losing her balance in the dinghy, Thea hollered: "Margot, what is it?"

Margot wailed like a dying animal.

The dinghy had drifted, so Thea rowed it as close to the sailboat as possible. The hull was half below the water, the stern tipping under now. Thea jumped into the deep water, swimming with large pulls to the sailboat. Margot moaned, then yelped, falling forward once, then a second time. With the boat slowly sinking, Thea wouldn't be able to push herself up and onto the deck. Margot had to come to her. And fast.

"Come on, Margot, you can make it! It will be okay."

Margot stumbled once more, and as she came into view, she was holding her upper left arm, the lower part hanging limp like a piece of spaghetti. The dinghy was at least six feet behind them, which might as well have been twenty miles since she was hurt. Felix had told Thea once that to save someone in the sea, you had to carry them under one arm and do the sidestroke, and she positioned herself to tuck Margot under her arm. "Just ease yourself down. Be careful now, the boat is slippery."

Thea reached for her as Margot dipped her ankles into the water, wincing all over again as she moved in the wrong direction, her entire body stiffening up. Margot couldn't swim now if she tried, and Thea feared she would sink to the bottom if she didn't grab her as she came into the water.

Thea's body had failed her lately. The miscarriage had made her feel weak and beat down, as though none of her parts were working together. She'd started to think of her physical body as a house with crooked shutters and missing shingles, the inside lacking working appliances, the plumbing frozen from the cold inside her heart. But Thea wouldn't accept that right now. She was stronger than she realized, maybe, and all at once, she felt the force of her body switch on, a sudden burst that pumped blood through her veins, her muscles, her brain.

Thea gripped her as hard as she could across her breastbone, swimming with her even as her head dunked under the water herself, unable to stay afloat with the weight pulling her down like the heavy metal lures her stepfather used the few times that he took her fishing. But Thea kept going, thinking of Penny and imagining that she could hear the Beatles singing "Penny Lane" on the radio, her lungs burning with breathlessness. She remembered Felix telling her that she was a fighter, and that's why he fell in love with her, because she wouldn't give up, even after all she'd been through. She wouldn't give up now, either.

Her body was strong. Her mind was powerful. And she didn't need a second baby to prove that to herself. Because she was proving it to herself right now. She would win this battle against the sea. She would save Margot's life.

Minutes later, her hand reached up to feel the wooden side of the dinghy and she yelled at Margot to try to push up with one arm. It would hurt, but it was the only way. Margot grimaced. Thea placed her friend's hand against the wood for support. Then Thea eased herself up and into the boat, careful not to rock Margot off with her weak grip, the smooth feel of a large fish grazing her leg.

Thea needed to stay focused, she thought, as she dragged Margot up and onto the boat, Margot crying out with pain with every change of position. And then they were coughing and sputtering and trying to clear the water out of their lungs, shivering and feeling as though their clothes were stuck to their skin like cellophane. Nearby, the water gurgled into the sinking sailboat, gravity pulling the bow lower.

Thea helped Margot lay down in the dinghy. Her chest filled with relief, or maybe it was victory. And still, they were merely on the boat, not back at shore. Thea had to use her hands to drive them to the small beach where they'd agreed to park the dinghy. Where she'd get her car and drive to Dale's and pick up Penny.

"You have to tell me how to start this thing, Margot." In the far distance, there was a late showing of pink fireworks, a Roman candle bursting near the shoreline. A reminder that there was life nearby. Her life nearby.

Thea tasted salt in her mouth, the goop of her nose, remembering how Felix had once pulled the choke over and over on a boat until the engine sputtered alive. Margot closed her eyes, whispering: "Steer toward the four lights on the horizon. Then follow the shoreline until you can make out the abandoned Coast Guard house on stilts."

All Thea could think of was Penny. How she was everything to her. How her daughter loved hearing the Beatles song, too, and how she'd put her small hands in Thea's and dance around the living room to the chorus.

She would make it home to her little girl. She would carry her daughter into her bedroom tonight, and she'd climb under her Holly Hobby coverlet, and she would stay there beside her. The entire night.

She wished she could celebrate her survival with Felix. She'd want to tell him how she knew her body was resilient, how she believed once more that her body was tough enough to weather what they'd been through, that it would find a way to do it again. But this was yet another secret she would keep from him. To protect him and everything they'd already built.

Chapter Eleven

July 1967

The shop door at Sunshine Records dinged after lunch, and Thea looked up and saw him. The young man who was working the party at Margot's house a few days before.

She nodded a curt hello, but it was Margot that spun on her heels to greet him, registering from across the store that Thea was sinking lower into the stool behind the register. It was always like this when he arrived: Thea went out of her way *not* to talk to him, a lurching in her midsection when he came into the store, even as she took mental notes on him. How his brown curls flopped off his forehead as he traveled through the aisles, his eyelashes so long and dark it looked like he used a wand to apply mascara to them, his green knapsack with the zipper partially undone, hardcovers and marble notebooks stuffed inside. Out of the corner of her eye, she noticed Margot still chatting with him, and then she said something like, "Let me know if you need anything else," and he returned to sifting through rock albums.

Would it be too much if Thea played the Righteous Brothers over the shop's speakers? Counting six etches and dropping the needle on the romantic "Unchained Melody" track? She recoiled into her stool. Never. He carried a Doors album to the record players in the back as Thea moved to the front, knowing without staring that he was positioning the headphones on his head. She tried to seem busy rotating the albums in the shop's front windows.

So lost in her thoughts was Thea that she jumped when Margot bounced her hip into hers. "Why don't you just talk to him? He's really nice."

Thea darted her eyes back to the listening station. "I wouldn't even know what to say."

Margot leaned against the window ledge, smiling, her pin-straight hair parted down the center, the roots as blond as the length. "Let me introduce you."

Thea's cheeks grew hot once more. She shushed her. The shop wasn't that big. "NO!"

"I know his name, you know. I got it for you."

Trying to hide her interest in the young man in the record shop, Thea rolled her eyes. "Okay, fine, Margot. What is his name?"

"Feeeeelix. Oh, feel me, Felix." Margot laughed so loud it caused Shelly to look at her, smile, then turn back to her pencil and accounting ledger.

"STOP." Thea smacked her friend playfully, although she was laughing too.

Margot twisted the beads at her neck, three strands made of tiny round colors strung in a rainbow. "Here's what you should do. Go up to him at the listening station with this record by Cream." She reached through the window and held it out for Thea to take. "Ask him if he's ever heard it. Poof. Conversation started."

Thea tugged at her miniskirt and actually considered approaching him, letting Margot nudge her toward the back carrying the record.

The shop door dinged three times in a row, and it was clear that Margot and Thea needed to help other customers. They reluctantly separated to opposite sides of the shop, Thea beginning a conversation with a woman about an old album her mother used to listen to. She forgot all about the young man at the listening station, and when she looked for him at some point later, he was gone.

Margot and Shelly were already behind the cashier's desk. Pulling a small round pin from a clear plastic bin on the counter, Thea attached it to Margot's dress, grinning at the slogan: *We Shall Overcome*. They'd been handing out a myriad of political buttons to anyone who took them. Shelly said it was how they could do their part to stop the hatred of colored people.

"You two are beginning to remind me of Lucy and Ethel," Shelly joked, as the two of them bantered about which pin was most appropriate to who they were, which somehow turned into a friendly argument about which beach had the best people watching. There was some truth in the comparison to the *I Love Lucy* characters, Thea thought. Ethel would have never survived her depressing marriage if she hadn't had Lucy and Desi's apartment to escape to. It was how Thea felt about Margot's summer home. It offered her refuge.

"You're not going to believe this," Margot said to Thea, lighting a patchouli incense stick in a small wooden boat, the scent wafting between them like connective tissue. "Shelly and I know a lot of the same summer residents."

Shelly squinted her eyes and wrinkled her nose as if to say she was tortured by whatever she was about to say. "I grew up going to the Maidstone Club where Margot's parents are members. It's this pretentious beach club that makes very rich people feel comfortable being rich."

Thea smiled but she backed away from the strand of smoke created by the incense, standing outside of the circle where it was burning. Why did Shelly assume she'd never heard of the Maidstone Club? Unlike the summer residents who spent eight weeks at the beach each season, Thea knew every curve of the road, every change in the height of hedgerows, every which way the people in these towns divided themselves up for everyone else to see. She knew every beach and yacht club she'd never set foot in. Every exclusive restaurant she couldn't afford. She knew that the Maidstone Club was the most expensive and snobby beach club in all of East Hampton. She also knew that it occupied some of the most beautiful oceanfront acreage this side of Long Island.

Thea pinned a button on herself that read: "Use Your Voice." "I know the Maidstone. I have friends there." It was true. They might work at the ostentatious restaurant in the Tudor clubhouse, but still, they were there.

"Who do you know?" Margot was genuinely curious, and Thea couldn't even be upset because she understood that her friend was being earnest. That she would love it if they shared someone in common since it gave them even more to talk about.

Shelly raised an eyebrow. "Please don't tell me you spend time there."

"Oh god, no," said Thea. The thought of donning a fabulous beach cover-up and walking through the grand gates entered Thea's mind; she imagined herself stretching her clean-shaven legs out on a lounger at the gleaming pool, smiling at the passing waitstaff carrying small round platters, waving a uniformed gentleman down for a cocktail with an umbrella floating in it. Doing nothing other than passing a languorous summer day. *Someday*, Thea thought. *Someday I will live with this much ease.*

Jay came out of the stockroom. "I'm telling them about the Maidstone," Shelly told him.

"How? You've been barred." He looked like a science teacher in his plaid shirt and black trousers, like he was announcing the key element in a chemistry experiment to his much cooler poet wife. Sometimes though, Thea heard him playing folk songs on the guitar in the back storeroom.

"I'm not *actually* barred, just discouraged from attending." Shelly tried to keep a straight face, her large hot-pink hoops pretty against her navy blouse. "Okay, here it is. I led a revolt against modest bathing suits and I made all my friends parade around the pool in skimpy bikinis because we were tired of how stuffy the rules were. Why should anyone tell us how to dress?" She was quite serious, and Thea dissolved into laughter.

"Our Shelly is a true rebel. You should be wearing this." Thea pulled one of the round buttons they stored in a bin on the counter onto Shelly's collar. In block letters, it read: "Act Up."

Shelly laughed harder. "I should snap a photograph and send one to my parents. They'd *die*. But even small rebellions matter sometimes."

Small rebellions. Thea couldn't think of a single thing in her life that counted. She wracked her brain for something to rebel against. Or maybe she needed to take a step back since she wasn't sure rebelling would even get her what she wanted at all: enough savings to help her move out of Dale's house and maybe even a chance to return to college to meet professors who believed her life could be bigger than this beach town.

Thea tried to keep up with them as they compared notes on people they knew. *Margot's parents and Shelly's parents knew each other? Shelly was a rich summer resident with a record store?* It was disappointing, and while it shouldn't have changed how she saw Shelly, it did. She'd assumed that Shelly started the record store with a meager savings cobbled together on her own, that she and Jay were part of the group that served the summer residents. But this conversation had brought Shelly into focus. She probably borrowed money from her parents to start the store, and she didn't need it to turn a profit to be successful. It kept Shelly busy, nothing more than a vanity shop.

"If you hate the club so much, then why don't you stop talking about it?" Thea turned the music up on the turntable, didn't wait to see their faces fall, and slipped off to the opposite corner of the shop. She couldn't listen to them cackle anymore.

Thea didn't ride her bike that morning to work, so she climbed into the passenger seat of Margot's dark green Mercedes convertible with Bee already in the back. She loved being in this car, sometimes even tricked herself into believing it was hers, yearning for someone from high school to see her in the passenger seat. She and Margot only had an hour before Thea needed to go home, so Margot whipped into her driveway, parking near the arbor where a tangle of roses grew up and over the white lattice.

Margot went back into the pool house, emerging with a vodka soda in each hand. She rejoined Thea, who was already nibbling from the fruit and cheese plate the housekeeper left them under cellophane on the picnic table.

"Why hasn't your housekeeper told your parents about Bee?" Thea sipped, gagging at how strong the vodka was, swallowing it anyway. She wasn't as worried about Margot getting caught with the dog now that Shelly and Jay had asked if Bee could move in with them, but still, it had been so easy for Margot to get away with. They hadn't even worked that hard to conceal the dog.

Isn't anyone even paying attention to her?

Margot stared up at the imposing back of her wood-shingled estate. "The staff doesn't care what I do as long as they get paid on Fridays. My last nanny was the same way. I turned fifteen, my parents let her go, and we never heard from her again. Anyway, listen to me, I'm talking as if I actually care."

Clearly, Margot was old enough to live on her own; but the idea of her spending a summer in an empty beach house creeped Thea out. The estate was set back from the road and isolated from its neighbors with tall thick hedges. If she were to scream inside the cavernous first-floor rooms, Thea doubted anyone could hear. Her own house was small, but at least she recognized every sound in it.

Across the rolling lawn, she spied the Walrus's cottage, his truck parked behind a shroud of tree cover. "Who would notice if you didn't come home one night?"

"You would notice. Okay? Now stop worrying about me, *Mom*."

"Okay," Thea said. These last two and a half weeks, though, it had been Margot who had been looking out for Thea, and her attention had lessened the loneliness Thea didn't even realize had settled into her. She'd started to look forward to their nightly phone calls after work, with Thea chatting away while she cooked dinner; Margot calling back after Thea got her sister off to bed. They always made plans to see each other again, and it was a comfort knowing Thea had somewhere to be the next day. "I'll pick you up for work at ten thirty," or "Meet me at Asparagus Beach at four on Wednesday." The other day, when she saw Margot waiting for her—in her usual bare feet, floral dress, and floppy hat—on a park bench in the village in front of the ice cream shop, Thea felt a warmth spread through her. The mysterious universe had taken her mother, but it had also sent her this friend, and for that, she was grateful. Thea had greeted Margot with a tight hug.

Thea glanced at her watch, setting her drink down on the round copper table next to her lounger. It was nearly six. She reached for her bag, its contents rattling as she tossed it over her shoulder. "*Bewitched* is on at eight-thirty. Shall I call you?"

Margot yawned. "Oh, Thea. Let's *do* something. You know the groundskeeper, Shawn? His band is playing tonight. They do mostly rock covers, but some originals."

The Walrus was in a band? It added up for Thea, though. He seemed like the kind of egotistical guy who might talk to his own reflection in a mirror. "Nah. Not tonight."

Margot strode off toward the house. "How about I get us both a bathing suit and we swim? I can't bear to be alone."

"Margot, I'm not swimming," Thea yelled after her as Margot disappeared inside the kitchen door. Cara was probably playing hide-and-seek outside with the neighbor's kids while waiting for Thea to return. Thea had been spending less time with Cara lately, much to her sister's dismay, and she promised she'd be home on time today. Dale would predictably pull in at half past six, sniffing about for dinner like a raccoon.

Margot returned wearing a purple striped one-piece, tossing Thea a canary-yellow swimsuit. She encouraged her to go to the pool house to change. Instead, Thea tapped the scratched face of her mother's crystal watch. It had been her grandmother Susan's, who Thea's mother left behind in Ireland when she immigrated here at about the age Thea was now. Even though Thea had never met her, she'd heard stories of how talented "Zuzu" was at drawing, her keen ability to capture faces and human expressions. She'd always felt close to her, like they were one and the same, simply because of their shared drawing skill.

Margot dove into the swimming pool, a wave of water parting before her. Thea wanted to jump in, to swim in this pool for days, hours, but she had something Margot didn't have: obligations. What would happen now if Thea let herself fall face-first, soaking her clothes down to her bra? The silken quality of the water, the glide of her body pushing off the underwater walls, a sense of wonder at the simplicity of staying afloat, how much easier life was in a pool.

"It's just, my sister waits for me all day. I feel bad when I'm late."

"Bring your sister here!"

She imagined Cara's big round eyes growing into a lemur's when she saw the pool. "Really?" Thea said.

"Of course," Margot yelled. "Tell Dale to make his own dinner tonight."

Small rebellions, Thea thought. It was tempting to go home only for her sister, leaving without setting a foot in front of the stove. Then Thea remembered that she'd be stuck inside with a grouchy Dale all week, and who wanted to start the night with a fight?

As soon as Thea walked across the weedy front lawn of Dale's house, her sister ran across the street from Mrs. Greeley's house and fell in step with her. Mrs. Greeley was one of their mother's good friends, and she'd been kind to let Cara play with her three young daughters during the day.

Cara chattered on about the most fun game of hide-and-seek she'd ever played, as Thea boiled hot dogs in the kitchen. The one window over the sink could never let in enough air on these hot, sticky days, and when Dale arrived home minutes later, setting his tool belt on the hook by the back door, there seemed to be even less air than before. He said hello, then disappeared into his bedroom. Thea heard the shower turn on in the hallway, and fifteen minutes later, he was back in the kitchen dressed in his orange-and-blue Hawaiian shirt, the smell of Hai Karate aftershave, something he sprayed only on special occasions.

"I'm going to dinner at the clam bar on the Flats," he said, popping a kiss on Cara's cheek, meaning he was in a particularly good mood. Her sister, whose knees were muddy with grass stains, was already devouring a hot dog, while Dale's dinner was waiting on his favorite dish in his usual place at the kitchen table, the newspaper folded beside it. Thea supposed she could eat it.

"You look nice, Daddy," Cara said. Thea could be annoyed at the fact that she'd come home to make dinner only to have him announce he was going out, but she was not, not even one bit, because all she was thinking about was Margot's pool. The invitation to bring Cara back for a swim.

When the ignition of Dale's van rumbled to a start, Cara wrapped her arms around Thea's waist. "Daddy has a date," Cara said, making a *blech* sound to show her disgust.

He's not my daddy, Thea thought, biting into her hot dog, which was drowning in sauerkraut and mustard. "Well, whoever this mystery date is, she's not prettier than Mom."

"I think it's the nice waitress named Becky at the diner. After we had pancakes last Saturday morning, we went out to the car, but Daddy said he forgot something. I saw him talking to her."

A date? How was it possible that another woman would actually be interested in Dale?

The walk along the manicured lawns to Margot's went fast, even if they'd been honked at twice since Thea and her sister were walking in their swimsuits and shorts and carrying their change of clothes. When they dropped their stuff on the slatted loungers in Margot's backyard, Margot came running out in bare feet, hugging them both. She showed Cara where the diving toys were kept in a bin and tossed in three plastic mermaids to sink to the bottom for scavenging.

"I'm so glad you came back," Margot said. "It's so lonely here sometimes, even when my parents are here. Aw. Look at your sister. She's so happy." In the shallow end, Cara dropped backward into the water, standing up straight, then dropping once more.

"You seem that happy most of the time," Thea said, trying not to fiddle with her halter straps. She'd saved up to buy the new swimsuit, her very first bikini with pink gingham checks.

"Sometimes yes, but sometimes I want to do something all at once, like drive to Boston on a moment's notice or buy every book by Ernest Hemingway and read them in a row. Do you ever feel that way?"

Thea smiled. "Only when I'm trying to drown out some restless feeling inside me."

"Well, maybe that's it for me too. Can I tell you something?" Margot sat up on her lounger, running her hands up and down her legs like she was cold. "One time I was in Grand Central and a woman got up from a bench holding her suitcase, but I noticed that she forgot her purse."

Thea remained still on her lounger. "Did you tell her?"

"Well, seeing it there ignited this curiosity in me, like I cared less about returning the purse and more about knowing who this woman was. On impulse I slipped the purse on my shoulder, carried it into the bathroom and stood in a stall, looking through it. There were photos of her children, a husband with a pug nose. A pink Chanel lipstick. Her license said she lived in Newport."

Thea would have instantly hollered to the woman: *Ma'am, your purse!* "That's awful. That you didn't give it to her." Cara did a cannon-ball, splashing them.

Margot laughed. "Don't worry, I'm not a monster. I mailed it back to the address on her license, but I always thought it fascinating how exciting it was to glimpse the details of someone else's existence. For a moment I could pretend I was her, and I could imagine what it was to live in her shoes, go home to that husband. Sometimes I wish I could do that, start over with a new name in a place where no one knows me."

"But you would miss your family."

Margot cocked her head to the side, looking at her like she was funny. "Would I, though? I'm not sure they would miss me. I think I'm the biggest disappointment in my mother's life. She likes you, though, says you're a good influence."

"You may be wrong about that," Thea laughed, sensing the empti-ness in Margot's heart. She decided to lift the mood. "Let's go in the water!"

Margot smiled. "We'll go in at the same time."

On the diving board, Cara cheered for her sister as she sprung up once, twice, and penciled her body straight into the deep end. The rush of water pulled Thea deeper, and she felt triumphant when her toes grazed the bottom before pushing up for air and surfacing with a grin. The three of them played Marco Polo until sunset turned the air cool, the game sending them into fits of laughter as they tried to tag each other, Cara outmaneuvering them every time. Thea and Margot dried off with the cabana towels, their fingers pruned, while Cara refused to come out.

"You know, it's nice to see you having fun tonight, Thea. I hope you know you're entitled to it." Margot applauded after Cara jumped off the diving board, landing in a belly flop.

There was judgment in Margot's tone, and it sent Thea's gaze into the champagne flute Margot handed her minutes ago. The bubbles popped. "I have fun all the time."

"No, I'm not saying you're not fun to be around. But since we're always so honest with each other, when it comes to your family . . . do you really think your mother wanted you to give up doing everything you enjoy?"

Thea prickled as Cara yelled at her from the diving board to watch her jump, and after she clapped for her sister, Thea snapped, "You don't know anything about what my mother wanted."

Her tone came out angrier than she intended, a jagged edge of accusation, and Thea was ready to apologize when Margot snuggled under her towel, turning toward Thea in her lounger like she was on the pillow next to her in bed. "Remember when you told me that the only reason you didn't finish college is because you had to come home? Your mother wanted you to stay and take care of everyone for her?"

"Yes," Thea said. It was the other night on the phone. She and Margot had stayed up later than usual, their voices burning like candles in the night, and Thea had let down her guard. She went into a long-winded account of her mother's last days, about the promise she'd made her in the hospital room, the responsibility she'd felt to take care of her sister, especially with the challenges she faced at school with reading. How Thea wanted to move to Boston or Los Angeles or New York, or maybe she just wanted to return to college or go to art school. But leaving without Cara wasn't an option. It had felt good to admit those wants, and she'd woken the following morning feeling so light that a child's balloon might have lifted her off the ground.

But now Thea sunk her eyes into the illuminated water, staring straight through Cara, who was practicing handstands in the shallow end. She hated Margot for bringing up her secrets in the open like this.

"Well . . ." Margot treaded carefully with her words, delivering them slowly and with gentle intent. "What if caring for Cara isn't what your mother really wanted? What if it's not what she actually said?"

"I was sitting right there. I know what she said." Thea's mother had made her wishes known: she wanted Thea to cook shepherd's pie and wipe down the bathtub tiles, to snuggle Cara if she woke from a bad dream, to pack her sister lunches, and urge Dale to sign school permission slips. Her mother may not have given those exact details, but she'd known what Thea quickly discovered: someone needed to take care of everyone, and it wasn't within Dale's abilities. Thea needed to step up.

Now Thea wanted to leave. "Do you mind if I use the bathroom?"

Margot didn't seem to realize the weight of what she'd been suggesting, and she plopped back into her chair, disappointed in the break in conversation. "The pool house toilet needs fixing. Use the one in the house and ignore the trash bags. It's stuff for the church sale. Hopefully, Mother doesn't notice anything gone."

There were large bouquets of fresh flowers on every table in Margot's house, and Thea stomped through the hallway, winding her way around the row of neatly aligned trash bags. She peered inside one—she had to—and she discovered several Chanel suits. In an open cardboard box was a blue-and-white soup tureen, a stack of plates, and a blender. Her head was beginning to pound. She needed aspirin.

After washing her hands, she pulled open the medicine cabinet. Inside was a bottle of Pepto-Bismol, an unopened box of Campho-Phenique, a small tin of Excedrin. The latter would do, and surely no one was going to mind if she popped two. Not with all that stuff going to charity out in the hallway. *Am I part of Margot's charity, too*, she wondered, *a local girl who needed fixing?*

She snapped open the small tin case, disappointed to find it devoid of pills. There was something else inside, though, something she never thought she'd ever hold in her hand. The crown of her head tightened, and she balanced the pill case on the edge of the ceramic sink, lifting out a sparkly diamond tennis bracelet, at least twenty-four tiny stones with an emerald-clad locket at the clasp. A nervous laugh slipped out of her as Thea dangled it from her fingertips. Were these people so rich they had left a priceless piece of jewelry in a rusting pill box in the bathroom? It was unfathomable, and yet another reason to be angry at Margot. Having money didn't give her the right to question Thea, to cast judgment about the choices she had made. To question what her mother actually said in her dying days.

She'd been the one hiding in a train station bathroom with someone else's purse!

Outside, the cool air whipped Thea's face as she hurried back to the pool. Margot was wrapping Cara in a blanket-sized towel. *Perfect*, she thought. Thea was ready to go anyway, grateful that Cara had gotten this swim despite everything. Still, Thea's voice was stony. "It's nice of you to donate all that to the church. You're very generous with your things."

There were large fluffy robes in the pool house, and Margot had one on, the material dwarfing her small frame. "I just hate all this stuff, Thea, it's horrible." She motioned to her robe. "Even this, there's so much in this house that no one uses, and there are people I pass in the city on my way home who are sleeping on subway grates and they don't even have a warm blanket."

Thea couldn't stay silent. "Do you hate the diamond bracelet in the aspirin tin in the medicine cabinet, too? Because maybe that should go in a jewelry box."

Later, Thea remembered Margot's reaction. That she didn't respond with, "What bracelet?" or "What are you even talking about?" Instead, she held Thea's gaze for an awkward beat, then responded with only a single word.

"Yes," Margot said. *Yes*, she hated the bracelet, or *yes*, it should go into a jewelry box?

"Thea, I'm cold." Cara's teeth were chattering, and Thea sent her sister into the pool house to change.

When her sister was out of earshot, Thea felt the fury rising before the words do. "I don't know, Margot. You sew your own clothes and say you hate your parents' money, but you drive that flashy Mercedes around like it's a Chevy."

Margot curled into herself on the lounger, her voice quiet. "Look, I know my whole life is a lie."

Thea couldn't help it. She had been holding too much in, and now it was flooding out, lava oozing out of her in one ugly flow. "Is that what you write in that journal of yours? That you wish you were *without options*, a girl like me living in her stepfather's house because she has nowhere else to go?"

Margot rose, took a step closer. "I only want to help you."

"I don't need help! I'm not some broken-down car that needs a jump!" She wished she hadn't shrieked like that.

Cara came out holding her wet bathing suit and saw Thea's wide stance, the way she was bracing herself for a gale. "What's wrong, Thea?" she said, and Thea wrapped an arm around her sister's slight back. "Nothing. Let's go."

Thea walked through the side gate to the front yard, Cara trailing alongside. Margot's voice came up just behind them.

"I'm sorry, Thea. I didn't mean to upset you about your mother. But just think about what I said, will you?"

At the end of Margot's driveway, the road twisted around a bend before joining up with the towering row of elm trees that Thea always looked forward to walking through. Thea thought about how clingy Margot was, how possessive she was with Thea's time; why did she care if Thea had to go home each night to care for her family? Then there was her façade of confidence but need for constant reassurance, rehashing every little interaction she had with Shelly and Jay at the record shop, looking for Thea to compliment the dresses she made, needing her approval on every little thing she said.

From the front yard, she and Cara could still hear Margot yelling after them: "Maybe you're being too literal in your interpretation. Thea!

Stop! Listen to me. Can't song lyrics mean different things to different people? Look at 'Eleanor Rigby.' Is Father Mackenzie as lonely as the old lady throwing rice in the church? It's up for INTERPRETATION!"

Thea ignored her, and she was happy she was wearing her Keds then, and not one of the pairs of sandals that tripped her up when she walked. She and Cara could run. Sprint, even.

They ran without stopping until they got all the way home.

Chapter Twelve

There was one circular table in the cheery Children's Room at the East Hampton Library, and as Thea settled her little sister into it, she noticed Cara's hands wringing in her lap. "Relax. You're going to do great today."

She gave her sister an easy children's book called *Imagine Flowers*, something basic to warm her up before Miss Porter arrived. Her sister read it with ease.

"You see," Thea said, pride shining in her eyes. "Now let's try this one." She handed her a much harder book: Frances Hodgson's *The Secret Garden*, which made Cara's small frame recoil so much she nearly fell out of her chair.

"I can't do it, Thea. Don't make me."

"Just try." Thea tied her sister's hair back to ensure she could see the page clearly. "I'll start." She read about Mary Lennox shipping off to Misselthwaite Manor to live with her uncle, how she was the most disagreeable-looking child.

Disagreeable. It was how Thea had felt since storming off from her conversation with Margot on Tuesday night, profoundly disturbed by the suggestion that she was reading into her mother's words. Thea was certain of what she'd heard. She was sitting right there, alongside the reliable whir of the oxygen machine and the tubes that ran straight out of her mother's nose, full of a longing to erase herself with the pencil she was sketching with.

"They'll keep her from moving on to sixth grade," Miss Porter had told Thea after she had evaluated Cara's reading last spring in the same room at the library. The teachers had discovered the problem after Cara was asked to read aloud from the *Swiss Family Robinson*, but Cara had fallen silent, refusing to look at the pages at all because some of the harder words tumbled together like clothes in a dryer. The children had laughed at Cara's perceived petulance, and the teacher sent Cara to the principal, where a phone call went home to Dale. Word blindness didn't make any sense to him, and he had told Cara to try harder, whatever that meant. But Thea had thought to call her old English teacher, Miss Porter, who she remembered worked with kids who struggled with reading. It was agreed that Thea would pay her an astronomical six dollars for two hours of tutoring every week.

Miss Porter instructed Cara to open her notebook, and Thea gave her sister a thumbs-up, slipping into the library hall. She had off from work yesterday and today, and with two hours ahead of her, she'd lose herself in the biography section, hoping to read about somebody else's sorry life. Running her fingers along the drab-colored spines, Thea recited the names of American actors, a few politicians, a surgeon telling his story. Finally, her eyes landed on a book about a woman rather than a man, and she slid out *The Autobiography of Eleanor Roosevelt*, studying the photograph on the cover. The former First Lady's words captured her interest immediately and she sunk down into a cross-legged position on the stiff woven carpet, the book resting in her lap.

It was engrossing. She learned about the death of Eleanor Roosevelt's parents, how she was an orphan of a different kind, raised by her wealthy grandmother upstate. Then something in the next aisle piqued her attention—two women talking in hushed voices, their conversation carrying an air of secrecy. When Thea heard Margot's name, she listened more closely.

"I didn't steal that necklace!" It was a woman her age with a high ponytail, soft tendrils framing her sunburned cheeks. Thea recognized her from Margot's party. She was talking to a statuesque woman with a gingham scarf tied around her neck, who stood chewing on the end of her long brown braid.

"Of course you didn't. But you slept over that night."

"I swear I didn't," the other whispered.

High ponytail sighed. "You have an original Cartier. Why would you?" Thea knew they were talking about the investigation into the jewelry thefts, that maybe the police were looking at party guests—rather than just the help—as suspects.

"Did Margot tell you anything else?"

The girl seemed on the verge of tears. "No."

Margot. She'd dropped a kind note under Thea's front door last night: *Sorry, I just want you to be happy. xo Margot.* Thea skulked off to the other side of the library. She'd been trying not to think about her so much. Yesterday, she'd even taped an index card to her makeup mirror that read: *Don't call Margot.* Of course it was all Thea wanted to do. They were like two queens facing off on a chess board, and Thea wouldn't be toppled first. Margot had pressed on a tender bruise in Thea's heart, asking a question that Thea had asked herself many times: Why *was* Thea still taking care of everybody?

Thea glanced at one of the library workers and scooted in her chair to allow his pudgy bespectacled frame to push the cart past her. She needed to think. Taking a brisk lap around the library, she remembered her mother in the week before she died, how she'd turned her head toward Thea, smiling at her daughter, telling her that stuff about "carving out the nooks and crannies" of happiness. Thea had heard that part loud and clear; it was why she'd had the courage to apply to Sunshine Records when Shelly offered the job. But the other part now blurred like the watercolors that her mother painted outside in the yard all summer long, the blue of the sea always blending with the sky.

Passing through the fiction section, the exact words came to her: "Promise me that you'll look after Dale and Cara. They're going to need someone to love them, and your heart is so big, Dorothea." Her mother had never mentioned cooking shepherd's pie or taking on the bulk of the household chores. Her mother hadn't left behind a will granting

Thea custody of her sister. Thea had simply started doing all of it. Who else would? It seemed like an act of love. Thea could see her mother's expectant look in her own reflection, waiting on Thea to get up from her place at the table and soap the dishes. Was it wrong that she had?

On her second lap through the library now, Thea stopped at the water fountain in the narrow entryway. She drank the cool water, remembering a conversation with her mother when she was in ninth grade. The two of them had come to the library for summer books, and they'd fought over what Thea should check out. Her mother's dreams of being in movies made her loyal to the classics, believing that little else was worth reading. "How are you going to get into college if you don't read Jane Austen?" her mother had said, her reddish hair in a French twist, her peridot-collared housedress neatly pressed. "Or Charles Dickens. These authors use the past to teach us important lessons about the present."

The memory made Thea squeeze her eyes shut trying to picture the soft features of her mother's face, her peach lipstick and carefully plucked eyebrows. She longed for her mother's sweeping opinions and her confidence that all was well if only Thea did what she said. How much her mother loved books, even complicated stories where she'd read sentences more than once to glean the meaning. How often she encouraged Thea to do the same because she wanted her to be so much more. How she had attended night school to become an accountant just so that she could afford to squirrel away money to pay for Thea's first and only year of college. How she had said to Thea on the day she left for school: "This is what us women do, little lark. We help each other."

It dawned on Thea then why she stepped into her mother's shoes a year ago, why she didn't fight against the crushing tide. It was what her mother would have done. It was what she in fact had always done: put everyone else first. "Reenie, you have to take care of yourself," Mrs. Greeley, the neighbor, had told her mother one night a few years before she died. The two women were at the kitchen table while Dale was out at a poker night, and Thea had pressed her ear to her bedroom floor to hear her mother's response. "There just isn't time," her mother had responded. "There's never enough time."

As her mother lay dying last July, Thea had stared at a stream of cars crowding the roadways outside the hospital window. Tourists funneled from the city, hurrying about their lives, just as life as Thea knew it was coming to an end. Without her mother, she'd thought, why fight to return to college at all?

But now. Now Thea stood in front of the water fountain at the public library and for some reason, she could see more clearly all the things her mother had wanted for her, for her heart.

How upset her mother would be to know that Thea hadn't followed any of her dreams—their dreams. How upset she would be to know that Thea had nearly given up.

Chapter Thirteen

"Welcome to Sunshine Records," Shelly spoke into a microphone when Thea entered into work at eleven on Friday. She was relieved that Margot wasn't there yet. She knew she had to apologize and dreaded the confrontation, worried that Margot wouldn't forgive her so easily. "Here is our favorite shop clerk Thea in her sexy sundress and sandals, along with rather scandalously large silver hoops. Tell us, what has gotten into you today with those unusual earrings?"

The cool silver handle of the microphone, which was wired to a big rectangular amplifier, was suddenly in Thea's hand, and even though there was no one else in the store yet, Thea clammed up. "Um, I wanted a change." She laughed, touching her finger to her impulsive drug store purchase.

Once again Shelly's voice boomed from the speaker. "And tell us, what is your favorite album of all time, Miss Thea Hayes?"

Thea set down her paper-bag lunch behind the counter, then her purse. Her mind drew a blank. Then Shelly ran into the pop/rock aisles and fetched a record. When she was behind the counter again, she held up a copy of the Beatles' *Revolver*.

Thea smiled. "Yes, most definitely *Revolver*," she heard her voice echo in the store, "because my favorite song 'Eleanor Rigby' is on it."

Thea handed Shelly the microphone back like it was hot. While she wanted to feel different today, she didn't have that much moxie. After switching on the turntable, Shelly dropped the needle on the album, the haunting notes of 'Eleanor Rigby' drifting around them. "Thank you, Thea. Now let's get listening."

Jay came out of the stockroom carrying three cardboard boxes, and this caused Shelly to pick up the microphone again. "It's Friday, folks, and today we received the newest and latest albums in from the record companies. Expect long lines and lots of new tracks coming from the turntable."

"We need to unplug you," Jay laughed, leaning across the counter to speak into the mic himself. "Hi Thea," he said. "We might have gotten that new Beatles single you've been looking for." He pulled out a razor blade and cut the seam to open the boxes. The door dinged and for a second, Thea thought the rush had come early, but it was Margot. Thea pretended she was looking for something under a stack of papers on the cashier's desk.

"Morning, everyone," Margot called.

"Hi," the three of them said in unison as Margot laid her eyes on the microphone, her expression brightening. Thea wanted to say something, apologize, but they had an audience. "How is your week going?" she finally asked.

Margot's hair was braided into a crown roping her head. "It's okay," she said. "How was your time off?"

"Fine." *Lonely. The new* Bewitched *episode was boring. I nearly called you twice. Then I had an epiphany.*

Margot pulled out her green leather notebook from her suede slouchy purse, her initials engraved on the cover. She flipped through the pages.

Without catching on to the awkwardness, Shelly talked into the microphone again, announcing each record that Jay pulled out of the boxes. Somehow this inspired Shelly and Margot to banter about various singers, and at some point, after Shelly accused her of favoring male singers, Margot blurted out that she wrote music herself. Then the strangest thing happened.

Margot dragged one of the wooden stools out from behind the counter, positioning it to one side of the cash register so the microphone's cord could still reach. She sat down in her wide-leg rayon jump-suit, the orange, floral V-neck bodice as pretty as the bottoms. Thumping her hand against her thigh, she grinned at Shelly, speaking into the mic: "This is something I've been working on."

Jay stopped what he was doing. No one knew what Margot was up to, although she seemed as though she'd just transformed herself into Cher. She parted her lips.

> *I don't need the house, I don't need the car*
> *What I need, baaaaaby, is you.*
> *A gift of the soul, baaaaby, is you.*

Thea and her bosses exchanged glances. Margot looked down at the green notebook for the lyrics as she sang. She had told Thea recently that she recorded all her thoughts and feelings in this journal, but Thea had no idea that included lyrics. It was a surprise, a delight, that she was so musical. Her voice had a bell-like quality like Joni Mitchell's, but also a husky tone like Brenda Lee's. Suddenly, Thea wondered if she talked too much about herself when she was with Margot, if she'd been as interested in Margot's life as Margot had been in hers. Thea knew she played piano, only because she'd seen her that night at her parents' party.

They applauded when Margot stopped singing halfway through the song. She made excuses for how "terrible" it was, and yet Thea could tell she knew it was good.

Jay returned to unpacking the new releases. "Is that what you want to do? Write songs?"

"And sing them?" Thea asked, thinking that Margot had so many secret talents; how did her parents not see that? "Your voice is really good, Margot."

"Thank you." Margot covered her mouth with embarrassment, and Shelly put an arm around her.

"You should learn to play guitar, Thea, and then you two can form a band."

"I've always wanted to learn." Music had always seemed so similar to drawing, another way to tell a good story.

"I can teach you how to play guitar." Margot dragged the stool back behind the counter as Jay and Shelly mooned over the new Bee Gees single on the other side of the store, scanning the back cover.

For the first time since she arrived, Thea and Margot were alone. Lifting her pencil from the notebook where she tracked which albums sold last week and which ones they needed to reorder, Thea didn't look up from the lined pages as she said, "You were right about what you said." She paused, sensing that Margot had rested her elbows on the counter, listening in Thea's direction. "I'm sorry for getting so mad and saying those things about your parents and your money and everything . . . but have you ever looked back and realized that the one thing that made you so mad is also the thing you actually needed to hear?"

Margot nodded. "All the time, and I'm sorry too. I shouldn't talk about things I know nothing about." Earlier Margot had dropped her suede shoulder bag in the wooden milk crate they used for storage behind the counter. She lifted the purse out and searched through the insides. She pulled out a black velvet jewelry box, popping it open and pulling out a pair of delicate gold chains. From each one hung a matching round locket the size of a nickel, two hummingbirds engraved in black on the front. "This one is for you."

"Really?" Thea was a little uncomfortable at the thought of her giving her something that looked so expensive, and yet she still lifted her hair on Margot's insistence so she could clasp it around her neck. "Where did you even get these?"

"We can put pictures of us inside, see?" Margot popped open the locket after putting the other one on herself, and sure enough, there was a place for a teeny picture. "My grandmother gave me the set years ago—it was her and her sister's—and one day when I was little, I was crying about not having a sister, and she said that sometimes friends get so close they can feel like sisters. That I could give the other one to my best friend someday, but I never really had one before."

The locket felt heavy—*it must be real gold*, Thea thought—and she didn't want Margot to feel she had to buy back her friendship. But she felt closer to her than ever.

Thea unhooked the necklace and placed it back into Margot's hand. "We are like sisters, yes, but I can't possibly take one of your family's precious heirlooms. Save this for your daughter, and maybe even her friend someday."

"You know what we should do?" Margot put a hand to her hip, her excitement for whatever idea she had in her head making her shoulder wriggle to an invisible beat. "We should wear them now, and then when we have little girls, they can be best friends too. We'll pass them on, two friends creating two more friends."

Thea imagined the little girls she and Margot had once been, the big girls they had become, and how they might someday have little girls of their own. The thought of all these little girls growing up made her dewy-eyed. So did the idea that she and Margot would find their way forward together. The chain was silken in her fingers as Margot handed it back to her.

"You're right," Thea said, repositioning it around her neck. She smiled. "We have to take the perfect pictures for these."

Margot cheered. "Let's get really decked out. Go to the salon and get our hair done up."

Once again everything was right.

After work that night, Thea planned to visit the cemetery. With all the big thoughts she'd been having lately, she wanted to sit at her mother's grave and tell her everything. Thea had prepared earlier that morning like she was meeting up with a friend, packing herself a peanut butter sandwich and a Yoo-Hoo to eat if she got hungry, a small bouquet of her mother's favorite garden roses, and one of her beloved books to read aloud.

The cemetery was a thirty-minute walk from the record shop, a fifteen-minute bike ride, and when Margot packed up for the night beside

Thea, she'd offered to give her a ride. Driving there saved Thea the trouble of bicycling on the main road. "I appreciate it, thank you," she'd said.

"You always visit alone?" Margot said once they were in the Mercedes. She steered the car down Cedar Street. "You don't bring your sister or anyone?"

"Typically, I like to go myself." Thea saw the church's white gothic spire coming into view. "Then I can speak directly to her."

Margot parked the car in the paved lot, turning off the ignition. "I'll wait for you here."

Making sure that the flowers weren't getting crushed in her bag, Thea said, "No, really, I may be a while. You should go home."

Margot leaned back against the headrest, waving her off with a smile. "It's too far for you to walk back later. Besides, I'm happy to wait. I can't imagine this gets any easier."

Thea clicked shut the car door. She had the sense that she'd pulled on her comfiest sweater. What Thea hadn't told Margot about going to the cemetery was that sometimes it made her feel lonelier. That standing at a grave and talking to the memory of her mother was a comfort only until she remembered that she was actually talking to a patch of scrub grass. "Okay, thanks."

Thea hurried past the tidy graves, wanting to get out of Margot's view, a little embarrassed at the emotions welling up inside her. She hated letting people see her cry, and tears came rather swiftly on these visits. When Thea spied the familiar small square headstone under the extended branches of a pretty oak, on came the usual mixture of relief and disappointment that the headstone was actually there. Sometimes she fantasized that she'd get here and find an empty spot where they'd buried her, her mother waiting at home.

"Hi Mommy," Thea said, plopping down to her knees, then adjusting her position to get comfortable. She brushed the grass bits and pollen off the cool stone, her fingers feeling the indents in the granite where her mother's name had been etched. Dale was still paying the headstone off monthly, seven-dollar installments he dutifully dropped off to the nice priest at the first of the month. "I'm sorry that I didn't come see you these last two weeks. Remember that friend I told you about? Margot. She's keeping me busy, actually. I think you would like her. She's dramatic, a theater type like you. Anyway, I'm sorry."

A voice popped into Thea's head. Her mother's, the one she'd use when she rubbed circles on Thea's back. *It's okay to take time away from me, sweetheart.*

Tears pricked at the corners of Thea's eyes. She pulled the small bouquet she'd brought from her sack purse and rested it against the front of the granite. The birds chirped in the tree overhead; somewhere there was the distant rumble of a car.

"I underlined that passage you love," Thea said, holding up *A Tree Grows in Brooklyn* for her mother to see. She opened to the page that she'd marked:

"'Dear God,' she prayed, 'let me be something every minute of every hour of my life. Let me be gay; let me be sad. Let me be cold; let me be warm . . . Only let me be something every blessed minute. And when I sleep, let me dream all the time so that not one little piece of living is ever lost.'"

As Thea read it, her mind slipped off to her mother's happy face when she'd handed her a Christmas gift she was excited for. When her mother twirled her in the kitchen to a song on the radio. When she'd crossed her eyebrows at Thea's disappointing math score. She would take her mother's anger over losing her any day.

Thea closed the novel, wiping her eyes with the back of her wrist, looking about to see if anyone was near her, but the graveyard rarely had other visitors in the evenings. She wondered if most people organized their grief into a checklist, shedding their feelings first thing in the morning. Thea missed her mother when she woke up, too, but the evenings were equally hard, those times when she was away from home and remembered the situation she was returning to. Thea was about to tell her mother that she was sorry that she'd started daydreaming about leaving East Hampton. She didn't really want to go far, but it was becoming harder for her imagine a life here. In Dale's house.

Then she'd heard something, the snap of a twig. Thea shot up to see who was there, and it was Margot. She hurried to crouch down beside Thea, handing her a handkerchief, and giving her a look that asked: Is this okay? When Thea nodded, Margot sat cross-legged beside her. They remained quiet for a few moments holding hands, until Margot asked Thea if she could say something to her mother. "Of course," Thea said, pulling her hand back into her lap.

"Hello, Mrs. Hayes. Reenie, right? That's what Thea said everyone called you." Margot looked down at the ground, where she began pulling at the grass. "My name is Margot, and I just want to say that you have a wonderful daughter. But you know that, you raised her."

Thea smiled through the tremble in her jaw, and when Margot continued, she felt a flutter of appreciation. Margot had come to comfort her, but she was also speaking to her mother like she was here in the flesh. Thea felt a warming in her heart.

"Honestly, Mrs. Hayes. I don't think I've ever seen a daughter love her mother like Thea loves you, and I want you to know that I'll watch over her for you. I won't let her be sad like this forever."

Thea smoothed the front of her shorts. "I'm not sad all the time, Mommy. Just sometimes."

The friends smiled at each other then, a spaciousness spreading inside Thea's center. It was her turn to talk. She had to tell her mother what she'd come to say.

"Mommy, please don't think I'm leaving you or Dale or Cara when I say this." Here, her voice wavered, but she pushed on. "I'm going to keep saving my money, and I'm probably going to leave home. I think that I may still have some dreams deep down inside me somewhere, and I think they have to do with drawing. I won't really be happy until I figure out what they are."

Her voice trailed off into the quiet, and the friends sat in the grass with their knees pulled in, their bodies breathing in the gentle breeze that ruffled the trees. They picked at the grass some more in the quiet.

The bright light began to fade, the blue sky turning white. It smelled of rain. Margot stood up, putting her hand out for Thea to put in hers. She pulled Thea up.

"Don't worry, Mrs. Hayes," Margot told the gravestone. "Don't worry about her one bit. Once I care for someone, I never give up on them."

Thea blew her mother a kiss, unable to say the words, "Goodbye, Mommy," and they began the walk to the parking lot leaning on each other.

"It's true, you know," Margot said. "I'm here if you ever want to talk about her more, even if you want to share a memory of her or call me and just say you're having a shitty day."

There was that comforting sweater again. It made Thea smile. "There was this one time . . . ," she began.

Thea told her story after story that night as they drove home to Thea's house, and even after they'd parked in her driveway, Margot had turned off the car and listened, laughing at the right places, frowning at the frustrating ones.

"I would have liked to have known her," Margot eventually said, rubbing her eyes and yawning. It was midnight.

"I would have liked that," Thea said. That night, for the first time in a long time, Thea slept soundly.

Chapter Fourteen

Before long, the store was packed with customers. They'd already had several people come in looking for the "All You Need is Love" single that arrived earlier that week, and all ten copies were already gone, except for the one that Jay set aside for Thea. They had been playing the song on repeat and the store was abuzz, a few lifeguards popping in to see what came in since last weekend, a woman from the summer colony with a trio of children in tow asking after a Temptations record.

By four in the afternoon the store quieted enough that Thea could get to a stack of albums that needed shelving. Some days passed by in a blink, and this was one of them. She wished Margot would help her, but she was engaged in a long conversation with a customer about everything that a recent *Time* magazine cover story on "The Hippies" got wrong.

"They talk about us like we're from another planet," said a preppy-looking kid wearing boat shoes; *he was certainly* not *a hippy,* Thea thought.

Margot nodded along with them. "Exactly. Why is it so far out to suggest that we all hold hands with our friends and neighbors in a national show of peace? Think of the love we'd all feel."

Well, "feel" being relative considering half the people would probably be on some kind of psychedelic drug, Thea snickered. Shelly said she tried LSD once and it hadn't been the best experience. Psychedelics

had never interested Thea anyway. Why complicate an already complicated life?

"Excuse me."

A man's voice addressed her, and when Thea turned around, it was
him.

Felix. His short brown curls were windblown, and he'd tied his yellow windbreaker around his waist, his leather backpack hanging open
and bulging with books.

"Hello," she said, and her nerves made her swallow hard. *Just treat
him like any other customer*, she reminded herself while straightening her
blouse. "Can I help you locate a band?"

He glanced over her shoulder where she had just dropped the *Jimi
Hendrix Experience* back into place. "Have you listened to it? I've never
heard anyone play electric like him."

She smiled, trying to impress him by passing on a piece of rock
trivia that Jay taught her. "Do you know that Hendrix lived with the
Isley Brothers when he was first starting out?"

Felix didn't seem surprised. Instead, he broke into the Twist, singing
the Isley Brothers' hit "Twist and Shout." He looked like an utter goofball, and then he noticed that she wasn't really giggling, so he stopped,
his cheeks pinker than she'd ever seen them. "Now here's one for you.
Do you know the Isley Brothers didn't even write 'Twist and Shout'?"

She shook her head no, grinning. "Really? Who did, then?"

"Songwriter extraordinaire Bert Berns," Felix said, a dimple forming in his cheek. "He based it on Ritchie Valens's 'La Bamba.' Can't you
hear the similarities?"

"That's funny, yes." From across the shop, Thea felt Margot's eyes on
her, so much so that she was almost embarrassed to have this conversation out in the middle of the store. Margot would want details of what
they talked about, even if Thea was already forgetting what she had
been saying while she desperately tried to think of something else. She
inhaled. "Anyway, what can I help you with?"

He hiked his backpack up onto his shoulder. "Did you get The
Young Rascals' record in today?"

"Not yet." She sauntered toward the cashier's desk, leaned over the counter, and pulled out a notebook where they wrote down orders. "You're not the first person to ask, either. We should get it in next week. Come back Tuesday, and I'll put it aside for you. What's your name?"

"Felix Lind." The backpack must be heavy—he kept lugging it up— and as Thea wrote his name neatly, one of the books inside tumbled out. *Contemporary History of the 1950s.* Thea reached to pick it up.

"I'm Thea," she said, handing it back to him. "Okay, you're officially in our secret notebook. Why are you carrying all those books around?"

"Research, for a book I'm writing," he said, his cedarwood cologne a little too strong. Had he planned to talk to her today?

"You're writing a book? About what?" Working hard to sound calm and collected, she spotted another customer enter the store, relieved when Margot rushed over to greet him.

Felix pushed his hands into the pockets of his slightly rumpled shorts. "It's about people like us. You know, the regular folks."

"Oh," she said, feeling the color leave her cheeks. *And what is that supposed to mean?* "The regular folks?"

"It turns out even boring people like us have a story to tell."

Did he really just call her *boring?* "Well, everyone has a story to tell, but that doesn't mean it's interesting," she said, tempted to erase his name from the Young Rascals waitlist. Why would someone so pompous deserve to be first in line for anything?

Offering a curt goodbye, she didn't stick around to measure his response. *The nerve!* Thea knew she may not look like a movie star, but she couldn't help but feel offended that he lumped her into such a broad category, pinning her down as something so vanilla, so "regular."

Out of the corner of her eye, she watched him stuff his books into his knapsack and zip it up. Then he left the shop, and she let out a breath. At once, Thea hurried to the notebook where she wrote his order and erased it. The arrogance! To think she'd been daydreaming about going on a date with him.

At closing time, after Shelly and Jay locked up for the night, Thea fell into the passenger seat of Margot's car; they somehow squeezed her bike into the trunk. It was too risky to ride home with the new Beatles single in her basket anyway, and Thea cradled it protectively by the sides on her lap, afraid it might scratch.

She studied the content expressions on Paul, John, Ringo, and George in the pictures on the album's cover. They always seemed to be having so much fun. "We should do something different tonight," she said.

Margot turned the key in the ignition: "You're in a particularly good mood. Is this because of your conversation with *Oh, Feel Me, Feel Me* Felix?"

"Sort of," Thea laughed. "But you've got it wrong." Thea told Margot about the strange interaction they had, and Margot seemed immediately annoyed, too. It's one thing Thea loved about her: she was quick to take Thea's side.

"He's writing a book? About the regular people? Who does he think he is, Hemingway?" Margot hit the gas. "We did see him at my house serving cocktails!"

Thea grabbed on to the door handle to steady herself as Margot raced her car through the back roads. "It's like he thinks he's better than me. 'Regular people.' What does that even mean?"

The wind blew back Margot's hair. "It means he's full of himself."

"Anyway, maybe he will write a book worth reading, but it doesn't matter because I'm not reading it." It was payday, and Thea couldn't wait to deposit the check in her purse into the savings account Dale had opened for her; the bank had refused Thea when she went in with her first paycheck months ago and the clerk had insisted she return with her father to co-sign. With this twenty-eight-dollar check, she'd have nearly two hundred dollars saved. By the end of the summer, she was hoping that account might offer her a chance at a fresh start. Wouldn't it be swell if she could enroll in classes again? Maybe even art classes.

A duck waddled into the street and Margot slammed on the brakes, letting the animal pass. They watched as four ducklings followed their mother across the road to the weeping willow tree on the other side. Thea willed one of them to return to the pond, to find its own way. The thought made her smile, and she threw her head against the seat. "I wish there was a party happening in this town tonight."

Margot turned up the radio, a bluesy song by Dee Dee Sharp. "My dear, there's always a party happening in this town, and tonight there's one at Melissa Hollander's. You want to come?"

"Yes, I want to come!" Thea assessed her denim cutoff shorts, wrinkling her nose. Perhaps she could borrow something of Margot's.

There was no way that Thea could step inside the suffocating angled ceilings of her bedroom right now. There was no way she was going straight home.

At least not tonight.

They drove along a road that cut straight through dusky potato fields to get to the party, the horizon opening to a row of houses on the ocean. Before they left, they'd bumped into the Walrus in the driveway. He'd been coiling up a hose while tidying the property for Julianna's arrival, and Margot invited him to come with them, Thea rolling her eyes at her immediately. Now she listened to their flirtatious banter from her perch in the passenger seat.

"I'll introduce you to my friends," Margot was saying. To which the Walrus had lit a cigarette, responding with, "I hope it's not a bunch of wise-ass rich kids at this party."

"Oh, they are certainly that," Margot said. "But you, me, and Thea will poke fun at them. Besides, I'd much rather be with the two of you. The party was Thea's idea."

"You like parties, Thea?" the Walrus asked her. She didn't even care if he saw her roll her eyes again.

"Doesn't everybody?" she said, rolling down her window to release his cigarette smoke.

A valet parked Margot's car at the end of a tree-lined driveway, and another tuxedoed gentleman opened the home's double-wide front doors to welcome them. Thea wondered if she was underdressed in her borrowed wide-leg pants with cadet stripes and navy tank. But Margot skipped up to the large Arts and Crafts mansion wearing a patchwork sundress, barefoot as always.

There were shiny silver balloons weighted around the slate patio, and so many people milled about that Thea didn't know where to go first. She coughed on an acrid smell, a twist of smoke exhaled from joints and cigarettes. On one side of the pool, two men with long hair played folk music on acoustic guitars, and Thea struggled to see their faces, to see if she recognized anyone from the record store. Margot walked with the Walrus over to the band, introducing her beau to the musicians, saying he played amazing acoustic guitar. "Groovy. Pick one of ours up," said the guy with a long brown ponytail down his back. "Play with us."

Thea noted that Margot blushed when the Walrus started to play a Buffalo Springfield song.

"I'm NOT blushing," Margot corrected her. She said hello to a few other people who hugged her, then pushed on. "I just like playing music with him sometimes. Do you want to get drinks?" But then the Walrus started singing to Margot, and Thea slipped off to find drinks on her own.

There were people going in and out of the house, so Thea followed. Inside, partygoers had dropped off numerous six-packs of beer atop the polished mahogany dining table, and there were three drunk women falling into the glass doors of a China hutch. She reached for two cans of Red White & Blue and hoped that by the time she got back outside, Margot was ready to leave the Walrus's mediocre guitar performance. Every time Thea thought she knew everything about her friend, she realized how much time they spent apart. How often did she and the Walrus play guitar together?

The singers were playing "Blowing in the Wind" by Bob Dylan when she returned outside into the din of voices, the air sweet with the smell of citronella torches. With her eyes on the band, Thea's mind tumbled back to the first time she heard the song—at sixteen, on the radio, her mother driving her to work at the diner—when suddenly Thea accidentally bumped into someone, the broad chest of a man wearing a Dartmouth T-shirt.

"Sorry," she said, rubbing her cheek. "I was just looking for . . ." He didn't seem to register the collision, stepping around her to go inside.

It was then that she looked over and saw Felix standing with two other guys his age, holding his can of Budweiser over his mouth to try to hide his laughter at her slamming into the lumberjack. It only reinforced everything she already thought of him, that he was smug and full of himself.

Thea pretended to be unscathed and tilted her chin upward, looking around for Margot, who was suddenly nowhere to be found. She finally spotted her in the gazebo, leaning back against the chest of the Walrus, holding her hand up to cup his angled cheek. Irritated and uncomfortable among this particular set of strangers, Thea slumped onto an empty lounge chair. This wasn't the gathering she had imagined. Instead, she'd assumed she and Margot would flit about together through the crowd, dance in perfect sync until their feet hurt, poke fun at the men checking them out on the sidelines, tumble into laughter when one tried to talk to them. But this, this was lonelier than if she'd remained at home.

"So this is how the filthy rich celebrate their birthdays." Felix sat on the chair opposite her, a glint of sarcasm in his dark brown eyes, and then: "Look, it's the future of America." He pointed at a muscled guy wearing a plaid shirt standing under a spewing keg tap, beer spilling into his mouth, a group of people cheering him as though he was scoring a touchdown. Thea didn't laugh.

"I'm surprised to see you here," she bristled. "I thought you were only interested in the 'regular' people." She used her fingers to make air quotes.

By the way he stared down into his beer, she knew he was uncomfortable now, too. "Why did you take offense to that? I didn't mean it as an insult."

She sipped her beer but didn't meet his eye. "Because it is insulting."

He pushed his hat off his head, a ridiculous pageboy cap that men a decade ago would have worn. "I completely disagree. These people are so predictable—even the long-haired ones who claim they're all love this, love that. They'll go to college, rebel from their parents for a couple of years, and then settle into cushy corporate jobs with houses in the suburbs. What I meant to say earlier, if you let me finish, is that I'm more interested when ordinary people accomplish great things. People like my mother."

"What did she do? Sail around the world?"

He laughed, shuffling his feet. "Do you actually want to know, or are you going to keep giving me that smirk telling me to go away?"

"Fine, tell me." Thea stared hard, her lids painted with blue shadow and thick eyeliner. "I'm *dying* to know." Her tone wasn't serious, but she actually was. She let her hair fall over part of her face, a flirty gesture she hoped he noticed.

But he didn't tell her. He motioned to a brunette with long smooth hair parted at the middle, a strapless satin dress undulating around her. "That's the birthday girl. We met at the beach club where I teach kids to swim. Her father is in publishing. Nice guy. He even gave me his card. I came tonight because I was so curious. This town can be so different, can't it?"

"Sure. We certainly see a cross-section at the record store."

"That's who you came with, your friend from the shop."

"Is it that obvious that I don't belong?"

He grinned, a single dimple at the corner of his smooth cheek. "In the best kind of way, and I hope you take that as a compliment."

She felt a prickle at the back of her neck. It took everything she had to keep from smiling. "So what is this book you're writing about?"

A song by the Beatles kicked up, and it was one of Thea's favorites, "Penny Lane." As she hummed along, Felix nudged her. "You're actually curious about my book, aren't you?"

"Well, when you said it was about your mom . . ."

He told her that his parents had driven their VW bus to seaside Amagansett last year on a whim and they loved it so much they rented a shabby Cape in town, fixed it up, and stayed. "They're kind of the great American love story, my parents."

This made her chortle. A boy, talking about his parents being in love. "Oh really? Would you care to elaborate?

"Sure."

She couldn't believe he was serious. In earnest, he said that his mother's family immigrated from Puerto Rico when she was a child, while his father, who was from Scandinavia, had come as a teenager. They'd met in Manhattan working onstage, where his mother was singing backup for a big band in which his father was playing the sax. His father was blond as could be, his mother cocoa-skinned. "Everyone told them it would never work between them. 'Too different.'" He said it like an old woman, imitating an accent Thea had heard in *West Side Story*. "But my parents surprised everyone. Do you know that my father still waits up for her in the living room while she works in the garage on her paintings. He won't even go to bed without her."

Felix's understated features made sense to her then; a melting pot of facial structure that had aligned into something sweet and tender, a pair of truthful eyes that searched her face for a response. He brightened when she smiled.

"And this is what your book is about?"

A flush crept across his cheeks. "Well, sort of. It's mostly about how I grew up on the road. But that's another story for another day."

He suggested that they play a game then. Felix said he would point to a person at the party, and she had to predict where the person would be in ten years. First, he motioned in the direction of a shaggy-haired guy in a pink paisley Nehru jacket. *Easy*, Thea thought. "A cinematographer making a film about some famous musician."

Felix tapped his beer to the beat against his folded legs. "That's actually pretty good."

Satisfaction rolled over her. Thea pointed to a woman in thick eyeliner, skinny as a twig, a washed-out look to her. They squabbled over whether she'd be a movie star, as Thea said, or six feet under in ten years from a bad Coke habit, as Felix predicted.

"You're dark," Thea accused him.

"Just being honest." He shrugged. "A lot of people these days don't want to see what's really going on around them."

"Which is why many of them are choosing to exist in their own fever dream," she said, thinking now that about half the people at the party might be on some kind of hallucinogen. "I suspect that John and Ringo have done stuff. But what about Paul? He seems so straight-laced."

"Like you?" Felix adjusted the frames of his glasses.

"Yes, like me. Don't fault me for wishing my favorite singer isn't off disappearing into a mushroom cloud. I find that depressing."

Felix paused a moment to watch the crowd, then said, "I do too. Why do people need so much help getting to the root of who they are? It's like, just be. Don't feel like you can't live your dream unless you've taken a hit of something. People are so afraid to sit with themselves."

Thea considered his point: he was right, it was so hard to sit in the quiet and listen to your own thoughts. It was hard to admit that you were having a crummy day or that your life hadn't turned out quite the way that you imagined, or maybe your life had turned out right, and it still wasn't enough. Thea thought about how many bad things she'd witnessed, how hard she'd worked to bury those moments deep inside her, and the terror she would feel if she had to face them every day. It would be so much easier to take a drug and make it all go away. But something kept her from doing it: she didn't want to feel like she didn't have control. Her life was already spinning.

"My stepfather numbs himself with a couple beers nearly every night, and it does nothing for his happiness levels, so I guess that's why I don't bother."

A pair of jocks strutted past in letter jackets, a stark contrast to Felix in his short sleeves and patterned cravat. "Besides, grass makes people incredibly boring. You should hear how my mother goes on after she smokes a joint. I always tell her that if she put the time she spent high into her paintings, she'd be at the Met by now." He flicked at the grass. "Well, and if she wasn't Puerto Rican."

"That shouldn't stop her."

"It doesn't—the world stops her." Felix looked out over the sea of faces in the crowd, and Thea registered that he was the only person there who wasn't lily white.

And she had thought she felt out of place. "I'm sorry," she said, unable to ignore the niggling voice inside her saying it was time to tell him the truth about her own parents. "Well, I don't want to be a downer or anything, but I lost my mother last year."

"Oh, Thea." He edged closer, an apology in the downturn of his eyes. "Here I am complaining about—"

"No, really. It's okay." She hadn't meant to make him feel uncomfortable. "It's just I didn't want you to think that I wasn't saying anything about my own mother because she was terrible or something."

He stared into her eyes when he said, "I bet she was as great as you are."

It made Thea grin. "She was better."

Silence settled between them. He took his cap off and turned it over in his hands; he certainly had a unique style, a cross between a surfer and an intellectual. "You know what I'm thinking, Thea? I'm thinking that there may be enough of my mother for both of us."

Thea waited for him to look at her again; it was a silly notion, this idea that his mother could be on lend, and still, she knew how kind he'd meant it. She played along. "You'd share her with me?"

He hesitated, some of his earlier bravado disappearing entirely. "I think it would be nice to share lots of things with you."

There was a momentary awkwardness, and they looked about at the crowd, their bodies six inches and a world apart, waiting for it to pass.

"Want to go for a walk by the ocean?" he asked her.

"Sure, but give me one sec. I'll be right back." She should check on Margot. Out of the corner of her eye, Thea had spotted her enter the house when she was talking with Felix.

There were crowds of people gathered amid the swirl of smoke inside the windowed living room of the estate. The first floor was a warren of formal, decorated rooms—a living room with a pair of wingback chairs, a library with shelves climbing to the ceiling, then a grand foyer. From the hallway, she saw Margot through the hall by the stairs, her small bare feet traveling up the carpeted steps. She yelled after her, but with the loud music, Margot didn't hear.

Thea didn't want to go any deeper into the house. Was Margot in one of the bedrooms with the Walrus?

Thea knocked on the first door she came to, then the second, listening for voices inside before opening and closing each one. "Margot? Are you up here?" Thea moved swiftly past tropical house plants and more framed photographs. At the fifth door, she peered into a bedroom with a large white canopy bed and saw the back of a woman. A whiff of Chanel perfume. She closed the door once she realized someone was inside, but Thea knew already that it was Margot's long sundress, her long straight hair falling down her back. Margot, standing at the dresser with a large jewelry box open in front of her, her finger pushing around inside. No sign of the Walrus.

Backing away with a feeling of panic overloading her senses, Thea flew down the stairs, the beer rising in her throat.

She prayed that the hunch developing in her mind was wrong, that Margot had absolutely nothing to do with the jewelry thefts, that she was only being nosy. And still, as she pushed through the partygoers, she remembered the Excedrin tin with the diamond bracelet in Margot's bathroom. Had Margot attended every party where jewelry had gone missing?

Outside, the Walrus stood listening to the musicians, beer in hand. Thea found Felix waiting at the edge of the patio, and she didn't mention anything about Margot or the Walrus. They walked the Hollanders' wooden boardwalk, which snaked through the dunes to a private stretch of ocean. A gentle breeze tickled her face as she and Felix climbed onto the sand. Thea drew them in her mind the way she would have if she had paper. From the back, a man with a narrow frame, his hands pushed into pockets, his chin tilted toward her, and a woman carrying her sandals, angling her head toward him. She would have made delicate pencil lines in the blank space between them because she'd need to signal her attraction to him somehow, her interest. She'd need to illustrate that there was something invisible drawing their bodies closer, something she could feel but couldn't see.

"You want to go for a swim?" he said. The sand was cold at night, and the waves were dark, moonlight casting a spotlight on the placid water. "It's not even rough. Come on."

"I don't have a bathing suit," she said, folding her arms protectively against her chest.

He smiled, his hair falling forward over his temples. "So what? No one can see anything, anyway."

Reaching for her hand, they ran to the edge of the ocean where he let go and they kicked off their shoes. In a hurry, he peeled off his T-shirt, but when it was her turn, she pressed her heels into the sand, deciding. She liked him, but she didn't know how much. And yet . . .

A voice in her head encouraged her to prove, even just to herself, that she was capable of being spontaneous. That she was ready to be something entirely different from who she was before. Tugging her shirt over her head, Thea left on her bra and modest, beige panties. She would dive in the water just like this, stripped of clothes, but not completely naked. An act her dead mother, if she was watching, would approve of.

Bolting toward the water, Thea yelled out with glee and terror and adrenaline, diving in. A wave crashed over her, cleansing her anxieties and reinvigorating her, and she let the water carry her up. It was only her third swim of the summer, and she scolded herself for being too busy. It felt so glorious to float.

"You cheated," Felix joked when Thea emerged, popping her head out like a seal. Another wave rolled in, lifting her up toward the starry night, and when she was lowered back down, her toes grazed the sandy bottom. She was facing Felix, who was smiling so wide it was as if he'd just won Olympic gold. He swam closer, and for a moment, she thought he was leaning in to kiss her.

Instead, when another wave approached, he placed his hands on her delicate shoulders and pushed her down, dunking her under the foamy crest. "Hey," she laughed as he swam away from her.

She caught up to him in the deep and jumped on his smooth back, his body rolling into the surf. They played this way until they tired of the water and her entire body was so cold that she was shivering. He took her water-logged fingers in his hand, running back up onto the sand. He covered his eyes and handed her his T-shirt, and with a nervous laugh, she slipped it on, feeling instantly warmer. Rose colored her cheeks, even though it was night and there was nothing but moonlight shining down on them.

Chapter Fifteen

July 1977

The first thing Thea did when she got up in the morning after sinking the boat was take another shower. At midnight last night, Thea had picked up Penny, groveling an apology to Dale for the late hour, and then she'd driven home with a battered Margot hidden under a blanket in the back seat. Pulling into the driveway, her headlights flashed across Felix's car. He was home? He'd only left that morning, and he was supposed to stay in the city for the duration of the week. Thea thought she might cry.

Felix's mother used to say that her son slept so deep that a burglar could roll out a television, record player, and multiple pieces of furniture, and Felix wouldn't wake up—"It's been true since the day he was born," she'd muse. It was certainly true now, as Thea found him sound asleep in an armchair in the living room, a novel called *The Shining* open on his chest. She tiptoed upstairs—avoiding the creaks in the boards, no need to test his mother's theory—and tucked Penny into her twin bed so she could hurry back down and help Margot get from the car to the barn. Margot could walk, but she was afraid to move her arm too much since a shooting pain traveled up it when she changed positions. She'd also refused to go to the hospital, and Thea was too tired to argue with her, bringing her aspirin and cringing when Margot lowered herself on the couch, wincing with pain. It was one in the morning when Thea finally stepped into the shower, delirious and cold, her body shedding sand into the running water.

Thea left Felix snoring softly in the armchair—it would be easier if he wasn't looking for her in bed—and then she had slowly gotten under the coverlet with Penny. Thea marveled at the smell of baby powder on her daughter's neck, the warm and rhythmic breathing of Penny's sturdy chest, feeling incredible wonder that she was alive. That she was home, that nothing could hurt her here.

And yet her mind paced with how much worse it might have gone. How Margot might have died out there. How they both could have. She tried to sleep, willing the muscles in her back to relax, but she heard the same line on a loop: you've been so incredibly stupid.

Penny was watching *Scooby-Doo* on television when Thea came downstairs the following morning in a dress. She wanted to feel put together and hide her guilt and her gloomy mood from her husband. Felix was sitting at the kitchen table reading the paper in the filmy sunlight filtering through the windows. Thea had already applied mascara, brushed her hair down her back, and tucked the wet chunks behind her ears.

"That was quite a night," Felix said, lowering the front page to the table. "Why did you sleep with Penny?" Feeling his eyes on her, Thea filled up a small glass with orange juice. Was her head spinning? Her stomach was certainly empty, and she worried that coffee might make her sick.

"It was late—I was with girlfriends," Thea said, thinking it was perfectly reasonable that she'd been at Midge's, that Penny had been playing with her friends until she fell asleep on the couch. "I didn't want to wake you." Thea gave him a kiss on the cheek.

His trousers were tailored, his white collared shirt tucked in, loafers on his feet. "What time did you get in?"

She couldn't take the small lies. They were anything but inconsequential. She needed to tell him. "Felix, I have to tell you something." Thea wrapped her arms around herself like a shield, both afraid of Felix's reaction and simultaneously trying to keep herself from falling apart. Maybe she should race out the front door, hitchhike into Manhattan. Disappear into a sea of strangers without ever having to tell Felix anything. How could she admit that she'd been lying to him these last two weeks? If she explained that Margot had been here—was still here!—if she told him that Margot was on the run from authorities or her husband or whoever, he would want to know why. Why she'd just helped her sink her father's boat. Then Thea would have to rewind her life like a cassette tape. She would have to return to the beginning, to the first lie she had ever told Felix. The lie that explained why she and Margot grew estranged ten years before. The biggest lie of all.

"Honey, are you okay? You don't look so good." Felix came to her side at the kitchen sink and held the back of his wrist to her forehead. They both knew that sometimes her blood sugar crashed, that she could get shaky if she didn't eat three square meals. "A quirk of the body," the doctor had told them when they'd checked it out, making sure she didn't have something wrong with her blood pressure. It didn't happen often, but she'd fainted at least five times since meeting her husband. He knew when he should sit her down, pull a 100 Grand chocolate bar out of the pantry, and feed her bites of it.

"Just rest a minute," he told her, helping her down to the wobbly kitchen chair and handing her the chocolate. He checked his silver sports watch, a gift she'd given him for his twenty-eighth birthday. A happy night when they'd had dinner at Bobby Van's in Bridgehampton. Felix had been giddy when they'd spotted Truman Capote at the bar.

"What are you doing home from Manhattan?"

The tension in his shoulders loosened, and he collapsed back into his seat like he was no longer made of bones. "The talks with the writer fell apart. Phil and I didn't think there was much point in staying."

"Oh honey, I'm sorry," she said, nibbling at the chocolate like a squirrel. She could feel her arms flaring up. Margot was in the barn, and she was hurt. Why couldn't Thea tell her husband, the person she trusted the most? But it was Felix's predictable response that scared her. *You need to call the police. What if she's putting us in some kind of danger?*

Because it was in the back of Thea's mind, too. It was within the realm of possibility. Mostly, Thea believed that Margot was in danger, and it was her job to help keep her oldest friend safe. At least for a few more days. But she knew Felix wouldn't understand that. He'd remind Thea of all the things he had said about Margot ten years before, right after she left for California: "Margot takes and takes, but she never gives. She's magnetic, Thea, but that doesn't mean she's worth your energy."

Thea was not in the mood to sit in the glare of Felix's judgment. She couldn't throw Margot to the wolves when she was hurt and Thea had been keeping secrets from Felix for more than a week. What was a few more days?

"I have a meeting at nine." Felix glanced at his watch, planting a kiss on her lips. He grabbed his toast. "Wait." He pushed open the back door, then stepped back inside. "What did you want to tell me?"

"Nothing." She forced a smile, watching for his reaction. How far would he push her? Was he curious about what she needed to say? "It can wait."

His face lost its concern. "I meant to tell you, I went to Vintage Vinyl in the city yesterday and picked up the first Elton John album, the one with 'Your Song.' That melody is simple, the words so innocent, and when I listen to it, I've been thinking of us."

"God, I love that song." Thea couldn't help but smile, a bit frustrated by how easy it was for him to move on, like passing a stranger on the bus to take a different seat, and a bit charmed by his nostalgia. How Felix could disarm her with his sweet side.

"The lyrics are strange if you really listen, a man making his own potions and such, but he sings that chorus with so much belief in love, you feel like you're falling for someone alongside him. Do you know he won't admit who it's about?"

She nodded, half smiling. "Maybe he hasn't told the person."

In the doorway, Thea saw Felix more plainly than she had since Penny was born. It was as though they had been separated for weeks. Felix was no longer a young editor on the rise, he was well-established now. Felix labored over the words of his writers, and every work he edited, he said, was a chance to deepen human understanding, connect people through well-crafted sentences. It was this empathy, this ability to go deep into someone else's heart and mind, that Thea had always loved most about him. But she wondered now why he didn't try to get inside her head more. Didn't he ever consider the story he would tell if he wrote about her, his wife?

Still, she could see this wasn't a good time to tell him what was going on. His entire day would have been thrown off, and he was already upset about the falling-out with his writer in the city. "I love you."

"I love you too." He popped back in once more to kiss her. "I'm sorry I've been so distracted. I'm just so wrapped up in this author, but hopefully that will end now." When he was gone, she rose to watch him back his car out of the driveway.

The phone rang. Then rang again. Rather than rush to pick it up, Thea felt immobilized by dread. *Somebody knows.* Somebody saw her and Margot take the sailboat last night. Someone saw them sink it, or someone heard the screams as Margot fell, her arm limp and lifeless. Someone called the police. But it could also be Dale or Penny's camp counselor or Cara. She picked it up.

"Hello," Thea pulled the long-coiled cord from the wall to the living room, where her little girl was lying on her belly watching TV.

"Hi. May I speak with Thea Lind?" asked a woman.

"This is she." On the wall near the phone, Thea had framed one of her smaller drawings. A charcoal pencil sketch of her mother's garden, her mother hunched over her tomatoes, a pretty white arbor framing the view. But now the light pencil marks suddenly looked dark and foreboding, the thick shadowing of the plants thorny.

The woman on the phone couldn't be with the police. Could she? She was talking so fast that Thea had asked her to repeat herself.

"I said, this is Mimi from the former Church Estate, Eothen. You did write us a note applying for the assistant job, didn't you?" the woman said.

The woman's words clicked into focus. The Classified ad Thea had responded to the day that Margot arrived. With everything that had happened these last couple weeks, she had forgotten. This had to be a joke. A part of her wanted to hang up on the woman.

"Sure, sorry, it took me a minute to remember," Thea said.

"It's okay. I have good news for you. Andy wants an interview. This Monday. Eleven a.m. Up here at Eothen in Montauk. He may ask you about art. You said you can draw?"

Thea felt the rise of every tiny little hair on her body. Everybody knew that the artist Andy Warhol lived in an oceanfront compound that once belonged to the heiress of the Arm & Hammer fortune in Montauk; the first summer Warhol had come out here, a few years before, he'd rented parts of it to Jackie Kennedy, her sister, and their kids. Now only the artist was living there, throwing wild parties at his house while inviting a long list of local celebrities. Mick Jagger was one of them.

"I mean, I doodle on napkins for my little girl, sure. But I'm not really into art in the Andy Warhol sense. Is this some kind of prank?"

The woman laughed. "We're not looking for Picasso. We just need someone who knows the lay of the land. Help us get supplies and whatnot. You said you're a local?"

"Yes." Thea scribbled down the address on the back of an electric bill envelope for an interview, eleven a.m., Friday. There was no mention of hours or what it paid, and Thea knew she wouldn't go, already planning on calling back and canceling later. It was silly that she even wrote down the address. Thea knew exactly where his house was. You could hike up to the compound from the surfer's beach in Montauk. Still, Andy Warhol wasn't going to hire her. He'd take one look at her and laugh her out the door.

After putting the phone down on the receiver, Thea brought her daughter a bowl of Wheaties. "Thanks, Mama," Penny said, snuggling up next to her. "You're going to watch my show with me?" Her smile revealed two missing front teeth.

"For a few minutes," Thea said, although even as she kissed her daughter's tiny shoulder, her mind slipped off to last night. In the wee hours, she had left Margot moaning in the barn on a pile of blankets on the couch. Her arm had to be broken.

Ten minutes passed. Fifteen.

The phone rang again, like an alarm sounding, and Thea rose to answer it, the anticipation enough to make her want to pluck one of the hairs out of her head. But it was only Felix. He'd arrived at work and received an apology from the novelist and a plea for him and Phil to come back to the city. "I'm sorry, honey. We're getting on the ten-ten. I still have my overnight bag in the car and I'll probably stay until Friday. Don't worry about dinner," he'd said.

In the kitchen Thea grabbed a plate, arranging a banana and buttered toast on it. She made two cups of coffee and balanced the plate on one of the coffee mugs. Outside, Thea momentarily put the food down in the grass to open the heavy barn doors, the sun slicing through the room like the beam of a flashlight.

Margot was lying on her back on the couch, staring at the ceiling, her hurt arm resting on the beat-up coffee table. Thea and Felix had only ever used the barn as a recreation space, opening all the doors and windows on weekends and playing ping-pong. They kept their bikes there, along with a baby pool and sprinklers. Now it looked like a make-shift infirmary. Margot had a once-frozen bag of peas on her arm. There was an empty glass of water, a bottle of aspirin open and spilled over— Thea didn't remember giving her the whole bottle.

"I brought you something to eat," Thea said, placing the plate on the coffee table near the mess of the aspirin, which she began picking up. God forbid Penny find the pills and mistake them for candy. "Your arm looks swollen."

Margot moaned as she adjusted her position. "I can barely move it."

It was worse than she'd imagined. Had Thea really thought that she'd wake up this morning and discover that Margot only had a minor bruise? She was seriously hurt. Which meant that there was no way that Margot was getting on a private sailboat in two days to go to the Cayman Islands, no way she was leaving Thea's house. And that was only half the worry: the biggest priority now was getting Margot to a doctor. Her injury would force her out of hiding.

"What will we do now?" Thea asked.

Margot had dark circles under her eyes. "I honestly don't know."

The response hit Thea like a bat to the chest. Margot always had a plan B. She needed to tell Thea what to do. Penny was inside watching cartoons, and Thea had helped her friend sink a goddamned boat, and now they were at a loss. It was unthinkable.

"We should call your father. He's here, right?" Was Thea the only one who understood that made the most sense?

Margot grabbed her arm. "Don't you dare. Besides, he'll just send you a check. That's his answer to everything."

"So? Maybe it would help."

Margot's face strained. "I would never give him the satisfaction."

With Thea's help, Margot sat up to nibble on some toast. She tried to describe the pain in her arm: that it hurt most when she tried to bend it.

Margot begged to take a shower. Unlike Thea, she hadn't washed off the salt water from the night before. Even though Margot's legs were in working order, Thea felt like she needed to follow her up the stairs in her house to make sure she was okay. With the television on, Penny wasn't paying attention, still immersed in *Scooby-Doo*.

I need to get her out of here. If there was going to be a plan B, it would be up to Thea now to figure out what it was.

She called Midge to ask if she could take Penny for a few hours, making up a story about how she was terribly hungover and needed to sleep it off. Midge said they were going to the Maidstone pool; did Penny want to join? Thea dressed Penny in her strawberry bathing suit while she watched the end of the television show, braiding her hair while the credits rolled, then sent her outside to the car with a brown bag containing a peanut butter–and–honey sandwich. With Penny in the back seat, she dashed back inside to help Margot out of the shower, handing her a towel to dry off. "I'll be right back," Thea called behind her, charging downstairs and grabbing her purse off the kitchen table.

"You ready, peanut?" Thea started the engine of her station wagon. She expelled a string of deep breaths, repeating to herself, *We are okay. We are okay.*

"Mama, why did you tell me a lie?"

Penny kicked the back of Thea's seat with her white sandals as they drove past the pink house she loved, with its large elm trees in the front yard—the one her daughter called "The Flamingo." "You lied about the lady in the barn."

"I didn't lie to you." Thea steadied her voice, trying to sound motherly, like someone her daughter could trust. On the inside, she felt like she'd been shot with a dart.

Penny kicked harder at the seat. "Then why was that lady taking a shower in our house?"

Clicking on her blinker, Thea turned onto Main Road, passing the windmill standing at the edge of town. She sank deeper into the driver's seat. "The lady you saw in the house is my old friend Margot—she's different from the other woman. That was a gardener." Another lie.

In her rearview mirror, she watched Penny cross her arms. "But no one even cut the roses."

"Penny, STOP." Thea pumped the gas. The Maidstone was just around the corner. She raced the car around the bend, nearly blowing a yield sign. She wanted her daughter to stop asking questions. There were so many questions she couldn't answer. Thea's own mother came to her then, how she couldn't always give Thea the answers she wanted, either. Her mother had told her that her father was leaving them while they were in a car on the way home from school. Even with all the platitudes—"We still love each other," and "We'll remain close friends, for your sake"—Thea had known her mother was lying. Her mother kept rubbing the back of her neck and fiddling with the radio, and her voice was nervous and scattered, like she didn't really believe what it was saying. Children could always tell when their parents were hiding something.

As they pulled up to the elegant club's gatehouse, Penny sniffled in the back seat, and Thea's guilt and anger dissipated as fast as it started. Thea wouldn't leave her daughter without some sense of what was going on. After parking the car in the lot, she waited for Midge's own wood-paneled station wagon to pull up. She got out and pulled Penny out of the back seat, balancing her on her hip.

"You're too smart, you know that?" Thea said, the corners of her eyes growing damp as she nuzzled her daughter. Then she placed her softly down on her sandaled feet and strapped the child's swim goggles around her forehead. "Okay, listen. Remember how you and Sarah used to be very close, and then she moved away, and when she came back, you made sandcastles on the beach? Do you remember that?"

Penny sucked on her bottom lip, nodding. "Is that who the lady is? Your Sarah?"

Thea touched the tip of her finger to her little girl's straight button nose. "Exactly. And it's about time that you meet my Sarah. I'll introduce the two of you tonight. Just don't tell anyone at camp or the pool today that she's here. Okay? I want it to be a surprise." Spotting Midge's car driving into the lot, she saddled Penny with a small beach bag, kissing her goodbye.

"Okay, Mommy."

"Promise," Thea said. Then, calling to Midge as they drew nearer to her car: "Thank you, Midge. Truly. You're so good to me."

Midge wore an aquamarine beach cover-up and a large yellow beaded necklace. She pulled out her own beach bag, her boys already running with Penny toward the pool. "We'll be here until about four. Want to get her then?"

"That would be great. Really. Thank you."

Thea turned back to her own car. She felt like screaming, thinking about what she had just promised her daughter. How would she introduce Penny to Margot? A cozy relationship between Margot and Penny—and ultimately, Felix—could not be part of plan B.

Just as she was about to get into the driver's seat, Midge called Thea back over. "You didn't let me know about the barbecue next week. Can you make it?"

"Oh, right, I'm not sure. Sorry, it's just . . ." Thea noticed the worry lines around Midge's eyes momentarily deepen. "My sister in LA had her heart broken and needed my help. I feel like I've been on the phone with her for days."

Midge folded her arms over her chest. "Thea. Did I do something wrong? You haven't called me back in two weeks, and then all of a sudden you need someone to watch Penny because you're hungover?"

"I'm just figuring some things out, honestly. I've been thinking."

Midge rubbed her hand along her belly. "Did you have . . ."

"Another miscarriage? No, it's not that. There are things . . . more than my sister." She wished her tone hadn't come out so short.

Midge glanced around her car, even looking into the back seat. "Okay. But what about our racquetball match tomorrow? Thea, I nearly called Felix. I'm worried."

"Please don't call Felix."

For a second, Thea tried to see herself from Midge's vantage point. Thea typically waited for Midge after camp drop-off to gossip for a few minutes. They had lunch at least once a week, played racquetball on some weekdays. In between, Thea might drop off a book she'd finished or call to laugh about something on the television. But since her birthday party two weeks before, Thea hadn't reached out to Midge once. She had been rushing home to catch up with Margot. She honestly never thought Midge would even notice.

"Don't worry about me," Thea swatted her away, attempting to sound playful. "I'm not mad at you. I'll be at the match tomorrow. Promise."

A sigh from Midge. She fiddled with the chunky yellow beads at her neck. "Okay. But I'm here if you need to talk. Don't think I don't miss you."

We are good friends, Thea thought as she turned over the car, an ABBA song playing on the radio. Margot's arrival had been so all-consuming that Thea had spent the last couple of weeks writing off the mom friends that she'd spent the last ten years accumulating. Women like Midge who didn't share her complicated past, who didn't know her when she was younger. For all these years, she had put her friendship with Margot on a pedestal, believing that friends like Midge were replaceable, and friends like Margot were not. But if your childhood friends helped reinforce who you once were, your adult friends accepted you as you were now. You no longer needed people to help define you—

you required friends that lightened the emotional load of everyday life. Midge was imperfect—maybe she'd never wanted to talk about what was *really* going on in their lives—but still, they did talk, griping about kids that didn't sleep and husbands that left toothpaste on the sink. Maybe Midge didn't need to know the darker side of Thea's heart to feel close to her. They could lean on each other when they needed one another, lean on their husbands when they didn't. Friendship in these years didn't have to be all-consuming.

"I'll call you, I promise," Thea said. "And I'll tell you what is going on. I just need a little more time."

It turned out that getting Margot to a doctor was more complicated than it should have been. When Thea parked in the emergency room lot at Southampton Hospital, Margot clutched her arm in the passenger seat and flat-out refused to get out of the car.

"I've come too far to get caught," she said.

Thea scratched at her inflamed arms; her eczema was flaring again, and she wished she'd brought a long-sleeve shirt. "Come on, Margot. You're not making this easy."

Margot leaned into the door with her weight, flinching. "I'm sorry—I can't even give a fake name because they'll ask me for identification. As soon as they check me in, every cop in New York will be headed this way."

"That's a bit dramatic." Thea leaned her forehead against the steering wheel, the leather seat creaking under her weight, sand sticking to her thighs. God, she wished in that moment that she could dump Margot at the beach. "So what if hospital officials ask you for identification? Show them your identification. If someone was going to find you, Margot, they would have found you by now. It's not that hard."

Margot turned her head to look out the window. Two nurses in white aprons and dresses breezed by, laughing. Two friends. In happier times. "It's more complicated than that."

Ambulance sirens blew by, the paramedics parking the truck and jumping out of the van, rushing around to open the back. "Well, you need to tell me how it's more complicated. Because I'm not going to keep helping you like this. You need a doctor. I'm not going to be responsible for you dying of something scary like internal bleeding and then I go to jail because I was the idiot that kept it all a secret. All for a story that doesn't even make sense."

A doctor in scrubs parked next to them in a blue Chevy and glanced in their direction after catching the volume of Thea's voice. She rolled up her window.

"There's more, okay?" Margot thumped her fingers against the leather seat, her anger coming out in a burst. "Willy stole from me. I don't talk to my shit-for-life father, but my mother left me a nice inheritance when she died. Enough that I could find my way into a good life on my own, if I ever needed to. Three weeks ago, I went to the bank to withdraw money and it was gone. All of it. Willy had used it to pay back debts, and it didn't even cover them all."

Thea imagined Margot in a sprawling Park Avenue apartment in the city, in that big summer house in East Hampton that her parents used to own. The fabulous parties, the designer clothes, the cars. She had always had everything. *Everything.* "You said Willy was wonderful."

"Well, Willy is nothing like Felix. He's a coward, and I was so angry about the money. I told him I was leaving him for good. That I deserved better, which isn't something I even believed, but I wanted to hurt him. I loved him, and I still love him, even if I feel pathetic saying that. The night that he disappeared I found a note from him on my nightstand. 'Go somewhere safe. I'll find you when I can.'"

"So he's fine, then?"

"Maybe?"

Worried for her own well-being, Margot had traveled to the safety deposit box her mother left her at Chemical Bank on Park Avenue. "I hid the key in a hatbox in my closet for years," she said. Inside the unlocked box was a neat row of minted gold bars that her mother had invested in and stored there in cases of emergency. Margot stashed a few of the single kilogram bullions in an extra handbag she'd carried into the bank and got on the subway.

"I took them to the King's Armory uptown to cash them in," she said. "The pawnshop is not exactly a bastion of morality, but someone decided to show some scruples." After Margot left with a wad of cash, the owner must have called the police. Later, she'd walked away from her apartment building, suitcase in hand, seconds before two cop cars sped up to the front. She ducked straight into a taxi, boarded her father's sailboat, and headed to Thea's harbor. Then she'd heard the radio bulletin in Thea's kitchen reporting she was wanted for questioning, putting two and two together.

"So this is why the police are looking for you. It has nothing to do with Willy?"

"It has everything to do with Willy. I'm certain they think I sold the gold bars to help him, that I'm collaborating with him."

A tingling danced up the back of Thea's neck, her fingernails biting into her palms. "Margot, don't you see? You are collaborating with Willy. The cops have every reason to come after you."

Her friend talked fast, pinching the skin at her throat. "Yes, you don't think I know that? I have no idea what's going on with him either. That's what made me think of the Caymans; I can safely stash this money I've been carting around with me. Willy could find me there. He knows I love it." Margot turned to her; she suddenly looked younger, sitting in a heap in the passenger seat, alone and trying to find her way in the world. "Please, Thea. Don't make me go into that hospital."

Thea shoved open her car door, stomping her feet on the pavement. She screamed like she was hurt, passersby in the parking lot stopping to stare. She smiled politely, then got back into the car. "Where is the money you got from pawning the gold bars?"

"I-I . . ." Margot's stammer only made Thea more frustrated.

She slammed her hand against the steering wheel. "Don't tell me it's in the barn. Please tell me this money isn't in my house." It was one thing to shelter a friend. It was another to have police raiding her house and discovering money there.

"I packed it in a box of frozen waffles and hid it in the back of your freezer."

Thea stretched her neck out, her face contorting. "You lied to me so many times."

"I didn't lie," Margot said. She moved an inch, sucking in a breath from the pain in her arm. "I just omitted details that I knew would worry you."

"That is LYING."

Thea needed a minute. She got back out of the car and walked to the edge of the parking lot where there was a patch of grass. She sat down, biting her nails, suddenly grateful for how boring life normally was. It made her think of Felix and how much confidence he had in Thea, how much she had in him. If they were in the same circumstances as Margot and her husband, she would never doubt that he'd do the right thing. Any lingering resentment from the morning dissipated—how could she be mad at the one person in her life who was as structurally sound as a Manhattan skyscraper?

What would Felix do if he were in her shoes right now? Would he leave a friend in severe pain who was refusing to go to the hospital? No, even if he was angry, he would get his friend to a doctor.

She strode back to the car. That was what she would do, too.

Thea steered the car out of the hospital parking lot. There was a local doctor who might see Margot instead. After passing the old movie house in the quaint village—Peter Benchley's *The Deep* advertised on the marquee—they drove to Sag Harbor, passing the brick office building where Felix worked. After going over the drawbridge toward Noyack, they came to the gates of a large house sitting in open marshland on the Peconic Bay. A crane stood in the reeds, watching them as they traveled up the long, twisting driveway. Thea parked the car.

"Where are we?"

"You'll see." Thea hurried up the elegant stone steps to the large shingled house, a pretty front door painted the color of the sea. One ring of the bell and dogs began barking, someone shooing them away.

When the door swung open, Thea saw her old boss's signature bangs and long brown hair, three petite dogs running about her bare feet. "Shel, I'm sorry to bother you without calling, but—"

"You know I love to see you, always." Shelly picked up one of the dogs, asking Thea if she'd met "Fish" yet. As Thea pet the dachshund, Thea smelled something sweet baking from inside the kitchen.

"It smells lovely."

"Lemon poppy seed cake. I'll make coffee."

"Okay, but there's someone here to see you."

Shelly's eyes traveled to the car. She wore much less blush and eyeshadow than she once did, and she squinted behind her wire-rimmed glasses. She put the dog down, then descended the steps in quick succession in her bare feet and white linen bell-bottoms. "You came back, you little vixen," she hollered to Margot, padding to the passenger door.

Thea smiled despite her earlier frustration, following her. "Shelly, we need to see Connor. I'm sure he's at the office now, but maybe you can call him?"

After Shelly and Jay split up several years back—the couple citing "irreconcilable differences" and selling the record store—Shelly had reconnected with a man she'd summered with since she was a kid. He was a local doctor, and she had started an animal rescue group in Bridgehampton called Happy Paws. She had never been happier herself.

Margot stood up, gripping her sore arm, while Thea explained, without offering too many specifics, that she had been injured. Shelly carefully pulled Margot into a hug so as not to hurt her arm. "I'll call Connor's front desk straightaway," she said.

Shelly took a step back and they surveyed each other. Thea guessed each was studying the way a woman's life was told in the lines around her eyes, the creases of her mouth. Shelly was nearly forty, and her skin was clearer than Margot's. While Margot remained stick thin, Shelly had bulges on either side of her hips and in her middle—changes that she'd told Thea once was evidence of how content she was.

"I did something stupid on the water last night, but please, Shelly, if anyone ever comes to ask you about me or Thea—tell them that Thea had no part in it."

"I shouldn't have gone with her," Thea said, wondering why Margot didn't just tell Shelly the truth. She was the kind of person that would take it to her grave.

"She wasn't a willing member," Margot shot back.

Shelly raised her eyebrows, the same way she would have if Thea told her she was putting on an album by Queen but then actually played one by Elton John.

"My, my," Shelly said with a laugh, a wide grin overtaking her rosy cheeks. "Lucy and Ethel have certainly gotten themselves into a pickle."

Chapter Sixteen

With the salt air of low tide stalled in the marsh, the women returned from the doctor's office in Shelly's white Volkswagen Beetle convertible with Margot's arm in a cast. Shelly's husband, who set aside waiting patients to examine Margot, said she had fractured the ulna bone of her forearm; she would need to wear the cast for four to six weeks. He gave her something stronger for the pain.

Thea yawned as she pushed open the passenger door. The last twenty-four hours had felt like an entire lifetime, and she wanted to go home and drop into bed. Instead, she followed Shelly and Margot inside Shelly's un-air-conditioned house, a quirky warren of rooms that Shelly had decorated with tables and furniture she'd picked up at local flea markets and painted herself in a variety of colors. Nothing was formal at Shelly's house, and nearly every chair and couch was layered with a soft top sheet, so the dogs could sit on the furniture. In the kitchen, after pouring all three of them iced teas in tall skinny glasses that she kept in her butler's pantry, Shelly chopped salad components and tossed lettuce and toppings into individual wooden bowls, dressing them with vinaigrette.

With the house situated beside the marsh, they only had to carry their lunch down a short reedy path down to a private beach. Clustered together were four teak lounge chairs and a round wooden table with a trendy marigold-colored fringed umbrella centered over it. Margot and Thea sat at the shady table while Shelly leaned back into one of the loungers in the sunshine. Her dogs yapped and chased after seagulls. Thea wished that Bee was here to run the beach too.

"Is someone going to actually tell me what's going on? Or do I not want to know?" Shelly asked, mixing the dressing into her salad.

Margot glanced pointedly at Thea, indicating she would do the talking. "We were out on a boat and I fell off the side like a complete and utter klutz." She used her right hand to eat; she was lucky she'd hurt her non-dominant arm.

"I got that much already," Shelly said.

"It was an accident, and you're not a klutz." Thea crunched on green pepper slices while looking out over the Peconic Bay. The sea was so placid and clear that they could see the stones and pebbles along the bottom. How many of Thea's secrets did this single body of water hold? Even as a teenager she would walk these beaches with whispers in her head, looking to the open horizon for answers. The water rarely let her down until last night when she'd nearly been swallowed whole by it.

"But what is going on with your husband, Margot? I'm worried." Shelly wasn't stupid. She wouldn't let the question of what really happened blow by her.

Margot sighed. "Okay, well. There's another woman."

Thea's attention shot up from her food. "What? He cheated, too? Let me guess: Another thing you left out to protect my nerves?" She wished she could read Margot's diary. It was hard not to wonder what other truths it held.

"Well, there it is. I said it out loud." Margot flopped back in her chair. "I was ashamed, honestly."

Shelly stabbed at her salad. "I'm sorry, old friend."

"When did it start?" Thea had so many questions, even as she shooed a seagull swooping low near her food.

"I'm not sure, to be honest. But I found the woman's Breck shampoo in my shower, which was the worst part. She'd been in my apartment. She'd been in my bed." Margot reached into her pocket and pulled out an amethyst crystal, caressing it with her thumb. "It's exactly what my father did to my mother, sneaking around right under her nose. I understood my mother's anger a lot better once my husband did it to me."

"Did you confront him?" Shelly asked.

"I did. He didn't deny it, but he complained that I'd been distant, which I guess I had been. When my mother died, I couldn't stop crying about a woman I never even liked very much, and I didn't know why I was so upset. Because I hated her. Then I wondered if maybe having a baby could fix me, maybe even change my sour views of motherhood. Because I would do it differently. I could love my baby in all the ways my mother never loved me." Margot pushed her salad bowl away and ran her fingers through her bobbed hair. "So maybe I can't blame him for cheating on me."

Before they had a chance to say more, Margot changed the subject, raising the topic of Jay. After he and Shelly split, Jay had moved to New York City and opened a record store on the Lower East Side. Margot wanted to know: When did Shelly know it was over? How did he react to the news that she'd wanted a divorce?

"We married too young." Shelly lowered her fork from her mouth, stirring it around in the lettuce. "He was everything my parents hated, which was part of the appeal, but one day I realized that he was nothing that I really wanted. I've come to believe that so much of our youth is wasted on trying to fill the holes our parents create in our lives. I mean, Jay and I were great record store owners. We were great friends. But I never had googly eyes for him. Remember when you first started dating Felix?" Shelly laughed, glancing at Thea. "We couldn't shut you up."

The memory of it made Thea smile. The first time Felix kissed her was on an ocean beach in Amagansett. How they'd fumbled, their lips not fitting at first, but then finding the perfect spot. How she could have stood on that beach for hours. It wasn't the kiss at all that drew her in. It was how he'd held her in his arms—how no one had ever held her so steady. How song lyrics had come into her head, John Lennon singing in her ear: *There's nothing you can do that can't be done.*

"Felix and Thea met so young," Margot said. "From what you describe, Thea, you seem like the perfect couple." Thea stopped smiling—it wasn't as though she and Felix were darling porcelain dolls for everyone else to admire.

"Our relationship is just like everybody else's, you know—we're just as riddled with potholes," Thea said. Nobody knew what went on in a marriage. Every relationship evolved, every relationship changed.

"Enlighten us," Margot challenged.

Thea considered this. She knew they didn't have serious problems. They still had fun together. She believed they were still in love. But with Felix gone at work all day and Thea home with Penny, Thea sometimes felt invisible. She was like the Montauk Lighthouse, sending out strobes of light for him to see. Sometimes he noticed, and sometimes he didn't. They fit in time together when they could, but the world didn't revolve around their resounding love story. When was the last time they'd stayed up all night listening to records? When was the last time they went to a concert, or even on a dinner date? It was as though by thirty they'd decided they knew everything there was to know about each other.

"Well, I suppose it's more about me. I'm just so impatient and frustrated with my body lately, failing me with those miscarriages," Thea said. "Felix doesn't understand any of that, and I resent him sometimes for getting up and going to work and not having to think about any of it."

Shelly extended a hand over Thea's and smiled with tenderness. "The quickest way to end a marriage is to stop talking."

The women picked at their lunch, the dogs sniffing around their feet, jumping up on their legs, begging for bits of food. Margot turned to look at Thea like she wanted to say something, then thought better of it.

"Jesus, Margot, what is it?" Thea said.

Margot crossed and uncrossed her legs; there were tiny little blond hairs where she hadn't had a chance to shave. *Peach fuzz*, she used to call it. "Don't get mad at me."

Thea wasn't sure she wanted to hear what came next. "Here we go again. Margot spouting off her big insights."

"Just hear me out," Margot said. She paused. "Remember on the boat last night when you said you weren't always happy with yourself. I think it's because you don't want a second baby. Maybe you want something else."

One of the dogs jumped on Thea's lap and she stopped eating to pet it, grateful for its smooth fur under her fingers. She thought of her birth control pills, how she wasn't taking them anymore. "You know that I love being Penny's mother."

Margot dug her toes into the sand, her tone more gentle than knowing. "You're an amazing mother from what I can tell. Why do you need another child to prove that?"

Shelly sipped her iced tea. "Why do I need a third dog to prove that I love animals? Sometimes it's just what you want."

A flurry of small sailboats began to glide through the bay across the inlet. A sailing school, the voices of happy children carrying off the water. "It's true, we want what we want," Margot said. "And I'm not saying you're against a second child. But is it possible that you're having a second baby because it's what you're *supposed* to do?"

Thea used her napkin to dab her neck. The air could be stagnant on the bay, not reliably cool like it was on the ocean. "Yes, it's what I'm supposed to do. But I also want to do it."

"Come on, Thea." Margot rolled her eyes, chuckling in disbelief. "Are you sure?"

"I don't know why you're laughing at me, Margot. I'm telling you the truth. I can't think of one single thing that I want that Felix doesn't want too." As soon as she said it, Thea coughed on the briny air. What kind of thing was that to admit to someone? That you didn't have any dreams of your own? Thea felt like the saddest person in the world then.

Margot brushed invisible lint off her shorts. "See, now that upsets me. Because the Thea that I knew had a spark, she seemed destined to get out of here, share her art with the world. But I think I've always believed in you more than you believed in yourself."

All she could hear was Margot's judgment, and Thea's voice wavered. "The girl you knew grew up and took on life's responsibilities. My options have always been different from yours."

Shelly held up her palm: "Ladies, stop. We all think we're going to be something different at twenty than we end up becoming, and that's what makes life disappointing but also inspiring. You don't fail by changing as you grow."

Margot turned her head to look at Thea, her gaze steady. "I don't think you failed, not one bit. But I do wish you'd acknowledge that there may be something else you want. You keep trying to convince me that you're some boring housewife, but I don't see that. You're still under all that scaffolding you've built up."

The water lapped against the shore, a rhythm so soothing Thea's breathing slowed. Scaffolding. They all had some, didn't they? After a large, slow sip of her iced tea, Thea held up a mirror to Margot's. "Do you think you'll get back together with Willy? If he comes for you?"

Margot tucked the crystal back into her bag. "I don't know. Shelly, you're the divorcée. Is there anything better on the other side?"

Shelly laughed, glancing back at her house as though she worried for a moment that her husband would materialize and overhear her thinking. "All I can say is that I settled with Jay, and I knew it. The night before my wedding, I went to my little Italian grandmother in tears." They held hands in the hotel lobby while she told her grandmother that she loved Jay, but she wasn't "in love" with him. That he didn't make her heart skip a beat. *Do you have fun with him*, her grandmother asked. Yes, Shelly had said. *Is he your best friend?* Yes!

"'Well, then marry him.'" Shelly tried to imitate her grandmother's raspy voice. "'You should marry your best friend because the attraction will dim in a matter of months.' Obviously, that was a bit dramatic, but I got her point."

"And do you agree with that?" Thea asked.

Shelly got up, encouraging them to wade into the water with her, the sea hitting their calves, the sun turning their skin golden. How calm Thea felt in the water, how different from last night when the sea had been cold, dark, threatening. Even with Margot's declaration hovering in the back of her mind, she could have stayed talking to Shelly and Margot long into the afternoon.

Shelly considered the horizon. "I did for a long time because it made me feel good about marrying Jay. But then I realized it shouldn't be one or the other, friendship or attraction. Sure, I should marry someone I can count as a friend, but a marriage is different from a friendship. You need to be attracted to that person to start because at some point there's going to be this man living in your house, leaving his socks on the couch, and you're going to have to want to sleep with him still."

"Willy is both for me." Margot lifted her hair off her neck, fanning herself with her hand. "No matter how much he messes up, I still think of him as my confidante and my one true love. I still want him to be the last person I see before I close my eyes at night. Is that strange, considering he's beyond forgiveness?"

"It's love, baby," Shelly said, shrugging. "It's not always good for us, but my advice is know when to let go. Don't let him trample you."

It was because Thea trusted these women so fully that Margot's voice circled in her head. The house on the hill, that had been what Thea had wanted. Finding someone as kind and steady as Felix, that had been what she'd needed when she felt so uncertain. Having a child she could raise to adulthood, to give everything to her daughter that her mother had never been able to give to Thea. A lifetime of love. Those had been her dreams.

Thea wasn't sure there was even room in a marriage for two people's dreams. Maybe each person had to take a turn. It sounded outlandish to her. Why had everything that Felix wanted in a career and in a family felt serious and worthy, while anything she thought about felt like child's play?

A cloud floated by, casting Thea in a stamp of shade, and when it passed, Thea shook her head. Why did she have to consider Penny in every decision she ever made, while Felix came and went as he pleased, keeping up a schedule of lunch dates, managing a staff, meeting authors for drinks? Hadn't they had this child *together*?

She stopped listening to Margot and Shelly as they packed up the dishes from lunch and walked the sandy path back to Shelly's house. Thea's mind had settled on something, an idea she couldn't ignore. She thought of Felix announcing that what he wanted for his birthday was a chance to write the novel he'd always dreamed of, how that was just one more notch in a belt he'd been punching holes in from the start. But Thea was entitled to be someone other than who she'd become in the house on the hill.

Shame stopped her heart, a burst of possibility turning into a steady beat. Surely she couldn't just tell Felix that it was her turn to go back to college to study for a career. She couldn't possibly tell him that he'd have to give her a chance to go after something she wanted, too. That there was time in this life.

"Maybe you're right," she told Margot, pausing at Shelly's back door and facing her. "Maybe I haven't been so truthful about my life. Maybe there are things I want."

Margot beamed. "Remember what I told you? Finding satisfaction is a full-time job. I can help you talk this out later." They exchanged a hand squeeze.

Margot climbed up the stairs to take a nap, and Shelly called Thea into her sunroom, closing the glass doors. They'd agreed that Margot would stay there that night while Thea went to fetch Penny from Midge at the Maidstone.

Shelly's thick dark brows knitted together. "I know you love her, Thea, and I love her too. But don't let her take over your life again. It's not healthy."

Thea knew what Shelly was talking about, how Margot's needs were so big that sometimes they began to feel bigger than everybody else's. "It's different now," Thea whispered, as though Margot might hear them. "I feel like her return has forced me to face things about myself I've been ignoring. Now that her arm is fixed, I'm going to help her get out of here. She's obviously not sailing to the Caymans on Friday with that arm, but we'll think of something."

Shelly picked up Fish, the dog, nuzzling her neck. "See, honey, now that's exactly what I'm afraid of. I want to help her too. But I wouldn't keep helping her if it could bring the police to my front door."

*   *   *

That Saturday, with Penny sound asleep and Felix, who had returned from the city for the weekend, in bed upstairs, Thea sat on her living room couch listening to her favorite Joni Mitchell album, "Clouds." Under the glow of lamplight and with Bee snuggled at her feet, she held the folk-pop album cover in her lap as the haunting chords of "Both Sides Now" played softly through the speakers, the brutal honesty of the lyrics hitting Thea all at once. The beginning of the song spoke of puffy white clouds, innocent and fantastical to a young girl, and how those same clouds went on to produce rain and snow, dampening the sunny times. Thea took that to mean that there were two ways of looking at everything, even the weather. Whenever Thea listened to this song she thought of her formative years, her memories from the distance of a rearview mirror. But as she stared at the album cover, which Joni Mitchell had drawn herself—a self-portrait sketched to perfection—Thea could see herself from both sides, too. She remembered how she used to draw alternate album covers when she was bored at Sunshine Records. She would sit at the cashier's desk and dream up illustrations to match the mood of the songs, the personality of the band. She wondered if she could still do that.

In the kitchen drawer, Thea kept a sketchbook. She grabbed a handful of Penny's colored pencils and positioned herself on her sofa so she was leaning against the armrest. In the center of the page, she sketched a close-up of a car's rearview mirror. In the reflection you could see scattered clouds in a blue sky, the blond hair of a young woman blowing into the mirror, the road stretching out behind the car—and in front of it.

When she finished it, Thea set the drawing down on the living room table with a sense of pride. She went to her bookshelves and slid a novel out of the shelf, analyzing the cover, then looked at another, analyzing that cover, too. All this art all around her—and she hadn't designed any of it.

She wondered about the people who designed book covers and album covers and cereal boxes and even advertisements for Oil of Olay. What kind of training had they had, and had any of them ever been a woman?

Chapter Seventeen

July 1967

It was after nine on Sunday night and Thea was upstairs in her slanted-ceilinged bedroom. Cara was asleep in the twin bed beside her while Thea sketched on scrap paper at her desk under a single desk lamp. Picking up a pencil and putting it to drawing paper was a type of reflex for her, especially once she was alone. She'd been a doodler since she was a child, and as she got older, years of practice honed the fine muscles of her hands. Her drawings had grown more complex over time, progressing from bunnies to landscapes, scratch figures to faces.

Tonight she was looking at a black-and-white photograph of her and her mother wearing bathing suits and eating strawberries on the beach—it was her favorite picture, even if their backs were to the camera. Maybe that was what made it more powerful, what was unsaid between them. How close they were sitting, their sides pressed together, their heads positioned upward like they were looking at the same thing in the sky. At this time, when Thea was six, they were one beating heart.

The television was still on in the living room, and last she checked, her stepfather Dale was asleep on the plaid couch with his new girlfriend, Becky, watching a Dick Cavett interview. Becky had a son, a boy named Matthew, who was nine and stayed with his father every other weekend. That was what Thea learned yesterday when she'd met Becky, still wearing her white-trimmed pink diner dress; she'd also discovered that Dale had been dating her for a month.

Thea glanced out her small window at the flash of headlights through her attic window, and outside, she saw Margot's Mercedes, the top down, pulling in behind Dale's van. After her walk with Felix at Melissa Hollander's party, she couldn't find Margot, so Felix had given her a ride home. That was when she had come home to find Dale and Becky—with her false eyelashes and peacock-green eyeshadow—sharing a bottle of E. & J. Gallo wine at the kitchen table. Thea had felt as though she'd walked into someone else's house entirely. In the morning Cara made clear that she was devastated by Dale getting a girlfriend. He was Cara's father, and as far as Cara saw it, this woman was auditioning to be her stepmother.

"How could he forget Mom?" she had pleaded with Thea. This had set off a conversation about all the things she and her sister missed about their mom. But Thea wasn't sure Becky was such a bad thing. Another woman seemed to blanket the household with a calm hush, and all of them, even Dale, remained respectful and kinder to one another. Becky had made dinner tonight, and she'd cleared and washed the dishes. Thea dried, feeling guilty leaving this strange woman to do the work alone, but Becky had asked Thea about her job at the record shop. She told her that she loved rock and roll, even if most people her age thought it was just a bunch of noise, and she seemed genuinely interested when Thea found herself sharing the details of the Beatles concert she had gone to last summer. Thea didn't like that Dale was looking beyond her mother either—but it wouldn't be terrible if Becky lightened Thea's load.

Thea leaned out her bedroom window. "Come to the back door!" She ran downstairs and passed Becky on the sagging couch, noticing how she rested her head against Dale's sleeping chest. Pushing open the aluminum screen, Thea kept Margot from rapping on it.

"What happened to you at the party?" Thea said, catching her breath. "I was worried when you didn't call me back."

"I'm sorry, I got sidetracked." Margot peeked inside to see if anyone was there, her balloon-sleeved, mauve dress too pretty for a casual get-together. "I had the best idea. Let's pierce Cara's ears. I can do it, you know, with a needle and rubbing alcohol."

Thea stepped outside and closed the door. "Cara is asleep; she was in the sun all day."

"Oh." Margot rattled the bangles on her wrist. "I'm just bored. Hey. Can I sleep over? My parents decided not to come this weekend, and being alone is getting to me."

"You know how small this house is. We don't have the room." What are they going to do, cram into her twin bed in her tiny attic bedroom? With Becky sleeping in Dale's room downstairs?

"Okay, well, can you come and sleep over my house?" Margot nibbled at the skin on her thumb. She tried to sell her on a girl's night, making popcorn and listening to records. "Please."

Thea had been miffed at Margot for ditching her at the party and she was upset that she'd found her rifling through the jewelry boxes. Yet she wasn't ready to give up on her either. She'd called her that morning, leaving a message with her housekeeper, even though she knew that Margot's parents insisted she spend Sundays at the beach club with them. Thea felt terrible leaving Cara alone with Dale and his new girl-friend—her sister would wake up and be livid with Thea—but sleeping at Margot's tonight would feel like running away from home, a fantasy craved. Even if Thea had diligently held back on numerous extras in her commitment to build a meager nest egg, she still only had enough to fund a few weeks away, rather than an apartment. Plus, the last thing she wanted was to hear the amorous sounds of Dale and his girlfriend in her mother's old bedroom.

"Let me pack my bag," Thea said, and minutes later, after leaving Becky and Dale a note on the kitchen table telling them where she went, Thea was in the convertible under the night sky, stars twinkling overhead.

After Margot parked the car, Thea followed her through the back sliders, which were unlocked, Margot flicking on the lights in the kitchen, then the hallway, then the living room. "I'm so glad you're here," Margot said. "I felt so bad about the party."

"Did you stay out with Shawn?" *The Walrus.* Thea fell onto the over-stuffed, floral-patterned couch. If she could own just one couch like this in her lifetime, she would be a full woman, Thea thought.

Margot said they came back to her house and played music. "He's so cool. We wrote a song together last night."

"With your lyrics?" Thea wasn't sure she should admit to her how much their age difference bothered her.

"It's a mix of mine and his." She seemed impressed with herself.

They decided to make popcorn and went to the kitchen, and as Margot poured the kernels into a pot lined with thick yellow oil, Thea said, "Did you see who I was with at the party?"

"Was that Feel Me Felix?"

Thea burst out laughing. "You have to stop calling him that." Although she kind of loved it.

"Why? It's precious." Margot went inside to put on a Supremes album in her living room, the speakers loud enough that it was audible even two rooms away in the kitchen. "So? What happened?"

There was so much Thea wanted to say at once, her cheeks turned pink. "I think I like him, Margot."

"Duh," Margot poured them each a tumbler of vodka over ice with a splash of cranberry juice from her refrigerator. "You've liked him from the minute he offended you. Maybe even before that."

"I find him such an authentic person." Thea sipped the drink, feeling festive. "And he's caring, too. When I told him about my mother, he didn't change the subject or awkwardly look away. He told me his mother could take care of both of us."

"That may not be a good thing," Margot quipped, pouring the popcorn into a bowl.

"I know, but it was his knee-jerk instinct to be kind. Like he wanted to take care of me, and maybe it's weak to admit this since I'm a strong woman and all, but I wouldn't mind someone taking care of me."

Margot shook salt into the popcorn, her voice feigning offense. "C'mon. I take care of you!"

"We take care of each other." Thea smiled, and they drank to that. "He didn't make a move on me or anything. It wasn't like that. But I felt like I could talk to him all night. I didn't get home until after midnight."

"You two are already the most adorable couple." Margot shook her head.

"Well, we're not a couple yet, but . . . I'm open to it."

They ate popcorn standing up at the counter and debated if they should watch *Mission Impossible* at ten on television, but neither one was in the mood. Instead, Margot offered to teach her to sew her own sack dress, and Thea jumped on the idea. She'd always wanted to learn to sew, but she didn't have her own sewing machine.

"It's a rather easy shape," Margot said of the McCall's pattern after Thea selected the fabric she wanted to use, a gauzy blue-and-white stripe that looked like a print you'd wear out for a day of sailing. "It's my only preppy pattern," Margot teased.

"Maybe I'm a secret prep."

"How about this?" Margot unrolled a black fabric with hot pink and yellow half-moons emblazoned on it. "Stop being so safe and show how bold you can be. You can wear this with little white ankle boots!"

Thea loved the style, but somehow it felt like a dress groovier people wore. "You don't think I'll look silly?" she said, the prospect of wearing it exciting, even if she was uncertain about it. Margot laughed: "No! You'll look fab." Thea used sewing pins to connect the crinkly paper pattern to the cotton, cutting the shape with a pair of jagged scissors. On the turntable, Margot put on that summer's hit song "San Francisco (Be Sure to Wear Flowers in Your Hair)," Scott McKenzie's voice pulling Thea into a contemplative mood. The emotional quality of the song reminded Thea of the party, walking in on Margot rifling through the Hollander woman's jewelry box in the bedroom upstairs, the distrust that had been lingering inside her since. She'd checked the papers this morning to see if there were any thefts announced on the front page, but there had been nothing.

"Can I ask you something?" Thea asked as Margot threaded the bobbin of the sewing machine.

"You can ask me anything," Margot said, holding a sliver of white thread between her front teeth.

Thea was nearly done pinning the brown paper pattern. "I followed you upstairs at the Hollander party. I was coming to tell you that I was going for a walk on the beach with Felix." She paused, steadying herself. "I saw you in one of the bedrooms." She can't bring herself to say the last part, about seeing her hand dipping into the open jewelry box.

Margot used the foot pedal to check the bobbin, and it spun without problem. "Were you following me?"

The question surprised Thea, making her feel silly for confronting her, like she'd done something wrong. "No, I just didn't want to leave you alone." Although Margot hadn't had any problem leaving Thea all alone, had she?

Margot left the sewing machine for a moment to restart the record. "Here, bring your pattern over. I'll show you what to do next."

Thea sat in the squat, wire-backed sewing chair, a small yellow cushion with buttons on the seat. After removing the paper pattern from the fabric, Margot positioned the edges of the sleeve under the needle. "Anyway, the younger sister Lacey and I are old friends, and she borrowed a record from me a while back. She told me to go up to her room to get it."

"But you were in her . . ." *Jewelry box.* Margot had started the song from the beginning, the singer crooning about how everyone should come to San Francisco.

"She had my Bobby Sherman album," Margot said. "I was mad, too, because it had all these scratches on it."

"Oh." Thea focused on pressing her foot into the sewing pedal. But she knew she'd seen Margot in the jewelry box, not in the albums, and that was the problem. She pretended that there was nothing else in the room to give her attention to other than these stitches, deciding if she should press her on the detail or not. Even if her gut was telling her Margot was lying, she chose to drop it for now; she would have to trust that Margot had a good reason to be in this woman's room.

At first, it was easy to guide the fabric through and sew the lines of the arm perfectly straight, but then the needle moved too fast and a tangled pile of loops formed at the surface.

"Margot, help!" Thea cried. After fixing the stitching and getting the sewing machine back on track, Margot cut the fabric for the dresses' matching belt. She stopped to put the "San Francisco" song on once more.

"You know, I've been thinking."

Thea looked up from the sewing machine. "Yes," she said.

"Let's go somewhere together."

"Like a vacation?" The thought was actually funny. People like Thea didn't go on vacation. She had never gone on vacation. Once, when she was seven, she remembered her parents renting a hotel room on nearby Shelter Island, but they went without her, leaving her with a neighbor.

"Let's take a road trip. We'll drive across the country to San Francisco and stay there. Start a new life together." Margot plucked a flower from the vase Thea assumed that the housekeeper left on her dresser—Margot stuck the pink flower above Thea's ear while she sang along with the record.

For a second, Thea considered it. The two of them in Margot's convertible, driving the open roads of America. She'd be able to see the entire country. Her mailing address would include the state of California. It nearly took her breath away. Then she imagined the reality: pulling into a gas station, Margot turning to her for gas money, and Thea forced to use her meager savings on something as aimless as a road trip.

"Argh. I wish I could. But I couldn't afford it. I have to keep saving up money."

"How? Working at the record store for the rest of your life? It's an hourly job that pays crap. Shelly and Jay will tell us we should go. Hell, they'll probably take up a collection to help us out."

Thea said all the things she had said before because it seemed like Margot never remembered. How she needed the job because she couldn't just leave home without savings that would give her the freedom to do what she wanted to do. That she couldn't do something crazy like drive cross-country *just because*.

"Maybe someday," Thea finished with a sigh. She pulled the dress sleeve out from the sewing machine, examining the neat row of stitches. Laying in her bed at night, Thea had started thinking maybe she would save up to get an apartment in town, decorating it with items from Labor Day yard sales. She could even take her childhood bookshelf and use it to arrange her favorite novels, sketchbooks, and colored pencils. If she didn't take classes, maybe she could keep designing concert posters for local bands, offer to draw ads for local businesses.

"No, Thea, you're missing the point. I have money, plenty of it, and we can make more money when we get there." Margot would sew a stack of dresses, and Thea could draw landscapes or inspirational sayings or song lyrics with psychedelic lettering, and they could create a stand and sell their artwork on the sidewalk or at one of the flea markets Margot had heard about in Berkeley. They could perform, too; Margot would sing, and she'd keep teaching Thea a few chords on the guitar to accompany her. "Look, if I sell these dresses for three dollars a pop and we sell ten of them—that's thirty dollars. How far we could go on thirty dollars!"

Thea laughed. How far *she* could go on thirty dollars was one thing—she wasn't so sure about Margot. Thea wished she could go, but it seemed impulsive, unplanned. She needed to be smart with her next step. It needed to feel like a sure thing. And yet . . . she didn't want to say *no* either. A trip, leaving everything behind and looking for her future out there in the big world . . . it was incredibly tempting. "You're right. I don't want to work at the record store for the rest of my life, but I do want to be useful in some way. I need to feel like I'm on the path toward something."

"You will be! You'll be starting a new life in California, the place where dreams are made, Thea."

She thought of her mother then, how she'd always believed she would be something more if she'd only set foot in Los Angeles. "How long would we be gone?"

A gleam surfaced in Margot's eye. "Six months, a year, maybe two. And don't worry, I'll make sure we're not homeless or sleeping in my car. I'll get us an apartment in the Haight. It will be fabulous."

Thea placed the seam of the dress back onto the sewing machine. "Margot! This is silly. You should go without me!"

"But it will be so fun if we go together. The two of us driving across the country and camping at national parks and stopping in cities along the way to check out the local record stores. C'mon, Thea! We have to go."

Thea *had* decided she wasn't going to live under Dale's thumb anymore, and she wasn't going to live in fear that she was disappointing her mother, either. A few days ago, she'd declared a *revolution* within herself and then she had done little to change anything. What Margot was proposing was the move of a lifetime. If Thea's mother was alive, she would want her to see the country, to do all the things she'd never gotten to do herself. Maybe they could even take a detour to Los Angeles, and Thea could see for herself the Hollywood stage sets that her mother had always dreamed of performing on.

Still, there was Cara, and that was the sticking point. At the very least, Cara would need to be back in school full-time to soften the blow—Thea needed to continue to pay Miss Porter, the tutor, as well. But Cara could last a few months without Thea, maybe two, if Thea promised to come back for her.

Thea needed time to prepare. Even if Margot wanted to leave right away, Thea didn't feel capable of that kind of spontaneous action. Plus, Shelly and Jay might be excited for the plan, but Thea wouldn't leave them without any help at the record store through the busiest time in summer.

Thea pushed down on the sewing pedal again. "I'll go, but I can't leave until just before Labor Day weekend."

Whipping open her nightstand drawer, Margot pulled out a salmon-colored planner, a series of formal obligations written on coordinating dates. "Okay, that works. That gives us four weeks, a little more, to prepare. It's better that way, anyway. I can sew more dresses for us to sell."

Thea would need to start sketching, too. Was she really going to drive to San Francisco with a box of art prints to sell at flea markets? Perhaps she'd start with a series of postcards. She'd always loved to draw small animals with whimsical sayings: A monkey standing on top of a box with a question beside it. *What did the monkey do?* She thought of them as "whimsies" and could sell them for a quarter each. The happy thought sent the spin of a record inside her stomach.

"Are you being serious, Margot? Because I'll start figuring out how to do it. And we'll take your car?" At least that seemed like a sure thing; Margot's car was new. It certainly wouldn't break down on them, stranding them in the middle of nowhere.

Margot fell backward onto her bed laughing, clutching the belt she'd been working on. "Yes, yes. I'm serious. I've never needed a change of scenery more."

Thea lifted her foot from the sewing pedal. "And what will your parents say?" *What would Dale say?* Honestly, she didn't think Dale would care, especially now that he had Becky.

"They'll tell me to have fun while I can. Because you're only young once."

Tilting her head in a show of doubt, Thea raised an eyebrow. "You sure about that?"

"Absolutely certain."

They fell asleep around two in the morning. Even with six empty bedrooms on the second floor of the estate, they slept together in Margot's large double bed, listening to the hum of a window air-conditioner. While Margot dropped into a deep sleep, Thea tossed and turned. She'd never slept in a house this big.

San Francisco. She was going to California.

After they'd finished sewing Thea's dress, she'd tried it on, the two of them laughing when the lower hem was crooked and needed to be fixed. Margot had re-stitched it for her while they'd munched on Dippy Canoes, wondering if Native Americans actually invented the corn chip or if it was some man in a suit dreaming up snacks for teenagers. Then they'd mapped their route with a road atlas of the United States that Margot had pulled out of a glossy mahogany bureau in the library, the pages crisp and unused.

Margot had used a thick black pen to mark the highways, and they'd agreed that after driving west to Chicago, stopping only once and staying at a cheap roadside motel to sleep, they'd spend one day in the city. ("You just have to see the Magritte at the Art Institute!") She also had friends with a house on Lake Michigan, and Margot had said it was even more beautiful than the ocean. They could stay there and swim and "catch our breath a bit," as Margot put it. Then they'd drive to South Dakota until they got to the Black Hills, camp a night, and cut down to Kansas to head into Colorado, where they would stop in Denver and see who was playing at the amphitheater there. Margot had gotten so excited then that she'd called the theater straightaway, even though it was eleven at night, disappointed to discover that they would miss a performance by Simon & Garfunkel. "We could have seen Paul Simon!" she whined.

There was a crescent moon tonight, and Thea watched clouds drift past, shadowing Margot's bedroom with light, then darkness. The ever-changing moonlight kept her awake, and Thea fiddled with the hummingbird locket at her neck, popping it open and snapping it shut. When she met Margot a month earlier, she had no idea she'd be the catalyst to change her life. She had done so much for her already, urging her to talk about things she'd been avoiding with her mother, a gnawing ache that no one else wanted to explore with her. But more than anything, Margot had forced her to see that she needed to take care of herself.

Thea scrunched the plump feather pillow under her head. Why, after all that, did Margot always feel so unsteady? Sometimes she wondered if Margot was a house of cards, if at any moment she would collapse onto the floor in a thousand pieces. Thea was excited to take this cross-country trip with her, but she feared that after all their planning, Margot might change her mind, that something else would capture her attention, and Thea would suddenly be back where she started. Margot could decide halfway through the drive that she wanted to go to New Orleans instead, and what would Thea do then? She wouldn't have the money to get home.

Then again, in two months' time, she could be staring at the Pacific Ocean for the first time in her life, watching a different sunrise than the one she was accustomed to on the East Coast. She wondered what Felix would say about her trip.

Thea's eyes were wide open, and as she stared into the darkened hallway, she heard another creak in the floors under the Persian hallway runner. At first, Thea brushed off the sound as a wall popping with heat. But then she saw the silhouette of someone standing in the doorway. A large man. Thea smacked her. "Margot?!"

Thea clutched the soft blanket to her chest and she shrieked so loudly that Margot fell out of bed.

Her hair in a long loose braid, Margot pushed up the satin mask over her eyes. "Thea, what on earth?"

Thea pointed toward the door. "There's a man!"

He retreated into the hallway, but Margot didn't seem scared. She yawned, throwing off the blankets. "Oh, sorry. I didn't think he'd come over tonight."

Thea's eyes adjusted to the light in the hallway as Margot padded downstairs in her baby-doll pajama tank top and matching shorts. The red numbers of the alarm clock read 2:43 a.m. Thea shivered from the cold blowing out of the air-conditioning window unit, pulling the covers higher and suddenly longing for the comfort of her own room where she and Cara slept with both windows open, the humidity surrounding them all summer long.

From the bed, she struggled to listen to their voices, both Margot and the man downstairs. With a sigh, she shoved off the blankets and crept to the edge of the stairwell banister. From there she could see it was the Walrus in the living room. She felt queasy then. He'd let himself in; did he have a key to the house as groundskeeper? They were arguing, something about Margot storming off, Margot saying that he didn't own her. Finally, their voices quieted, and he said, "I love you. You know I do." There was the wet lap of kissing, and Thea dove back into Margot's bed so she didn't have to hear anymore.

After an hour of restless thinking, delirium finally set in and Thea fell asleep, dreaming that she and Margot were crossing a river. But when they got to the other side, Margot told Thea she could not come. That she needed to go without her.

When Thea woke up, she was alone in the large white canopy bed. The sun shone through Margot's salmon-colored pom-pom curtains, and Thea still remembered every bit of the dream. The brackish scent of the water, the beads of sweat at her temples. And the part of the dream that frightened her most: When Margot got in a strange man's car at the dock and drove off, leaving Thea standing all alone on the raft, waving goodbye.

Chapter Eighteen

Thea was the first one at Sunshine Records that Thursday. It was quarter of eleven, and Jay and Shelly were usually already inside with the lights switched on, the cash register humming, but there was no sign of them. Thea deadheaded the pansies drying up outside in the shop's window boxes from the mid-summer heat. After a few minutes, she walked around a cluster of hydrangea bushes to get to the back door and saw Jay leaning against the shingled siding, smoking a cigarette. He didn't see her at first, and Thea noticed how his head hung low, his tattered canvas boat shoe tapping against the dirt. She said hello, and he startled, her voice pulling him out of his thoughts.

"Oh, hi Thea," he said, tossing his cigarette on the ground and grinding it with his heel.

His yellow Chevy Impala was parked behind the shop, but there was no sign of anyone else. "Where is Shelly?" she said.

"Who cares?"

Thea didn't say anything as he turned the key in the lock of the shop, slamming his body into the back door to open it, though no extraordinary force was required. Jay walked through, turning on the lights, even if the day was bright enough to illuminate the aisles, and Shelly simultaneously came in the front door, slamming it behind her. "Hi Thea," she mumbled, her eyes puffy and red.

"Are you okay?" Thea said. Shelly watched Jay slip into the storage room and close the door.

"I don't want to talk about it." Shelly had brushed her thick hair up into a ponytail, her bangs a curtain-like row above her eyebrows, while large aqua hoops popped against her serious black shift dress. Behind the counter, she lit a cigarette. "We had a spat."

"Okay." Thea didn't really want to talk about what was on her mind either.

She'd run into the Walrus in the kitchen just before leaving Margot's house yesterday morning; Thea had slept over again Tuesday night. Margot was slicing a grapefruit in the kitchen, giggling, while the Walrus entered in his work clothes and planted kisses up her neck. "Good morning, Thea," he had said, offering a mischievous grin. "Sorry I scared you the other night. I needed to see my girl."

Margot had her hair tied up with chopsticks. "He likes to surprise me."

"It's okay," Thea had said, a bit speechless being that close to him while wearing her pajamas. Margot had admitted earlier in the week that she had more of a relationship with the Walrus than she'd let on, that he climbed into bed with her sometimes to keep her company on her loneliest nights, and now she looked forward to his evening visits, even though he was ten years her senior. But yesterday she'd said she might be falling in love with him and she hadn't told Thea because she worried Thea would disapprove of their age difference. Thea pretended not to be appalled, but Margot had seen through her: "I know it's unconventional, but I can't stop who I'm attracted to. He said with a little more practice, maybe I could join his band, as a lead singer."

So that's what this was about? The Walrus was going to take her on a wild journey through rock and roll, even if his band could barely land a gig in Montauk? Thea didn't want to be such a harsh judge, but when she'd heard him playing at the party, he'd played the same three chords—what Jay once told her was the first sign of a mediocre musician.

The front door swung open, and Margot came in wearing one of her signature handsewn dresses: flowy, patchwork, floral. She launched right into a whirlwind of thoughts. "I have the best idea," she said. Her eyes had dark circles underneath.

Margot convinced Shelly that they needed to catalog their large collection of music in fresh ways. She wanted to set up a table up front called "Women in Rock and Roll." Last week, Shelly had mentioned that she'd read an article in the newspaper reporting that women musicians didn't get as much radio playing time as their male counterparts. "Let's give some of our favorite woman singers more visibility," Margot suggested. "We'll help them sell more of their albums."

Everybody loved the idea, and the store felt sunny again as Shelly put on a Peter, Paul and Mary album, stubbed out her cigarette, and lit some lavender incense.

The shop wasn't busy, so the women got to work on the display. In addition to some younger, lesser-known singers, Thea and Shelly began making a list of who to feature: Mama Cass, Dusty Springfield, Grace Slick, Aretha Franklin, Joan Baez, Janis Joplin, Cher. Margot collected their albums and arranged them on the table, which she'd covered in a paisley tablecloth. Thea offered to hand-draw the signage: she'd paint an electric guitar with swirling lettering hugging the edges of the instrument. She wanted shoppers to take the sign as seriously as they should the women performers.

After lunch, Shelly entered the stockroom, closing the door with Jay inside. Margot seized the opportunity to stand beside Thea to chat. "A friend of mine in Arizona is organizing a concert just as we'll be passing by. Do you want to go?"

Thea nodded, even if she felt a little wary of adding another stop on their growing journey across the country. "I'll go anywhere you want. I'm just along for the ride, remember? What about your boyfriend?"

Margot laughed. "He's just a guy, not my boyfriend."

After they finished the women's table in the shop, Shelly came out of the stockroom, humming. She seemed unburdened, and Thea knew that whatever happened between her and Jay had been resolved. "How about we do another special display?" Thea proposed. "We can call it 'Sounds of Summer,' and we'll feature records that are quintessential summer picks."

"Yes!" Shelly applauded the idea. They started throwing out their favorite summer hits: Margot's was "A Summer Song" by Chad & Jeremy, which sends Thea and Shelly into a fit of giggles. The song had such a sappy feel—the musicians seemed like coeds singing wistfully about a summer fling, compared to the hard rockers of the day—but they put it on the record player anyway. She and Margot danced around the empty shop like fairies flitting about in a glen.

What was most interesting, Thea thought, as she and Margot playfully spun each other around the shop, was how much her relationship with music had changed since she began working in the store. In high school, Thea enjoyed pop hits because they were on the radio, the songs were catchy, and singing the hooks instantly bonded her and her friends. But the record shop had forced her to think about music with more depth. Who was singing? Why were they putting those particular lyrics out into the world? To Thea, music was no longer about singing along to a hit song—it was about delivering a musical experience. People came into the record shop looking to rock stars and jazz singers to enhance their mood and personality, even providing them with an identity. *The kind of music you listen to,* Thea thought, *can tell you everything you need to know about a person.*

The idea that Thea herself mostly listened to the Beatles before this year made her blush as the song ended, and she returned to making a sign for the "Sounds of Summer" table, a big sunburst with colorful psychedelic lettering. Shelly must have found her record choices so predictable each time she carried one up to the counter for purchase. Then again, so many of the teenagers that Thea met in the store these days made similar choices. They came in for the songs on the *Billboard* Hot 100 chart.

Lately, Thea had only wanted to listen to new bands fresh off the radio waves. Singers like Mick Jagger made her want to break free of everything she thought she knew. Then there was the Velvet Under-

ground—only their moody guitar riffs could capture the angst she was
feeling on some days. A single song could release an emotion long buried, could offer renewal. The lyrics drew her in more than the melody.
Lately, she'd fixate on one line in a song and listen on repeat, feeling the
emotion building, the freedom of the words bursting inside her.

Thea wondered what kind of music she would discover in San Francisco, if she and Margot would meet musicians just walking down the
street. She imagined herself befriending exotic rock stars, offering to
draw them concert posters, becoming a well-known artist designing for
local bands.

The phone rang, and Shelly answered it, calling over to Thea. She
shrugged: "Someone named Felix?"

"Feel Me Felix!" Margot yelled, Thea murdering her with her eyes.
She ran over to the front counter and grabbed the phone, crouching
down so no one could see her, little fires burning her nerves on the
inside. After they said their hellos, there was an awkward second where
Felix didn't say anything. The silence made her feel a bit wobbly. Then
he said: "I have a request. Find the single by the Drifters. The one with
'Baltimore' on the flip side."

"'This Magic Moment'?" This was the song on the other side. Thea
knew this because one old timer had come in for a copy to gift his wife
for their anniversary. It had been one of the sweetest things she'd ever
seen.

Felix sounded amused. "How did you know that? Anyway, I left
something for you there."

Thea felt Shelly's and Margot's eyes on her back as she hung up and
went to the shelf holding the *D* albums. When she located the Drifters
album, she lifted it up, a single piece of loose-leaf paper drifting down.
Thea caught it in her hand. In blue ink, Felix had written: *Will you come
to my house Saturday tonight and listen to records with me? I live behind the
pizza shop in Amagansett. White house, dark shutters. #4. Any time after
six. Felix.*

Thea laughed out loud, Margot immediately at her side, ripping the
note from her hand. Shelly leaned over her other shoulder.

"Should I go?" Thea asked, loving that Felix wrote the note in an elegant script. Her mother used to joke that a man with beautiful hand-writing should always be trusted because he'd care for you with the same care he moved his hands along the page.

"Of course you should," Margot squealed.

Shelly had the palm of her hand resting across her heart. "Do you think I should tell Jay to set up a scavenger hunt for me in the record shop? Oh, the romance."

"Why not? We have to tell people what we want, don't we?" As Thea said it, she thought about how changed she sounded. Telling people what was on her mind. Is that something she was able to do now? She certainly hoped so.

The door of the shop dinged, only their third customer of the day, and after Thea tucked the note into her purse, she noticed that two uni-formed officers had entered the store.

"Hi Joshua," Thea said, while Shelly returned to her spot behind the cashier's desk. "I mean, Officer Barley."

"Hello, Thea. You can call me Josh. You know that." Josh Barley was one of three brothers that she'd attended high school with; he'd had a crush on her when she was in ninth grade and he was a senior. The other cop was older: tall, mustached, a chip in one canine. He reached out to shake Shelly's hand.

"I'm Officer Kapalo. Our boss sent us over."

"To buy records?" Thea played innocent as she returned to her let-tering at the counter. She noticed that Margot was arranging the sum-mer hits table, Shelly right next to her, listening. When Josh said "Nah," Thea's voice wavered. "Is everything okay?"

"Everything is fine." Josh folded his arms across his chest.

"Thea, were you at a party last Saturday at the Hollander house in Bridgehampton?" Thea could see the judgment in his eyes: *Why would someone like you be in that part of town?* "Yes, I went with Margot, my friend. She's right there." Thea nodded in the direction of Margot, hop-ing that no one could hear how loud her pulse thumped in her chest. "Margot, this is Josh, Officer Barley. He's a childhood friend."

"You were both there?" Josh held a yellow-lined notepad and began to scribble something down. He took out a list of names. "Oh yes, here you are. You're Julianna and Brett Lazure's daughter, right?"

"I am." Margot sauntered over, the hem of her dress swishing, and she leaned over the cashier's desk, twisting the quartz crystal hanging from a leather cord around her neck, the hummingbird locket just below it. "My family is close with the Hollanders. We grew up riding horses together."

"I spoke to your mother two weeks ago—she gives a nice donation to the precinct every year, doesn't she?" Josh chewed on his pencil.

"Sounds like Mother."

Shelly motioned to the new customers, a young family, and said to the officers: "Is this something you could finish later? I'm afraid my patrons will feel uneasy seeing you in here."

"It'll just be another minute." The kids belonging to the family began running in circles in the aisles, and the mother tried to corral them.

"Why are you asking about the Hollander party?" Thea smelled the banana peel she'd tossed in the trash early this morning, the sweet, sickly smell turning rancid now. Her stomach flip-flopped.

"Ladies, I'm sure you've heard of the burglar that's been poaching pieces from people's homes during parties." Josh stopped, waiting for them to nod along. "Well, we've been keeping it out of the papers, but a gold bracelet went missing at the Hollander party. It's a gold bangle that wraps around your wrist twice, a snake head at one end, emeralds for eyes."

Thea glanced up at Margot, who didn't flinch. "That's awful. Her father gave her that bracelet when she turned sixteen," Margot said. "Do you think one of the caterers took it?"

Josh emitted a frustrated grunt. "Did either of you see anything that night?" He seemed to speak directly to Thea.

Margot glanced at Thea. "I was in my friend's room retrieving an old Bobby Sherman album. I didn't see anyone else upstairs. Did you, Thea?"

Thea had to lift her jaw off the floor. Did Margot just confirm that Thea had been upstairs too? *Relax. You did nothing wrong.* If anyone was guilty, it was Margot.

Josh was waiting on Thea's answer, but Thea felt trapped. Margot's easy admission that she was upstairs at the party—in one of the bedrooms, to be exact—made it difficult for Thea to tell the officer that she saw her hunting through a jewelry box. Not that she'd turn her in even if she could. Who had a clearer motive: Margot, a woman whose parents made more money in a week than most would earn in a lifetime, or Thea, a local who was pinching pennies to move out of her stepfather's house?

"There were so many people at that party, Josh—there must've been over a hundred, and they were drunk, high, falling into rooms to make-out. Whoever took that bracelet didn't need to be too sneaky about it," Thea said. She looked up, met his gaze, and saw the officer as she always would: a pimply teenager popping wheelies on his bike in the neighborhood.

He stood like a cop now, wide stance, cheeks puffed. "That's the problem with all these thefts. Each party has so many people that no one seems to notice if anyone slips off."

The tight knot in Thea's chest loosened slightly. She smiled, tried to switch gears. She knew his wife was a bank teller, that they lived in the Springs, that they had a new baby called Bitsy. "How's the baby, Josh?"

"Finally sleeping through the night." He winked, snapping his gum. "I'll tell you this much, ladies, get your sleep while you can."

The officers thanked them for their time and pushed open the shop door. Thea was relieved at the sight of his hulking form stepping back onto the sidewalk, adjusting his visor, because he would find someone else to blame for these crimes.

When he was gone, Margot returned to arranging the albums on the front table, and Thea was immediately at her heels, feeling as though if she didn't confront her now, she never would. "You stole that jewelry, didn't you?" she whispered to Margot. "Why? It makes no sense."

Margot trained her eyes on the Beach Boys album on the shelf in front of her. "Lots of things don't make sense, Thea."

*　　*　　*

On the way home that night, the road held the fragrance of a forest outside the car windows, the elm trees tunneling over the convertible. Nature usually calmed Thea. It was what a lifetime of running barefoot in the forest did for a child, but not now. Not sitting beside Margot. Neither one spoke.

Finally, Thea blurted: "Did you tell the cops that I was up there on purpose? So they'd think I was the thief?"

"No." Margot took one hand off the steering wheel, her hair loose and blowing in her face. "How could you think that? I thought we'd look less guilty if we were upstairs together, to make the point that people were wandering up and down the entire night."

Thea slammed her body back into the leather seat, groaning. "I still don't know why you're taking this stuff. You don't need anyone's jewelry."

"Why are you so convinced it's me? Anyway, if I were to take such things, it wouldn't be to feed my own impulse. Do you know that if the thief were to sell the Hollander bracelet to a pawnshop, it would probably fetch enough cash to fund an orphanage in Vietnam for an entire year?"

Thea grinded her teeth. "And do you moonlight at pawnshops, too? I'm not stupid, Margot. Your parents could fund an orphanage if you asked them."

The car sped over a pothole, their bodies lifting, slamming down. "My parents don't care about anything but building up their own wealth. They actually talk about these things at dinner. When I spoke to them about the orphans that I read about in *my mother's own* paper, she talked about how I needed to think more responsibly. In her mind, Thea, wealth doesn't mean sharing." Margot pulled into Thea's driveway.

She remembered the officers standing in the record shop earlier. "Well, your parents give to the police association."

"And why is that, do you think? Because they're kind? No, it's in case they get caught speeding on Sunrise Highway. They don't share, Thea. They don't share like I want to share." Margot folded her arms against her chest. She lowered her voice. "I'm sorry for yelling."

Thea rubbed the side of her arm. "It's okay. Relationships are complicated. Parents are complicated."

Margot gave her a weak smile and wiped her nose, resting her hand on the gearshift. "I need to run home to see Shawn. I only have one more night until my parents get here."

The Walrus. *Dear god,* Thea thought. "Okay, thanks for the ride."

Saturday night couldn't come fast enough. She'd thought of little else other than her date with Felix at work that day, and when Thea completed her shift at the record shop, her stomach was full of butterflies. Margot dropped her home after work, agreeing to give her a ride to Felix's house in Amagansett in an hour. After rushing through the back door, Thea found the kitchen cleaned, thanks to Becky. With Cara and Dale at a barbecue with one of Becky's friends, Thea could focus on prettying herself. Lathering her body with her prized Princess Dial soap bar, Thea shaved her legs, then rinsed and dried off. She applied thick eyeliner and mascara and zipped up her sundress. After drying her wavy hair straight, she pinned a pretty piece to one side with a small pinch clip.

Just before seven o'clock, she heard a horn. "Right on time." Thea took one last look in the mirror. Lip gloss. She quickly applied a shimmery pink to her lips. Margot was outside in her car with the top down, her hair in a loose ponytail.

"You're acting funny. Are you still mad at me about the Hollander party?" Margot let her aviator sunglasses fall down her nose, the convertible open to the air.

Thea pulled the door shut. "Maybe a little. I just wish you would tell me the truth. Can we put this top up so I don't ruin my hair?"

Margot tossed her a scarf from the glove box, a sheer one that women from a decade ago might have worn. "Tie it back," she said as she backed out of the driveway. "This night is too beautiful. And anyway, you can't be too upset with me. I got you your first assignment at the paper."

Thea knotted the scarf, confused. "What do you mean?"

Margot grinned. She'd talked to her mother about Thea's illustrations, and her mother said they needed a new logo for their Dear Virgie column. They'd already seen a few ideas from their stable of illustrators, all seeming too dated for the youthful vibe they wanted for the column. "She said if you sketch her some possibilities, she'll take a look."

"I don't believe you." Thea felt like her insides were vibrating.

The car crested over a hill, a glimpse of the sea in the distance. Margot laughed. "Well, believe it. She needs them by Friday."

Thea bounced like a child in her seat, clapping, a smile brighter than sunset. "A week? Oh, Margot. Thank you." She scooted toward her, hugging her. "I can't believe you talked to your mom about me."

The timing of an act so generous couldn't have been worse. As excited as Thea was, she couldn't pretend she wasn't unsettled by the events of the week. When the police came to the store on Thursday, Thea had answered each question the best that she could. But when she'd asked Margot if she'd taken the jewelry, she hadn't denied it. She'd deflected. *Lots of things don't make sense, Thea.* And then in the car that day, she'd talked about what the money from a bracelet could fund. It made Thea uneasy. If she outed Margot for her crimes, she'd have to live with herself for ruining Margot's life—and they'd never go on their trip to California. But what if they did go and Margot continued to steal along the way?

What if she tried to pawn off any of the crimes on Thea?

She sighed for whatever unknown consequence might come in overlooking Margot's indiscretions. "Okay, but about the jewelry. Just promise me," Thea said, leaning forward so Margot looked her in the eye, "that if you are stealing, you'll stop right now, and you'll never drag me down with you. I'm trying to get out of here, okay?"

Margot pushed at Thea's shoulder with a playful toggle, like she couldn't believe how silly she was being. "Oh, Thea. Don't worry so much. I love you too much to hurt you like that."

There was an American flag flying from the porch when they pulled up to Felix's darling white house, blush-colored roses growing along a white picket fence. The driveway was narrow, lined with tall hedgerows, and could fit only one car, an aquamarine VW bus. Margot parked out front. "This must be it," Thea said.

Margot handed her a bottle of Binaca breath drops, and Thea squeezed a drip onto her tongue, puckering her face from the awful taste of the freshener. "I'm going to smell like I swallowed a tube of tooth cream."

"It's better than smelling like whatever you had for dinner." Margot waved her out of the car.

Felix must have been watching from the windows because he came outside just as Thea climbed the steps, Margot disappearing down the road. "You came," he said, a copy of Walt Whitman's *Leaves of Grass* tucked under his arm.

"Are you surprised?" Thea fiddled with the waist of her dress.

"Just happy." He was wearing green, white, and blue plaid shorts, and a white collared shirt with vertical panels in front. His hair was cut straight in a line above his eyebrows, choppy around the ears, looking a bit like Ringo Starr. "My parents are at an art opening in town. I told them you were coming over."

She followed him inside, stepping directly into the living room, a small narrow staircase facing the front door. There was a television with a large metal antenna, a pea-green velour couch, flowery wallpaper. He led her beyond the cramped kitchen, which looked similar to Dale's, and brought her down into the basement, which he called his "study." Here, the walls had been lined with wood paneling, there was a white shag rug on the floor, and a lopsided couch. There were crates of records, a hall table holding a turntable, a writing desk outfitted with a typewriter, and a stack of books he referred to as "the greatest novels of all time." In the stack was his very favorite, *Great Expectations*.

"Can I get you something to drink? I make a damn good G & T."

"Sure." she smiled, sitting on the couch awkwardly as he climbed back up the stairs. A spoon clinked inside a glass, ice was shaken in a tumbler. "Do you need help?" she hollered up.

But he was already coming down carrying two highball glasses. "I kind of feel like my parents right now." He seemed proud of it, too. "They drink one every night after dinner."

"Right. The lovely couple." They clinked their glasses together. His parents. He had both of them. How lucky he was. She nodded to the pile of albums, giving them a purpose in the awkward pauses. "Where should we begin?"

Felix set down his glass. "I have an entire song list that I've created for you. You probably know many of these songs, you know, being the record store girl and everything." He scrunched up his face, pushing his hands into his pockets. "But maybe not in this order."

This made her laugh. "I just started listening to the Velvet Underground, so you may be surprised how little I know."

The needle dropped on Otis Redding's "These Arms of Mine" and already, Thea was intrigued. This song was not on her usual rotation. Felix nodded along with the opening notes, then looked up at her under his tortoiseshell glasses.

"I've always loved how Redding sings the song with so much yearning, like he wants to hold this girl he likes more than anything."

"It's sweet." Thea smiled, heat flushing her cheeks. She pretended to hold a microphone and sang with the same depth of emotion, then plopped down on the fuzzy rug, giggling. He sat cross-legged beside her.

"You're a goofball," Felix laughed. He tapped his finger to the beat on her arm. "This was the song we were listening to when my parents and I first pulled into New York. I remember driving all night from Florida and the sun was rising over the city when we went over the George Washington Bridge, and I knew, even though I hadn't ever been to the city, or to the state, that I'd found home."

"You never want to leave here?" It was the opposite of how Thea felt. How could someone want to stay in a town where nothing ever happened?

"I plan to attend graduate school, so I'll be back in Manhattan for the next year. But after that, yes, I hope I can live out here by the ocean. When all the summer people leave in August, I love how quiet it gets. Like the sea is ours to keep."

Her mind wandered during the next song, and they listened instead of talked, Thea picturing the years ahead as one gelatinous blob she needed to tunnel through. "Sometimes looking into the future scares me. What if it all turns out rather plain?"

"You? Turn out plain? Sorry, can't see it." A smile overtook his face, revealing deep dimples, as he elbowed her softly. "Anyway, we're just dreaming."

She returned the smile, feeling inspired by his optimism. "Two kids who will make their dreams come true."

Their fingertips grazed. Thea realized how close they'd been sitting, both of them leaning against the couch. He rose to switch albums. The next song was one of her favorites: Stevie Wonder's "Uptight (Everything's Alright)."

"I have a funny story about this one," she told him. It was when she was at junior college Upstate. She and a friend had boarded the campus bus to make curfew after smoking a joint, but this song was playing on the radio. The bus driver must have known they were high because he repeatedly drove the traffic circle, and they laughed so hard that Thea nearly threw up in the green leather seat. "Something about this song makes me feel like I'm about to get into mischief," she laughed.

"Did you make curfew?" He smiled again.

"Barely," she said.

His next few songs were fun to listen to together, and they lay down on the rug beside each other, him running his fingers up and down the smooth undersides of her arm in between changing records. Sam Cooke's "Cupid," and The Kinks' "You Really Got Me."

After a while she saw a pattern emerging in his song list, and she blushed thinking about it. All the songs made her feel like she was falling in love, seeing the possibility of it. Two warm bodies sitting close, listening to some of the best love songs from the last several years.

"I'm trying to pinpoint your tastes," she said, focusing on the musicality of the songs so as not to embarrass herself. "You've got some soul, some jazz, some rock."

He had sun-browned skin, the warm scent of something vaguely cedar coming from his clothes. "My parents introduced me to all different types of music growing up, and I latched on to some of the songs at different points in my life. Sometimes I come down here when I'm writing and choose songs that I know will make me feel something."

The ceiling of the basement had foam tiles with crisscross lattice, and it seemed as charming as the picket fence outside. "I do the same thing. A song can call up a specific moment in time, an entire set of feelings. Whatever I'm listening to influences what I draw, too."

He looked at her with great interest. "You draw?"

Thea nodded but went back to the music. "And some of those songs help me go deeper into myself."

"If it's raining and I'm reading a novel, you can bet I've got Otis Redding on. If I've got my car windows down on a gorgeous day, I'm blasting the Stones."

"Yes, definitely Mick Jagger. Jay keeps telling me at the store: 'Enough with "Ruby Tuesday."'"

"For me, it's all about 'Paint It Black,'" he laughed.

Three hours passed in a blink, and she was surprised when she heard the front door latch upstairs. There were footsteps on the floorboards overhead, someone getting water in the kitchen. "Fefe, you down there?" his mother said from the top of the stairs.

"Yes, Mami," he called up. Felix sat up and pulled Thea up to stand with him. He turned to her and asked, "I want you to meet my parents. Do you want to go get a slice of pizza after?"

She was surprised when she met his father, Stefan, who was blond, a Scandinavian who moved to Long Island to become a fisherman but ended up running an Irish pub, and his mother, Olivia, a petite woman with skin so smooth she could be in a cigarette ad. She hugged Thea tight, stepped back and smiled with tenderness. "I hope I'm not overstepping here, but Felix told me about your mother. I want you to know that whenever I was upset as a child, and even in later years, my grandmother used to say to me in Spanish, 'This bruise will heal soon with my love and care.' And so will your bruise, sweet girl. My Felix will—"

"Mami! Too much." Felix draped an arm around his mother, who was shorter than him by at least five inches.

"Olivia, give the girl a break," his father said with his head buried in the fridge.

Thea could have stayed in this strange woman's embrace for an eternity, and Felix laughed self-consciously. "I told you, there's plenty of her to go around."

Thea squeezed his mother's hand in return. "Thank you, Mrs. Lind. I can't tell you how much that means to me."

Felix seemed eager to get to dinner and he rushed her out onto the sidewalk, the music inspiring a giddiness inside them as they walked down a side street to the small main strip of Amagansett. "They're wonderful," Thea said, imagining how easy it would be to attend Sunday dinners at his house. To watch his mother paint. To talk to her.

"I knew you'd like them." Felix grazed her fingertips as they walked. "Why does it feel like we've known each other forever?"

There *was* an ease between them, a familiarity. And yet, Thea wanted to know more of him. All of him.

Under the fluorescent lights of the pizza place, they laughed after ordering, because Dylan's "Visions of Johanna" was on the radio. It was the last song they'd heard before they left Felix's house, both of them declaring it the best song Dylan had ever written. They loved the harmonica in the song, wondered what Dylan was really saying when he talked about the ladies playing blindman's bluff—what he was talking about at all in the unusual lyrics.

This is amazing, Thea thought. They each lifted a greasy slice off a paper plate, biting into it. She wanted to come back to this pizzeria every night of the week. Nothing had ever tasted so good.

Chapter Nineteen

"Every time I look at you, you're smiling," said Shelly. The store was empty of patrons that August morning, and even quieter than usual since Margot had off today and Jay was picking up a collection of albums from an estate sale. Thea and Felix had gone out two more times since their first date and she felt lit by a hundred light bulbs.

"It's like we are the only two people in the world." She'd been so giddy that she filled an entire sketchbook with drawings. A boy and a girl, simple lines of summer, nothing that could capture how breathless she'd felt when they had that slice of late-night pizza. She'd also finished three sketches for Margot's mother, dropping them off with her last night; the newspaper woman thanked Thea with an encouraging smile, saying she would review them with her editors in the office on Monday.

Shelly ashed her cigarette into a ceramic dish made to look like a tiny record. "I remember that feeling." On the turntable was a record by Simon & Garfunkel. The soft voices of the singers drew out every little detail of the night in her mind: how the edges of her body glowed when his grazed against her, the way he opened his mouth with surprise when he laughed at something she said.

Thea spun in the sack-style dress she had sewed at Margot's house. She wouldn't have worn something so modern—with its bold geometric print (and imperfect seams)—even a month ago, but now the style, which could be seen every weekend on American Bandstand, gave her the sense that she was stepping out of one version of herself and into another. She couldn't afford the white ankle booties that Margot had suggested pairing with the dress, so she had put on wedge sandals she had in her closet. "I want this feeling to last forever."

For the millionth time since last week, she thought of how the music, the intimacy, and the conversation of the nights with Felix had unlocked even more doors into her creative self. How much she suddenly wanted to draw sketches of the record shop, a close-up of the East Hampton windmill, her sister sleeping in her twin bed. A cartoon strip came to her, too. Not a traditional comic, but a farce, one that follows two hippy friends, young women working at a Manhattan corporation, and the scenes that emerge when they collide with strait-laced middle America. She showed the storyboards she'd drawn to Shelly, and while her boss flipped through, Thea gauged her reaction, how Shelly tapped on one of the squares with a chuckle when one of the women wore a belly shirt to a boardroom meeting, the company president asking the room: "Can someone tell me what's going on?" A scared-looking vice president standing up and saying: "The advertiser said we need to *understand* them."

Thea wasn't sure it was even funny. "It's my first try, but I was thinking that each week the women would get closer to their full potential, forcing the stiff corporate executives to take them seriously, mirroring this tension between our parents' generation and ours."

"You have to get Margot to show her mother this." Shelly handed her back the storyboards, and Thea slipped them back into her tote bag, thinking that it seemed like a good possibility. If Julianna Lazure liked her floral-designed Dear Virgie logo, with the serious-looking block print lettering, maybe she'd be open to seeing more from her.

At the end of the day, feeling brave from Shelly's input, Thea decided she'd draft a letter to the local newspaper as well and include some of her drawings. *Why not*, she thought. It had become her motto.

"See you Monday," Thea told Shelly, the shop bell dinging as she walked outside to the bike rack. She hadn't even pulled it out to ride when Shelly stuck her head out the door.

"It's Margot on the line. She's hysterical and wants you to stop by."

Thea balanced over the center of the bike. "What's wrong?"

Shelly seemed concerned. "Something about her parents."

With a knowing look, Thea said, "Typical." Then she hurried back into the shop and borrowed a copy of an old record by Buddy Holly with the song "Everyday" on the flip. The song always made Margot happy when they put it on at the shop; maybe it would cheer her up today.

After a fifteen-minute ride, Thea dropped her tote bag on one of the pool loungers in the backyard of Margot's house. The housekeeper had sent her here to wait, and Margot eventually emerged from the kitchen doors in a cream satin kimono, her hair pinned into a bun with two chopsticks. There were large red rings around her eyes, her nose the color of fire. She plopped down next to Thea, her cheeks stained with tears.

"Did you see the news?"

"What news?" Thea pulled the Buddy Holly album out of her tote, handing it to her. "I brought you this, by the way. I thought it would help cheer you up."

"Those bastards at the *New York Daily Mirror*." She glared through her watery eyes. "They put this awful photo of my parents in the paper, my mother looking like she might bite my father's head off, and another picture of Dad and Alexandra McKinnon looking all happy. With the headline: 'Media Mogul's Divorce Shakes Industry.'"

Bringing the record, Thea thought, was a bad idea; this was beyond the realm of something fixable with music. "Well, is it true? About your dad leaving?"

Margot wiped her nose against the gauzy sleeve of her robe. "Does it matter?"

"Yes it matters. A hurtful headline is different from your family actually falling apart."

Margot rubbed her foot back and forth on the smooth surround of the pool. "Daddy didn't come out last weekend, which is odd because he comes every weekend. He didn't come last night, either. Mother said he was in Washington covering the protests. He is—I saw his report on television. But *she* was there too. I saw them on TV together."

"What does your mother have to say about all this?" She shuddered, imagining poor Mrs. Lazure picking up the newspaper that morning and discovering her husband's betrayal, along with the rest of Manhattan.

"She lied to me. Apparently, Daddy filed for divorce just after Memorial Day. They were waiting for the 'right moment' to tell me."

"Really? That's awful of them to keep you out of the loop like that. Didn't they realize how it would hurt you?"

"I don't know. Maybe they didn't think the papers would cover it." Margot tied her hands together at her back. "But there's more. My mother said she's selling the house. This house."

"Oh, Margot," Thea said, an image of her friend packing up her sewing machine, her stack of fabrics and album covers. "You love it out here."

"Want to know the irony of it all? My father bought this house to apologize for a previous affair. Mother was going to leave him, but he said they'd start anew in a house by the sea. We had this one incredible summer. I was fourteen, and we did everything, just the three of us. I remember sitting on the kitchen counter and watching my parents coo over each other as they cooked these grand French-style meals from Julia Child's cookbook. But he's done it to her so many times since. Of course it's with that dumb television reporter, as if she cares that he has a *family*."

"Maybe your father will keep the house for you."

"He doesn't care about this house either. He'll buy something else out here, probably with his *new girlfriend*. I bet he already bought her an engagement ring."

Thea couldn't imagine living in a house purchased as a promise of enduring love, but then witnessing yourself falling *out of love*. There would be emotional triggers in every corner. "But you have another home, an apartment, in the city, right? Someday you can buy your own house out here. We can be neighbors."

Margot brightened through her tears. They walked the perimeter of the yard, the salt pond flat and glassy in the distance. "This house is my happy place where I keep my horses and swim. Where we celebrate Christmas in winter and my birthday in springtime."

Thea could relate. As much as she hated living at Dale's, it was still a place where she could see her mother everywhere.

Thea glanced toward the Walrus's cottage to their right. He was outside in a button-down work shirt, golden-skinned, hair pulled in a low ponytail, carrying a weed trimmer through the yard. He waved at them, his teeth straight and white. They waved back. "But this house isn't everything. You said it yourself. There's a great big world out there. Remember, we're going to go see it."

Margot took Thea's hands. "That's the thing, Thea. About our move to California. I want to leave this week, tomorrow even. I need to get out of here." They traveled beyond the rose garden with the large statue of an angel, a vast amount of lawn before they'd step onto the thin slip of sand.

"But what about him," Thea said, nodding back at the Walrus behind them. She was stalling. Thea couldn't leave tomorrow. She wasn't ready. They'd agreed they would go the first week in September, once Cara was back in school, once Shelly and Jay settled into the shoulder season. It was only the first week in August.

"Maybe he'll follow me out there so we can play music, I don't know," Margot said, turning around and walking backward so she could see him again. "Anyway, I can't be here anymore and I can't move in with him in the maintenance shed. That's where I draw the line."

"Thank goodness you said that." Thea exhaled. She didn't want him following them to California, either. The idea of Margot ending up with the groundskeeper felt like something akin to her throwing her life away. No matter what Margot saw in the Walrus, whether she was looking for a daddy or a deft musical partner, Thea knew they weren't right for each other. Still, she couldn't leave now simply to get Margot away from him. Thea had to be selfish, even if her friend was in distress and she was asking her to endure it. For her own personal timeline. "There has to be a friend you can stay with?"

"Not unless I can stay with you," Margot said, shaking her head, then burying her face in her hands. "The house is going on the market tomorrow, and I don't want to be here when movers pack up all my childhood memories and seal them into boxes. To think, just last week, I thought I was having the best summer of my life."

Thea felt the same. July had turned to August with so many possibilities opening up for her. She'd started drawing artwork to sell in California, compiling elaborate drawings of animals along with funny snippets of what was going through their heads. Her illustration for the newspaper advice column could be chosen by Julianna Lazure the following week. Thea had a glamorous new friend in Margot, and she had a plan to leave East Hampton. She was moving to the West Coast. Shelly hadn't even laughed when Thea said she might want to be an illustrator—maybe even an animator—and under her encouragement, Thea decided she'd visit the library to research art schools she might attend in San Francisco, if she made enough money to pay her way.

Then there was Felix, the nicest guy she'd ever met.

Still, happiness could vanish in an instant, and when it did, Thea knew how unsteady it felt.

"The way you feel right now is temporary." Thea attempted to sound wise. "It will make you stronger. Hardship always makes us stronger."

Margot waved her off. "I don't care about being strong."

As empathetic as she was, Thea knew she wouldn't leave tomorrow. How would she explain her sudden departure to Felix?

They'd circled the yard and returned to the pool, both of them sitting in loungers. Thea stared into the bottom of the water. "It's just too soon for me."

Margot glared at her. "But I can't stay here."

Thea wished then that the pool was an ocean, that a big wave would sweep her out to sea. What she hadn't told Margot, what she couldn't admit out loud, is that every night this week she had gone to bed with her stomach clenched in knots so tight it felt like a sailor tied them. She couldn't shake her unease with Margot's character. Did Margot even have an inner compass? Even with their cross-country route outlined in that road atlas they found in Margot's parents' library bureau, would they ever get to Chicago or Denver or San Francisco without drama following?

Thea knew that Margot genuinely cared for her. Giving her the opportunity to try her hand at the Dear Virgie logo was practically philanthropic. But moving up their trip seemed too convenient. Margot would be on the other side of the country before anyone questioned her more seriously about the missing jewelry. By the time investigators landed on her powerful mother's doorstep, Julianna Lazure would be ready to shut down any lines of inquiry.

"I'm sorry. I can't go, Margot," Thea said. "Not tomorrow."

She flicked her eyes back to Thea, the mascara making a mess of her face. "You can bring Felix. It's fine."

Thea was instantly irritated at what Margot was inferring. She sighed, then pulled gently at the hummingbird locket with her fingertips. "It's not that I don't want to go. You know that."

Even with her doubts, Thea cared about Margot too much. But it was true that the timing of meeting Felix *had* been lousy. Leaving to go to California meant leaving behind the possibility of him. What if he was her one chance at romantic love? If Thea just had a few more weeks to explore her feelings for him, she would know whether or not leaving him behind would be the biggest mistake of her life. Thea continued: "I know you're upset about your parents, and rightly so—but I can't turn my life upside down because you need me to. I still have responsibilities."

Margot wrapped herself tighter in her kimono. "You and your responsibilities. You hate those responsibilities, and no one is making you stay but *you*."

Again, it was true. Thea could march home, pack her bags in a jiffy, and drive off into the sunset with Margot tomorrow. But she wouldn't do that to Cara. While Cara knew Thea planned to take a trip, Thea had presented it as something happening in the far-off future—not an absence as close as tomorrow. "Can you give me at least two weeks? I'll try to be ready by mid-August."

"Fine." Margot rose off the lounger and crossed her arms, her white-blond eyebrows arching into sharp mountain peaks. "But you should know that these next couple weeks will be the hardest of my life, and I'll always blame you for making me live through it."

Thea woke up in her bed the next morning, panicked that she'd over-slept. She threw on shorts, buttoned up a floral blouse, and rushed down to cook breakfast. In the kitchen, she found Dale wiping Cara's nose, her eyes red, her father rubbing her back. There were four empty cereal bowls in the sink, juice glasses cleared from the table.

"We were just talking about some changes around here," Dale said. "Becky is going to move in here with her son."

"But we don't have the room," Thea protested, shooting her sister a look. Cara ran from the table into Thea's arms. Outside the kitchen window Thea could see Becky. Her son tossed her a football, the woman catching the pigskin and throwing it back.

"We'll make the room." Dale screwed the cap on the orange juice and pushed it away from him, like the discussion was closed, too.

"How could you do this, Daddy?" Cara wailed, and Thea hugged her sister tight while Dale stared out the kitchen window, sighing.

I can't leave now—I can't leave ever, Thea thought to herself, even as she knew with all of her being that she had to get out of this house, too.

Chapter Twenty

July 1977

As Thea steered her station wagon along the dirt road up to Eothen in Montauk, she was struck by the fact that there wasn't one house on the artist's compound. There were six. One main house—with white planking and white shutters—that sat atop the cliff overlooking the ocean, and five small matching cottages around it. Today was cooler than it had been earlier in July, the ocean whitecapped and rough, and Thea was happy she'd chosen her white button-down blouse and denim bell-bottoms. After she parked the car, uncertain which house to approach to find the woman who had called her on the phone, Thea checked her teeth in the mirror. No food bits. Then she applied lipstick, a pale peach that wouldn't stand out too much. She wiped it off with a tissue from her glove box and tried a brighter pink instead. She regretted it immediately, quickly dabbing it off and reapplying the peach color.

Thea emerged from her car into the salt air, her long hair blowing about her face. For a second, she considered driving back home where Margot waited; her friend had practically forced her to come to the interview today. She and Margot had stayed up late on the patio last night talking about how Thea wanted to pursue her creative side, what types of art she'd always loved, why it was so scary to put yourself out there. Thea told Margot that while she wanted to meet Andy Warhol, she worried he'd think her drawings too amateur. "At least see what the job is about," Margot had pleaded, her arm feeling better on her steady diet of aspirin. "You know when you go to a hotel and you try out being a different person for a day? Well, that's what you're doing."

The interview had seemed easier to pull off with Felix in the city; she didn't tell him anything about the potential job before he left early that morning. She wasn't sure she'd even get it. Inhaling the crisp ocean air, Thea tucked the portfolio she threw together under her arm. It contained a few of her newer drawings, nothing remarkable, and the realization made her feel like an imposter standing there. Still, she let herself wonder if this job could turn into something worthwhile. An apprenticeship, maybe. Something from her wildest dreams. Maybe she could start out as an assistant and soon enough be helping Mr. Warhol.

Don't get ahead of yourself, Thea thought, walking away from her car so she might slow her thoughts. It wasn't as though she could really work anyway, since she only had free time when Penny was at camp or school, Dale couldn't babysit very often, and she doubted the pay would be enough to cover a sitter.

Footsteps sounded on the white pebbled driveway, and Thea shielded her eyes from the sun, smiling at a woman in her midtwenties wearing a denim jumpsuit and flip-flops.

"You must be Thea Lind," the woman said with a thick New York accent. "I'm Cecelia. I'm helping out here this summer."

"Nice to meet you." Thea had the sense that someone was watching her, as though she was going to get caught doing something she was not supposed to, but when she turned around, there was no one there. "Thank you for having me today."

Thea followed Cecelia into one of the small cottages, and they sat at a simple kitchen table with expansive views of the turbulent ocean. Cecelia explained that their last housekeeper had just left, and they needed someone to grocery shop, keep the houses clean, cook, and restock art supplies. Lately, Andy had been interested in painting animals, she said, and sometimes Thea's job would be to walk the dogs in between shoots.

All the excitement and anticipation building inside Thea fell flat, like she was a tire and she'd just rolled over a nail.

"Oh, I thought you said I needed some drawing experience," Thea said. The job was no different from what she did every day at home, except now she'd be doing it for someone else. She didn't know if that would be better or worse. Worse, she supposed.

"Andy likes when his staff has some interest in art. It weeds out the nonbelievers."

"That makes sense," Thea said, her swallow deafening in the quiet.

"Okay, Andy will see you now," Cecelia said, and she walked Thea to another one of the cottages on the estate. This one wasn't as bright as the last one, and Warhol was standing on a large ream of unfurled white paper, wearing a purple velvet blazer and petting a Jack Russell terrier. He didn't turn around, and the dog must have been old because it didn't react to Thea's arrival. Cecelia let Warhol know that Thea was there, talking to him as though she was afraid she was interrupting him, and Thea waited near the doorway, gripping her folder of drawings. She wished she could dump them back in her car.

There were shelves piled with books, a human skull on a table next to a tufted armchair, a large picture window looking out over the same swirling seas. When he didn't say anything, Thea said: "Hello, Mr. Warhol. My name is Thea Lind. I'm here to talk to you about the job." Cecelia excused herself.

From the back, Warhol's hair reminded her of Margot's—short and white blond—and when he talked, his cadence was slow and deliberate, utterly strange. "Do you know anywhere out here to find caviar? I'm having a craving these days. Spaghetti with caviar."

Thea cleared her throat, staring at his unfinished painting. A small dog with canoes for eyes on a photograph, paint streaks right on top of it. To think that she was one of the first people in the world seeing this artwork, that she could be at a gallery someday, staring at the finished version on a wall, bragging to everyone around that she'd seen it when it was in its earliest form, the beginning of something incredible.

"Caviar? Maybe at the specialty food shop in Southampton." Thea said. "I go there when I need anchovies."

But she wasn't thinking of fetching him caviar or doing his laundry or wiping down his kitchen counters. She was thinking of herself. She was thinking how different her life could have been if she'd actually gone to art school. When Felix was finishing graduate school in the city, she'd taken a few classes at Pratt, but she had gotten so immersed in helping Felix become an editor. Then they'd wanted a child. Art was something that Thea always said she'd come back to but never did. If she had kept up with those classes, she might have been standing there with one of the greatest painters of all time for a reason other than doing his laundry.

The studio smelled of turpentine and oil paint. "Are you punctual? Will you come Saturday and Sunday mornings to pick up after our parties? Of course, you're always invited to the parties too." Warhol still hadn't turned around, and it was strange having a conversation with his back. The man seemed more interested in putting the animal at ease than her. Thea stepped closer to him, wanting to see the painting up close. She couldn't come on weekends, and as much as she was in awe of being around this man, she didn't want to clean up after his good time. Coming into the studio had inspired her to reconsider her choices in an instant. Thea's restlessness suddenly made sense to her.

She fidgeted with her denim belt loops to keep her hands from touching the dried brush strokes covering the canvas, wanting to feel the layers of texture, bending in close to see the colors blend and separate.

In the clarity of that moment, Thea wanted to reclaim herself. It wasn't that she wished she was famous. What she aspired to was something she might see in the supermarket or record store, a bookshop or a clothing sign. Commercial art—designing album covers or illustrating books, drawings that a newspaper features editor asked her to draw, an image that told a story. She was a long way off from doing it. Years, even. But just having the goal made her aware of how badly she'd wanted it all along.

There was a hot feeling in her body, like she was on the verge of a fever. She needed to go.

"I'm sorry to waste your time, Mr. Warhol, but I didn't realize you were looking for a housekeeper. I do enough housekeeping at home." Thea turned to leave.

That night, she called Felix in his hotel room in Manhattan. He always stayed in a modest boardinghouse near Washington Square because he preferred being near NYU and it was cheaper than the soulless Midtown options anyway. Thea was happy he picked up on the first ring; he was often early to bed when he was in the city, the sheer number of people alone exhausted him. During their city years, he'd often refer to himself as a "country mouse."

"How is Penny?" he asked. A cab honked in the background.

"She insisted on painting my fingernails tonight." And Margot's, too. They had become fast friends, Penny giggling at all the stories Margot was telling her about Thea when she was younger. *One time after work we stuffed pillows under our shirts and walked down the road pretending to be pregnant* . . .

Thea could hear the smile in Felix's voice when he said, "That's our girl."

She asked about the manuscript he was working on with the legendary thriller writer Arthur Willens. After rising in the ranks and leaving Doubleday, Felix had landed a job with a small Sag Harbor publishing house that specialized in fiction. The publishing house was a vanity project of his wealthy boss, a finance titan who retired early in East Hampton and decided he wanted to publish the next great American novel. Felix had thrived there, determined to acquire bigger name writers, like Willens.

"He's impossible," he said, and Thea could tell by the phone's staticky background that he was cleaning his glasses with the phone tucked under his chin. "The guy thinks winning a literary prize makes him immune from critique, but he could do better. Much better."

I could do better. Thea pressed her eyes shut, leaning against the frame of the living room doorway. There was so much she wanted to share with

him about just how much had shifted inside her since leaving Andy Warhol's estate earlier, but she didn't know where to begin. She didn't know
how he'd react, and it was strange feeling uncomfortable talking to Felix,
who was truly her best friend. Still, this new mindset, this new side of
herself, made her feel like she and her husband were on a first date.

"I miss you," she heard herself saying. Through the window, Thea
could see Margot outside on the dock. She did that sometimes after
Penny was asleep—lowered herself down with one arm onto the slats,
staring out into the blue nothingness at dusk. "When are you coming
home?"

She knew the answer: this Wednesday, so he could be home the rest
of the week. She didn't want to hide any of this from him anymore. She
would tell him everything, all the uneven thoughts churning inside her.

"I miss you too." He yawned, and she imagined him lying on a
scratchy polyester quilt wearing his beloved Ramones T-shirt and blue
cotton sleep shorts.

"Remember that time you and I were the only ones on the train
home from the city after Ronkonkoma, and we hid under our coats and
couldn't stop kissing?" He'd slid his hand into her skirt and they had
made out as if they couldn't care less if their train crashed straight into
the ocean.

His voice sounded deeper. "I miss those days."

"I do too." Thea blushed saying it aloud. These days she would prefer making out in the comfort of their bed. Still, Thea knew that it was
spontaneity that made life fun. She hated that Felix no longer wrote
her love notes, that in the aisles of the grocery store it was *easy* to keep
their hands off each other. That they talked more of Penny than they did
of their own connection. This was why women read so many of those
trashy romance novels, she thought. Everyone wanted more love, more
fun, more spontaneity in their lives, even if they'd forgotten how to find
it. She wouldn't turn to the books. She would turn to herself. To her
husband.

She paced the kitchen, stretching the phone cord. "There is something on my mind."

His pencil scratched at paper; he was probably marking up a manuscript as they spoke. "What is it?"

Thea sprayed her counter with cleaner, wiping it with a sponge, even
though it was already clean. "I was thinking. Maybe I could start drawing again and try to get work as an artist."

"Wow, Thea. Wow. That's great news." He seemed giddy. "You could
approach Sally Maye at the *Star*, I bet she'd give you a chance."

She hadn't expected this response. "Really? But what about having
a second baby?"

He sounded confused. "Well, just because you're drawing again
doesn't mean we can't have another child. Right?"

Thea bit her tongue. If she got pregnant, if she had a newborn in her
arms, she would definitely not be asking Sally Maye to give her a chance
at the *Star*. Plus, she had bigger ideas. She would have to tell him about
those, too, someday. "Right," she said softly.

On Tuesday afternoon, Thea called her sister and asked her for advice,
pulling the phone into the coat closet when she picked up. *If you're playing the role of someone who is trying to be convincing, to get someone to do
something big for you, what do you say?*

Cara crunched on celery sticks, dipping them in peanut butter, her
favorite: "You start by being very clear. Don't beat around the bush."

"But what if they get upset or angry?"

"Then you should reiterate why what you're saying is important,
how it may benefit you both. Thea, what is this about?"

Thea shared her realizations about art and Felix and her life, but
after the part of the story where she snubbed Andy Warhol, Cara
sounded only sad. "Is that really how you feel? That you've never had a
chance to take care of yourself?"

"No," Thea soothed her sister, realizing her mistake, and she tried to
backpedal. "You're missing the point. The stuff with Warhol was *funny*."
But Cara still tried to assuage her own guilt for the rest of the conversation.

"I hope I'm not a burden on you from out here?" Cara said. "I try not to be."

"You are my sister, Cara. I'm as much of a burden on you as you are on me. That's what love is, remember?"

Her sister half-heartedly agreed. "Be kind to Felix, though. I think he may be shocked by what you're about to tell him."

"I told him some of it already. He seemed happy."

"But when you say you want everything to change, it can feel like you're saying 'I don't love you anymore.'"

"It's not just my feelings I'm dealing with, you're right. You know I love you, Cara." A swirl of nerves tornadoed through Thea's body as they said goodbye. Thea stumbled out of the coat closet, stepping back into the light to find Margot staring at her quizzically.

"Do you always talk on the phone in there?"

Thea readjusted her shorts, smiling at Penny, who smiled back. "Just when I speak to Cara."

Margot laughed. She began to bounce from one foot to the other with excitement. "Penny and I have a surprise for you."

Thea wasn't sure she needed any more surprises. Still, Margot and Penny led her through the kitchen to the back door, turning every couple of seconds to make sure Thea was following as they stepped from one gray slate slab stone to the next, until they were at the barn. "Close your eyes," Margot said, leading Thea by the hand up the old tractor ramp and inside. Thea smelled the white oak of the barn walls, sensed the plankboard flooring underfoot. Margot walked her toward the back corner of the structure, and as they approached, Thea felt the sunlight brightening through her eyelids because of the window there. Penny giggled.

"Okay, now you can look."

Thea fluttered her eyes open, first glimpsing Margot's broad smile, then noticing what Penny was pointing at. In an area under the window, Margot had rearranged a pretty braided rug and positioned a rectangular, yellow-painted table on top, a simple white lamp to one corner. A wooden chair Thea recognized from her basement was tucked neatly underneath. On the table were a row of Mason jars, one with pastel pencils, another with charcoal and graphite versions, and the last one with erasers, an Elmer's glue, and tiny knives with which to cut paper. There was an oversized tapestry of a sunburst, each beam a different color, that had been nailed up behind the table for decoration.

Thea's mouth fell open and her heart swelled. *Her very own workspace.* She heard herself stutter: "Th-This is for me?"

"Of course it's for you. I figured if you were going to take your art seriously, you needed a serious room to work out of." On one wall Margot had positioned a bookshelf, lining up Thea's records and turntable as well as neat stacks of paper in various surfaces and sizes. This was all for *her.*

"How did you do this with a bad arm?" Happy tears rolled down Thea's cheeks while Bee wagged her tail, flicking her with it. "Where did you get this stuff?"

"I helped!" Penny said.

Margot's eyes were shining. "I hit up a couple of yard sales with Shelly and she took me to get art supplies and helped me carry things. Can you believe I found you a yellow worktable? The color is said to inspire creativity."

Penny was sitting in the chair.

"Honey, can I sit down?" Thea gently shooed her little girl off, sitting at the desk. She ran her palms along its smooth surface, thinking about how lovely it would be to put on the Beatles, spread her supplies out, and create.

Margot rested a hand on the top of her shoulder, and it sent a warm glow of connection through Thea's body.

"I hope you like it," Margot said.

"I can't stop smiling. Thank you." Thea stood and hugged Margot tightly. Then she kissed Penny on the cheek.

Margot had her flaws, but at her core, she was a good person, and there were times when she was a very good friend.

*   *   *

Finally, it was Wednesday. After Thea dropped Penny at camp, straightened up the house, showered, and blow-dried her hair to mimic the waves of Farrah Fawcett, she pulled into a parking spot in front of the American Hotel in Sag Harbor. Felix had traveled back from the city that morning, heading straight to work without stopping home. She hadn't come to see him at work since the first year they lived here, back when Thea was pregnant, and they would sometimes eat club sandwiches at a local diner. Once Penny was born, who had time for leisurely lunches mid-week?

Penny. Thea had nearly given up her dreams of becoming an illustrator, just as her mother had given up her dreams of becoming an actress to have Thea. It made her think about all the women who wanted things when they were young, only to realize they'd never have them as they grew older. This heartbreak that women suffered. It was no wonder that all of her mom friends talked about how they couldn't sleep, why they popped those little "happy" pills. They were haunted by their wants. Thea wanted to know what they thought their adult lives would look like when they were younger, how they had pictured themselves before they were forced into a great reimagining.

The offices of the publishing house where Felix worked were a few doors down from the National Hotel, housed in a brick building that didn't look all that different from the others on the street. She stepped inside the glossy mahogany double doors, greeting the office's secretary, and traveled up the gray carpeted steps. Felix looked up at her from a stack of pages when she knocked on the door. He stood to give her a kiss, then returned to his seat. "Is everything okay?"

"More than okay," she said. She needed to tell him about Margot, but first, there was this. "It's just, I was hoping that we could take a walk."

Felix looked down at the stack of pages on his desk, and she relaxed when he made a note in one of the margins, then placed down his pencil and stood. "Sure," he said, pushing his hair off his forehead, just like he did when she'd watched him at the record shop the very first day she had seen him. "Where do you want to go?"

"Just around town."

When they were on the sidewalk, Felix turned to her.

"You have me worried sick. What's wrong?"

Thea continued down the sidewalk with him. "I met Andy Warhol the other day," she said.

Confusion knitted his brow, then a smile. "What? How?"

She told him that she had applied for a job in the Classifieds that she thought it was an assistant job but was really more for a house-keeper. Then she shared the realization she'd had while standing there, the urge to better herself. "I don't want to doodle in a notebook, Felix. I'm talking about enrolling in classes in the city, and it's too far to com-mute, so I was thinking we might live there for a while. You could cer-tainly find work in publishing, and I could find someone to take me under their wing in the art world. What I'm talking about, Fe, is really going after something."

"Hold on. Slow down." He paused, shaking off what she had said with a frustrated pivot of the head. "But Penny? Her school. We can't just uproot her."

"You said you were happy for me to be drawing again."

She could see the way Felix struggled to keep up with her. "But the city? Where is this even coming from?"

Margot. That's where it had come from. But her arrival, that she was here, was a bigger conversation. The dreaded one. As they passed the movie theater, Thea breathed in the smell of buttery popcorn, a line of children ready for a matinee. "It's just that Penny is getting older."

"Penny is six! She's a little girl."

"I know, but she's not a baby anymore. It's given me time to see things. Holes."

Children. It was the sticking point between them. How could Thea think of anyone else but Penny? For Thea, it was why she'd been so blinded these last few years. There hadn't been anything else she wanted to be doing than raising her daughter, or if there was, she'd been too tired to see it. Of course, Penny would always be her priority, but she needed Penny to be Felix's priority, too. They'd started their relationship so equitably, but somehow their relationship had crept into the same old traditional gender stereotypes of decades past. It made her think of the editorial Gloria Steinem had published in the *New York Times* years before: "The first problem for all of us, men and women, is not to learn, but to unlearn."

That's what she and Felix would need to do to move forward. They would need to unlearn whatever roles they'd fallen into. She just wasn't so sure she'd be able to convince him to do it.

They walked to the small beach at the end of town, the two of them sitting on the sand, staring out at the sea. Over the quiet lap of the water, Thea said: "Remember early on in our relationship? We tried surfing in Ditch Plains, and when we laid on the beach blanket afterward, I told you that I loved to draw, and you said—I never forgot this—you said, 'Then you need to draw for the rest of your life.'"

"We weren't married then, Thea. We didn't have a child." Felix's eyes narrowed on something in the distance. "Why haven't you talked to me about this before? I need time to figure out how I feel too."

"It's just that I was afraid if I didn't act quickly, if I didn't tell you this, I might keep it inside me forever."

His voice was as tender as a bruise. "Well, I can't just leave, I can't just quit my job."

There were smooth stones on the small beach all around her, and Thea picked one up, gliding her thumbprint along the soft contours. "But you have more than the house, more than Penny. Why can't I have more, too?" She lobbed a rock at the water.

"That's not what I'm saying," he said.

But wasn't it? How did he have no idea how unhappy she'd been? Perhaps he only saw what he wanted to see. It was partly why she had gotten angry after they'd gone berry picking recently. "You should make a blueberry tart," he had told her. An innocent remark, she knew, and yet—why couldn't he announce *he* was making *her* a blueberry tart?

Felix pulled his knees in toward his chest; he looked young and uncertain. "I've done everything for you, Thea, and now I feel like you're giving it all back. Telling me, 'Thank you, but it's time to move on.'"

"I'm not moving on from you, Fe. I love you. I'm just raising a simple question: Will you follow me this time?"

Felix's wedding ring shone in the sunlight. A simple band. He wore
it everywhere, even in the shower, even while he slept. He had been
a good husband, a good father, and she could see she'd hurt him. She
wished she could hear his thoughts right now, what he was yelling in his
mind, because she needed to know what she was up against.

"I do want a second baby, maybe someday, but not now," she said,
breathless, almost to defend herself from whatever he said next.

"But you want to move to the city? And have us live in a tiny apartment? Do you even hear yourself? It's so irresponsible."

My mother was never irresponsible, Thea thought. Her mother used
to laugh at herself when she made a mistake. She would dish out com-
pliments; she'd say she was sorry if she yelled too loud. When Thea gave
birth to Penny, she vowed she'd never do anything to hurt her, and for a
long time, Thea had fantasized about having many little bodies to love
and care for, to mold in all the ways that her mother missed out on
molding her. There had been a hole in her heart, she could see that now.
But Felix and Penny had filled it.

Penny. As if Penny wasn't Thea's everything. His accusation filled her
with so much anger, years of resentment building like the pile of sand
she'd been collecting at her feet. "I've done nothing better in my life
than have Penny, and you know it. I've counted my greatest victory that
you wanted to marry me. We've created a beautiful life. But life can
change. It can take new shapes and forms, and it doesn't mean I'll love
you any less."

Thea stood up, facing the sea, and waited for him to say something.
But he only mumbled that he had to get back to work.

Brushing sand off his feet, he said, "You can't just wake up one day
and decide you want our entire life to be different."

"You're not hearing me," she said. "I don't want everything to be
different. I just need me to be different."

He shrugged, pushed his hands in his pocket. "But I don't really
want us to change."

"Oh, Felix. That's not fair." Her eyes searched his for what exactly he meant, if he wanted her to shelve her discontent entirely or if he was simply disappointed that she felt that way at all. He strode off, and Thea collapsed back down against the sand. She stared up at the cornflower sky, watching the watery clouds paint streaks overhead. How fast the atmosphere moved sometimes, she thought, and yet, how slow the earth spun.

Thea imagined lying in this spot for the rest of the summer, the world creeping by as she remained perfectly still, and nothing changed at all.

Chapter Twenty-One

Monarchs flitted around the tall, purple plumes of butterfly bushes lining the patio while Bee chewed on a stick near the picnic table. Penny and Margot played with Barbies on a blanket in the grass while Thea finished up dinner in the kitchen, checking the clock every few minutes.

It was inevitable that Felix's arrival home would only make things worse. She'd have to tell him about Margot being here. She'd have to tell him right now, in fact, since Felix's car was pulling into the driveway. After turning off the burner and draining the potatoes, Thea slipped out the front door, rushing down the white porch steps to the driveway. He was rolling up his window while Thea waited at the driver's-side door. She nibbled her cuticle, eager for him to step out of the car.

"We need to talk," she said.

Felix bent into the back seat to grab a stack of papers. "I'm so tired, Thea, and I'm sorry for my reaction earlier. But I don't think I can handle any more today."

"I know the timing is bad, but there's something important, something I didn't tell you earlier. Not about me. Well, it is about me, but . . ." Thea tucked her hair behind each of her ears, her eyes caked with liner and eyeshadow and mascara, anything to hide how much she'd been crying. "Remember Margot?"

Felix's forehead wrinkled. He leaned down to give Bee a quick pet. "Margot the Mess? I meant to tell you I saw something in the news about her."

At some point, Felix had nicknamed Margot to make Thea feel better. But now, with Margot playing in the backyard with their daughter, it felt particularly unkind. "Yes, that Margot. She's here."

Felix had only known Margot a few weeks back then, and he'd spent the better part of that long-ago autumn convincing his then-girlfriend Thea to move on from their friendship. He didn't really have anything against Margot, other than that she'd hurt the woman he'd fallen in love with.

Felix drew his head back, glanced up at the house. "Thea, isn't she in some kind of trouble?" It was taking everything Thea had not to wrap her arms around his neck and kiss him. To apologize for everything. The regret she'd felt after admitting those deeply guarded emotions seemed worse, and now standing there with the one man she'd ever loved, she had never felt more alone.

"Yes, and I didn't know how much at first. I was happy to see her, but things have spun out of control and we're trying to figure out how to get her somewhere safe."

It was half-true, but mostly, it was another lie. "Thea, you haven't seen her in years, and you just said yes? You didn't tell me she was here?"

Thea's gaze flicked upward. It was hard to look at him. "You would do the same if Eddie or Mike came to the house."

"But after she hurt you?" From where they stood, they could hear Penny and Margot giggling like schoolgirls, and Felix reached out to touch her cheek softly with his fingertips, like he might lean down to kiss her. "There were probably ten people she called who said no before she called you."

"That's rather cruel," Thea said. She took a step away from him, plucking a mulberry leaf off the bush.

The squeak of the front door announced Penny's arrival onto the front porch, Margot following close behind. Felix waved like he was saying hello to a stranger, and Margot smiled, gripping her lame arm across her chest like she was wrapping a sweater tighter.

"Daddy!" Penny bounded down the steps, jumping into her father's arms.

"She has nowhere else to go," Thea said to him through gritted teeth as they walked toward the house.

"Everyone has somewhere else, especially her," Felix hissed back. He lifted his daughter, flying her through the air like an airplane. "I missed you, kiddo," he said louder.

The tension subsided later when Felix, always a gentleman, brought two gin and tonics to the outdoor picnic table, handing one to Margot as they stood and made chitchat.

"What happened to your arm?" Felix inquired.

Margot sipped her cocktail, her voice cautious. "I took a rather unfortunate spill back in the city."

Standing at the kitchen counter inside, Thea mixed hard at the potato salad, smashing the potatoes more than she needed to, beating the mayonnaise in with a wooden spoon. She'd spent the latter part of the day in her new art studio, a blank page in front of her, her pencil doing nothing but sketching the spiraling feelings in her head. At some point, she'd given up, and she and Margot went down to the loungers at the small beach out back while Penny splashed in the shallow water. Margot thought Thea had done the right thing telling Felix how she felt, but that only made Thea take her husband's side: "All these years, I haven't shared my true feelings with him. I expected him to read my mind, and now he has no idea where I'm coming from."

Margot hadn't seemed convinced. "I bet Felix knew how you felt all along. It's easier to assume everything is peachy than dig around in your wife's heart for the truth. You know what I realized last night, Thea? That Willy blamed *me* for his cheating. Can you imagine? He said that my desire to have a baby consumed me too much. Well, if that was the case, then how come he didn't ever try to make me feel better?"

Why couldn't Margot see what seemed so clear to Thea? "Because maybe Willy didn't know how to comfort you. Maybe you were out of reach—and maybe Felix didn't know how to bring me back either."

She plated the barbecue chicken and potato salad in the kitchen now, calling out to Penny to help her carry the dishes outside to Felix and Margot. Thea had made Felix's favorite summer dinner in the hopes that it would placate him. Something would have to.

There had to be a middle road for them. The more she'd thought about it, the more Thea believed that she'd been too quick to get angry with Felix this morning. She'd talked about babies and art school and uprooting their lives, but she could see now that she'd only briefly touched on what she really wanted, which was the freedom to evolve.

Music. Thea needed to put on casual dinner music to put everyone, or maybe just herself, at ease. "Penny Lane" by The Beatles. That would cheer them up. She positioned the speaker in the kitchen window so they could hear it on the patio.

From the minute she and Felix met, she hadn't asked him for anything she was asking for now: to be her cheerleader rather than her provider. She hadn't asked him to support her in going back to college or to encourage her to take charge of her passive friendships. She had only asked him to love her, to give her a steady place in this world—a place far away from the pain of losing her mother, of her lonesome stepfather, of her needy sister—even if it was a mere mile down the road. That had been enough for her—until now. Even if Felix did have an inkling that she was dissatisfied all along, as Margot had suggested, he had never stopped her from doing the things she wanted. She had stopped herself.

It shouldn't have mattered, either, if Felix had asked Thea for so much more. The gift of her time, her innermost spark, the attention necessary to run a happy household. She'd wanted to give it to him. But what she'd been trying to say this morning—what she'd failed to express— was that he had started to treat her like a bank with an unlimited number of checks to cash. The dynamic of their marriage had worked for Felix—what incentive did he have to change? And she wouldn't *make* him change that much—just enough to allow her to grow.

In an instant, Margot sailed into the kitchen. "There's a cop car outside," she said, dumping her cocktail into the sink. Thea instructed her to go to the third-floor bedroom to hide in the crawl space behind the moving panel in the closet.

Penny. Thea turned on the television, singing to Penny that she could watch . . . *Little House on the Prairie* . . . it was on right now. And then it was Felix who stood in the kitchen, his hands on his hips, the crease in his forehead again.

"Thea? What is going on? Penny said that she and Margot have been having sleepovers all week."

Thea wrapped her arms around her husband's neck, pleading with him to go along with whatever she said as they heard the officer's footsteps on the gravel driveway. "I told you. I'm helping a friend. Just nod along."

His arms didn't return the embrace. "Thea!"

She pushed open the screened front door to step onto the front porch, Bee wagging her tail and barking at the stranger. It was Josh Barley, her old friend from high school. Since she had known him in his early days on the local force, he had risen up the ranks to captain.

His badge caught the fading sun. "Hi Thea. Sorry to show up like this."

"Hi Josh." She pretended to be interested in picking up two dice Penny left on the step while saying, "Don't tell me you're trying to recruit Penny to the boys' baseball team?" Josh managed some of the local Little League teams. Thea had taken Penny to some of the boys' games, wishing they had a league for girls.

The cop laughed. Felix popped out onto the porch, and he and the officer made small talk about how hot the summer had been. *Your footsteps need to be slow and measured,* Thea thought. In her head, Thea said a silent prayer that Penny didn't come outside during a commercial. That Felix didn't give something away.

Josh leaned against the white column. "Remember that rich summer friend of yours? The one you worked with at the record store years ago. Margot Lazure?"

A prop plane flew overhead, and Thea's heart beat faster than its puttering engine; she wished it could swoop down and pick her up, take her to some isolated stretch of sand and leave her there. "We had a fall-ing out years ago. It was sad, really. We had been very close."

Felix pegged her with his espresso eyes, and Thea wasn't certain what she'd done wrong. Was her voice trembling? Had she said too much? She assumed cops were trained to pick up on body language, too, so she unhooked her arms, dropping her hands to her sides. That didn't feel right either, so she rested her hands on her hips. *Stop fidgeting!*

"Well, I got a call from the feds in Manhattan. Apparently, her husband worked with some bogus investment firm who has been taking money from restauranteurs and doubling the returns, allowing them to borrow against what looked like big money, but they were fudging the numbers. Half the accounts were made up. Anyway, he went missing and so did your friend." Josh had no reason to suspect Thea had done anything wrong. No one who knew her would categorize Thea as a rule breaker, and she would use that to her advantage.

"We always did call her Margot the Mess," Felix laughed, clapping the officer on the back.

Thea pretended she didn't hear him. "Is Margot okay? Did some-thing happen?"

Cops always had pin-straight pants, as Josh's were, and Thea won-dered if his wife ironed them, if she watched game shows to pass the time as the steam hissed near her face, if she dreaded a chore like that, wishing she was doing anything else. "Hard to say, but it seems like it all comes back to her husband. They want to see what she knew and when."

Nerves propelled Thea up. She went to the side of the porch and leaned over to pick hydrangea to put in a vase. Out of the corner of her eye, she saw a shift of light in the attic window, but when she looked up, there was no one there. "Huh. She hasn't telephoned, if that's what you're asking." It wasn't a lie. She had shown up on a boat. They'd sunk it. She had nearly died.

The officer snorted. "Didn't think so, but let me know if she turns up. When I went to her father's house in Southampton, he told me he hadn't spoken to her in years. Rotten kid."

Thea could smell the noxious mud flats of low tide. The boat. Had a portion of Margot's father's sailboat washed up on shore? Would someone discover scraps of the bow's wooden planks and confirm that she'd been on these shores? "Do you need a picture of her? I probably have one around."

"Nah," said Josh. "But Midge mentioned she saw a woman here. That she'd driven up to drop off a racquet, and there was someone on the dock?"

Heat flashed up Thea's neck, but when she looked up, Josh's expression only seemed curious, not suspicious. "Maybe she saw our babysitter? You know Midge, she's always so good at stirring the pot."

That made the officer hoot. Midge did have a reputation.

Felix walked the officer to the squad car. "But listen, on another note, I have an idea. You want to start a men's softball league? I've been talking to Peter Triller about it."

A men's softball league. Brilliant, Felix. He didn't even like baseball. He said he found it the slowest sport in the world, and here he was hatching plans for a league to distract Josh Barley from taking a look around their house. Midge! Why would she tell Josh there was a strange woman here?

It seemed an eternity that the two men talked in the driveway, but when the officer heard something on his CB radio, he jumped in the car and peeled out.

She handed Felix a plate when he came into the kitchen. "Thank you for that," she said.

Felix didn't even glance at the food. He put the plate on the counter, then rested his hands on Thea's shoulders. "This isn't going to end well," he said.

Her nerves were frayed, too, and she knew that Felix was upset, but why believe it would go bad? The cop said that they weren't certain about Margot's complicity in the Ponzi scheme. Besides, selling the gold bars she'd taken from her family's safety deposit box hadn't done anything to prove, legally, that she was guilty either. Thea felt relieved knowing that it was Margot's husband that was the true bad guy.

"I'm very sorry. I shouldn't have come." Margot entered the small kitchen, her lower lip red and puffy where she'd been biting it. "I didn't think anyone would look here."

"And no one has found you, either," Thea said. "It's okay. There's no need to worry."

"Of course there's reason to worry," Felix yelled, loud enough that Penny ran in from the living room, hiding her face in Thea's middle. "We just lied to the police."

"I'll be out of here tonight." Margot hurried out the back door, scurrying across the lawn to the barn, and Penny began to cry, perhaps from the big emotions of the adults. After rocking Penny and calming her, the three of them sat down for dinner, Penny and Felix polishing off the barbecue chicken. Thea didn't take a single bite. Later, after Penny was bathed and sleeping, Thea and Felix met in their bedroom, laying on their backs on the coverlet. Both of them stared at the threadlike crack snaking across the ceiling. *They had a lot to fix, didn't they?*

"How long has she been here?" Felix whispered.

"She sailed here the night of my party. Do you remember seeing that boat in the harbor?" Thea could guess his next question: Why hadn't she told him that Margot was there? She kept talking. "I didn't tell you because she was so scared that someone was coming to hurt her, and I was still trying to figure out what was even happening. You were in the city, and I was lonely, and I'd missed her, Felix. You know how much that whole thing with her hurt."

Felix blew at the hair stuck to his forehead. Their room didn't have air-conditioning and while Thea preferred it that way, Felix needed a fan moving cool air around him at all times. "There's only one reason someone doesn't want to be found, Thea. You know that, right? Because she's guilty of something."

Thea didn't want to fight. She didn't have it in her after their tense conversation on the beach. "Some days I hate that Margot showed up here and put this on me, but mostly, I've just been grateful to see her. This might sound crazy, but being with her has restored a piece of myself that went missing when she did."

He rolled onto his side, talking like someone waiting on a line that wasn't moving fast enough. "Nothing about you went missing."

The only way to feel closer to him, Thea thought, would be to come back to him, just as Shelly suggested. "Felix," she said, rubbing the chest of his Ramones T-shirt while gazing up at him. "So much of what we have here is all I ever wanted. You and I built this life together. But I lied to you these last couple of weeks because hiding Margot gave me something that was just mine, too. The way you have your authors."

He opened his eyes to her—he was truly listening, so she continued. "Somewhere in these last few years, between the diaper changes and Christmas eggnogs and conversations about your work, I just let myself melt into you. Do you know that I realized the other day that I only buy ice cream flavors you and Penny like? I just eat your favorite flavors to keep you both happy."

He rolled away from her onto his back, lowering his hand off the bed to pet Bee. "You hid a possible fugitive in our house, Thea. Stop shortchanging the situation."

In the distance, the buoy bell sounded, a chime that lulled Thea to sleep nearly every night. She listened to its predictable rhythm, trying to figure out which direction the wind was blowing, while watching the rise and fall of Felix's back, waiting for him to say something. Anything.

"I can see what you're saying about putting yourself aside for me. It's been hard to admit that to myself, that I had some part in your unhappiness, but I can see it." He moved to turn off his bedside light, one of the chinoiserie, ginger-jar-style lamps she'd found at an estate sale. When she'd positioned them in their room a few years ago, Felix had said: "They look like something from Miss Havisham's house." *Well, then they're perfect*, she'd laughed, since *Great Expectations* was his favorite novel.

His brow furrowed now. "But what I can't see, Thea, is how you can decide overnight that we should move to the city and you're going to art school. Don't you think that's a conversation, not a proclamation? And the lying? It's so confusing. I'm so utterly confused."

Thea wiped at the corners of her eyes. "So that's it? You'll never forgive me for this?"

Felix sat up in the dark, his back up against the pillows. "Our daughter knew Margot was here before I did. Our daughter kept a secret from me. I'm not dismissing you, Thea. I'm just realizing how much you've been dismissing me."

He waited a beat, then got up and turned on the oscillating fan. He fell hard back into bed. "And Margot needs to go, or I'll call the feds myself."

Chapter Twenty-Two

August 1967

The next time that Thea rode her bike past Margot's house there was a "FOR SALE" sign in the front yard. Margot was supposed to come to work that day, but when she didn't show, Thea called her from the counter at Sunshine Records. Margot's voice sounded strained when she came to the phone, like someone was listening. It wasn't her mother. She'd returned to the city on Sunday night but planned to return that Wednesday to help pack through the weekend, Margot complained.

"I'm going through my closet and organizing everything because the movers are coming end of the week," Margot said, sighing. "I'm putting a few things aside for you, like that trench coat you love."

"Thanks." Thea felt funny, though, about taking Margot's castoffs.

After work, she rode home and collapsed onto the couch, turning on the television. Dread turned her muscles achy as she thought about leaving, mostly because she'd have to tell her sister soon. Then there was Dale, whose van had just pulled into the driveway; she glanced outside to check if Becky was in the passenger seat. It was empty.

On Becky's first night in the house, Cara had refused to eat dinner with the woman's son, and in a show of solidarity, Thea had joined her in the backyard. Now Thea couldn't go anywhere in the house without bumping into items belonging to the two interlopers: the woman's jacket draped over a chair, the boy's Hot Wheels on the living room floor, like the house was no longer Thea's or her sister's.

Dale barely waved hello to Thea from the kitchen. Leaning against the doorframe, he cleared his throat, like he did whenever he had something to say. There was the sound of applause coming from the TV, a game show Thea didn't care about. "Becky told me about the trip you're planning," he said.

Thea hadn't purposely kept it from him; she just hadn't known how to tell him. Instead she'd mentioned her plans to Becky in passing at breakfast the other day, knowing that it would get back to Dale. "I'm not even sure I'm going anymore," she said, uncertain of his reaction. Dale couldn't really tell her not to go—she was old enough to make her own choices—and yet she wanted his approval, even if she didn't know why.

He shifted his weight to his other leather work boot, crossing his arms over his polyester uniform, his voice competing against the murmurs of the television. "She'll be okay without you, you know?"

Surprise rushed through her, that Dale knew she was worried about leaving, that he'd even noticed. "Like I said, I don't know if I'm going anywhere." It was a lie. An utter lie. Thea was going. *She had to go.*

"This last year, you've done more than your fair share around here," he said. Dale wiped away an invisible milk mustache. "What I'm saying is. Cara is *my* girl. She's yours too, of course. But you can check up on her. Even from there."

Thea nodded, and Dale nodded back like he'd been given an order, before patting the wall and excusing himself. He went into the bathroom, the sound of the shower emanating from behind the closed door. On the television, a woman on the game show won a power boat, and Thea jumped up, a bouncy feeling inside her, too.

In promising to take care of Cara, Dale had given her permission to go. She only needed to break the news to her sister. She and Margot were leaving together.

But first. First, Thea wanted to make sure that Margot hadn't invited the Walrus on the trip. She'd hinted as much the last time they'd spoken, and Thea needed to be clear: she wouldn't drive across the country in the same car as him. After leaving Dale a note on the kitchen table while her sister played Manhunt with neighborhood kids, Thea escaped into the humid night, crickets trilling, and walked toward Margot's. In her right hand she carried a flashlight, the fading beam illuminating the sandy roadway. Gosh, how she'd miss these trees when she left—the towering elms formed a canopy over her head and she'd started to feel like they were trusted elders guiding her to a better place. They kept her company now as her footsteps were the only sounds in range.

There was thundering rock music coming from Margot's backyard as Thea walked under the arbor, jubilant voices at the pool. Hurrying past the familiar marble Venus de Milo replica, then a line of shrubs blinking with fireflies, Jim Morrison's voice got louder, crackling on a stereo speaker. Thea rounded the bend, and when the garden opened up to the pool, it was Margot that Thea saw first.

She was completely nude. There were subtle sunburn lines where her bikini normally rested, her alabaster skin even more fair on the smooth of her stomach, a brown triangle between her legs. It was not her nakedness that alarmed Thea so much as the way Margot twirled around, smiling at nothing in particular. She nearly teetered into the pool, then regained her balance, laughing. Someone out of view grabbed her elbow, a man stepping into the pool lights. The Walrus. All six feet of him. He wasn't wearing any clothes either, his chestnut hair swinging about his neck, and he looked magnificent standing there in his chiseled nakedness. For a moment Thea considered what it would be like to draw a man like him, his muscles as defined as a Michelangelo sculpture. He held Margot's hands around his waist and kissed her, his white backside gleaming in the moonlight.

She couldn't watch. Thea inhaled sharply and spun on her feet, rushing along the daisy-lined path and out of the arbor before hearing a thud, then more strained laughter. *Oh no*, Thea thought. *She must be on something.* All along she'd been afraid that Margot would interrupt their trip to California with a trip of an entirely different kind. Thea grumbled to the trees. *Look! She was already doing it.* Then she narrowed her anger on the Walrus. What had he given her?

She would go home and call Felix. Earlier, he'd phoned the record shop to apologize for not calling since their last date. His mother had been in a fender bender, and while she was okay, he'd taken her to the hospital, then the auto body shop. He asked if he could pick Thea up tomorrow at nine and take her to the arcade in Sag Harbor.

Halfway around Margot's circular driveway, rushing home now, Thea fantasized about driving her friend away from all this, even if only for the night.

That's when she heard a woman scream, a yell so hysterical that Thea was reminded of someone being pushed in front of a subway car or falling off a cliff. She wished the housekeeper was still in the house, that she wasn't entirely alone going back there.

Thea turned back, running under the arbor and past the sculpture, into the open grass of Margot's backyard. The couple were on a lounger now, the Walrus on top of Margot, her straight blond hair strewn out across the plastic slats.

"What are you doing? Get off me!" Margot yelled. She tried to push herself up, smiling at him like she was trying to be polite, but the Walrus pinned her back down. Margot's face wrinkled with frustration, and she tried to clamber out from under him.

"Shawn, STOP, you're hurting my back. I—" The Walrus pinned Margot's shoulders down with his hands, leaning against her, and they talked quietly like that a moment. Margot whipped her head from side to side while trying to use her abdominals to propel herself up, but without effect. He was too big. Too strong.

"You told me you'd help me," he yelled.

Margot heaved against him, her middle barely lifting an inch off the chair. "I already gave you so much. I'm not a bank, and the plan was to give that money to those who need it. You agreed."

"Maybe *I* need it." His voice cut through the music. "As soon as this house sells, I'm out of a job." He finally let up on her, and when Margot scooted away from him, he glared at her from the opposite side of the lounge chair. Margot rushed to put on a geometric print dress she'd discarded on the ground.

"Say you'll give it to me," he said in a tone that frightened Thea.

Margot buttoned the top of her dress. "I can't believe I thought I was falling in love with you."

The Walrus rose, taking a few steps closer to her on the patio. "Say. You'll. Give it to me."

Margot remained silent, turning away from him. She walked in the direction of her house like she didn't have to answer him at all.

All at once, the Walrus rushed after her, yanking her to face him. He clapped Margot so hard across the cheek that it sounded like thunder.

"I hate you," Margot screamed. A splat of blood oozed from her left cheek. She lunged at him, but the Walrus threw her back against the ground. His foot pressed down on her chest.

"Where is the money?" he barked.

Thea looked around for a weapon. There was an outdoor tool shed close to where she was hiding, and Thea slinked over so she couldn't be seen opening the door. A leaf blower. Lounge chairs. She snatched up a beach umbrella, the sharp spiral point of the pole enough to do some damage. On her way out, she tripped. *Faster. Move faster,* she scolded herself. Thea came up behind him, the Walrus aware that Margot registered someone in view. When he turned, Thea aimed the umbrella pole at his throat like a trident. Thea could no longer feel her toes, her arms, her hands; she didn't feel like she was anywhere in her body when she ordered: "Leave. Her. ALONE."

The man took a step forward, without shame of his naked form, his lip curling like this was one big joke. "You want to join the party, baby girl? I've been asking Margot to invite you."

"I've already called the police," Thea said with a shudder.

He moved to grab the umbrella, but Thea backed away, moved quickly to his right, and anger flashed in his eyes.

"Thea, it's okay. I can handle him." With his foot off her chest, Margot flew to Thea's side.

The Walrus took a step toward them, a suggestive grin on his face. He still hadn't reached for his pants and seemed to enjoy making Thea uncomfortable, pushing out his lower half for her to see.

"With you playing guitar now, the three of us should form a band out in San Francisco," the Walrus leered, striding toward Thea like they were old friends. "It would certainly give us all a reason to spend time together."

Thea backed up, nodding in the direction of his small house on the property like she was in charge, but when she spoke, her voice came out quiet and powerless. "You need to go now."

He grabbed the umbrella out of her hands, tossing it into the grass like a child's plastic sword. Her wrists were in his grip in an instant. She closed her eyes to the heat of his breath on her cheeks, listening to Margot sobbing. Margot pounded her fists against his back, but the Walrus used his shoulder to knock Margot away. Somehow, he'd pinned Thea to the damp grass, her hands locked down on either side of her head, but even as she twisted and turned her body away from him, the Walrus was too overpowering.

"You smell nice, like baby powder," he said.

Thea's stomach turned like she'd eaten a dead fish.

He would not. She wouldn't let him.

His comment ignited an anger inside her, and she pulled harder to escape, kneeing him, wriggling out from under him, and rising. She ran a few paces before he tackled her back down to the ground. If Margot was still there, Thea couldn't hear her or see her. It made Thea sad to think that she'd risked everything to stop the Walrus from hurting Margot, but where was Margot when Thea needed her?

Thea's chest hit hard into the earth and at first, she didn't realize that he was reaching his hand around her body and into the front of her dress. He tugged at her breast, and she squeezed her eyes shut. She should fight harder, and yet every time she moved under him, he gripped her tighter. The wet grass spread a damp spot on her belly, and her mind went black when he pushed her legs apart with his hand. She squirmed them closed before he did it again. Thea worked to remember her mother's face. She hoped if she just imagined her mother, none of it would hurt. That she could pretend she was merely tucked inside her mother's embrace. But then his penis rubbed up against the outer walls of her underwear and she screamed as loud as she'd ever screamed in her life.

Suddenly the vice loosened and she could breathe again, blinking through glassy eyes to see him staggering away from her, blood spewing down his head. He pressed his palm to the top of his skull. Margot gripped a large rock in her right hand over her shoulder, poised to hit him once more. He winced before lunging at her.

"I won't let you hurt her," Margot cried, snot slipping down her lips, her soft features distorted with panic, and Thea saw that she hadn't lowered the rock. She'd lured him toward her. It would give Thea time to run inside, to call the police, to end this night once and for all. Thea attempted to sprint, a burning sensation in her chest, but it was like one of those dreams where her feet wouldn't go fast enough. She turned back toward the pool, choking on her breath.

Even from here, she smelled the chlorine, how it mixed with the stale smell of fertilizer and blood.

Margot raised the rock higher like a hammer, slamming it on the Walrus's hunched form. He tried to gain his footing, getting upright for a second before staggering to one side. His body fell against the side of the pool.

"Margot, NO!" Thea screamed.

Margot stood over him, huffing, while Thea hurried to the pool, and now she was beside her friend, who had fallen against her in a tight ball. The Walrus was splayed out on the patio, one of his legs dangling in the pool, his head and torso lying on the gray stone. Thea had seen his head slam against the cement trim, just beside the aluminum ladder into the deep end. She'd seen Margot smash his forehead with a rock.

Thea's pulse skittered, and she grabbed Margot's hand. They ran inside her house, sliding the door shut and locking it. They clung to each other, and after a few seconds, Thea whispered: "Do you think he's dead?"

Margot bit her nail so far down that it was bleeding. She opened the sliding door. They moved stealthily toward the body, afraid that he might sit up and chase after them again. Once they were next to his long naked legs, black hair from his navel to his neck, Thea could see the blood. First from the cut on the back of his head where Margot hit him the first time, then a smaller gash on his hairline from the second. But it was the dark puddle gathering under his right ear that alarmed Thea most.

Thea clenched her jaw so tight it felt like her teeth might snap. "Margot? What did you do?"

"Nothing. He, he, he was hurting you."

"I thought you loved him, but how could you love someone like that?" Thea bent down and raised the Walrus's wrist while Margot bit deep into her cuticles, staring at the unmoving form by her bare feet.

"I don't know. He kept slamming me down and I thought it might get worse, that he might . . . and then you came, and I couldn't watch . . ."

"I know." Thea positioned her finger against the spot on his wrist where his pulse should be. No beat pushing blood through his veins, no breath causing the rise and fall of his chest.

It was self-defense, of course it was, but what did that mean for two young women? Wouldn't the police have questions for them—namely, why was the man naked? A frown would certainly cross the officers faces as they deemed both women loose.

Margot sunk down onto her knees. "Oh my god. Oh my god."

The umbrella pole was on the ground. Had Thea hit him with it? She couldn't remember now. "All I did was try to get him off you at first."

"He was just so strong," Margot whispered. "If I didn't hit hard, it may have been worse."

Then Thea began to cry. How would she tell Cara that she was going to prison? How would she explain what happened in a way that Cara wouldn't believe she was capable of awful things? It was an accident, they'd tell the police. He'd tried to hurt them; he'd tried to rape her. She would have never pushed him, but then . . . it had been unthinkable.

A car passed by, and Thea worried it was Margot's mother, who was set to arrive later that night, but it never slowed.

"We have to get rid of him," Margot said. She attempted to drag the Walrus by the hand, but his body was leaden. It was like trying to move a thick rubber mat.

"We can't get rid of him. It's bad enough that we've killed him. He has a family!"

"He has no one." Margot wiped her cheeks clean. "You hear me. He has no one." Margot strode off to the gardener's shed. She pulled it open, stepped inside, and there was clanking. Things being moved. She emerged pushing a wheelbarrow. "Come on, help me get him in."

They would drag him into a wheelbarrow and dump him somewhere that no one could find him. *Of course they'd be caught*, Thea thought. She was definitely going to jail for murder, and she'd never even been able to kill a spider. But no one would know that. They would hear the facts, and she'd be found guilty. "Come on!" Margot screamed at her, her sobriety snapping to attention. "Help me."

Using their body weight to lift him under his shoulders, the women grunted as they attempted to inch him toward the night sky. But he might as well have been a whale.

Headlights flashed through the front windows of the house. Margot's mother. "God dammit. She isn't supposed to be here until eleven. Stay here."

Staggering to the edge of the lawn, Thea vomited into a hydrangea bush, her mind a jumble.

There were sounds at every corner of the yard, shadows stretching across her sneakers as night set in. Thea feared that the Walrus would come back to life, like a zombie from a horror film. Women's voices came toward her, talking, yelling. Thea squinted, making out the silhouettes of Margot and her mother. Heading straight toward her and the Walrus.

"I-I have no idea how it happened, Mommy. I s-swear," Margot stuttered. "We got home from a bonfire and he was here. Dead in the pool."

Julianna Lazure marched across the patio like she wasn't sure what she'd find, and when she stopped, taking in the scene of the naked man, her nostrils flared. She turned her beady eyes toward Thea and her rumpled dress, her dirt-caked knees, frowning.

"Is that right, Thea? You just found him here?"

The woman emitted a statuesque calm, projecting her confidence with as much weight as the gold in the chain links of her austere necklace.

Thea worked to steady her voice. "Yes, Mrs. Lazure. We got here a few minutes ago, and he was . . . here."

Julianna stared a beat too long at Thea. She crossed her delicate arms across her chest and noted the wheelbarrow positioned beside the body. After a long pause, the only sound the rapid rise and fall of their breathing, Margot's mother turned and walked toward the house.

Margot shot Thea a questioning look, and it was then that she could see how puffy Margot's eyes were, how her cheeks were hollowed out with fear. "We did find him here, didn't we?" Margot said, searching Thea's expression to see how far she'd go to protect this secret.

There was a tingling in Thea's scalp. "Yes, we did."

Margot's mother marched back outside carrying a wet washcloth and duffle bag. "Come here, girls," she said. She dabbed at the dirt on Margot's clavicle, washed at her hands, scrubbing at her muddy fingernails. "You will need to change your clothes before I call the police. Brush your hair. You too, Thea. I want you to fill this bag with everything you wore tonight, then put rocks in it. You will drive to the marina and haul it on your father's boat. You will drive the boat as deep out into the water as you can get, and you will dump it. You will take the rock with the blood on it too."

The words made Thea flinch. Had they been so stupid to think she hadn't noticed the large rock next to the body? But she was willing to rewrite their reality right then and there. Julianna motioned for Thea to stand in front of her. Her breath smelled of red wine. Had Julianna gone inside and guzzled a glass?

Margot's mother scrubbed awkwardly at Thea's dirty cheeks, like they were children coming off the playground. It was uncomfortable having this woman wipe at her face, and yet what power did Thea have at that moment other than to submit? When Julianna was finished, she pressed the rag into Thea's hand, pointing at her knees, and Thea began to scrub her own legs.

Julianna's voice didn't rise or fall; it was as though she was telling them something insignificant. "Make sure you park the wheelbarrow back into the shed and fix the order of the loungers. I will call the police once you go. I will say that I found our maintenance man unresponsive at the pool when I arrived, and that some of my jewelry was missing, too. You will not talk to police. You will not mention that you were here. You will never speak of this night again."

Margot collapsed against her mother, who steeled her fisted hands by her sides. "This is awful, Mommy. Just awful."

She didn't respond. Instead, her mother addressed Thea, making Thea feel even more wobbly. "There will be an investigation, but I'll be sure it is short. If police question you, you say: we were out on the boat to watch the sun set. We started to gossip about boys and lost track of time. You play the dumb little girl. Police will write you off almost immediately. Understand?"

Thea would not mess this up, even though she felt dazed, a survivor of a plane crash she had helped cause. "I do."

Julianna never did ask who struck the killing blow, and she never did return Margot's embrace. Instead, the glamorous newspaper woman, still dressed in a tan pantsuit, removed her daughter's hands from her waist. "Good night, girls. Enjoy your boat ride."

She turned her back on them. They watched her saunter in the house—her job was complete—and Thea rolled the wheelbarrow into the shed, while Margot changed her clothes by the pool house. Thea lined up the loungers. Had one of the most respected journalists in the entire country decided to lie to police to protect her daughter? Margot always said her mother didn't love her, but there it was, right there for Margot to see. Her mother didn't think twice about taking on the murder of a man to help her daughter avoid ruin. Or maybe it was about avoiding headlines.

The ten-minute drive to the marina passed in a blur, the boat rattling to a start in the tar black night when Margot turned the key. She backed the boat away from the creaking dock, turning toward the mouth of the sea, its small headlight casting a square of light ahead.

With a subtle rev of the engine, Margot drove the boat straight into the Gardiners Bay.

Of course Margot's mother should be the one to tell police that she'd found the Walrus. They'd believe her. She wouldn't be involved with a grifter who had stolen from her—and had the gall to use her pool! But as they sped farther from shore, Thea wasn't sure they were doing the right thing. It had all happened so fast. Now they were indebted to one another, a lifetime of obligation to keep a secret that would allow both of them to come out in one piece.

Salty tears ran into Thea's mouth. "We should go back and tell your mother the truth. That he attacked us. That we needed to protect ourselves. She can explain that to police."

"NO." Margot slapped her with her words. "We have to listen to her, Thea. We will do what she said."

The boat zipped across the sea now, and Thea couldn't catch her breath with all the salt air blowing into her mouth. "Margot, you didn't have to get him off me. You could have called the police. He might still be alive."

There was no regret in Margot's voice. "He deserved what he got."

They dropped anchor far from shore where the water was choppy. Thea heaved the duffle bag of their belongings over the side. The white-trimmed bag floated a moment before slowly sinking to bottom.

Then Margot turned the boat around. As the speedboat neared the shore, Margot at the helm, a police boat stopped them for no reason other than they were the only boat out at this time of night. An officer shined a flashlight in their faces in the dark, both women squinting their eyes to see. That they were in the same harbor as the police awakened Thea to how different her life would be now. How she'd have to live with the fact that she'd watched her best friend kill a man, and Thea had helped hide her crimes.

Margot pretended to have lost her way, and somehow, she convinced the cops to let them follow their boat back to Three Mile Harbor. Then they moored in the deeper part of the inlet, letting the boat drift in the gentle waves for a couple of hours. At midnight, when they finally parked at the marina's dock, they climbed back into the car, shivering on the drive home to Margot's.

Thea was so cold on the walk home that she couldn't feel her fingertips. At some point, she crawled into bed, and in the morning, she didn't remember getting home at all. The night before pounded in her mind like a hangover she would never be rid of. And still, she rose early that morning like it was any other day, so as not to arouse suspicion. She went to work and talked to Shelly about music and she helped a customer find an album by the Byrds. She called Felix and canceled their date, saying she was too tired. They agreed to meet in a few nights.

"Margot was having a meltdown about her house, and she made me go out on her boat and we lost track of time." Thea hoped to God that he'd give her another chance.

"Rain check for Sunday?" he said, a tinge of vulnerability in his voice. "I promised my mother I'd go to the city with her Friday to Saturday."

She wavered at the thought of facing him, even if she never told him what transpired.

"I can't wait," she said.

Trudging up the steps to her attic bedroom, Thea crawled into bed with her sister, the springs squeaking as she lay down beside her. Sharing the narrow twin wasn't the comfort Thea hoped for, though, and she fell asleep only after settling on a thought that offered more solace than family.

Perhaps Thea could live with this secret simply by pretending that there was no secret at all.

Chapter Twenty-Three

July 1977

Margot didn't leave the next morning. It was Felix who announced his departure. He decided to return to Manhattan after office hours that day to work on the novel with his famed author. While it was quite possible that Felix had to report to meetings in the city through the weekend—he'd been there on and off the last few weeks—Thea had also intuited that Felix needed some separation from her, from this unruly situation. So into his garment bag went four dress shirts. Thea saw the shirts as a deadline. She had four days to get Margot out.

"But you just got home, Daddy," Penny said, hugging his leg at the entrance to her camp's summer carnival day.

He kneeled so he was eye level with her. "Don't worry. I'll be back in a jiffy." She hugged her father, then ran off to join one of her counselors.

Thea drove Felix to the train station, and as the car idled near the train tracks, he didn't kiss her goodbye like he had every single other time he'd left. "Please think about what I said last night," Thea had pleaded, leaning over the gearshift to hug him. He kept his hands in his lap until she pulled away. Then he took off his glasses, rubbed his eyes, slipped them back on: "I might not be the perfect husband, I can see that now. But I have never lied to you. Not once."

In a small voice, Thea said, "You did lie, that time you told me you were taking Penny to your mother's but you went—"

"To the mall to buy your birthday present. That wasn't a lie." He laughed, his familiar dimple loosening the knot in her chest, and she smiled back at him.

"I knew I could make you laugh."

It was unlike Felix to hold a grudge, but they had never been in a fight this big. She held his hand. "Listen, I'm sorry, but you know when you feel like you have to listen to that voice inside you, and after you do, all you want to do is take it back?" She grasped for a better way to say it. "Like when John Lennon said he wished he didn't release 'Run for Your Life' on *Rubber Soul*. Felix. I regret all of it. Taking in Margot. Lying. Saying I want to live in New York."

"'Run For Your Life' is a good song." Despite the tension, that made her laugh now, too, and he glanced at her over the leather messenger bag on his lap, with the beginning of another smile. It felt like an olive branch, since that song had always inspired a friendly debate between them. Thea had hated the lyrics, while Felix saw promise in its guitar riffs.

"You shouldn't want to take it back, Thea—those are your feelings and now you need to stand by them. My mother always said, 'If you feel it, say it.' It was just really hard to hear." He pushed at the passenger door to open it, shaking his head. "Honestly, I need more time to think this through, but what I want most is Margot gone. She's trouble."

The chambers of her nose began to burn, like she might cry, even as her heart swelled at the possibility of Felix's forgiveness. "I will. I'll have her gone before you get home. Promise."

An elderly man in a bow tie opened the wooden train station doors for Felix, and he'd turned around before going in, watching her drive away. She wanted to blow him a kiss, to yell she was sorry through her open window, but instead she waved, nodding, like she knew what she had to do and she planned to do it.

Home. A very hot shower. Letting her hair dry in the sun. Blasting the Rolling Stones. Fearing that Margot's husband would never come for her. She hadn't seen Margot leave the barn yet, but she had an idea about where she should go next. Thea couldn't believe she hadn't thought of it before. Amtrak. Margot could ride the passenger rail to Florida and get off at some pretty seaside town to wait. When she offered up the idea later that day, Margot wrinkled her nose.

"Well, we have to come up with something to get you out of here!" Thea grabbed her sketchbook, doodling spirals on the page, unable to hold in her frustration any longer.

Her friend pressed her face into her hands. "I know. I'm thinking Oregon. I just don't know how to get there yet."

Oregon, Thea thought. That meant she still didn't have a plan at all.

On Saturday morning, Thea braided Penny's hair and dropped her off at a friend's house to play. It was a good day to catch up on house work, Thea thought. She stopped at the market to pick up fresh blueberries, pancake mix, slices of ham and bread. After putting away the groceries, she vacuumed and fluffed the couch pillows, changed the bedsheets and wiped out the bathtub, trying to keep her mind off Margot, who was in the barn supposedly planning her escape route. Thea's thinking was interrupted by the sound of the doorbell, and then someone's voice called Thea's name. A familiar voice. Her favorite voice.

It couldn't be.

Cara came through the front door holding a suitcase covered in travel stickers, dropping it beside her flip-flops and running to Thea, who was already running to her, both of them embracing. They took a step back, Thea rummaging through her denim shorts to find a tissue, wiping the corners of her sister's green eyes. Thea's questioning look met with Cara's pleading one. Her face was tired and puffy, and she looked like she might apologize. Thea hugged her sister again, struck, like she always was, by how similar Cara looked to their mother. "What are you doing here?"

"I decided to come home for a while." She was laughing, crying, then laughing again.

"What do you mean, come home?"

Cara let Thea take her suitcase, following her inside to the kitchen. "Home. Here. I missed the East Coast."

Thea positioned the suitcase in the living room by the stairs, spotting Cara's brown Gremlin in the driveway, the one that she and Felix had lent her money to buy a few years ago. It was filled with so much stuff that she couldn't see through the car windows. "Come. I have my sun tea ready. Let's have a glass."

Cara sank into the blue corduroy couch, sipping the iced tea with lemon slices, then yawned. "What a couple of days! I drove straight here." As Thea expressed her shock, the two of them chatted about the endless highways and the truckers who veered into her lane while falling asleep and the strange rest stop in Tennessee where she'd slept in her car. Cara glanced around the living room, her eye springing from the telescope for stargazing to the framed Mary Cassatt print over the bookshelf. "This is what I want, Thea. A home. It's so beautiful here. You know, I think what I had in Los Angeles was a layover."

Thea heard her sister's comment as a bad joke. "A layover? No it wasn't—it was an entirely established life. I hope you're not here because you let some jerk shred your self-esteem."

"It was so many things, actually." Cara was tired of waiting on call-backs that never came. She had to waitress six days a week to pay her bills, so she didn't even go outside all that much. And while she had plenty of friends, they all seemed to be getting married or giving up on acting or moving back home and actually starting real life, not chasing a pretend one. "I'm at a crossroads, I think. Just like you are. Talking to you the other day made me ask myself all the same questions you've been asking."

Thea wrinkled her nose. Gosh, how she regretted being so honest with her sister on the phone earlier that week. "But Cara, you were in a commercial and you had an apartment and you loved it out there. At twenty, you've already lived a hundred times better than I have."

Since she was a little girl, Cara had puckered her lips when she was pouting, and she did it now, sounding petulant. "Thea, you have lived a hundred times better than me. You have people that love you. All I have are people who never call me back."

Cara had never admitted to feeling that lonely before—*but*, Thea thought, *you never really knew a person, did you?* Felix hadn't known about the discontent brewing in Thea, and he slept a foot away from her. "But you were always telling me how much the sun shined, how every single street led to the ocean."

Cara lay back on the couch and closed her eyes. "I know, but I mostly called you on my good days. The other night after we got off the phone I drove up into the Hollywood Hills and parked in this random dirt lot, staring out over the twinkling lights of Los Angeles and smoked a joint. California is beautiful, Thea, and you would love it out there. Mom would have loved it." She sighed. "That night I could see the Santa Ynez Mountains, the illuminated grid of highways, but what I couldn't see in all of it was the reason why I was there. It was Mom that wanted to be an actress, and you who told me I could do it. And I love you for that. I moved there, and I tried. But I heard Mommy's voice up in the Hills the other night. *You don't have to pick up on my dreams, baby doll.* And that's when it hit me. I didn't just inherit Mommy's dream. I inherited yours, too. Mommy's dream of being in Los Angeles, your dream of living somewhere else. I'm not even sure I even had a choice of what to do after high school."

"That was the joint talking." Thea's judgment made Cara roll her eyes.

"Ha, ha. But think about it: Why was I actually there?"

It was as though someone threw a bucket of cold water over Thea's head. Her sister didn't have a choice? Cara had had so many chances to reinvent herself in Los Angeles, to find a life beyond the one she'd been raised in.

Thea could empathize with Felix now.

It was easy to feel betrayed when someone you loved didn't feel the way you thought they did. Thea had done everything to make sure that her sister had what she needed to get a solid start: she'd spotted her the occasional rent, she'd sent her Hallmark cards just because. All this time, she thought her sister had it all, and now, to think that Cara hadn't wanted any of it, Thea felt foolish.

"But you were in every school play, Car. You had your head in TV, and you worked at the movie theater. You were always talking about characters and plot twists, and you can sing."

"I cannot sing," Cara laughed, harder than she needed to. "You should see how the casting director's faces fell when I tried to carry a tune."

"Well, you're a fine actress."

"Maybe," Cara said. "And you're right. I did love acting. But people change, Thea. You told me as much on the phone the other day."

Perhaps the truest way to love someone, Thea thought, staring at her sister lying there, was giving them permission to change on you. "What do you think you want to do?"

"Don't flip out. Okay?" Cara opened her eyes, sitting up like one of those sweet dolls whose eyes fluttered as they switched positions. "I want to get my degree and become a teacher. Kindergarten or first grade. Help kids who struggle with reading, and I want a baby, too, so I guess that means I need a husband."

Thea laughed, and Cara waited on her response. She could tell her sister was worried that Thea wouldn't approve. She scooted closer to Cara and snuggled into her, the way they used to when they were children. Thea would accept Cara as she was, just as Thea wanted Felix to accept her. Plus, it made sense, all of it. Her sister had always wanted to work with children. When she didn't work at the movie theater, she'd worked at a local camp. "And you want to live here?"

"Yes, with Dale at first, until I can get my own house. I always loved Montauk and its little school."

The back door opened, and Cara leaned over to see who it was. Thea sensed her friend's arrival. "Margot? What are you doing here?" Cara said, looking at Thea for reassurance that it was okay. Thea nodded. "We've been catching up. It's been nice." Even though she thought: just what I need, one more person laying eyes on Margot. Would Willy ever call her?

"Oh, hi honey." Margot used her good arm to squeeze Cara tight over the couch. Cara never did forget that magical evening at Margot's pool when the three of them had played Marco Polo. "I heard you're a big Hollywood star these days."

"I'm moving back here, actually."

The conversation between the women beat on, and Thea couldn't believe they were both here. It was Cara and Margot who carried her through the summer after her mother died. It was Cara and Margot who would carry her through now.

On the stereo, Thea lowered the needle onto a Carly Simon album. She had to hear the song, "Haven't Got Time for the Pain." The song was the perfect emotional soundtrack to process the highs and lows of the last twenty-four hours. Just before lunch, when all of them had gone into the kitchen to prepare a chicken salad with leftovers from the other night, Cara said she needed to get something from the car.

The song changed, and Thea popped another slice of bread in the toaster.

"Is everything okay?" Thea asked Margot, noting how fast she was spooning the mayonnaise into the bowl.

Margot lowered the glass jar. "I didn't want to say anything in front of Cara, but he contacted me."

"Willy?"

"Yes, Willy." Margot looked like a racoon caught in a light. "We have this answering machine—it's hooked up to a phone number that he wrote on that note he left me, and I've been calling it occasionally. This morning, the message changed. It's Willy's voice, and he said he was ready. That I should leave my number, and he'd get in touch."

"Will you give him this number?"

"I don't know. Can I?"

"What about a pay phone in town?"

"I can't possibly stand there all day into the night, though."

Thea really didn't want to give Willy her number. "Okay," she said.

As Thea used a knife to lift the chopped chicken to the bowl, Margot put her back to the sink and crossed her arms over her tank, whispering: "He's my husband, Thea, and I love him, and I just know that we're going to be okay."

Thea wasn't so sure.

Chapter Twenty-Four

August 1967

Thea could mostly pretend nothing ever happened the other night, even if her insides rattled like an old car. Margot hadn't shown up to work again and Thea called her once more from the counter at Sunshine Records after lunch, whispering into the phone: "You can't leave me alone like this. I'm terrified someone is going to find out what we did."

"I know, we shouldn't have taken my father's boat out without asking. My mother is furious," Margot said, her words coming out louder than they needed to. "She won't even let me come to work."

Thea was not amused. Margot was skirting the issue. "Will she let you go to a movie with me and Shelly tonight? I need to talk to you."

Margot cut her off. "I can't. I'm too busy packing everything for the move," Margot said, like Thea needed to be packing, too. "I even put aside a bag of peanut butter and crackers for long shifts in the car."

"Okay, great." Thea felt a sinking sense, like she was plunging to the bottom of the ocean. She covered her mouth to muffle her voice: "Should we even still go to California next week?"

Margot groaned. "Of course we're still going."

When Thea hung up the phone, Shelly handed her a stack of records to reshelve, pausing like she was a doctor examining a patient. "Is everything okay? You seem distracted."

Thea alphabetized the albums in a row on the counter so they'd be easier to put away, lowering her voice so the customers couldn't hear her. "Margot is just so devastated about her parents. I'm worried what selling the house might do to her."

She didn't share her bigger worry. What if the two of them packed up the car with their belongings and a secret so big they crumbled under the weight?

With Cara sleeping at a friend's house, Shelly picked Thea up around seven and drove them to see the Bond movie *You Only Live Twice* at the theater in town. Thea was grateful for the distraction but struggled to follow the plot. So much had been going on that she hadn't really had time to process it all. After the movie, Shelly suggested they get milkshakes. They sat on a park bench across the street, Thea chattering away with nerves—what she liked in the movie, the latest shipment of albums at the shop—so Shelly wouldn't notice how fractured she was feeling.

Her plan backfired, though, because as Shelly used a plastic spoon to eat from her strawberry milkshake, she said: "You don't seem very excited about going to San Francisco."

"I am, but I'm beginning to feel like this move is really about Margot." Thea kicked a pebble with her sandal, sipping her egg cream. She guessed Margot would want to get as far away from here as she could now, and Thea probably should, too. But the night with the Walrus had confused her, terrified her, and she wasn't sure she was ready to leave home for good. The world seemed more frightening than it had days ago. The image of the Walrus lying bleeding against the pool popped into her head sometimes, and she'd feel a tremor. "And it's okay if it's about her because I'm just going along for the ride. But it's like even if I didn't want to go, I can't stay here, either."

"Two so-so options, but neither one what you really want." A young couple walked by canoodling, both dressed formally, as though they'd just left a dinner dance. "Thea, you know that I love you both, but here's what I've noticed watching the two of you this summer."

Thea rested her elbows on her knees, curious. Even before the traumatic events of the week, she'd felt like they were teetering.

A smile shined across Shelly's face when a puppy walked by with its
owner. "I know that you look up to Margot, but I also know that Margot
wants you to believe that you need her to survive. That she's been the key
to your transformation these last few weeks."

"But she has been."

"Yes and no. Other things have been at work, too."

If she hadn't met Margot, she'd be right where she was at the beginning of the summer: in a funk. Then again, if she hadn't met Margot,
she wouldn't be carrying this terrible secret either. "I don't know what
you're saying."

"Well, it's you that's asking all the questions. It's you that's searching for your next steps, and Margot is a fantastic sounding board. But
don't mistake your friendship with her as your sole purpose. She's here
to enrich your life, not define it."

As Thea grasped what Shelly was saying, she felt a little embarrassed. "I'm not in awe of her, if that's what you think." *Not after what
we did.*

"It's just that she's a fabulous person, yes, but I hope that you can see
that so are you. That you give her just as much as she gives you."

"What do you think she gets from our friendship?" It was a question that had been gnawing at Thea. What did Thea add to Margot's life,
and what did Margot bring to hers? She'd wondered continually if the
events of the other night would draw them closer or drive them apart.

Shelly said with kind eyes, "It's simple. You prop Margot up. She
may be the glamorous one from your point of view, but from her stand-
point, you're the strong one. Do you think we haven't noticed how you
hold up the sky around you?"

Perhaps that terrible night was another burden Thea would bear.
Quickly wiping her nose with the back of her shirtsleeve, Thea gulped
down her egg cream, afraid that if she tried to say something with this
much emotion beating in her heart, she'd jumble up her words and
cry so hard she'd hiccup. She might even tell Shelly what happened to

the Walrus. Instead, Thea watched people pass, trying to parse Shelly's words: Thea had been pinning her entire future on Margot, as if she could single-handedly save her. But Thea didn't need to be saved. She already knew what she had to do to redefine her life, and the only one who could do it was her. She didn't need Margot to believe in her. All she needed was to decide she was going to do it.

How had Thea not seen that before?

Even though she waited a full minute to respond, Thea's voice still came out trembly. "I'm really not that strong, Shelly. Without Margot, without this job and you and Jay, I'd still be waking up depressed every morning, missing my mom, trying to take care of my sister and stepfather."

"Maybe that's true. Maybe Margot is the kind of friend that helps another person bloom. I'm just saying that you shouldn't move to San Francisco because you think it's the only way to get out. You are strong enough, Thea, to follow any path you wish for yourself. This trip won't be the sole opportunity you have."

Thea tossed her empty cup into the trash can, making the shot. "What's my other option? Dale's girlfriend moved in."

Shelly frowned. "Obviously step one is leaving home. I'm just saying that you don't need to run from your past. You can walk."

It was true. She knew it was. Even with her knowledge of what happened the other night, even if she lived the next few years on eggshells around police, Thea would move on. There could be another plan—and Thea didn't need Margot to strike out on her own. She could rent a room in a dormitory-style house for women. There had to be one nearby. Then she wouldn't have to leave her sister, not entirely. Thea knew her sister would benefit from having a steady female presence in her life. One that would never leave her.

Still, Thea wanted a road trip to the West Coast. To inhale the Pacific Ocean. She wanted to watch the sun set behind the Hollywood sign and the Golden Gate Bridge. She wanted to talk out what happened while on the car ride, then leave the painful memories in the rearview mirror.

But she didn't want to move away for good. She didn't want Margot to pay for her apartment. She didn't want Margot to have that much of a say in her life.

At the end of their journey, Thea would buy a plane ticket or hitch a ride back home. Her home, right here on eastern Long Island.

Chapter Twenty-Five

July 1977

The foghorn sounded in the distance, the ocean night expelling mist over the east end of Long Island. Thea pulled a shawl around her shoulders in her art studio to warm herself, a sketchbook on the table and Bee curled into a ball at her feet. In the glow of the lamplight, she inked a second drawing in a series she'd named "Awakenings"—the first image detailed the smooth plane of a newborn's face, a look of wonder in its alert little eyes; the second was a more abstract drawing of boulders on an unnamed shoreline, a young couple playing chess on the rocks while waves crashed. Using charcoal pencils, then inking pens, Thea worked to insert depth in the lines and shading, hoping to capture longing and love and regret in the smallest of details.

Thea wasn't certain if she could have produced these drawings at twenty. There was wisdom in creativity, and these last few years, she'd garnered plenty of it. Even more so these last few weeks. For one, Margot's reemergence had shown her that it was lucky to make one or two great friends in life, and while the two women had been cleaved apart by traumatic circumstances, what never, ever left was their ability to sit together doing absolutely nothing and somehow enjoy every minute of it. To Thea, the great friends, the truly great ones, didn't need finger sandwiches and tea. They didn't need plans. All they needed was time.

And she and Margot were running out of it.

For the last twenty-four hours, Willy had known Thea's number, and still, he hadn't phoned.

Earlier that morning, filled with impending doom, she'd told Margot over bowls of Wheaties: "If Willy doesn't call, I will have to drive you to the train station tomorrow."

"I know." Margot drank the milk in her bowl. "And I will go."

Cara had decamped to Dale's house after sleeping over in Penny's bed on her first night, and Thea missed her already. She lowered her pencil and returned to the house; it was nearly Penny's bedtime. In the living room, Margot brushed Penny's hair with her good arm in the armchair, Penny paging through a picture book. "Remember, every night is one hundred strokes. Just like Rapunzel," Margot said. "Don't let me hear from your mother that it's tangled again."

"Let's make me a crown," Penny begged, her bottom lip puffing dramatically.

"After this, it's bedtime." Thea poked her daughter gently with her stuffed bunny.

It was after nine o'clock and the sun had dipped below the horizon, chiffon clouds casting an eerie hue in the sky. Summer days were seemingly endless, this day particularly so.

Thea marched Penny up to bed, and just as she kissed her daughter goodnight, she heard the phone ring. She rushed down the stairs, meeting Margot in the kitchen. "You have to answer it," she begged Thea, as if she would refuse. Thea nodded, lifting the earpiece from the wall phone.

"Hello," Thea said.

It was a man's voice, a polite, smooth inflection that didn't sound at all menacing, and yet felt dangerous when he said, "Put Margot on, please."

Thea reassured herself that her daughter was in the next room. She wasn't in harm's way, although she couldn't stop herself from glancing about the dark corners of the yard from her kitchen windows, as though Willy might be calling from a neighbor's house.

"Who is this?" Thea demanded, even though she knew who it was. Margot paced.

When he said it was Willy, Thea nearly yelled at him, "How could you steal from those people? How could you do this to Margot?" But what good would blame do now? She mouthed to Margot, *It's him*, handing her the phone and listening from the couch in the living room, where she couldn't stop tapping her foot.

There was so much nervous energy pulsing inside her that Thea swore she could feel her blood flowing through her veins. For one, Willy calling the house made her feel embedded in something more criminal now. But she was most upset because Margot was truly leaving, a little part of Thea's spirit withering at the thought, and Thea didn't know when she'd see her again. Thea was aware how easy it was to lose the people you cared about. Relationships were as vulnerable as a rowboat in the ocean in a nor'easter—if you weren't careful, they could slip under the water forever. While Thea knew how to win back Felix, and she was certain they would move on from this, what she didn't know was how to keep Margot in her life. Thea would need to express just how important it was that they remain in touch.

Penny called her name from her bed, Thea moving past the darkened kitchen where Margot was speaking in muffled tones. Upstairs, her daughter expressed worry that she wouldn't get to say goodbye to Margot, that she would leave too early. Thea's eyes usually burned at the end of her daughter's bedtime routine, but she was alert now, impatient to return downstairs. "She wouldn't do that to you," Thea promised.

When Thea came back downstairs, she found Margot eating handfuls of popcorn from the bowl she'd made Penny earlier. The popcorn had to be stale by now, on account of the fog. The two women went outside, sitting on top of the picnic table with their feet dangling, the fog creating a wall of white air all around them.

"Well, what did he say?" Thea said.

Margot stared out at the water, her hurt arm resting on one knee. "He said I need to get to the border at Niagara Falls. There's a Canadian Howard Johnson's motor lodge, and he'll be there waiting."

"And then?" It seemed unlikely that they would remain in Canada, too cold, too hard to access the hidden money in the Cayman Islands.

He'd stolen Margot's savings, but Thea guessed there was more, plenty more.

"And then we'll disappear." Margot shrugged. "And don't ask if it's a good plan. It's the only plan." Just the other day Margot had declared she deserved better than Willy, but she also loved people with a fierce loyalty. Willy was her make-it-work, no-matter-what person and following him was a chance at self-reinvention, something she'd always longed for.

"You don't have to take whatever dark road he's paved himself. If he stole money from people, Margot, then cut ties and move on. Unless you were in on it?"

Margot flicked at a lightning bug flying near her face. "I would never help the rich get richer, and you know it. We've always had plenty. I'll admit, I knew he was involved in something unscrupulous—I saw his wallet grow, his accounts swell—but I had no idea he was stealing from people, from our friends. Every year I made him donate large swaths of our fortune to the YMCA and the Boys and Girls Club of New York, and we were on all those boards together. When I asked him a few minutes ago about why he stole so much, he said, 'We had an expensive life.'"

"Last I heard, you were funding it," Thea balked. "And anyway, it doesn't sound like he understands you if he thinks you want to live in splendor." She remembered the note that Margot sent her years ago, how she'd referred to herself as Robin Hood.

"He enjoys the finer things." Margot pushed off the picnic table. "Anyway, Willy apologized for everything. He told me that we'd get a little casita in Italy and we would have a hundred babies." Margot glanced at the stars, like God was in on some private joke. "Just hearing him again made me realize how much I need him, even if he's imperfect. And I want to have a hundred babies."

The vision of Margot in some small Italian village with so many babies that she couldn't remember any of their names made them laugh and reinforced everything they had believed until that point: Even when no one else got their friendship, they got each other. But still, Thea wasn't certain Margot wasn't making a mistake.

They walked out across the lawn in the direction of the sea. "Margot. You could call the feds and help with their investigation. You could move to a house out here, and we could spend summers together."

For a moment, she imagined Margot living nearby, and even if it was the most selfish of responses, she reveled in it. They could take turns hosting dinner parties. They could go to musicals at Jones Beach and shop for cocktail dresses at Saks in Southampton. Her daughter would grow up knowing Margot, and Felix could introduce Margot to his responsible single friends.

But not if she went back to Willy.

Margot nudged Thea's side with her own, dropping her head on Thea's shoulder. "I need my husband, Thea. You need your husband. We can't keep living in this fantasy that our friendship is some kind of salve that heals all."

If their friendship wasn't a salve, what was it, then? A Band-Aid? Thea had thought of it as the latter lately. Margot's arrival had lessened the sting of whatever was hiding in the recesses of Thea's heart. She'd distracted her, and it had helped Thea see her life from an outsider's point of view.

Penny was at the kitchen screen door, nuzzling her bunny and asking for water, so Thea ushered her back upstairs holding a plastic cup. There were still dishes in the sink when Thea grabbed a cold piece of chicken off the kitchen counter, pulling off bites as she carried two beers outside. She cracked one open and handed the other to Margot, who leaned toward her.

"Okay, so I need a favor."

"As long as you don't ask me to drive you to Canada." The flame of the citronella candle danced with the breeze.

"Well . . ."

"NO." Thea knew this was next. She'd predicted it while listening to Margot say that she'd realized how much she missed Willy. "I won't take you." A part of her wanted to, though. A part of Thea believed it could be the road trip they never took. One last chance to say goodbye.

But now there was Felix. And Penny.

Margot chattered on. "We can bring Penny and Cara with us. I'll sit in the back and we'll play cat's cradle, and we'll go see the falls before you take me to the Canadian side. You can tell Felix you've always wanted to go there. He doesn't even need to know you're taking me."

"Don't try to appeal to my sense of nostalgia, and I'm done lying to him."

"But it would be fun. I've regretted it all these years. Not waiting for you. Please, Thea."

"I can't—I just can't."

Thea scooted off the picnic table to go inside. Turning on the sink, she squeezed a drip of Palmolive onto the dishes and waited for the suds. After soaping the sponge, Thea heard the screen door open. Margot came up next to her, helping her as best she could, to dry the dishes Thea put in the wooden dish rack.

"If we leave by eight in the morning, we'll be there by dinner. Tell Felix this is the fastest way to get rid of me."

A bowl slipped out of Thea's hands, a chunk of the edge breaking off into a triangle in the kitchen sink. She tossed it in the trash, somehow cutting her finger on it. "I'm sorry. Maybe you can rent a car. Take a bus. You can wear a big hat."

"Thea! I need you."

Thea tasted blood on her finger. "Margot! Stop."

Using a clean dishrag Margot pulled from a kitchen drawer, she wrapped Thea's bleeding finger with kindness. "You have a passport, right? You'll need one to cross the border."

"Of course I have one."

Felix made her get one a few years back when he had partnered with a London publishing house on a book that ended up falling through. She'd never even had a chance to use it. Well, until now. There was something so appealing about packing up a car and driving to Niagara Falls. She thought she might gain fresh perspective in leaving, even if for only two nights, and she would better appreciate what she had upon return.

Thea pressed the rag tighter to the sting on her finger. "I can't risk losing Felix forever," she said without registering anything else Margot said.

A bell buoy sounded in the distance once more, striking like a clock, reminding them that night was long, and they needed to sleep. Margot said goodnight, bringing a glass of water with her to the barn. Thea climbed the stairs to her daughter's bedroom on the second floor, watching her sleep in the glow of her nightlight. Felix would be home in the morning, and if she decided to take Margot to the border, she would have a lot of explaining to do. He wouldn't understand why she was considering driving her. But without knowing what happened with the Walrus, Felix would never appreciate the weight of what Margot had done for her years ago. Thea had been pinned to the ground, she'd been attacked and defended . . . and as such, their friendship carried historical debt. Deep down, Thea believed she needed to repay her. Driving Margot up north felt like they would finally settle a very old score.

In the attic room on the third floor, which was much too hot to sleep in during summer, Felix had stored their passports in a locked metal combination safe. Inside were other important documents: birth certificates, house insurance, social security cards. She spun the dial to the left, then twice to the right: 04–12–6, pocketing the navy blue booklet as she returned downstairs. She moved quietly through her bedroom, gathering a change of clothes and packing them into a duffle.

Thea left her passport and wallet in her suede tote next to the fruit bowl on the kitchen table, reminding herself that their station wagon had recently been serviced, the mechanic insisting on replacing two front tires, so the car should make the trip easily to Niagara Falls. She wouldn't bring Penny. Instead, she would have to call Cara and ask her sister to stay with her.

Here is why I'm going, she'd tell Felix in the morning over sugary coffee, the morning glories climbing the lattice outside their window. *I need a chance to think, and the open road is calling*. Maybe it was naïve, Thea thought, but she wasn't worried about getting caught. She and Margot were two attractive women traveling in a wood-paneled station wagon, the official family car of their generation. There was no reason to give them a second glance. Thea wouldn't drive over the speed limit. She'd stop for a full three seconds at every stop sign.

And after two days away, she would drive east along Sunrise Highway and finally have some answers for her husband. For herself. These long stretches of highway would carry her to some kind of realization. A destiny. In the end, the journey to Niagara Falls wouldn't be about Margot. It would be about Thea, once again, returning home.

Chapter Twenty-Six

August 1967

It was early afternoon, a few hours before her date with Felix. Thea rode her bike over to Margot's to make sure they were leaving the following Sunday but also to have the dreaded conversation about Thea's change of plans. She wasn't sure how Margot would take it, if she would be crushed by Thea admitting she was in for a road trip, nothing more, or if she would be relieved. Thea looked forward to being on the road with her for hours, talking about the present and past, and delving into that night. Thea needed reminding that what they'd done was necessary.

There was a "Sold" sign in Margot's front yard, a pool-cleaning van parked in the driveway. Three moving trucks were lined up in the white pebbly drive, each packed with stacks of brown cardboard boxes. Three burly men came outside carrying the overstuffed couch from the formal living room that Thea loved. When she asked if anyone was home, Thea was told that the family had already returned to Manhattan.

"Gotta get everything out by the end of the day," one of the men told Thea. "Some kind of nasty divorce."

The front door was open. Thea rushed through the empty hallway, then living room and kitchen, calling Margot's name. Perhaps she was upstairs. She waited for the movers to carry Margot's dresser down the stairs, then scurried up. The only thing left in her friend's bedroom was a bare mattress, Margot nowhere to be found.

Back on her bike, Thea rode home with a gaping hole in her stomach. She tossed her bike against the front steps, Dale raising an eyebrow
from the kitchen table when she hurried in and grabbed the phone,
dialing furiously.

Shelly picked up on the third ring. "Did Margot tell you she was
leaving?" Thea said into the phone.

Shelly said she hadn't heard from her either. "I'm sure she'll call
you," Shelly said. "Maybe she needed to go back to the city and see her
father. I'm sure she'll come out and get you on Sunday."

"It's just so odd," Thea said, embarrassed that Dale could hear rising
panic in her voice. "Why would she leave without telling me?"

Thea had only wanted to talk to her, but perhaps she'd pushed too
hard this week. Had Margot worried that Thea might tell? Maybe she'd
needed to reiterate to Margot that she would never.

"I need to get in touch with her," Thea told Shelly, knowing that
their families overlapped at the Maidstone. "Can you help me get the
number to her parents' apartment in the city?"

That night, Felix pulled up to her house in his parents' VW bus. When
he knocked on the door, Thea answered it, Dale coming to the door to
say hello as Thea slung her purse on her shoulder to go. "Have her home
by midnight, son," Dale said, with a fatherly tone he'd never used on her
before.

"That was strange," Thea said, turning to follow Felix down the
steps.

"He's just looking out for you."

Thea glanced back at the house. "That's why it's strange."

Following her to the passenger door, Felix opened it and waited for
her to sit. The window was already rolled down. "Off to the milkshakes,"
he said, grinning, and she giggled. He rushed across the front of the van
and slid into the driver's seat. He used both hands to smooth back his
hair, then started the van, the unmistakable putter kicking up.

"I'm not moving to California," she sputtered, not wanting him to think this date was their last. "We don't have to say goodbye for forever tonight."

"I don't think I could say goodbye for forever, anyway," Felix said, a goofy smile overtaking his face. They glanced at each other quick from across the upholstered seats, and Thea reached out to touch his dimple. "You're really cute, you know that?"

They drove to the diner in town for grilled cheese and fries, and as they talked about music and childhood memories and all the things they wanted to do together, Thea thought it strange how easy it was to forget all about Margot when she was with him. To push the Walrus out of her head and sink deeper into Felix's adoring gaze. Afterward they went for a walk along the sandy curve of Crescent Beach, a short drive over the bridge from Sag Harbor. It was when he'd hugged her in the cool night air that Thea's body began to tremble. *Not now*, she thought. *Don't let yourself cry right now.*

The night had been so perfect.

"What's the matter?" he whispered, stepping back and resting his hands on her cheeks, tilting her face up so he could see her. "Did I do something wrong?"

She raised her eyes up to his. "It's Margot. I have this bad feeling. She left her house without saying goodbye to me. I don't even know where she is."

He squeezed her tight against him once more and she let herself cry. She imagined his eyelashes, those beautiful long brown eyelashes, fluttering, trying to figure out what to say to make her feel better. But he didn't need to say anything. She melted into him.

Margot never did come back for her.

Thea waited for Margot to call her, and when that didn't happen, she called her repeatedly, leaving messages at her family's New York City apartment. One rainy afternoon after she and Felix had seen a movie, he'd handed her a newspaper clipping. An article in the *East Hampton Star* about the Lazure family selling their residence due to the couple's impending divorce, a short paragraph about an unfortunate event involving a groundskeeper at the property who had stolen her jewelry before slipping and falling by the pool. A quote from Mrs. Lazure: "I was quite shaken up. Imagine if he'd harmed my daughter and me?"

"Strange," Thea said, crumpling up the article and changing the subject, a patch of red itching up her arm. "Do you want to have a picnic tomorrow?" She smiled wanly.

The story never did appear in the larger papers; Mrs. Lazure owned one of the largest in New York. Margot told her once that she felt sorry for the Walrus because he was estranged from his family, and it must have been true because no one ever came looking for him. He was a soul the world was willing to let go of.

Sometimes the gravity of what transpired would hit Thea and she would cry in the shower or before falling asleep at night. It wasn't just the Walrus. It was that she'd lost Margot.

But then she'd imagine all the summers she and Felix had ahead of them. She daydreamed about following him to Columbia University in December when he began his studies and an apprenticeship at Doubleday with the father of one of the kids he had lifeguarded for. "Hard workers aren't easy to come by," the father had told him with a wink.

Sometimes it felt like she'd need to remain in these towns forever. To keep watch if anyone showed up looking for the Walrus, if anyone came forward asking what really happened.

One month later, Thea lost her virginity to Felix on a dark ocean beach. He'd pulled her up afterward and said, "You are the most incredible person I've ever met."

"I love you," she said as they held hands walking back to his parents' car. Her mind pulled to an alternate path: She and Margot leaving for their trip to California, returning home right around now. Pulling into

East Hampton with a fresh set of eyes, having rested her own on so many other places, having met so many other people. Instead, she'd met this one incredible person, and he was enough for her.

"I love you too," Felix said, squeezing her hand. "Do you want to come to my house for Sunday dinner tomorrow?"

"Tell your mother I'll make a pie."

Thea turned around on the path, tugging him back to the ocean's edge. There was something she needed to do. Standing in the swirls of moonlit seafoam, she unclasped the hummingbird locket around her neck, the cool metal dangling between her fingertips.

Some days she wished she'd gone on the trip. Other days she thought maybe it was better that Margot had left the way she had. With the Lazure family erased from East Hampton, Thea didn't have to think of that awful night.

The ocean wind whipped her hair into her face. Thea held the locket over her shoulder like a baseball and heaved it into the waves. *Goodbye, Margot,* she whispered, feeling droplets of sea spray dapple her skin. *Goodbye forever.*

Chapter Twenty-Seven

The weather turned cool that October, the stately elms transforming into fountains of gold, the ocean a deep vivid blue thanks to dimming sunlight. Thea packed the last of her clothes into one final cardboard box. She was finally leaving Dale's. There was a pretty old whaling house in Sag Harbor that functioned as a rooming house for single young women, and while it was a temporary fix, she was excited for her bedroom, a small square room at the back of the house with a private door to the back garden. Felix let her borrow his car so she could move out. As she carried boxes outside, she ran into the postman on the front walk. She'd sent away for information from two art schools in New York and had been eagerly checking for them.

"I didn't know you had friends in faraway places," the postman winked, handing over a package.

"Oh, thank you." Thea looked at the box, the return address from a post office in San Francisco. Even though there was no one home at Dale's house, Thea carried it up to her bedroom, which would now be Cara's bedroom. Using a box cutter to slice open the tape, she found it full of those annoying Styrofoam peanuts. Underneath there was a manila envelope. When she opened the seal, she found that there was a letter, but it was not an apology or a heartfelt page of handwriting. It was reporting, as if someone had written an article without a byline.

When he pushed Thea down to the ground, I tried to pull him off. I punched at his back, but I had to do something extreme or he would hurt her. I found a rock . . ." Thea skipped to the next page. *"It was my mother that decided that we should admit to the body but say that we found him this way, and Thea agreed to keep it secret."*

The truth as it happened, just as Thea remembered it. She crumpled the pages, then realized she couldn't put them in the kitchen trash. Later, she'd burn them.

Thea dug deeper inside the box, pulling out Margot's tan trench coat, the one that Thea wore running after the dog in the rain during Julianna Lazure's party—the first time Thea had ever met the Walrus. Margot had always planned to give her the trench, and now, slipping her arms in, smelling a bonfire in the seams, the hint of strawberry lip gloss in the collar, Thea wished her friend had hand-delivered it.

She moved to put her hands in the pockets, reflecting on what it would be like to reunite, when she realized her fingers were pushing up against stitching. The pockets were sewn shut. Thea remembered then that Margot had said she liked to hide stuff in the pockets of her coats. Downstairs in the kitchen, Thea turned the jacket inside out, then located a pair of shears. She cut open the white cotton lining of the pocket.

First, the coat slipped out of Thea's hands, then the necklace. Her gaze fixed at the sparkling gemstones at her bare feet. Then, with little earthquakes in her heart, she stared out the window at a bird jumping branches in a tree. *You always were an aspiring jailbird,* Thea smiled.

She recognized the glittery piece immediately. It was one of the stolen necklaces, the elaborate teardrop ruby pendant that had been printed on the front page of the *East Hampton Star.* Julianna Lazure had pinned the thefts on the dead groundskeeper; articles reported that they had found ten thousand dollars in cash in his cottage. Presumably, he got that from illegal dealings. Either that, or Margot's mother had planted it.

There was one more thing in the cardboard box. A simple white envelope, nothing on the outside. A paper folded into thirds, typed on parchment paper. A few lines.

You'll never fall on hard times now that you have this jacket and its contents . . . the King's Armory at Lexington and 112th doesn't ask questions. The rest is where it's supposed to be, the funds on an airplane headed to people who need it. And the reportage, well, that's just in case you get a conscience. I'll miss you. Xo Robin Hood.

Chapter Twenty-Eight

July 1977

Thea woke just before sunrise, twisted and slick with sweat in her white cotton sheets. The filmy remains of a bad dream lingered. She flipped onto her side thinking of Felix, wondering if she should call off the plan. Her body was too jittery to sink back into sleep, even if everyone else was still in bed. After several minutes of fighting the urge to get up, she finally rose from the mattress, her eyes still half-closed as she descended the carpeted steps to fetch a glass of water.

There was a quiet rustle in the kitchen, and she feared she would find a mouse skittering along the counter, so she stopped in the hall and listened.

The worn wooden floorboards near the refrigerator creaked, sounding like a rusted gate swinging shut. These were the home's original wide planks and they tended to hiss and pop as the mercury climbed or fell. But she heard it again—the subtle separation of a floor joist, the press of a footstep. A silhouette skulked past the doorway, an intruder. She felt her breath catch, her eyes adjusting to the light.

It was Margot. She had no idea Thea was watching from the hallway on the burgundy oriental rug that Felix's mother had gifted them for their five-year anniversary, their "professor" rug, as Felix liked to joke, since it made them feel like intellectuals. The scene in the kitchen was familiar too—Margot alone in her house, doing something Thea knew nothing about—and Thea was saddled with the same uncertainty she'd felt when she first discovered Margot in her house weeks ago. Only, unlike the last time, Margot had no idea that Thea was awake or that she was standing there, watching when Margot assumed she was concealed—that Thea was one step ahead, even if she hadn't thought things would go this way.

The milky gray of early morning cast sideways shadows, the birds just beginning to chirp.

Margot was dressed in denim and a simple blouse, standing at the table, her leather suitcase resting on the ground beside her espadrilles. She'd unzipped Thea's handbag, and one of her hands rifled through it.

Once a thief, always a thief—wasn't that how the saying went? A feeling of sorrow radiated in a line from Thea's sternum to her naval. *Let her go,* Thea heard a voice in her head, and she immediately decided it was her mother talking to her in the quiet, the tone that she'd used with her at bedtime, stroking her forehead with her fingertips. Thea was overcome with relief that she could remember her mother's voice—she hadn't heard it in years—and she wondered why she was hearing it now.

A sniffle developed in her nose, the beginning of a good cry. *Of course I'll let her go,* Thea responded in her thoughts. She already had plans to drive Margot several hours upstate; she didn't want her to stay. But even then, Thea sensed it would end in confrontation. Because her hand was in Thea's bag; she was looking for something. Her wallet? What? They'd already removed the hidden money from the freezer, Margot slipping it into her pocket before returning to the barn that night to pack.

Thea's eyes blurred, and she worked to refocus them on Margot's Louis Vuitton suitcase next to the table leg. It looked as though Margot had stopped to do something on her way out the door. She moved quietly, in near silence, as though she feared someone would wake.

Out of Thea's bag, she lifted the small blue booklet, the engraved golden seal on the cover. Thea's passport. It had been locked in the safe, and Margot had needed it. That was why she had asked Thea to drive her to Canada. Had she been searching for Thea's passport all along, growing frustrated when she couldn't find it? Was that really why she had stayed, why she'd concocted the road trip idea?

Now she hunched over the kitchen table, the two passports open in front of her. There was a small square photo of Margot on the tabletop, and she was cutting the edges straight with an X-Acto knife. Thea's yellowed passport photo had been removed and cast aside, and using glue, Margot was pressing her picture into the other passport. Thea's passport.

The betrayal she registered, knowing that Margot hadn't asked, that she had wanted something else all along, made Thea feel as though she was hanging upside down in the doorway, the world on tilt. A sharp inhale gave away Thea's place in the hall, and the bony parts of Margot's shoulders flinched at the sound.

Margot began to clean up the mess, stacking the map from AAA on top of a notebook, open to what looked like a long letter. "I hope I didn't wake you," Margot said.

"You didn't wake me." Thea padded to the table and picked up the map. "Are you going somewhere?"

"I have this letter. I planned to leave it, to help you understand." Margot said this as a way of explaining herself, moving Thea's purse out from in front of her, looking as though she was attempting to erase a wall between them.

Thea smelled her mother's Youth-Dew perfume, the distinct mix of peaches, cinnamon, and oranges. There was no question of Margot's intentions, and once again Thea had been played for a fool.

Suddenly, Thea was twenty years old again, waiting at the edge of Dale's lawn to get a glimpse of Margot's green Mercedes. How she kept walking back to Margot's estate after the Walrus died, hoping that she would come back to pick her up. The moment when Thea had unpacked her suitcase for California, the reality settling in that the trip was never happening.

Why had Margot come at all if she'd always planned on hurting her all over again? This was a textbook primer for a thief: grow chummy with the victim, case the house, take what you need when the victim least expects it. A drama series she'd watch on television—*How far would you go for a friend?* Margot had done so much for her, and yet Thea wondered if she would ever hit a limit in what she would do in return. How much was she willing to overlook to settle the score?

Thea carried her glass of water to the table, slumped into a kitchen chair, the rough cane sticking her in the thighs, and looked outside at the silvery sea, wishing she was looking out a different window, one on a train zipping back in time. Back to that night. She hated that her voice came out hoarse. "Sometimes when I can't sleep, I think that maybe we were wrong, and the Walrus didn't deserve to die."

Thea hadn't meant to make Margot lose the color in her skin, to make her feel small, but that was the result of her admission. Margot let out an odd laugh: "The only reason that I can get up in the morning is because I know that I stopped him from raping you, Thea. We didn't imagine that. Don't be one of those women apologizing when you're the victim."

It was low tide, the fog had dissipated, and from here Thea could see what was revealed when the water went out: a smattering of broken shells and muck-covered stones. How much she preferred high tide when all of that was hidden away. "But you could have just run inside and called the cops."

Margot dropped her face into her hands, rubbing at the tip of her nose before looking up at Thea. "Really? You're serious? He had you pinned to the ground."

There was no apology in Thea's tone. "You didn't have to strike him *twice*. He was already hurt after you hit him in the back of the head. He'd gotten off me. All this time you said that you did it to save me, but your motivations have always been more complex than that, haven't they? There was something in it for you too. There was a reason you wanted him dead."

Thea was surprised by her own assertion, irked by the sound of her own accusatory voice. But it had dawned on her long ago during one sleepless night that maybe Margot's intentions weren't as pure as she'd let on, and perhaps they never were.

The passport sat on the table in between Margot's two hands, her palms flat like she needed to steady herself. She pushed it close to the fruit bowl, halfway to Thea's position on the opposite end of the table, like a peace offering.

"I didn't mean to kill him, if that's what you're suggesting. Jesus, Thea. Don't you know me?" Margot twisted at the earring in her right ear.

"I'm not sure that I do." Thea was careful to keep her voice steady; if Penny came downstairs, it would break the spell, and Thea needed to push. Clarifying that night mattered to her: Why had they lived with this guilt unless it had been worthwhile?

"You were about to run out on me again this morning. I deserve to know."

Margot ripped the hair band out of her short ponytail—and threaded her fingers through her hair, her scalp pulling against her hairline. "When he found out that I had some of the jewelry, that I had taken it from those parties, he made me steal a couple of extra things so he could sell them. Remember when you found that Excedrin tin? Selling anything for his gain went against my reasons for doing it altogether. I had a crush on him, but I didn't understand what he was doing at first, that he didn't really like me—he was just manipulating me. Then he threatened to tell the police about the jewelry, and even though we had already been together, he started visiting me at night. I was always so embarrassed by how easily I gave in to him. I tried to put a stop to it, but he didn't allow it."

It was so much worse than she'd thought, but Thea didn't regret getting there. "What do you mean, did he force himself on you?"

She hadn't seen Margot's face ball up since the day she had told Thea that her parents were selling the East Hampton house, and the tears coming now were old, deep. Margot sucked in a breath, pressing her eyes shut. She exhaled. While she waited, Thea was consumed staring at a framed picture of a black tea kettle on the wall behind her friend's head; it was so ugly, and she'd kept it up all this time. What kept you from seeing the truth behind things you looked at every day? Why hadn't she noticed that Margot had been in such a terrible situation?

Margot cleared her throat. "After a while I just did whatever he wanted—I had started it between us, after all. I had thought it was funny to show up at his cottage in a short nightgown, asking him to change a lightbulb. But then it went too far, and I was a kid and he was a grown man. When I saw him on top of you that night, I felt like someone sawed me in half. I didn't want you to smell cigarettes and Certs on his breath or feel the sharp stubble of his chin. I didn't want to watch him do to you what he had been doing to me. I told my mother everything when I left you at the pool and ran inside, it all came rushing out of me, and she told me that I did the right thing. It was maybe the only time I did the right thing. But she was worried that you would go to the police, so she made me write every detail down, and she made me send you the pages, as collateral, and I listened."

"I didn't tell a soul." Thea thought back to how Julianna Lazure had marched out to the pool under the security lights beaming off the back of the house, quizzing Thea on what had happened, how she had stared at her one beat too long, as if she wasn't sure what to make of her. It was disappointing to Thea that she had been right—that there had been another reason Margot had killed the Walrus. She never felt as though she was enough for her, and this confirmed it. *Stop*, she thought. *Margot helped you.* She saved you from a lifetime of nightmares, from the greatest of violations.

Margot picked up the map to give her hands something to do. "I know you didn't tell anyone, and I knew we could trust you. I've always been able to trust you."

"Can I say the same for you?" Thea lifted her passport, Margot's photo fastened inside, holding it up like evidence of wrongdoing.

"You have a right to be angry."

But Thea wasn't angry. She was only sad. There was truth to what she sensed her mother's memory was telling her, that sometimes you really did need to let go of people, especially if they're no longer serving you. Thea had been forced to let go of her mother. It had been the only way for Thea to move on, to live her life. To be who she was meant to be. And yet—Margot was still walking this earth. It would be a different goodbye.

Thea's body felt leaden. "I always wondered why you wanted to be my friend. You could have picked anyone to spend that summer with, but you chose me."

Margot shifted her weight, seemingly annoyed. "Why do you say that? I liked you."

"The answer matters to me."

For Thea, friendship with Margot had felt more one-sided than she'd ever let on, and her devotion to her friend, before that one terrible night, had come down to one moment: the warm evening at Sunshine Records when they were about to lock up, but Margot happened upon Thea at the front desk drawing new versions of existing album covers. She had insisted on looking at every sketch, turning Thea's notebook around, studying the details. It embarrassed Thea to think about how much her ego had needed someone to compliment her artwork, but she *had* needed it. In her teenage years, she'd always hoped that an art teacher would see something special in her and submit one of her drawings to a contest, or that she'd meet an artist by chance at the record shop and he would offer her free lessons. But not every letter to the universe was answered. That day, though, Margot had truly seen Thea. She had witnessed her hand moving across the page and complimented the finished work. She had decided that Thea had talent, categorizing her as someone who had something beautiful to offer. Suddenly, maybe even to herself, Thea was more than just a caretaker of Dale and his sagging old house. She was a person who would use her mother's premature death as a catalyst, not an excuse to fail.

Wasn't that why it was always so hard for her to stay angry at Margot? Margot had made her believe all those years ago that she was worth something.

"Explain it," Thea pushed. "Why me?"

Margot sat down beside Thea at the table. "I don't know. I value you for so many reasons. Your kindness and easy laugh, the way you accepted me into your life like we were somehow related." The arches of her plucked eyebrows pulled up, and she smiled at Thea. "You know, I think it was because you thought I had everything, and I didn't, and it felt so good for once to think that maybe I did."

Thea pressed the soft tips of her fingers into the corners of her eyes, sighing out her disappointment. The answer was more about Margot than Thea. "You did always have so much."

Margot tapped on the table, getting Thea to look at her. "Yes, a nice car and a pool and a fancy address. Sure. But the truth is that you had everything that I wanted, not your house or anything. What I wanted was for people to like me for who I was inside. Without all those pretty things, I felt ugly. I was always trying to redeem myself, help people, take on charity cases. Then there you were with so much less than me, and yet everyone—Shelly, your sister, even my mother—saw so much beauty in you."

Thea listened more closely, watching the lines in Margot's forehead ripple as she continued to speak. "Don't you remember how much I needed Shelly to like me, how I gave Jay that signed record to impress him. How I flirted with Felix the first time I met him, and he quickly forgot me? I'm entertaining. I've always been entertaining, Thea. But you—you are the true north. You are everyone's true north because you carry every single person in your heart. You make us shine brighter when we're next to you, and that is why *everyone always wants to be next to you*. That's why I came back here. I needed you. I needed you to tell me I would be okay."

Thea couldn't stop biting down hard on her lip. It seemed impossible that Margot saw her like this, that anyone did, and yet it only shored up what Thea had always believed—that Margot could see things in Thea that she couldn't see in herself. That friends were the people you went to for belly laughs, for birthday drinks, for a person who would take your side no matter what, but more important, friends were the pillars of strength in our lives. A friend could remind you in an instant that you were likeable, that you were special, that you were so much more than what strangers saw when they met you for the first time.

Old friends—they were another kind of important. You kept parts of them inside you for a lifetime. All these years Thea had forgiven the dishonest, insecure aspects of Margot's personality because all she could see was the young woman who had taught Thea to live with joy, to live in the mindset that a daydream on a sleepover could become reality. Margot, in turn, had ignored the part of Thea that bent her morals to please a friend, seeing instead a young woman who didn't love herself, even if everyone else around her did.

And then.

And then Margot had come back into her life. Her arrival had brought a much-needed reminder that Thea could still be that girl who worked at the record store, that she didn't have to abandon her youthful ideals just because she'd grown another year older. She was still Thea—she was still a dreamer and she still loved music and she'd still take care of the people she loved the way she always had. She didn't even believe anymore that her mother's death had changed the direction of her life in the worst way possible. Because aside from the pain of the loss, aside from the fact that she might have finished her four-year degree, Thea knew she would still be right here. In this house. With Felix and Penny and Margot begging for forgiveness. In her heart of hearts, Thea knew it was where she belonged, and her desire to create was a way to make sense of all these emotions she'd collected over the years.

She could also see that the only difference between young Thea and older Thea was wisdom. And majesty came in knowing who you were at your core, being curious with yourself, like a sculptor carving lines deeper and deeper, and figuring out that what mattered most to you in this life was hope. Having hope, doling it out, living like every single day had the possibility of being the best in your life.

Leaning over her chair, Thea hugged Margot. She held on to her like she might turn to dust, and then she pulled back, both of them wiping their noses. "Have I ever told you that I think my mother sent you to me that summer?"

"Dear god. Don't get all weird on me."

They both laughed despite their wet cheeks. "No, but it's true," Thea said, rising for a tissue in the living room, then coming back to the table and handing one to Margot. "I know she did. She knew that I needed you. I can sense her here today, and I think it's why I have to ask you one last question: Why didn't you just tell me you needed my passport?"

Margot frowned, dabbing her eyes with the back of her wrist. "You must think I'm some kind of kleptomaniac." Thea didn't say anything, waiting, and Margot cleared her throat. "I knew you would say no. Any sane person would, and Willy said if you knew I'd taken it, you'd likely call the authorities. That I'd have no chance of getting past the border."

Thea shook her head with disgust. "There was never going to be a drive to Niagara Falls, was there?"

"There was not." Margot blew her nose. "Willy is in Canada, but he's leaving on a plane for Rome this morning. There's no extradition there, so the feds can't touch him. But to get there from New York, I needed this." She glanced down at the passport resting on the table between them. "It was a stupid plan. I'm sorry."

Thea wished there was a stamp inside. Instead, the small textured pages were empty of any kind of evidence of far-flung adventures. Last month, it had saddened Thea to think that she might never set foot on the soil across the ocean. Now she knew she would get there someday. She would see more of the world. Perhaps they could start by visiting London, bringing Penny with them, and ride a red double-decker bus in circles around Trafalgar Square. Then they could save up to visit Paris, maybe Rome.

Thea lifted the passport off the table, and in reaching for it, the first day she met Margot came rushing back to her. How Margot had lied about having a dog, how she had cursed at her mother, how she'd lain on the lounger at her pool, curled into a tight ball. Back then, Thea sometimes attended mass with Dale, and she'd thought of angels in the biblical sense, as spiritual beings who delivered messages to and from God. But she believed now, after these weeks with Margot, that there were other kinds of angels, that there were versions that walked the earth that were entirely human. And they could heal one another, and often did, sometimes in roundabout ways.

"Take it," Thea said, placing her passport in Margot's handbag. "Use it for as long as you need it."

The act surprised Margot, and she fished it out, shaking her head, apologizing under her breath that she was going to take it at all, saying that she had been desperate, that she hadn't known what else to do but she would find another way.

"Nonsense," Thea told her. "You gave me a second chance. You believed I was so much more than I thought I was, and that belief gave me the ability to find happiness. You deserve it too. That same happiness."

Margot struggled with what to say, remaining quiet. Finally, she said: "You always give more than you should."

"I want to—and I want you to have those one hundred babies." A laugh broke through Thea's tears.

Through the windows, the sun glowed in a sliver at the horizon, the water turning a shade of pale pink and gold. Thea announced that she would be right back and headed up to her bedroom, tugging at the trench coat she had kept in the back of her closet for nearly a decade, pulling the heavy jewels out of the pocket she'd once used a scissor to cut into.

The gems glittered in the early morning light, and Thea slid the necklace into the satin lining of the shorts she'd slipped on. While she wouldn't be driving Margot to Canada, she would take her to one of the first trains leaving the Long Island Railroad station that morning. Thea called her sister and asked her to come over right away. "I won't be long," she told her.

An hour later, Thea pulled out of the driveway with Margot in the passenger seat, headed for the village. Margot would board a train bound for Manhattan, then hop a cab to John F. Kennedy International Airport to start a new life in Rome. One of Willy's friends had left a ticket under Thea's name in a locker in the TWA terminal.

When they pulled up to the brick station, tidy rows of plantings in bloom, Thea switched off the ignition. It was quiet, and neither one said anything. The train chugged into the station; they had only a few minutes.

"I promise I'll write," Margot said, giving Thea one last hug.

"I know you will."

Thea noticed a woman in a pressed, tailored pink suit carrying a suitcase to the train platform. What would Margot's life look like from here? Would Thea ever really hear from her again, and did it matter? These were the worst good times, as Margot had said on the boat, and Thea would keep the memories close to her, discarding some of the more unpleasant ones as Penny grew into adulthood.

"You're going to need this," Thea said, pulling the necklace from her pocket, tucking it in the palm of Margot's hand.

"You still have it?" Margot examined the jewels, then closed her hand around them. "I thought you would have used it. To buy the house?"

"Never." Thea didn't say that the gems were more of a burden than a gift. She was relieved to be rid of them.

Margot clicked open the station wagon's passenger door, lifting her suitcase out of the back seat. She walked around to the driver's side and leaned into the open window. Her eyes were lined in thick mascara, an uncertainty in her uneven smile. She looked sad, and seeing that brought a weariness to the strong face that Thea had been putting on.

"Just call me when you get there. They have phones in Italy, don't they?" Thea felt as though Margot was going to the moon.

Margot reached through the window and put her hand over Thea's on the steering wheel. Then Margot took a step away. She picked up her suitcase to go. "You take care of yourself. I'm rooting for you."

There was something else Thea wanted to say; there was always more she wanted to say.

"Wait," Thea said. She got out of the car, pulling a photograph out of her pocket. "You said you came to me this summer because you wanted to know that everything would be okay. It will be, Margot." Thea handed her the picture, a Polaroid that Cara had snapped of Thea and Margot laughing side by side on the couch, Penny laying across their laps, grinning. On the back, Thea had written: *Remember, you're not alone.*

Margot cleared her throat, dabbing at her eyes just once, before tucking the photograph into her purse. "It will be okay, right?" she said, glancing behind her to the station doors. "Willy and me?"

Thea hated lying but she didn't know how things would end up for her. "I think everything will be just fine."

Margot hugged her once more. When she pulled back, she grinned. "I expect great things from you in that studio, okay? Don't disappoint me now."

Thea laughed, her eyes growing damp too. "I won't."

Then Margot disappeared into the train station. With a heavy heart, Thea returned to the car. She whispered to the empty passenger seat, "Goodbye, old friend."

Thea pulled back into her driveway at half past eight, staring up at the house on the hill, the light over the front step still burning, a trellis of morning glories at the front of the house, open to the sun.

Now let yourself go, the voice said to her.

Was it her mother's or her own? Thea wasn't sure, but she was certain what it meant. It was time to figure the rest out. Felix would arrive home later that morning, and she would have coffee ready, and they would talk. Her Felix. Her house. Her decision.

Thea wouldn't take back her interest in art school or retire her reticence about having a second baby. She imagined lying in bed beside Felix, caressing the chest of his beloved Ramones shirt, and telling him: I will not risk losing you too, but I will also not risk losing me.

Then she would show him the catalog she'd picked up from the local college, share her drawings and her plan to enroll in classes. They would find a way to do it. Perhaps it wasn't fair that Felix was so immediately against moving to the city for her. Perhaps Gloria Steinem would disapprove of Thea bending for her husband. But the truth, Thea believed, was that her love and her dreams could coexist. A balance of both was the only way to be happy. Without one, what was the other?

Thea heard the song playing in the living room before she saw who'd put it on. Felix had slipped in the front door, switched on the record player, and lowered the needle onto the first track. The lyrics emerged over the uneven vinyl. "These Arms of Mine," by Otis Redding.

When Thea turned to face him from her spot in the kitchen, the soundtrack of their lives evoking some kind of gravitational pull between them, Thea lowered the jar of peanut butter, which she'd been spreading on toast. In front of her was a man with an open heart, a tenderness in his stooped stance, a purpose in how he walked toward her now, like he wanted to kiss her all at once but didn't know if she'd kiss him back.

He reached out a hand, then dropped it, glanced around the kitchen looking for Margot, trying to discern if she was somewhere in the inner recesses of their house. "She's gone," Thea said, untying her apron. She felt the hairs on her arms stand on end. Oh, how she wanted to hold him.

Felix set down his briefcase, holding on to a small brown grocery bag. His caramel eyes had the depth of a man who had just returned from war. "Do you know that he wasn't supposed to record this song?"

"Otis Redding?"

His voice soft. "Yes, he was a chauffeur for a different band, not even discovered, and the band he drove for couldn't come up with another hit. Otis happened to be in the recording studio, and he just started singing. This song, our song. They recorded it right then and there. It was his first hit."

Thea stepped closer to him, seeing the last ten years of their lives in his laugh lines, in the way he looked at her with his utmost attention. She thought of them swimming in the ocean all those summers in between. How when they'd kissed for the first time she'd felt as though all the pieces of her heart had been sewed back together. "And you're telling me about Otis Redding because . . ."

His face was as serious as she'd ever seen it. "Because sometimes people don't realize what others are capable of. They don't know how badly they want something until they go for it. You've got some Otis in you, don't you?"

A pang hit Thea in the chest, the sensation of relief, of happiness. She smiled, her lips nearly touching his. "I think I might."

"There's something else I want to say," he said. He grazed her mouth with his, then lifted the grocery bag between them. "I got your favorite ice cream: butter pecan."

"You remembered?" The lines around her mouth turned up, and she could see his dimple. Thea pressed her fingertip to it, like she had when they were falling in love.

Felix pressed her forehead to hers. "I couldn't forget you if I tried."

It was what he had said to her the night before she was supposed to leave on the road trip with Margot. That night, they hadn't been able to kiss, but today they could, and they kissed deeply in their kitchen, the sun shining through the window and casting them aglow. The song ended, but they didn't let go.

When they pulled back, an idea unfolded in Thea's mind, the lines drawing themselves in her heart. Lunch could wait. She excused herself and hurried into the living room.

She reached for her sketchbook.

Acknowledgments

A very big hug to my rock star agent, Rebecca Scherer, who always reads the earliest drafts of my novels and never tells me to get another job. Thank you, Rebecca, for guiding my career as a novelist, offering astute editing in the earliest stages, and landing me publishing contracts from my wildest dreams. We've grown up together these last several years, and I value you as a friend, not just a business partner.

To my brilliant team at Gallery, you make my stories shine brighter than I ever thought possible. I feel incredibly lucky to have landed into the hands of smart and insightful Hannah Braaten, who loved Thea and Margot as much as I did. She guided this manuscript expertly and these pages fly because of the heart she put into this book. I needed you, Hannah! I'm thrilled that we get to work on another book together. An enormous thank you to the lovely Sarah Schlick, who helped shepherd this novel to print in Hannah's absence. To my publicist, Jessica Roth, your emails always make me smile, and Jen Bergstrom, your faith in my work has guided me from my very first book.

All the bookstores that have sold my books, both big and small, thank you. I also need to acknowledge the wonderful book lovers on social media who have shared lovely reviews and gorgeous photography featuring my novels. I'm so very grateful. To readers of my Substack newsletter, thank you for tuning in to my writing each week on Dear Fiction.

I have so much gratitude for writer friends who have offered up writing advice, a supportive email, read my novels for blurbs or feedback, or met for lunch and learns—or just lunch! My favorite part of being an author is connecting with other writers and hearing what they're working on. So I'm sending major thank-you vibes to Beatriz Williams, Natalie Jenner, Janet Skeslien Charles, Kristy Woodson Harvey, Nancy Thayer, Kristin Harmel, Susie Orman Schnall, Jamie Brenner, Karen Dukess, Annabel Monaghan, Lynda Loigman, Fiona Davis, Amy Poeppel, Elin Hilderbrand, and Patti Callahan Henry! You all inspire me. To Samantha Woodruff and Jackie Friedland: Our writing group powers me up every time we meet!

Without my mother's crystalline memories of being a teenager in Montauk/Hamptons in the 1960s, then a young woman in the 1970s, I may not have been able to see Thea and Margot so clearly. Thank you for a lifetime of great stories, mom! Thank you to my dad and sisters, too; you cheer me on every step of the way.

This novel is about friendship, so I need to thank all my closest friends, old and new; you know who you are. Carin: It's been thirty-five years since we hid in the girl's locker room to avoid running track. Who knew a lifelong friendship would be born of sheer laziness? To Nancy, you are my secret sauce; thank you! Kelsa: Thank you for picking up on the first ring and talking character motivations whenever I need you; and Laura: my original writing buddy!

To Harper, whose natural curiosity is an endless inspiration, and to Emi, whose determined spirit reminds me that nothing is out of reach.

John, you have been my best friend since we were nineteen. There is no better soul than you.